Escape From

Terror

Escape from Terror

A Novel

Dr. Glenn W. Brownewell, Jr.

Upper Dedication

This novel is dedicated our Sovereign Triune Creator God Who gave my wife and me the privilege to serve Him in Romania for 10 years with a Bible institute and church planting ministry.

This experience included the opportunity to see our miracle-working God prove that He meets the needs of those He calls to serve Him.

Lower Dedication

This novel exists only because my wife was willing to leave the comfort of my successful career for the potential hazards of life with untested promises after a ruthless Romanian Communist Regime.

Our children have earned recognition as well for supporting us. They recognized our decision as an extension of the theology in which they had been raised. God's will is to be obeyed by faith!

Table of Contents

Foreword by the Author

This is a work composed of two inextricably connected parts based on experiences as missionaries of my wife and two of our children living in Romania shortly after the revolution that took down the infamous tyrant, Ceausescu. It also helped precipitate the collapse of the Soviet Cold War Empire that had existed following the end of World War II.

I set aside a successful career of 24 years in the corporate world as a Certified Public Accountant and 4 years as a Bible college administrator and professor to take on the challenge of a lifetime.

My first exposure to life in Romania occurred 10 months after the assassination of Ceausescu and his wife on Christmas day of 1989 by members of the Communist Party who read the "handwriting on the wall." At the time of my trip, there was no significant change in the lives of the average Romanian, so I experienced firsthand the conditions existing prior to the revolution in the capital city of Bucharest. Bullet holes and burned-out buildings gave evidence of the recent revolution. The airport was in a state of unimaginable disrepair. When the first facility that a visitor would see upon entering the country was in such disrepair, one could only imagine the condition of the remainder of the country. A quick trip through the city gave strong evidence of the failed Communist design for the perfect world society.

In a follow-up survey trip with my wife, we visited the far southwestern part of the country along the Danube River. We experienced village life as it had existed during the tyrannical rule of Ceausescu. A short time later, my wife, two of our children and I moved to this region of the country and began ministry while living in the town of Orsova on the Danube.

Orsova was a town of approximately 14,000 people. On the other side of the Danube River was Serbia, one of the six nations incorporated into Yugoslavia in 1918 following World War I. The ethnicity of the people of Orsova was unusual, because of the Danube River, which had given immediate access to Romania from many other countries prior to World War II. It included a number of people of German, Hungarian, Serbian and Czech extraction. These people of other ethnicities were the descendants of those who were working in Romania, many in the logging industry, during the war era and were trapped when Russia had quickly established the Iron Curtain around the Eastern European countries taken over following the end of the war. These people had seen the Russians as co-liberators with the Allies of Britain, America, and France and thus, had made no attempt to make an immediate return to their native countries following the end of the war. Though they were trapped, they maintained their culture to the best of their ability.

We experienced the fact that the secret police (Securitate), which were not very secret, were alive and well, though the government claimed to the world that they were disbanded following the revolution.

The first three-fourths of the book is primarily fiction regarding the characters, but realistically portrays the conditions of life that existed during the Ceausescu reign in the 1980s as personally experienced and learned from the many people to whom I ministered.

The two escape accounts in the novel somewhat parallel the actual escapes made by two men I met when they came back into the country to visit relatives. The attempted escape in the novel is fictional but does reflect accounts of escapees who were not successful in swimming the Danube River. Over the years before the collapse of the Ceausescu regime, many attempted escaping over the Danube or over land through Hungary. Some were successful and some were not.

The account of the main character going to America is fictional, but many of the Romanian experiences in the novel reflect actual life experiences of the national pastor who took over the church I established. The Romanian churches in Atlanta, Georgia, and Chicago, Illinois, were real, and I preached in both of them. My wife and I were, in fact, raised in the suburbs of Chicago.

It is not my intent to offend readers of the Orthodox faith, but the noted confrontations with Orthodox priests were real, and the Orthodox grip on the culture was evidenced firsthand through the eyes of the many people with whom the author interacted over a decade. This is not to suggest that the Orthodox churches of America replicate our experiences in Romania. In fact, I do not believe this to be the case.

ix

In the autobiographical part, I reflect with great accuracy the experiences my wife and I had as missionaries living in Romania for 10 years. All of the events experienced by the missionaries in the novel are factual and without exaggeration. Detailing the retrieval of the automobile, the reception and unloading of the container, the events regarding the Bible institute, and the purchase of property when the church was planted certainly bring glory to God for His obvious intervention in our ministry. To record all of the obvious involvement of the Lord in our ministry would require much more information.

I believe that the novel realistically portrays the effect that the Gospel has had on people over the ages. It shows how a person can achieve a vibrant, personal relationship with his or her Creator God following a previous life of disbelief. Regardless of the particular evangelical background of the reader, it is hoped that the novel will bring glory to God, Who has reached multitudes of people via different denominations in unusual circumstances.

For those interested in the history and failure of Romanian Communism as one of the most ruthless regimes in the Communist world, this novel provides accurate information regarding life in Romania and other Communist countries during and after the reign of Ceausescu.

After the establishment of the church that was turned over to a Romanian national trained in the Bible institute, we returned to America to serve again in the Bible College in which we had previously served.

Acknowledgments

Our family has had inextricable involvement in the process of our lives and the events that have led to the writing of this novel.

I acknowledge the editing accomplished by our daughter Elizabeth Brownewell and Mrs. Carolyn Van Loh, friend, previous English Professor at Pillsbury Baptist Bible College and previous editor for two local newspapers in Minnesota and Mr. Randy L. Miller, Graduate and Faculty Research and Instruction Librarian at Jerry Falwell Library – Liberty University.

I also acknowledge Mr. Scott Roberts as Cover Art Director for "Escape from Terror".

CHAPTER 1 ESCAPE PLANS INITIATED

It was a beautiful moon-lit night that made Daniel nervous as he made his way through the woods near the Danube River. Even though this was an area few people traversed, he feared being seen by someone and being found out would have dire consequences. There were countrymen who were eager to turn anyone over to the Securitate as a way to get on the good side of the authorities, thus resulting in some form of benefit. Under President Ceausescu's rule, anyone found meeting in the night was automatically assumed to be up to nothing good. The Securitate had ways to extract confessions, even of things not committed or intended. Anything that sounded like disloyalty to the regime was to incur harsh penalty or death.

As Daniel approached his destination, he carefully looked around, and then ducked down into the large patch of thorn bushes overrun by vines. As he made his way through the hewn tunnel, a voice called out softly, "Is that you, Daniel?"

"Quiet, Radu! Who else would it be? You and I are the only ones who know of this meeting place. At least I sure hope so!"

As Daniel reached the enclosure, he was met by Radu's flashlight. "Turn that thing off. The leaves may not be dense enough to shield the light now that fall is coming. Now move over and give me some room."

As Daniel settled in, Radu said, "These exposed roots really provide a perfect cave, and these thorn bushes sure provide fine cover."

"Aren't you glad I was brave enough to crawl into these thorns and find this place?"

With a bit of scorn, Radu said, "Oh, aren't you the brave one! You were just lucky to find the passage under the vines. If your Brutus had not run in here chasing that rabbit, you would never have found it. Anyway, I am glad he chased the rabbit in here that day."

"Oh, how I miss him. He was a great watchdog. Parvo kills too many of our dogs. The vet who gives injections to our livestock told us there is an injection available for dogs, but they are only used with police or military guard dogs. Perhaps it was better for Brutus because when we escape, there would be no one in my family to care for him like I did. Mom and Dad see dogs only as a necessity to protect the livestock and garden from thieves, but for me, he was my friend. He followed me everywhere and sometimes I almost thought he understood me when I talked to him."

"I know, I know, you have told me many times, but let's get on with our plans. Every time I see the gunboat, I think of the people who have been shot over the years trying to cross the Danube, but if Eugene can do it, I am sure we can too!"

"I hope you are right, but I am not as confident. Just because Eugene made it, doesn't mean we can. I, too, keep thinking about those who have tried and didn't make it. If the military captured only the people trying to cross and punished them instead of killing them, I would feel a little better about our plans. Maybe it is better to live under these conditions than to die trying to escape."

"Daniel, we have to make the attempt for a better life. Our magazine shows us how much better life is in the West. That is what I want!"

"Ok, Radu, let's pull it out again."

As Radu carefully brushed the dirt aside and pulled out the plastic bag containing the magazine, he exclaimed, "Thank heavens it is dry after the rains last week."

"Why are you thanking the heavens? You don't believe in God any more than I do."

"Just in case we are wrong and there is a God, I want to get on His good side!"

As they carefully knelt over the flashlight to cover the glare and turned the pages, Daniel mentioned that he wished everyone in the country could see it and know the truth about life beyond their borders. "But, if we dare to tell even one more person, our lives are not worth anything. We must never tell anyone, not even our parents. It is easy to see why the penalty for having a magazine from the West will get a person thrown into jail for five years of hard labor or worse. If people knew the truth, I think Ceausescu and his loyal party members would be in trouble. Our people would pour into the streets and demand change."

"What a joke when they show the Laurel and Hardy films every evening on TV for our daily half hour of entertainment. It makes Americans look stupid and poor. Well, if they have the same things that are in this magazine, they aren't poor and they obviously aren't stupid. I believed those films until I saw this magazine."

"Man, I would love to see this car up close! I saw cars driven by the government officials that looked like these, when I was in Craiova and the people on the street said that the Russians made them. What a lie! I wish we knew English so we could do more than read the pictures. Say, Radu, what do you think this is? It has the word "computer" under it, but it doesn't make sense. It has keys like the typewriters in the school office, but the ones in the school don't look anything like this."

"I have no idea."

"Whew," exclaimed Radu when they turned to the pages showing furniture. "Every time we look at this furniture, I am amazed. How is it that we don't' have anything like this in our part of the country? Would these ever look nice in our house! Our rooms are probably too small for some of this stuff anyway."

"Oh, I am sure we have furniture like this in our country, but it is in the homes of the Communist leaders."

"Hey, Daniel, look at this large bottle of water on top of a box with an opening on the side. What a clever way to have water in an office. It must be nice not to have to bring your own water bottle to work. Can you imagine our government providing water for the employees?"

"Now, Daniel, after looking at these pictures again, do you still want to remain in this pitiful place when such things exist on the outside? You can be sure that there is more out there than what is in this magazine."

"Yes, Radu, but again, you keep forgetting how many people have been killed trying to cross the river over the years. And what about those who made it and were captured by the Yugoslavs and returned? The result is the same. They are dead."

"Perhaps the difference, Daniel, is that they hadn't planned as well as we have. Besides, have you forgotten that Eugene made it? I still insist that if he can do it, so can we. We are at least as smart as he is."

"Ok, Radu, so he got across the river, but that is no assurance that he successfully made it through to Austria."

"Naw, Eugene made it for sure. You, yourself, just noted that captured escapees are returned by the Yugoslavs for certain death. Well, he hasn't been returned after all these months, so obviously he wasn't captured."

"Why do you think the authorities have played this down? Yes, they have put the family and Eugene's friends through a lot of grief, especially the beatings that they gave to his father. But nothing has been said about him for months now. They are embarrassed for sure!"

"So, how many times do I have to tell you that Eugene made it?"

"But do you think our fathers will be treated any better than Eugene's?"

"Yes, I have thought about that too, but Eugene's father was not seriously injured. I figure our fathers are as strong as Eugene's. Besides, remember that they will benefit from our escape. When we earn enough money to purchase their freedom, they will consider a little beating well worth it."

"Well now, seriously Daniel, when do you think we should try?"

"What do you mean 'try'"?

"Ok, you got me! When do you think we should 'plan' to escape?"

3

"That's better! Anyway, it's too late now. With the fall harvest upon us, my family will count on us to help bring in the crops and prepare for winter. Besides, the water will soon be too cold, though that would be to our benefit because the police would not expect someone to try swimming across the river in such temperatures."

"You know, Radu, I heard that the military have what they call wet suits that the divers use when going into water rescues. They say that the suits keep the divers warm when they are in cold water, but how would we ever acquire such a thing? Anyway, even if we had such suits, they are only good for swimming over the river."

"The problem is that with the cold nights we will soon be having, we have to be able to stay warm after the swim. It could take weeks before reaching the Austrian border. Besides, since we must wait until next year, we have a lot of time to improve our plans!"

"Ok, Daniel, you are right. We had better get back home. My mother will be worried and ask where I have been. With the lights being turned off at dusk, she worries any time I am out of the apartment. It is a good thing my dad works the evening shift because he doesn't know when I am out. Mother doesn't tell him because she is afraid he would whip me. She protects me when I sneak out to meet you."

"Radu, be careful to wrap our treasure well in that plastic bag since we probably won't be back here until next spring."

"Of course I will, my worrying friend!"

"By the way, Daniel, when we leave, you must take the alley home behind the bakery and then cut into the woods on the way to your village. Stay away from the apartments. Petru told me that the night security police have shifted the locations of their evening surveillance in town."

"How does Petru know? Did he get caught?"

"No, his father had gone to his grandmother's house last week before dark because she was ill. On his way home, he was trying to walk slowly and carefully behind the trees when he was grabbed. He tried to explain why he was out after curfew, but they took him to the station anyway and beat and questioned him for two hours. They said, 'You know the rules. No one is supposed to be out after curfew for any reason.' Obviously, the fact that his mother was ill was not justification to be out after curfew."

"Anyway, Radu, it is not the police I am afraid of. It's the dogs. If they start their barking, I am in trouble because the night police always go through our section of the village since we are the closest to town. We know they are there because the dogs are barking during the night. That is why I carry some pieces of bread with me to throw to the dogs if they start to bark."

"You are lucky, Radu, that you only have to sneak into the back of your apartment building."

After whispering "good luck" to one another, the boys carefully crawled out into the open carefully looking to make sure no one was nearby. They pulled the vines over the opening and quickly headed home.

Radu quietly made his way, staying in the shadows. He was almost home when he thought he heard someone sneezing. He carefully dropped to the ground in the shadow of a tree. Someone was indeed nearby, and that someone was coming in his direction. It must be the night police because he was shining his flashlight this way and that as he approached. No one but the police would use a flashlight at night. Radu was sure he would be found and be a goner. His heart was beating so hard he feared the approaching policeman would hear it. Just as Radu was about to be discovered, a co-worker approached, offering the man a drink.

As soon as the policeman changed direction for the drink with his buddy, Radu crawled through the shadows until he was far enough to run quickly to the back door of the apartment. Out of breath, he moved quickly through the door to the kitchen and tripped over a chair, making a terrible racket. A hand reached out and grabbed his shoulder. He was about to yell, when his mother said, "Radu!"

"Yes, Mother?"

"Son, where have you been? You scared me half to death. I thought you were in your room. You can imagine my surprise when I discovered you weren't there. Where were you, son?"

"Mom, I went out to meet one of my friends."

"Which friend?"

"Aw, Mom, that isn't important. I wasn't doing anything wrong. We just wanted to get out of the house to talk and tell stories."

"I should tell your dad when he gets home, and then you would be in trouble."

"Mom, if you do, you know dad will whip me. You don't want that to happen to me, do you?"

"No, son", she said as she brushed her hand through his hair. "I just want you to be safe. You know we can't take chances."

"At the market today, some of the women were talking about an incident a couple months ago when a boy in a village north of us was caught by the night police. After being beaten, he finally admitted that he had been out with a friend planning to escape. He and the other boy disappeared that very evening, and the parents have heard nothing since then. Since Eugene's assumed escape, they want to make sure that they put the fear of God in anyone planning to escape."

"No, Mom, it isn't the fear of God; it is the fear of Ceausescu!"

"Well, son, you know that life is cheap in our country and that the police can beat a confession out of anyone whether it is the truth or not. And, if they don't like the excuse, they can make one up and use the person as an example to scare everyone else into continued submission. Son, I don't want that to happen to you. So, promise me that you will not sneak out again after the curfew! Do you promise?"

"Yes, Mom, I promise."

He crawled under the covers and thought of the close call he had. Being reminded by his mother about those poor boys, he had difficulty falling asleep.

The next day Radu quickly found Daniel and blurted out, "Did you get home ok last night?"

"Radu, are you crazy! Don't talk so loudly! What if someone hears you? I am telling you that we must be more careful. In answer to your question, I almost didn't get home ok last night. I came within an inch of getting caught. The neighbor's dog started barking. I threw him a piece of bread, but he kept barking. A policeman was nearby and flashed his light my way. I had ducked just in time, crawled around to the front door and into the house. The policeman shined his light at our windows and walked around the house. My family was smart enough not to even speak as he walked around outside the door. Whew, it was close, and did I get it later! I am not sure which would be worse, the beating I got from my father or a beating from the police."

Radu could hardly wait for Daniel to finish so he could tell him about his close call with the night police too! His adrenalin was pumping as he relayed to Daniel how he had almost gotten caught. If it hadn't been for the alcohol, he might have been in real trouble, too! Then he told Daniel what his mother said about the two boys in the nearby village.

Daniel reminded Radu of the danger they faced as they proceeded with their plans. After their stories, they became sober again, and Daniel suggested that they had better drop the discussion for the time being. They agreed that, with the fall season approaching, they definitely should not meet in their root cave till next spring. Now that the leaves from the vines and thorns were beginning to dry and fall, they could no longer risk meeting there and having the magazine fall into the wrong hands.

CHAPTER 2 ESCAPE PLANS DELAYED

The fall harvest was always a happy time for Daniel's family because their large garden gave them assurance of sufficient vegetables until the next harvest. This winter would be particularly comfortable as they had good rain throughout the year and the harvest promised to be very good. This would enable them to barter some of their produce for other things needed for the winter.

Because Daniel's father, George, was able to do extra work, they were able to raise two pigs instead of the usual one pig. As if that wasn't enough, their cow had twin calves, which was quite rare. This would mean more meat for the winter and spring seasons. The smoke house would soon be operating full time. It would take several weeks to smoke the meat from the two pigs and one of the calves. The other calf would get a reprieve and spend the winter with the cow in the new animal shed.

Daniel had built it after the two calves were born. Daniel showed skill working with wood and enjoyed the work. He was very proud of his accomplishment. The old one was in very bad condition, and the cow had a difficult time in the winter because of the drafts through the many rotted boards. This winter, the cow and her calf would enjoy luxury.

Daniel had gone beyond the call of duty when building the shed. He also constructed several compartments in one wall for the chickens. The original chicken shed was as bad as the original animal shed. Daniel was sure that the chickens would appreciate their new quarters, too. He predicted that they would lay more eggs in appreciation for better quarters. His sisters said he was crazy, but he thought it made a good story anyway.

Living in an apartment, Radu's family didn't have the opportunity to have a garden. They had once owned a house and garden plot in a nearby village that no longer existed. When Ceausescu created the large collective farms, their village, like so many others, was destroyed and they were moved into apartments built for that purpose. Daniel's family was lucky because their village bordered the foothills of the Carpathian Mountains and was not of value for a collective farm.

Because Radu would work long hours helping Daniel's family bring in the crops, his family would share some of the harvest. One of the harvest time activities was preparation of cabbage in large containers for use in making cabbage rolls during the Christmas holiday season. Daniel and Radu, respectively, were responsible for preparing the cabbages for their families. Radu's family cabbage barrel would remain at Daniel's house because they did not have room in their apartment for storage.

The process included preparing about 20 normal size cabbages by cutting out about two inches of the core. They would fill the cavity with salt and place the cabbage, core up, in the large containers. After carefully stuffing the cabbages in the container, they would place a few ears of dry corn in the container to hasten the fermentation process. Then the container was filled to the top with hot water, and the lid was put on tightly.

Every other week until the holidays, they would carefully empty the water through a valve and pour it in again. This would help assure the complete mixing of the fermented salt water with the cabbage. By the holidays, the fermentation would change the cabbage color, texture, and flavor.

The result would be much like sauerkraut. Oh, what meals would be made by rolling chopped meat with onions, garlic, and spices along with rice into cabbage rolls for slow cooking over the stove for several hours.

The harvest at Daniel's farm was not the only harvest activity that the family was engaged in. The collective farm, where Radu's former village was located, required much work. Each family in the town and village where Radu and Daniel lived was required to spend some time working in the fields on evenings and weekends.

The previous year, Radu and Daniel had devised a great scheme for retrieving potatoes from the fields when it was their turn to dig them up. There was a ravine at the edge of the potato field that led to the river. A lot of bushes protected the view. They decided to try their scheme again this year. They carefully watched the progress in the fields, and when the work was getting close to the ravine, Radu would volunteer to work so their scheme could be pulled off.

He would throw some of the potatoes into the ravine while digging and no one else was watching. Daniel would be lying in the ravine waiting with a large burlap sack. As the potatoes were tossed in the ravine, he would quickly put them in the sack and drag them down to the riverbank and hide them in the bushes.

After dark, Daniel and Radu would bring the potatoes home and divide them between both families. Because Daniel's home was between the fields and the town, there was less danger of getting caught. It worked great, just like the previous year. This year they were able to get almost 50 kilo (110 lbs.). Daniel had to make two trips in the dark to get them.

He had an alarm system devised using his sisters. They would play in the back yard, and if anyone was coming, they would sing a particular song. When all was clear, they would sing a different song. They couldn't be too careful with such a treasure.

At first, Daniel's mother Lidia didn't agree with doing this since it was stealing, but finally, Daniel and his father convinced her that it was only right since the government was stealing from everyone. After all, the government had stolen the land from Radu, and all the other families put in the apartment buildings. They didn't even get paid for the "volunteer" work put out by each family. Everyone knew that the government officials were using their positions to their own financial advantage. So, if one was clever enough to gain, why not? Finally, Lidia saw the "wisdom" of their argument.

The killing of the pigs and calf would be a special occasion. This year Daniel's family planned to butcher the first week of November. To wait any longer would risk cold weather, which would hamper the process. George would do the honors. He was an expert in "sticking" pigs and calves. Doing this was the process of cutting the arteries so the animal would quickly and painlessly bleed to death. The neighbors would be called upon to help in the process since the poor animals would sense their coming doom and would put up a valiant fight for their lives. It was a messy business, one that had gone on since the beginning of time in Romania and other Eastern European countries.

On the morning of the kill, they would start with the pigs. Daniel, Radu, and a couple neighbors would go back a bit from the house near the sheds. They would hold the pig while George would stick a large knife into the main artery. All the while the pig would struggle to get away and yell with a high- pitched squeal. If, as occasionally happened, his father missed the artery the first time and the pig got away, property was in danger and the pig would be difficult to catch. After retrieving it, George would have to do it again and then the poor pig would be in terrible pain. That part was not at all enjoyable, but there was no other way to accomplish the task. Daniel's sisters would sit in the house with their fingers in their ears during the killing process.

After the pigs were killed, they were hoisted up by the hind feet with chains over a rack constructed every year for that purpose. It was an iron pipe horizontally installed over a wooden frame. Then, George would get the blowtorch filled with kerosene and burn all the hair from the pig's body. From there, the pigs would be gutted.

This year, the killing was precise, and the pigs were immediately hoisted up to bleed into a pan. Nothing was wasted. The blood was used to make pudding, and some of the fat was used to make soap. The intestines were cleaned out and used for making sausage.

While the men were butchering the pig, they would cut out pieces of the fat near the skin and chew on it the whole time they worked, much like someone would chew tobacco. Daniel and Radu each got a large piece of fat to chew. It was warm with a strong pork taste. Now that was real living!

CHAPTER 3 A FRIGHTFUL CHARGE

In the middle of November, on an evening with no moonlight, there was a knock at Daniel's door. George told the family to be quiet and opened the door to face two angry policemen shining flashlights into his eyes. They pushed him aside and walked in.

"Where is the radio?" George responded that they didn't have a radio, to which they exclaimed, "We know different! One of your loyal villagers told us that you have been hiding one away to listen to broadcasts from the West." Again, George denied the charge. One of the men struck him across the face with his fist causing him to bleed. They ransacked every room in the house, and then dragged George behind the house where they spent an hour looking through the vegetable bin, the smoke house, the animal shed, the corn bin, and haystacks. Finding nothing, they took him to the police station, interrogating and beating him for several hours, before letting him return to his home in a very sad physical condition.

All the while, Lidia and the girls sat and cried. Daniel tried to calm them and assure them that George would be ok since he was innocent. Daniel was not very successful. When his father finally arrived home, it was like "the prodigal son" returning. The entire family doted over him and bandaged his wounds. They had prepared a hot snack. The family sat up for hours and discussed the situation. The big question was, had the police singled them out randomly, or had someone turned them in? Then the question was, why? As far as they knew, they were liked by everyone. George couldn't think of any enemies at his job.

George had no choice but to go to work with his injuries the next morning. When he arrived, he was shunned by the other workers and even his friends. At their break time, he tried to talk with Radu's father, Samuel (Sami), who was his best friend.

Sami told him to stay away. He whispered, "They are watching all of us and if we speak to you, they may come and do the same thing to us. Someone turned you in, and I think I know who it was."

George whispered back, "Who would do this to me?" Sami said that it would be dangerous for him to say.

The torment didn't end with George. Daniel was ridiculed at school. Obviously, the teachers were told to make things difficult for him, too. He could do nothing right in any of his classes. He was one of the best students in his grade, which afforded him a front row seat as recognition, but now he was moved to the back row in every class. He was asked questions he could not answer, and then ridiculed by the teachers. Other students were told to shun him because his family could not be trusted.

The only bright spot came when Radu brushed by him saying, "I can't talk because we are being watched, but I don't believe any of those things they are saying."

"Thanks", whispered Daniel in tears. Radu was truly his friend and he wondered what he would do without him.

The students accused Daniel's father of being a traitor. After class, Daniel was made to clean the blackboards and empty the trash in each of his classrooms. He did not get home till dark. He was stopped by the night patrol to explain why he was out alone.

Daniel, thinking the policeman was sympathetic, tried to explain the events of the day and the treatment he had received. Instead of sympathy, the policeman punched him, knocking him down and caused his books to fall to the ground. He quickly gathered them up and ran home, bursting into the kitchen with tears streaming down his face.

"Daniel, where have you been and why are you crying?" Lidia wept as he told her every detail of his day.

She explained that her day was not good either. She went to the market, like she did every day, to buy bread and other necessary things. When she knocked on the door of Mari, her best friend who always accompanied her to the market, there was no response. She thought it strange, but after a few attempts she went on to the market. When she spoke to other friends along the way, they turned their backs and didn't return her greetings. When she finally got to the market, she saw Mari. She approached her and said, "Mari, why did you come to the market without me? You have never done that before."

Mari turned her back on Lidia, who was in tears by this time. She said, "Please Mari, have I done something?"

Mari, with her back still turned, whispered, "I can't be seen talking with you. I am sorry but we will have to talk later."

Lidia turned and headed for the bread store. When she got there, the clerk told her that the bread was all sold and turned her back on Lidia. As she walked away, she saw another villager walk up to the bread counter and receive bread. Still in tears, she went to buy tomatoes and cucumbers, which were not in the best of condition at this time of year, and she was given only half rotten items. When she tried to object, she was told to take them or get nothing. She needed food for her children and husband, so she laid her precious money down for very poor goods and trudged home in despair.

As she relayed this incident to Daniel, his sisters, who were also treated badly in school, began crying. Soon they were all crying together and hugging one another.

Just at that point, George entered the home to see the dearest people in his life weeping. As they each relayed their stories, he just sat in silence.

Finally, he said, "I just don't understand it! We have always been highly respected, and Daniel has been a model student. Why are they doing this to us? We aren't happy with our government, but we are not traitors! Surely someone has made false statements about us, but who and why?"

"This is just another ploy by the Securitate to scare everyone from any thoughts of revolution. Ceausescu is a tyrant, and something should be done about him and his regime!"

"George, don't you dare say such a thing! That is traitorous talk and that is what you are being accused of."

"Well, it's true."

Lidia suggested that they go to bed early and prepare for the next day, which would probably be a repeat of this one. She pulled out one of her Orthodox Icons, made the sign of the cross, and chanted some well-used prayers.

Daniel said, "Mother, why do you do that? You know it doesn't do any good. Why do you believe in God anyway? If there was a God, He would not allow the terrible life we have in Romania. I wish I was never born in Romania! Why couldn't we have been born in another country, like America, where they have nice cars and houses and furniture, and other things?"

"What are you saying? What do you know about such things? Who have you been talking with? Is it your friend Radu?" Daniel realized he had made a foolish mistake, but he could not dare to let his parents know of the magazine and his plans to escape with Radu. He hated lying to his mother, but he responded that a couple kids at school were saying these things. Stepping into the conversation, George told him not to talk to those boys again, or he could bring more trouble for his family.

Daniel sighed inside and realized how close he had come to divulging his secret. He realized more than ever how careful he needed to be. He was also more determined than ever to escape life in Romania. The risk would be worth it! Because of the day's unhappy circumstances, he laid awake most of the night, wishing he could have revenge and thinking of his and Radu's escape plans.

Daniel's family was not the only family disappointed by what had happened. When Sami got home from work, Radu was relating how Daniel had been treated at school. When he finished, Grati told her husband and son what Lidia had gone through at the market. Lidia had stopped by in tears to speak of her disappointment with how Mari had treated her. Sami then relayed to them the events of the day for George. Before they were done relaying their accounts, no one had any appetite. They agreed that they must be careful not to be seen with Daniel's family for a few days or weeks until things blew over. Sami simply said that this was the way it was in Romania, and there was nothing that anyone could do about it. As Radu lay down for the evening, his thoughts also went to his and Daniel's plan to escape. Now, with more resolve than ever, he, too, was determined that they should accomplish their plans.

George continued to be verbally buffeted by the bosses and rejected by his co-workers for a couple weeks. His family also continued to be shunned and taunted.

Unfortunately, this process was followed by the Securitate against different families from time to time. It was done to keep them on edge and afraid to speak any words of dissatisfaction regarding conditions in the country. Ceausescu lived in continual distrust that the people would revolt against his regime, so he kept the pressure on everyone.

Daniel was determined that he was going to prove that he was being persecuted unjustly by studying harder than he had ever studied before. The teachers were having a hard time being harsh with him because he always had the correct answers to fair questions. They had received their orders from higher up and were sick at having to play the role of inquisitor. Radu would give Daniel a thumbs up at every opportunity, using care not to be seen by the other students or the teachers.

Daniel's father worked harder than ever to justify himself, too.

The family continued to be in a quandary over what and who had precipitated this injustice. Finally, during the last week of November, the mystery began to come to light. Late one night, the Securitate knocked on the door of the Popescu family a few houses down from Daniel's home. A search was conducted as had been done at Daniel's home a couple weeks previously. A radio was found along with some foreign magazines under the hay in the loft of their chicken coop. The entire Popescu family disappeared that night and was not heard from again. Their house was boarded up. That day, two mysteries were cleared up for Daniel and Radu.

The first was that Daniel's family might have been accidentally singled out for the violations. The second, known only to Daniel and Radu, was that Mr. Popescu was probably the man who had lost the magazine that Daniel and Radu found. A third mystery evolved from the clearing of the previous two. Who had turned Daniel's family in, and why? Sami had told George that he had a suspicion of who it might have been, but he didn't feel that he dared to comment on it. Will he feel comfortable to share his views in the future?

CHAPTER 4 HOLIDAYS GONE AWRY

As November turned into December and Christmas approached, Lidia began her traditional rituals in preparation for this special season. The problem was that it was not particularly special to Daniel since he didn't believe in God. He certainly didn't believe in a Christ Child born in Jerusalem, Who, as very God, came into the world to save sinners. He didn't see himself as a sinner either. He lived as well as anyone else that he knew, and better than most.

Besides, if there was any chance that there was a God, he assumed he was safe because he was baptized into the Orthodox Church when he was eight days old. He had been forced to take religion classes in grade school, as a result of the fact that the Communist government appeased the Orthodox Church in order to gets its help indoctrinating the Romanian culture with Communist ideology. He was always told that he didn't have to give serious consideration to Orthodox doctrine since he was baptized. None of his friends believed in God, either and rather prided themselves for their enlightened position. After all religion was the "opiate of the people," as they were often reminded in school, Daniel was too smart to be duped into believing something that didn't seem to have had any impact on the society.

After all, if all that religion stuff was true, why did so many people steal from their neighbor's gardens, etc. when they had the chance? Why did everyone lie to each other or the government if it benefited them? Perhaps the biggest inconsistency that Daniel observed was in the lives of the Orthodox priests. Why were they so often seen at the pubs in a drunken state with members of their church, telling and laughing at dirty jokes?

And then, even though they were married with families, why were some of them cavorting with other women in their parish? They especially liked the young girls. Everyone knew that the priests received special privileges from the government in the form of food, clothing, and wood for the winter. These necessities gave them bargaining power for sexual favors and other things. So, all in all, they didn't live any differently than the rest of the society. Well, that is, most of the rest of the society.

The exceptions were the "Repenters" who seemed to live by a different code. They got that name because they re-baptized people who repented for their sins and accepted Christ into their hearts, whatever that meant. After all, didn't the Orthodox believe in Christ? Everyone thought that the Repenters were strange, but one had to admit that their lives were more moral than the society at large. They seemed to take their beliefs seriously, but to no advantage, because they were often persecuted by the government and by their neighbors. Repenters were always passed over for the better jobs, even though they were usually more diligent at their jobs than their Orthodox counterparts.

The Orthodox priests mocked them and even threatened to put curses on the families of anyone who dared to attend their services. Not only that, when they met for the services on Sundays and Wednesday evenings, they were frequently harassed by the Securitate. They would stand outside the Repenters' meeting place, poking fun at them and shoving them or hitting them with the butts of their rifles.

The fact that they were willing to accept such treatment seemed to be evidence that they were, indeed, not very smart. Anyway, that was how Daniel had sized up the Repenters. Well, that was before he experienced a firsthand incident with John, who was from a Repenter family. John had been a fellow student as long as Daniel could remember, but he had never given him the time of day because of his religion. Daniel certainly didn't want to be associated with anyone who was considered somewhat of an outcast.

Daniel had been sent by his mother to purchase some ingredients for holiday pastries she was making. It was a particularly cold day and it had snowed the evening before. Daniel had made his purchase and was returning home. He decided to take a shortcut because of the cold and cross the creek that ran along the edge of the town. He had a favorite crossing spot that required jumping on large rocks placed in the creek for that purpose. He had crossed the creek many times in good weather without any mishap but on this day, conditions were different. The rocks were coated with a thin layer of ice. When Daniel hit the first rock on the run, his foot slipped out from under him, and the rest of the story could be guessed. He landed in the creek, hitting his head on a rock and splitting his scalp open. Daniel was stunned for a moment as he tried to get out of the water. He was totally soaked, and a brisk wind instantly chilled him to the bone. Because he was about a half kilometer from home, he was in trouble. His path took him past the home of John, who just happened to be playing in the snow with his brothers.

As John looked up at the approaching figure, he recognized Daniel was in trouble. He ran toward his shivering classmate, noticing that he was soaked, and his head was bleeding. He insisted that Daniel come into the warmth of his home. At this point, Daniel's predisposition toward John and Repenters, in general, was cast aside. He was in trouble and needed help. As John grabbed him and pulled him inside their humble home, Daniel could not have been more grateful. John's mother, who had heard her son's yell for help, met them at the door.

"Oh my, young man, what happened to you?"

Before he could answer, she whisked him into their living room in front of the fireplace where a large log was burning. "John, this boy is about your size. Go and get some of your clothes. He will need everything."

While John ran for the clothing, his mother took off Daniel's coat that was still dripping with water and wrapped him in a blanket. When John returned, his mother told him to help the boy get changed while she stepped out to get him something warm to drink. Soon Daniel was in warm clothing while his wet clothes hung in front of the fireplace to dry.

John's mother, Cristina, returned a few minutes later with a cup of hot tea and a couple biscuits. She also had a patch of cloth to put on his wound after she cleaned it with warm water and administered some salve used when their animals had injuries.

"Young man, what is your name and where do you live?"

He responded that his name was Daniel and that he lived at the next village. He related his mishap and then proudly noted that, although he was totally soaked, he had not dropped his precious purchase. They had a laugh over that.

As they talked, Daniel took in his surroundings with interest. He had never been in the home of a Repenter. Everything looked pretty normal, but he noted that there were none of the icons that his mother hung in every room of their home. He also noticed a worn book on a small table with the words Biblia on the cover.

Daniel said that he needed to get home quickly because he had been gone for some time and his mother would be very worried. "Can I wear John's clothes home," he asked?

"Well now, Daniel, I don't think you have any other option." Daniel laughed as he thought of the obvious.

"You can come back tomorrow to switch clothing."

Daniel thanked everyone for the hospitality and food and ducked out into the cold wearing John's old coat. It was old, but it was warm! He carried his precious purchase in one hand and held the cloth on his wound with the other.

After Daniel left, Cristina asked John if Daniel was one of his friends at school. John responded that Daniel was a classmate but not a friend. Daniel had always ignored him, probably because he is a Repenter. He noted that sometimes Daniel had made fun of him with some of the other popular students. He recounted one exception a few weeks back when Daniel had been ostracized by the teachers and some of the students because his father had been accused of being a traitor.

"Daniel found out what it feels like to be rejected by others. He deserved it after the way he has acted toward me."

"John, shame on you for saying such a thing! Haven't we taught you better than that? This boy is only acting like an unsaved person would be expected to act. He needs the Lord to change his heart like he has done with ours.

"I know, Mom, but it is hard to forgive people when they don't treat us right."

"I know, son, but the Lord has promised his grace when we follow His command to love our enemies. In a sense, Daniel is an enemy. He is an enemy of Christ, and the Bible teaches us that if the world hates Jesus, it will hate us. What you should do is pray for him to receive Christ one day."

"That is about as likely as having a hot summer day tomorrow."

"Now, John, remember that with God, all things are possible!"

At this point in their conversation, John's father walked in from work looking half frozen.

"Whew, this is mean weather so early in the winter season. I hope this doesn't mean we will have a bad winter. We won't have enough wood to keep warm. Speaking of warm, I am going to sit in front of the fire."

He had hardly spoken these words when John's brother blurted out the incident with Daniel. John Sr. chuckled at what he had missed.

"Now, John, shame on you for laughing at Daniel's mishap," Cristina said as she began to laugh. "He was really something of a sight, though." They all laughed as she said, "Well, let's go to the kitchen for supper."

When Daniel entered his home, Lidia asked, "Daniel, where have you been?" Looking at him more closely, she said, "What are you wearing and what happened to your head?"

Daniel proudly held up his purchase with a smile on his face. Then he quickly recounted his accident and the kindness shown by John's family.

"Mom, they really are nice people and treated me almost like I was a friend. I sort of felt guilty because I have never been John's friend. I have even made fun of him for being a Repenter."

"That is a good lesson to you, Son. Sometimes you are too quick to judge others. I have noticed that about you and especially your friend, Radu. If you want people to treat you nicely, you should treat them the same. I think that is taught somewhere in the Bible."

"Speaking of the Bible, I never see you reading our Bible. I haven't even seen it anywhere."

"It isn't necessary for us to read the Bible because the priests tell us what we are supposed to know. In fact, it is dangerous to read the Bible for ourselves because we might not understand it correctly. Only the priests, who have gone to the seminary, are able to interpret it. Why do you ask anyway?"

18

"Well, I noticed a Bible in John's house on a table in front of the fireplace, and it looked very worn, like it is read a lot."

"That is interesting." At that she walked into the kitchen to get something to change the dressing on his head.

When she returned, Daniel asked her why she had icons in every room of the house as he didn't see anything like that in John's house. She noted that they bring good luck.

"If they are supposed to bring good luck, then why did we go through all the accusations a few weeks ago?"

"I don't know, Son."

When George got home, Daniel again recounted the day's events.

George said, "Lidia, why not make some holiday pastry for that family in appreciation of their help."

"George, isn't that going a little too far? After all, they are Repenters!"

His response was rather sharp! "It seems like they went rather far to help our son, didn't they?"

"Dad is right. Didn't you just accuse me of being too quick to judge others? Maybe I learned it from you."

Daniel had gone too far with that remark and was told by his father that he would not allow his children to sass their mother, even if they were right! There was a glimmer in his eye as he made the statement, looking directly at his wife. Well, perhaps everyone learned a lesson at that moment. The suggestion of making pastries for John's family fell by the wayside.

The next day on his walk to school, Daniel took the long way so he could stop at John's house to switch clothes. He thanked them again, and since John was ready to leave for school, they walked together. As they approached the school, Radu was waiting for Daniel. He didn't even speak to John, but said to Daniel, "Where have you been and why are you walking with a Repenter?"

John quickly headed for the classroom to avoid being a part of the discussion that followed between Daniel and Radu. Daniel said, "Calm down, it is not what you think. I will tell you later, but first we better get to class."

Later that day, Daniel told Radu the events of the previous day that led up to his arrival at school with John. Radu didn't seem impressed, which bothered Daniel a little. In his brief encounter with John's family, he felt different about the Repenters and even wondered if their faith was more genuine than the Orthodox Faith.

In the Orthodox tradition, a lot of fanfare was made at Christmas. Cakes were taken to the church with lighted candles in the center. Lidia usually made several cakes so she could take a different one to the church each of the seven days before Christmas. She would make the sign of the cross several times, once for each member of the family, upon entering the church.

She would light candles for family members who had died and needed help getting out of purgatory, or so she said. She would leave the cakes for the priests. Regarding purgatory, Daniel never believed any of that stuff because if there was no God, there certainly was no heaven, hell, or purgatory. Daniel was too enlightened for that! After all, the younger generations knew evolution was a scientific fact. The problem with the older generations was that they were not trained in scientific facts. Daniel was very confident of his position because that was what everyone believed in his grade at school, that is, with the exception of John, who couldn't possibly be right!

In addition to cakes, many people took some of their home brew to the priests to buy their favor. George was no exception. He was known for his home brew. Daniel's family had several plum trees and plenty of grape vines, the kind for making wine. George had two stills, one for making whiskey from plums and one for wine from the grapes. George was so good at making whiskey that he could use just about any fruit with success. He had used apricots and cherries in the past, but because plums were always plentiful, he had used plums the last several years. This year was no exception.

George was always on very good terms with the priest in their parish because of his brew. It irritated Daniel that his father would buddy up to the priests to get spiritual favors that neither of them believed in. He had once challenged his father on the basis of his disbelief in God. George's response was that just in case there was a God, he wanted to be His friend.

Daniel's family always had a big feast for the Christmas holiday, which started on Christmas Eve with more food than one could imagine for the two days. Most families would eat like there was no tomorrow. This year would be the same. Their very traditional meal consisted of several courses. There was chicken noodle soup, salad, cabbage rolls, and pork and chicken with mashed potatoes and a vegetable.

This feast was followed by plates of sweet cakes of every size, shape, and flavor imaginable. The meal was washed down with a very strong espresso coffee, followed by wine or whiskey. This part was of no interest to Daniel, as he had never developed a taste for alcohol. His dislike was not a result of any moral considerations. He simply didn't like the taste, and he disliked the results of alcohol that he had seen too often. Radu was one who frequently could not control himself after he had a few too many. That was the only thing about Radu Daniel did not appreciate. He had to practically carry Radu home from many a party.

New Years was always a repeat of Christmas, with drinking well into the night. It seemed a little stupid to Daniel to make such a fuss over a holiday based on fables, and then have little to eat for the remainder of the month.

In John's house, there were also many preparations for the holidays, but from a very different perspective. Most of the food preparations were similar, except there would be no alcohol.

Radu and Daniel usually went to the forest together to cut down trees to decorate for the holidays. They usually decorated their trees on the morning of Christmas Eve in preparation for the evening festivities. While the women were in the kitchen, the rest of the family decorated the trees and ate small cakes and cookies with tea.

This year, Radu's parents were going to make the four-hour drive to Timisoara to spend the holidays with other family members. Radu and Daniel would not spend the holidays together, which was a real disappointment. They had so many days without school and would not be able to spend any time together during the happiest time of the year. Their goodbyes were said with sorrow.

Early the day before Christmas Eve, Daniel headed out to the forest by himself to cut down a tree, since Radu was out of town and his father had chores caring for the animals.

As Daniel entered the part of the forest where the best trees were, he noticed a father and son ahead. He decided to join them because he was feeling a little down. As he approached, he realized it was, of all people, John and his father. He thought to himself, "I am glad Radu is not here to see me with the Repenters."

They exchanged greetings, and John introduced his father to Daniel.

"I heard of your swim in the creek recently. I thought only polar bears did this in the winter."

Daniel was not sure how to respond, but when he saw the warm smile and twinkle in the father's eyes, he began to laugh.

"I wouldn't want that to happen again unless your wife had some more of those good cookies she gave me. It was almost worth the fall for the cookies."

They all laughed, and Daniel thought to himself, "What am I doing laughing and socializing with Repenters? I really am glad Radu isn't here! He would never forgive me."

As those thoughts were running through his mind, John blurted out, "Daniel, you are in luck! Mother made some cookies and a thermos of hot coffee for us to bring on our tree hunting expedition. I am sure my dad won't mind if you shared them with us."

"Absolutely, you will share with us," said his father. "This is the season to share, and besides, it is part of our faith to show kindness and share with others."

"Thanks," blurted Daniel, somewhat embarrassed.

As they entered the thickest part of the forest, they flushed out two wild boars that were digging out roots to eat. These animals were a problem in the area

21

because of the proximity to the foothills of the mountains. They would come out of the mountains and raid the gardens. In some of the villages closer to the mountains, villagers would have to share vigil day and night to ward them off. The people would keep fires going all night, and when boars came down, people would light sticks with pitch to chase them away.

They could be dangerous, and occasionally one of the villagers would be attacked, especially if there was more than one boar. When in numbers, they could really be bold. For that reason, only the older boys and men were allowed to take part. The rule was that there needed to be more than one person holding vigil for protection.

As the boars retreated further into the forest, Daniel said, "I am not sure who was the most surprised, the boars or us."

Soon they found the trees that they were looking for and cut down two that were approximately two meters tall. They sat on a dead tree stump and opened the coffee and container of cookies. Though it was quite cold, the thick tree shelter blocked the wind, making the conditions tolerable.

John, Sr. said, "I hope you don't mind sharing the canteen with us, as we didn't bring any cups."

"No, that is ok."

Then John Sr. really surprised Daniel when he asked his son to give thanks for the cookies and coffee. They closed their eyes while John gave a short word of thanks for the time of year, their safety, the cookies and the coffee. Daniel did not know what to do. When they closed their eyes, he wondered if he should, too, so he would not look like a heathen.

"But who is looking? What am I thinking anyway? I am a heathen by religious standards!"

After the prayer, they ate their snacks and decided it was time to make the trip back home. They swapped Christmas stories all the way. After leaving the forest, they parted ways for their homes and wished each other a Merry Christmas. Daniel repeated the greeting for the sake of being sociable, but he didn't expect this Christmas to be a merry one with Radu in Timisoara.

When John and his father reached home, the younger brothers were all excited with the tree and said, "Oh! I think this is the best tree ever."

John thought to himself, "They say that every year."

While his father was getting the tree set in the stand, John told Cristina about meeting Daniel in the forest and all that took place. "Mother, I think he was a little uncomfortable with us, especially when we prayed for the cookies and coffee we shared with him."

"Son, you must remember how the Orthodox feel about us, and as you said before, he has ignored you and even laughed at you in the past. I think he probably was uncomfortable. But it sounds like you and your father were a good testimony before him. You must continue to pray that Daniel and his family will put their faith in Christ someday."

"I think that would take a miracle since Daniel says that he doesn't even believe there is a God."

"Son, with God all things are possible. Here is your opportunity to show love to your enemy."

"Mom, I wouldn't exactly call him an enemy."

"You know what I mean."

John, his brothers and father decorated the tree while Cristina was busy in the kitchen. They also sang Christmas carols. Cristina's soprano voice could be heard emanating from the kitchen. Following the decorating of the tree, John, Sr. went to fetch his parents for the Christmas Eve feast.

What a grand time they would have when the grandparents arrived! Grandpa always read the Christmas story. They would sing carols, and then Grandpa would tell stories about what Christmas was like when he was a child, before the Communist regime took control of the country. Of course, they would feast on the sweets mother made while listening to the stories.

When Daniel got home with his tree, his three sisters were all excited as usual. George helped him put the tree in the stand. Having nothing else to do, he decided to help his sisters decorate the tree while Lidia was in the kitchen preparing for the meal. If Radu was here, Daniel would be hanging out with him. Lidia interrupted his thoughts by asking him if he had met anyone on his way to the forest to get the tree.

Not wanting to tell her who he was with, he responded that there was a man with his son.

"Well, who was it?"

"It was a boy named John and his father."

"Was it the boy who helped you the other day?"

"Yes, it was my luck to meet the Repenters. I am glad Radu isn't here. I would never hear the end of it, and he would probably tell the other guys at school. I would be the laughingstock with my friends."

He didn't share too many of the details, especially about the prayer they offered before eating the snack. He was a little embarrassed to admit to himself that no such prayers were offered for meals in his home, although his mother acted as if they were so religious.

After some moments, Lidia scolded him for his comments about the Repenters. "I think you are not being fair with that boy. He seems to be a fine young man. Whatever else Repenters do, they seem to raise their children to be polite and respectful. I will tell you one thing; you could learn some manners from them. You still haven't learned that you must learn to live in peace with everyone."

23

Daniel felt the sting of the criticism because in his heart; he knew she was right. He grabbed his coat and said that he was going out to get some fresh air. The curfew would be relaxed because it was Christmas Eve.

As Daniel left the house, Lidia mumbled to herself, "What am I going to do with that boy? He is always so critical of everyone different than himself. It is that Radu. I wish Daniel had a different friend. But since Sami is George's best friend at work, a different friend will probably never happen."

The air was very crisp, and Daniel followed his breath around for a while. He had to admit John really was not so strange after all. He was almost envious of John because he seemed to be close to his father in a neat sort of way. Daniel wished he and his father had the same relationship. George always seemed too busy to spend any quality time with him. As Daniel thought on this, he wondered if John's faith had anything to do with his relationship with his father. Daniel was a little haunted by his chance meeting with them in the woods. What if it was not a chance meeting?

Realizing the implications of this thought, he quickly pushed it out of his mind. If Radu had been here, none of this would have happened. It seemed that in the peace and quiet of the outdoors, his mind was overactive, so he went into the house to get his mind on other things. He decided trying to enjoy Christmas along with his family.

Back at John's home, the grandparents arrived with their son, and the family had a wonderful time celebrating God's greatest gift to mankind: the birth of the Savior. John and one brother shared the same bed, but on this evening, they would allow their grandparents to have their bed. They would sleep on the floor in front of the fireplace, wrapped in the warm wool blankets that their mother made.

Cristina made extra money from sewing wool blankets and selling them in the market. She would buy the freshly sheared wool and weave her own thread. It was quite an art, and John always marveled while watching her weave the wool into thread. She had learned the art from her mother who learned it from her mother.

As John and his brothers snuggled into the blankets, he thought, "It sure is easy to see how sheep have no problems with the cold winter weather. God surely cares for those He has created!"

The next morning, John and his brothers were awakened with the smell of cooking in the kitchen. Cristina was singing carols softly while she worked, trying to be as quiet as possible for everyone's benefit. Soon, everyone was up greeting each other with Craciun Fericit (Merry Christmas).

As they opened the few gifts John's parents were able to provide, they agreed that they were a blessed people, even though they had to live under Ceausescu's repressive Communist regime. After all, because of the holiday they were celebrating, they had the assurance of freedom in heaven one day.

John and his family spent much of Christmas Day at their little Baptist Church. When they arrived, it was packed. Extra wood had been brought by the members to assure a very "warm" fellowship for an extra-long service. John's family had been invited for dinner by one of the families in the village. Following a wonderful traditional Romanian meal, the children went out so the adults could fellowship until the evening service. The joy of the season blotted out the realities of life in bondage.

After arriving home, John came up with a great idea. "Mom and Dad, why don't we go Christmas caroling at Daniel's home? I sort of like him, even though he has not been very nice to me in the past. I bet they would be really surprised!"

Cristina replied, "I don't know. We really don't know them at all. Besides, it is getting a little late for such a thing."

John, Sr. said, "Well, we have had two chance meetings with Daniel in the last couple of weeks. Maybe the Lord wants us to be a further witness to him and his family. Everyone stays up late during the Christmas holidays."

"Perhaps." After a few moments of thought, she said, "Ok, let's do it. I still have some of those cookies that Daniel likes. We will wrap them up and present them to Daniel's family after we sing."

The grandparents noted that they would stay home, keep the fire burning until their return, and saying a prayer for their ministry of song to Daniel's family.

John, Sr. led the way through the darkness, with only the moon to light their path. John's brothers laughed and chattered all the way to Daniel's house. When they arrived, the dog was barking to signal their arrival. Cristina was the one with the good voice, so she began to lead them in singing Silent Night, Holy Night.

Lidia was the first to respond. "What in the world! Someone is singing outside our house." She opened the door to see John and his family.

"Come here," she said to the family. They all stumbled to the door.

Lidia asked Daniel, "Who are these people?"

"They are the Repenters who helped me when I fell into the creek."

"You cut the tree down with them yesterday?"

"Yes," was Daniel's reply as he thought, "I can't believe this, I can't seem to get away from them."

After singing half a dozen songs, John, Sr. extended his hand to George. Though their wives had not really met, they knew each other from working at the factory.

Cristina stepped forward with the cookies and said, "Daniel seemed to enjoy these at our home and in the forest yesterday, so I thought you might enjoy them too."

Lidia received them and awkwardly asked if they would like to come in.

"Thank you, but I am sure you are busy celebrating Christmas, so we will be on our way home."

"Merry Christmas!" they said as they walked away.

When they arrived home, they told the grandparents about their visit.

Grandpa said, "I think God was pleased with what you did tonight. We may never know what could come of that visit. Those people need the Lord, and maybe this evening the door to their hearts has been cracked open a little for the Lord to get his foot in, so to speak."

Back at Daniel's home, an interesting conversation was taking place. Lidia was the first to speak. Daniel, "I told you that those folks seemed to be good people for the way they helped you when you fell in the creek and shared cookies with you yesterday. Speaking of cookies, let's see if these are as good as your mother makes." They laughed as Lidia headed to the kitchen to make tea.

As they started eating, George said, "Mother, you need this recipe."

The week passed quickly as the New Year approached. It had been a particularly perplexing week for Daniel. Without the influence of Radu, and due to the unusual events of the past couple of weeks with the Repenters, Daniel found himself wondering what was happening to him. It scared him that he found himself liking John and his family, and he even missed their kindness.

As always, John's small church was planning to have a service on New Year's Eve. This was always a special time of singing and giving testimonies of God's grace throughout the year. Each family brought some sweets, and hot water was ready on the pot-bellied stove that heated the one-room church. John's family had prayed all week for Daniel and his family, that they would accept Christ. John asked his father if he could invite Daniel to the service that evening.

"Why, John, I think that is a wonderful idea."

"I am sure he will laugh at me, but that is ok. People laughed at Jesus too. At least I will feel better if I try."

"You are so right! I will say a prayer for you as you go to invite him."

Mustering all the courage he had, which wasn't very much, he headed out the door to Daniel's house. When he arrived, the dog was there to announce his arrival. He knocked on the door and Daniel opened it. Now that he was there, John didn't know what to say.

After what seemed like forever, he blurted out, "I know your friend Radu is not here, and I thought that if you didn't have anything to do tonight, you could come to our service at the church at 7:00. We sing and stuff and then have cakes and cookies with tea."

Daniel was so surprised that he did not know what to say. In fact, he didn't have any plans for the evening. He stammered that he would probably be busy.

"I know it is probably hard for you to be seen visiting our church, since I know you don't like Repenters. But I like you and would like you to come. If you decide to come, you can come in the back door with me so no one will see you entering the church. I will be by the back door waiting for you. We can sit in the back of the church. Well, bye," he said as he nervously spun around to head for home.

He thought to himself, "Did I really say that? I was embarrassed and he was probably embarrassed, too. "He will never come," John said out loud as if talking with someone. When he got home, he told his mother and father what he had done and how he had "blown it."

Noting the tears in his eyes, Cristina put her arms around him and said, "Son, I am proud of you. You are no longer a boy. You are becoming a man like your father. What you did is what a man of God would do. He probably won't come, but you tried." His father also commended him. Their responses meant more to John than they could know.

John couldn't wait for the evening service to arrive. How he hoped that Daniel would come! Seeing his anxiety, his father reminded him not to get his hopes up. Things were probably moving too fast to expect that Daniel would come.

John said he could hope anyway, to which his father said, "Yes, son, you certainly can." John left for the church before the family, just in case Daniel would come early. People began to arrive around 7:00, but no Daniel. The service started with prayer and then they began singing.

John slipped out the back door to check once more, but Daniel was not there. As he went back inside, his father looked back at him and smiled understandingly. John decided he would stay by the back door anyway, just in case. A half hour or so went by and then the doorknob slowly turned. John's heart raced. Could it be Daniel? As the door opened, John's heart leaped. It was Daniel! He could not believe it. Daniel had come. God had answered his prayer.

John grabbed the door and said quietly, "Hi Daniel. I am glad you came. Sit here with me."

Daniel had arrived while a hymn was being sung, so no one knew he was there except John, Sr. Secretly, he had been praying for a miracle for his son's sake and for Daniel's sake. He looked back, and with a broad grin on his face caught John's eye.

Shortly after, people began to give testimonies of God's goodness to them during the past year. Daniel could not believe what he was hearing. He had never heard such talk before. People were thanking God for blessing their lives.

In Daniel's opinion, there was nothing about living in Romania that would cause someone to thank God. After all, he was planning to escape with Radu because he couldn't see any reason to be happy in such a country. One testimony after another flowed, and Daniel felt like he was in a trance.

Then the pastor stood up to say a few words. As he looked over the small congregation, he quickly noticed Daniel sitting next to John. Before the service, John had told the pastor that he had invited an unsaved friend to the service. Seeing Daniel next to John. He breathed a prayer that he would say what Daniel needed to hear on this first exposure to the Gospel. The last thing he wanted to do was come on too strong with the Gospel and scare Daniel away.

He also noted that there were no Securitate agents in the service. They were all busy celebrating and getting drunk, so he would have liberty that he did not usually have. He started by thanking everyone for coming to the service. He agreed with the many who had testified of God's goodness during the past year.

"We have had a better than usual harvest this fall, and we have not lost any of our members through death." He then spoke for a few minutes about the greatest blessing of all, the coming of the Son of God in human form. He came to shed His blood for the whole world. The pastor said he was often burdened when he thought of the many people in Romania who did not have a personal relationship with Christ and the peace that comes as a result of that relationship. He reminded the little congregation that the difficulties on earth were no comparison to the joys of being in the Lord's presence one day.

Daniel could not believe what he was hearing. Never had he heard such joy from people who lived in such conditions as existed in their country. All he ever heard was complaining from everyone with whom he was associated. His friends all wanted to get out of the country, and even if these people were satisfied to stay in the country, he wasn't, and he was going to get out as soon as he could. Following the pastor's comments, it was time for the cakes and tea.

Daniel didn't want to meet people, so he took a couple cookies and told John that he had to go.

John thanked him for coming and blurted out, "What did you think?"

"Well, it was interesting, but I have to be honest with you. I don't know how you can sing and talk about God's blessing in a country like this. If God really exists, I can't understand why He allows us to live under these conditions. Well, I have to go." He slipped into the darkness.

John called after him, "See ya."

"We'll see."

John excitedly returned inside to enjoy the fellowship while Daniel walked home feeling very strange, like he was in a dream. He couldn't wait for Radu to get back. These had been a strange couple of weeks, and it would be good to get back to normal life in the New Year.

His parents didn't know why he had left. He told them he was going out for some fresh air. After all, that was true. It just wasn't the whole truth.

They knew his feelings about religion, and he would be embarrassed if they knew where he had been. It was his secret, and he certainly would not tell them or Radu. He couldn't bear the thought of Radu knowing what he had done. Their friendship would be in jeopardy if he knew the events of the past couple weeks. He would have to keep a distance from John so Radu wouldn't find out.

The next morning, New Year's Day, Daniel awoke after a night with very little sleep. He couldn't understand what was wrong with him. He kept thinking about the things he saw and heard the previous evening. Later that day Radu returned from Timisoara and immediately came to Daniel's home. They were glad to be together for a while before they returned to school. Radu had so much to tell him of his days in Timisoara. He had met several other teens, including some girls he had pursued. According to Radu's rendition of the trip, the girls thought he was the epitome of manhood.

As always, alcohol played into Radu's activities. According to Radu, he had one continuous party while he was there. Knowing his friend well, Daniel knew that there was a lot of wishful thinking in his tales. Of course, Daniel was not there to verify the details of what he heard, so he was at Radu's mercy. Daniel was glad that Radu was not at home to verify the details of Daniel's explanation of how he spent the holidays. He very carefully wove a tale of how he slipped and hit his head against a post in the back yard while he was helping his father work around the house and in the outbuildings. His tale seemed to satisfy Radu, and Daniel's secret remained just that, at least for now.

CHAPTER 5 ESCAPE PLANS ARE ON THE FRONT BURNER

January was colder than usual. As much as possible, people stayed indoors. During the week, Radu and Daniel saw each other only at school. Weekends were a different story. They spent a lot of time together dreaming of life in the West. They frequently, but very carefully, discussed their plans for escaping to a new life.

They acknowledged that the greatest threats were the fast gunboat that patrolled the Danube 24 hours a day and the towers that lined the Danube and were also manned 24 hours a day. At night, the guards shined spotlights over the water continually. Another problem to consider was the currents. In some places, they were alleged to be very strong with an undertow. Of course, they also needed to think through how they would get food, clothing, and survival implements across the river.

Language would not be a concern to them after reaching Austria, if they reached Austria! Because they were both of German heritage, they spoke German in their home. It was almost as much their mother tongue as Romanian. Since the Austrian language was related to the German language, they were not worried about their ability to communicate once they got over the border.

The problem was that they had to get through Yugoslavia to get into Austria. The Serbian portion of Yugoslavia, which made up more than half of the distance to be traversed, bordered the Danube River across from the area of Romania where Daniel and Radu lived. Some of the inhabitants on the Romanian side of the Danube were of Serbian extraction, so Daniel and Radu had learned some of the language just by growing up with Serbian children, but they determined to learn more key words. They had worked toward developing stronger friendships with their Serbian classmates.

It was difficult to conceal why they so often asked what certain words meant in the Serbian language. Radu and Daniel kept close notes and turned the project into a clever game. Each would look for or create excuses to ask about the language. At the first opportunity, they would write the words down and share them with each other. They each kept a small journal of the words they were learning. If someone saw their journal and the types of vocabulary words they were collecting, it might be clear that they were planning an escape. Therefore, they kept close control of their journals.

The danger of being exposed was made real in January when Grati was cleaning in Radu's room. She came upon some of the notes he had not yet entered into his journal, and when he returned from spending time with Daniel, she asked him why he had vocabulary words in the Serbian language. Talk about being on the spot and having to quickly create a lie! He blurted out that they were learning some of the Serbian language in their Romanian language classes because there were so many Serbians in their town. It only seemed right that if they had to take the Romanian language in school, that the Romanian kids should have to learn some Serbian. Even though she appeared a little skeptical, she seemed to buy his story. After all, his story was reasonable even if it wasn't true.

Radu told Daniel about his close call, and they both agreed that the utmost care had to be given to the care and location of their journals and notes. It was decided that Daniel would keep both journals at his home, and they would update them and study them on weekends. Living in a village with small sheds housing animals and hay, he had many places he could hide the notes. Living in a small apartment, Radu had no safe place to store something so sensitive.

In their discussions during the winter, it was agreed that if they were to safely navigate through the mountains and forests of Yugoslavia without getting caught, they would need topographical maps of Serbia and Croatia, and Slovenia. They would need to know the locations of the more remote villages, because survival depended on their ability to "borrow" food along the way. If they could master enough of the language, it might help them get close to the villagers without raising suspicions, while they determined how to extract what they needed to survive. They had laughed that it was too bad they did not have some Gypsy blood in them, since they were very adept at finding food they had not grown themselves.

Acquiring the type of maps they needed was not going to be easy, but they were confident in their skills of deception. They could go to their small library at school and try to find topographical maps in an atlas, but as seniors, they had already had geography, and thus, they would look suspicious if they tried to check them out or even look at them. Borrowing textbooks from students taking geography would also be rather obvious. They decided the best course of action was to get into the homes of their Serbian friends, see if any of them had any maps of their mother country, borrow them, and trace them. Their project for February was to acquire a few sheets of paper and a topographical map to trace.

Luck was on their side. One of their Serbian friends had been injured playing soccer in the snow. He had slipped and fractured his leg; thus, he required a few weeks of recovery time. It was decided that Radu, the cleverest of the two, would go to his "new" friend's house after school for a visit. While there, he wove Serbia into the conversation by asking Sache if they had any maps, so he could see where his family was from.

Sache asked his mother to get their old maps of Yugoslavia. They were exactly what Radu was looking for.

One of the maps was topographical and had different shadings to indicate hills, mountains, forested areas, and the location of villages in the more remote areas. He did not realize how mountainous the northern regions of Yugoslavia were. That map was going to be a great benefit. Now the challenge was how to trace it. Radu finally concocted a story of how his grandparents had some Serbian blood in them and they would probably be very interested in seeing these maps to locate where their relatives lived. Sache's mother said it would be ok for him to take the map home for the evening if he was careful with it, but he had to bring it back the next day on his way to school. It would be difficult for him and Daniel to find a place of secrecy long enough to trace the map.

After a short time that seemed forever, Radu told Sache he really had to get going because he had some chores to do.

Radu quickly headed for Daniel's home, and when he met Daniel at the door, Radu said, "I have our ticket through Yugoslavia."

"So quickly?"

"When you get the right man for the job, the job gets done right."

"It sounds more like we are talking about luck."

"Well, there may have been a little of that involved. I hope Sache and his mother don't find out that my grandparents are dead. I told them I wanted the map to show my grandparents because they had relatives in Serbia."

"Radu, your lying tongue will get you in trouble yet." They both laughed at Radu's cleverness.

"Daniel, where can we lay this map on a flat surface to trace it with some secrecy?"

"Let's try to use the dining room table. I'll ask my mother to keep the girls out so we can work on this as quickly as possible."

There was some risk, but in the dead of winter in the late afternoon, there wasn't another option. They would have to be on their toes with a great story if Lidia asked them what they were doing. Lucky for them, she complied with his request to keep the girls out of the room, and she was too busy in the kitchen to wonder what they were actually doing. In about 30 minutes, they were done and Radu prepared to leave. He suggested that Daniel hide the traced maps with the journals. Radu was leaving just as Lidia entered the room.

"That must have been some project if the girls had to stay out, and it only took a half hour."

"Oh, Mom, we just work fast."

At that, Radu ducked out into the cold yelling back, "See you tomorrow."

The next morning Radu told Daniel that he had taken the map back to Sache's mother. They discussed between themselves, before entering the school, that they were coming closer to the time when they could make good on their plans to escape. They agreed that they needed to make their escape as soon after their graduation as possible. They wouldn't have jobs yet, and thus would not be missed for some time. That is, as long as their parents didn't acknowledge their absence. Once the absence was noted by the authorities, their families would be put under significant pressure. Who knows what type of retribution would be placed against them? That was the one thing that continually bothered Daniel the most about their plans. As in their discussion last fall, it didn't seem to bother Radu much.

Then, he thought, "Radu has always been rather self-centered. Many other students don't like him because of his personality."

Daniel had always looked up to Radu for his independence and self-confidence. Frankly, if it had not been for those characteristics, Daniel might never have given serious consideration to escaping. Radu was so sure they could pull it off successfully that Daniel's fears were overcome.

In early March, something happened in Orsova that had the whole town in an uproar. One of the main Communist Party bosses was arrested one night. He and his family were taken quickly out of town like the Popescu family a couple months earlier. Their apartment was sealed, too. A few days later, rumors began to circulate regarding the Selescu family. Apparently, Mr. Selescu was involved in a plot with the Popescu family and others to do something about removing Ceausescu from power. Foreign magazines were also found in his possession. Rumor had it that extra agents would be moved to Orsova to ferret out other possible conspirators. This put panic and fear in everyone. The slightest wrong move or comment might bring arrest, interrogation or torture, even if one was innocent.

Sure enough, within a few days, there were some new faces in town. Anyone associated with the Selescu family was being questioned. Radu and Daniel were thankful that their families were not friends, or even acquaintances, of the Selescu family. As Daniel and Radu discussed the seriousness and dangers associated with having the magazine, they agreed that it must be destroyed as soon as possible. If they were caught with it, their plans for escape would be replaced by imprisonment or worse. With the present mood in the country, it most certainly would be elimination.

The problem was how they would destroy the magazine with all the additional surveillance. Anyone leaving the town would be watched very carefully. As usual, Radu, in his self-confidence, assured Daniel there was nothing to worry about. But worry was all Daniel did. It must have become evident because a few days later Lidia said, "Daniel, you have not been yourself lately. Is something wrong?"

"No, I am alright. I have just been thinking a lot about graduation and what kind of job I will be able to get afterwards."

"Daniel, are you sure?"

"Mother, I am really ok. Don't worry!"

Daniel thought, "Am I that obvious? I had better be careful to not arouse suspicion with others." With the suspicious environment in Orsova and the surrounding villages, anyone could turn him into the authorities if they observed a change in his countenance. Any change in behavior or mood would be cause for suspicion.

When Daniel saw Radu the next day, he told him about his conversation with his mother.

"Radu, have I seemed to be preoccupied or different in my demeanor?"

"Yes, you have been acting a little strange. What are you worrying about now?"

"To be honest with you, I will not rest easy until we have destroyed that magazine."

"Trust me, everything will be ok. No one will find our hiding place, and even if they did, they will have no way to know the magazine is buried in the dirt under the tree roots. The magazine will be safe until we can get to it."

He felt better after this conversation but decided that he needed to be more careful. If his mother and Radu had sensed something, perhaps others had too!

Almost as a fulfilled prophecy, George came home a few days later and shared with Daniel and Lidia an interesting conversation he had that day with Sami.

"George, do you remember back when you were under suspicion, I told you I had an idea who might have turned you in, but I couldn't say?" Yes, George had thought about it often and it had bothered him that nothing else was said.

"I suspected Mr. Selescu at that time because I had overheard him discussing something with another worker when I was in the bathroom. I don't know who the other person was, but I heard Mr. Selescu say, 'They may be getting too close, and I need to throw suspicion on to someone else to get the heat off of me.'"

"With Mr. Selescu's position in the party, I did not dare say anything. Now that he has been caught, I guess I have confirmation of my suspicion. The question I have, though, is whether or not the other person in the washroom was Mr. Popescu or yet another person. This purge may not be over yet."

George warned Daniel not to talk with Radu about this. He said, "If Sami wanted to share it with his son, that is ok, but if not, it is not your place to discuss what had been shared. That kind of talk could be dangerous, but it was good to have some closure on what we went through a couple months ago."

March came and went somewhat quietly. The extra Securitate agents that had been sent to Orsova left at the end of the month. A good number of families were put on notice, which was probably more of a scare technique than anything, but no more charges were made. The Securitate knew they had put sufficient fear into the populace to neutralize any thoughts of insurrection.

Daniel and Radu didn't spend a lot of time together those days. Both were trying to make sure that their academics were in order so nothing would hinder their upcoming graduation the first week of June. As a top student, Daniel really had no serious concerns. He was a favorite of the teachers. This factor was one thing that gave Daniel some confidence during the times he was concerned about his plans with Radu.

Radu, however, was a different story. He had a lot of unfinished projects to turn in before he could graduate. His friendship with Daniel came in handy as Radu got him to help with his projects. In fact, Daniel outright did some of the projects for him. After all, what are friends for? Everyone did this, and the teachers knew that the cheating was going on. They understood it was normal to do what you had to do in order to get through life.

Even with the help Daniel gave him, Radu still had to take a few "gifts" to his teachers to assure that he would receive sufficient marks to graduate. This was a great time of the year for the teachers. There were always a number of students who needed a little "help" along the way.

CHAPTER 6 ESCAPE GONE AWRY

Before they knew it, the Easter holiday was upon them. Daniel and Radu always enjoyed festivities surrounding this holiday. It meant a week of vacation from school and a lot of partying. Of course, there was no significance to the occasion for them. If they didn't believe in the birth of Christ at Christmas, they certainly didn't believe in His death and resurrection at Easter! But it sure was a great excuse for a holiday! As usual, their mothers would bake cakes and take them to the church a week before Easter Sunday, just like they did at Christmas.

The tradition they enjoyed most was going to the cemetery the Friday before Easter to place sweets and alcohol on the graves of loved ones. The idea was that their spirits came back at this time to eat and drink what was left for them. The event began with the priest putting on his special robe and going to the graveyard, followed by the children. He would make a terrible racket with a metal triangle and metal rod to scare away the evil spirits. Then the parents would enter and place the food and drink at the gravesites. The children would run around playing and waiting until late afternoon, when the families would eat the food and drink the alcohol.

The festivities would continue at home well into the early morning with heavy drinking. That was the part Radu liked the most. It would take him a couple days to recover. All in all, it was a ridiculous thought that spirits of the dead would come back to eat spirit food. Who had ever heard of spirit food? But nevertheless, it provided for some fun in an otherwise dreary existence.

It seemed to Daniel and Radu that April and May flew by with a vengeance, probably because they were facing graduation, which for a Romanian, was a big deal. Romanians were not all expected to graduate. Many stopped after two years of high school and continued with two years of technical school for a trade or dropped out altogether to work. Those from large families or of poor circumstances were the ones who usually dropped out.

When graduation came, Daniel received honors for his academics. Radu didn't receive any recognition for anything. The teachers were probably glad to get rid of him. His overly confident attitude irritated most of them. When the ceremonies were over, Daniel said, "Well, Radu, when we complete our escape, you won't be missed, but everyone will say, 'Where is that scholar, Daniel? What a loss he is to our country!'"

"Oh yeah, what will I care? I will have a new life in Germany!"

The week after graduation one of their graduating classmates got married. The groom's and bride's parents were some of the wealthier families in town, so the celebration was quite an event. Only the privileged participated in the dinner party after the service at the Orthodox Church. But the ceremony and preparations were open to scrutiny by all who were interested. All the party bosses and Securitate agents would be in attendance, which meant that surveillance of the outskirts of town would be pretty much nonexistent. Radu and Daniel planned to use this opportunity to go to their hiding place to retrieve the magazine and dispose of it.

Before carrying out their plan, they intended to watch the street ceremony. There would be plenty of time that evening while the private dinner party was taking place. This was a typical wedding for the well-to-do. The groom's family lived in one of the houses in town. A young bull was brought into town and tied to a tree in the front yard for all to see. The evening before the wedding, the bull was killed in the back yard. As always, it was a messy affair. The bull was hit over the head with a heavy mallet. Knocked unconscious, his throat was cut, and he bled out in the gutter that ran along the house to the street. Though the gutter was hosed down, blood and water ran down the street for some distance before disappearing in the street sewer that went under the street and emptied into the Danube.

Members and friends of the family cooked the meat all night, along with the traditional cabbage rolls, special salads, and other menu items. The desert delicacies would all have been prepared beforehand.

The street ceremony began after the service in the Orthodox Church where they received a blessing from the priest for money, of course. Everything the priests did was for money. Following this ritual ceremony, the wedding party, family, and friends would join hands and dance through the street while a paid orchestra followed along playing traditional folk music. This dance continued through the streets toward the banquet room. Sometimes they would stay at a specific location and dance in circles while bystanders clapped their hands. Then the party would move on in serpentine order, all the while continually dancing hand-in-hand or arm-in-arm. When they reached their destination, they would go into the dining hall with those chosen to party until the wee hours of the morning.

Daniel and Radu followed the procession at the beginning and made sure they got in the line of photographs to document their attendance. Then they both slipped from the crowd and headed for the center of town, doubling back a different way and not moving too quickly to cause any suspicion. They were laughing like they didn't have a care in the world. When out of sight of the last house, they cut into the woods and circled around toward their hiding place. From their vantage point above the trail below they could see if anyone was approaching. Already the leaves had filled out the thorn bushes and provided cover as they crawled into their cave.

As Radu reached into the hole where he had stuffed the plastic-covered magazine, he was horrified to find that it was not there. How could that be? They had not been there for several months.

"Daniel, we are in trouble. This is not good! Someone must have followed us and found the magazine!"

Daniel said, "One thing is for sure. We have not been visited by the Securitate, so whoever has it either does not know who put it here or is keeping it for some other purpose."

Radu agreed but suggested that whoever took it must know who put it there because with it buried in the dirt, it would never have been found. They decided to get out of there as quickly as possible and head back through the forest the way they had come. They agreed it would be wise to rejoin the wedding party. They made sure to get into other photos. They were having a very hard time trying to put on the front of enjoying the festivities. When the wedding party finally reached the party room, they quietly walked away discussing their dilemma.

"Radu, I told you we should never have taken that magazine when we found it. This will be the end of our plans and our lives if we are turned in to the Securitate."

The next few days were pure agony for both boys, so they met often to discuss their plight. They agreed they needed to execute their plans to escape as quickly as possible with the hope of getting out of the country before someone could turn them in. They gathered together the things they would need to take across the river and decided they would not try to keep their clothing or survival implements dry. That would be too difficult, and any such packages would undoubtedly float, thus hindering their secrecy. They would put their things in a sack and submerge them under water as they swam. The only things they had to secure in plastic were their maps, matches, Serbian vocabulary words, and some food snacks.

They decided to put notes under their pillows before leaving, telling their parents why they had not come home. It would be terribly difficult to leave without saying goodbye. They agreed that they would not tell the identity of each other in the event something went wrong. They picked out the spot, midway between two watchtowers, where they would slip into the water immediately after the patrol boat passed the spot and paddle backwards facing the towers so they could see the spotlights. As the spotlights swung toward them, they would hold their breath and duck under the water. When the light passed, they would come up for air. They figured they would be able to see the light from under the water and know when to emerge.

Just when it looked like they were ready to proceed, they were handed a bombshell. Sergiu, one of their classmates whom they hardly knew, approached them as they were sitting on a bench overlooking the Danube.

"Hi, fellows. I think I have something you were looking for."

Radu said, "What are you talking about?"

"I think you know. I know you guys are up to something, and I want in. My guess is that you are planning to escape over the Danube. We haven't been friends in the past, but I think that is about to change. This is my deal. Either you let me in on your plans or I turn the magazine over to the Securitate."

Daniel asked, "What magazine? What are you talking about?"

"Don't try to act innocent with me. I was watching you guys last year. You were always so secretive, so I decided to keep an eye on you to see what you were up to. Last fall, when you left town through the woods, I carefully followed and observed you crawling into the vines to your hiding place. When you left, I went in and found the magazine. I have to admit that you had hidden it well, but I noticed the earth had been moved, so I dug around and found it. You thought it was there all winter, but I have it. I have been keeping an eye on you. When you slipped away from the wedding party, I followed you again."

While Daniel was having a panic attack, Radu said, "That is blackmail." Sergiu agreed but added it looked like the cards were in his favor. They discussed the situation a few minutes, and it appeared that Radu and Daniel had no choice but to let Sergiu in on their plans. They did get one concession. Sergiu had to bring the magazine with him at their next meeting, and they would destroy it together.

When Sergiu departed, Radu said, "I don't like this at all. Three of us will increase the possibility of being seen when we cross the Danube."

"I don't think we have a choice. The longer we wait to cross, the greater the risk that one of us will slip up."

Radu agreed but said, "I say we ditch Sergiu when we get to the other side of the Danube. Three is just too many to travel together." Daniel agreed. They parted for a couple sleepless nights.

As planned, the three next met in the woods, burned the magazine, stamped the ashes into the ground and worked out the final plans. They agreed to leave the next Wednesday. According to the almanac, there was to be no moon. They agreed to put their things in their hiding place the next evening and then not see each other again until Wednesday evening at 10:00 p.m. From there it would take only about 15 minutes to get to the spot they had chosen to cross.

Writing the goodbye letter was the most difficult thing Daniel had ever done. He started:

Dear Mom and Dad,
    This is the most difficult thing I have ever had to do. I love you and my sisters very much and will miss all of you dearly. I have decided to cross the Danube tonight into Serbia, make my way to Austria and, ultimately, to Germany where I will seek asylum. Please do not be angry with me. I simply see no life worth living in Romania under the present regime. When I get established, my goal is to try to make enough money to buy your freedom.
    I love you, Daniel

On Wednesday, he put the note under his pillow, figuring his mother would find it when he didn't return home. He told his parents he was going out for some fresh air. It was hard for him to hold back the tears. He wanted to hug them in the worse way, but could not tell them what he was about to do. They would try to stop him, and things could get very difficult. He went to the shed to retrieve his belongings and slipped through the shadows into the woods, making his way to the meeting place. As expected, it was very dark, making it difficult for Daniel to make his way.

The other two were already there waiting for him. "We were beginning to worry that you had backed out."

"You don't think I am going to let you guys leave me behind? Besides, Radu, I would not escape repercussions from the Securitate when your absence was acknowledged. They would certainly be able to torture the truth out of me, and I think that would be the end of me. Enough of that! I am glad for the darkness, but I think it is partly because a storm is coming up and will make the water choppy."

"That is even better. The choppy water will help camouflage us. It is perfect," Sergiu agreed.

"But I am afraid it may be more difficult to swim."

Radu responded, "Come on, we have to go now!"

They made their way quickly, but quietly, to the water's edge and carefully stowed their shoes in their bags. Even though it was the end of June, the water seemed unusually cold. Perhaps it was their anxiety. They waited a few minutes and as planned, the patrol boat passed and headed up the river.

Daniel wasn't a very good swimmer, and he was having difficulty with the waves pushing against him from the Serbian side. They had not gone far when Daniel whispered, "I am sorry fellows, but the waves are too strong, and I am already getting tired. I don't think I can make it."

"You can't go back now," said Radu. "What if they find out you were in on this with us? Like you said, they will be able to beat the truth out of you."

"That is the chance I will have to take. I really don't think I can make it. I would rather stay behind and take my chances than drown."

With the wind and waves at his back, he quickly made his way back to shore and headed home as quickly as possible so he could retrieve the letter from under his pillow. His parents must not know of his plans. He made his way through the woods, and as he was about to exit on the other side, he heard gunfire and the racing of a boat motor. His heart failed him. He could only imagine the worse.

"Surely there was enough time for them to have gotten across the river. Perhaps they made it across, and the gunboat was shooting into Serbia. Oh God, please let Radu and Sergiu be ok."

"Why am I calling upon God?"

He hurried home, shaking from fear and from running through the cool air totally soaked. When he arrived, he wondered how he would explain why he was wet. He stepped inside the kitchen, hoping that he could get to his room and change clothes before anyone saw him. Seeing no one, he thought, "God is with me. There I go again," he almost blurted out.

A moment later, his mother called out, "Is that you, Daniel?

"Yes, I will be out in a moment."

He hurried into his room adjacent to the kitchen and quickly reached under his pillow for the letter he had written. He shoved it into a boot, changed into his pajamas, and went into the living room where the family was gathered to discuss the activities of the day. George had just gotten home from work.

"Daniel, you are in pajamas so early. Are you ill?"

"No, I am just tired. I went hiking this afternoon with Pavel (Paul)."

"Who is Pavel?"

"Oh, he is a guy I know from school. I ran into him on my way to town, and he asked me if I wanted to go for a hike with him. I figured that I could see Radu later, but the hike took longer than I thought, so I will see Radu tomorrow."

"Whew", he thought, "I haven't lost my ability to think fast on my feet. Radu has taught me well." There was no one named Pavel that he knew. But it sounded good, and his mother would never know.

His father said he heard what sounded like gunshots coming from the direction of the river. At this time of the night, he wondered if some unfortunate soul was shot trying to escape to Serbia. Daniel mumbled that he had heard the shots as well. After several minutes of small talk, Daniel went to his room, fearing the news of the morning. He lay awake most of the night. All he could think about was Radu and Sergiu, hoping morning would confirm that they had gotten safely over the river.

He kept mulling over in his mind the events of the day. Was it possible that they were killed? If so, he would have been killed as well if he had continued with them. Several times he thought maybe there is a God and maybe He caused him to turn back. But why would He cause him to turn back and not Radu and Sergiu?

"No, this is silly thinking," was his response each time these thoughts went through his mind.

Finally, he fell asleep, only to be awakened abruptly by his father telling him two boys were killed the previous evening trying to swim the Danube.

"The rumor is that one of them was Radu."

Daniel leaped out of bed. "Are you sure? How do you know?"

George said that he had gone into town early to get bread so Lidia wouldn't have to. When he got there, the streets were full of people talking about the shooting last night. Some of the men claimed that a couple of boys were shot trying to cross the river. One of them said Radu was one of them, and the other boy was named Sergiu.

Thinking quickly to divert any complicity, Daniel said, "Radu would never do something stupid like that, and he certainly would have told me if he was planning an escape."

Daniel hurriedly dressed and told his parents that he was going to see Radu. He blurted out that he was sure Radu was ok. He hurriedly left and headed for town, knowing all along that his father was right. In order to protect himself, he had to act totally surprised. When he approached Radu's apartment, there were people gathered around the entrance. As he approached, one of the men grabbed him and said, "Your friend Radu is dead. He tried to cross the Danube last evening with another boy and they were shot from the patrol boat."

"That is not possible. I just talked with Radu yesterday morning. He wouldn't do such a thing without telling me!"

He made sure he said this loud enough to be heard by everyone within hearing distance. It was critically important that he not be suspected. As it was, he knew he was facing interrogation. Everyone knew they were the best of friends and always together. He feared what was ahead. Having made his proclamation, he barged into the apartment where he found Grati and Sami weeping with friends gathered around them. He also noticed a man that he was sure worked undercover for the Securitate.

When Grati saw Daniel, she said, "Oh Daniel, I thought you were the other boy killed with our Radu." At that, she burst into tears and reached out for him. He could not contain himself any longer and burst into weeping as he clutched her.

After some time, she said, "Did you know Radu was planning to escape?"

"No, he never told me. I can't believe he would do such a stupid thing. It is unbelievable! We were always talking about our future and how we wanted to get jobs working together. We would talk about when we would have families and be best of friends. I thought he was my friend. I just can't believe he would do this!"

He made sure he was heard by the man he suspected to be a Securitate Agent. He had to distance himself from what had just taken place if he was to survive at all. He felt guilty about the lies he was fabricating by the minute, but he had to keep up the charade.

Finally, he left Radu's home crying and seeking out other classmates so he could continue his deception. The only part of his story that was true was his sorrow for Radu. He tried to be as visible in his grief as possible because he was sure his every move and word were being noted by the Securitate. They would be watching his reactions and listening to his responses to questions.

After he had spent sufficient time with the mourners and the curious, he headed for home. He had always prided himself on his ability to hold back tears in difficult times because he always perceived that a real man didn't cry. But in this case, he was glad he could not hold back the tears because it made his claims of innocence more believable. He loved Radu and would miss him more than words could tell. His life would never be the same without him!

By the time he arrived home, his father had already left for work. His younger sisters were playing in the front yard not aware that anything had happened.

Lidia met him at the door with tears in her eyes and embraced him tightly saying, "I love you."

"I love you, too! Mother, what brought this on?" She led him into the kitchen and through the kitchen door to the back yard, pointing to his wet clothes hanging on the line. "Oops, I forgot my wet clothes!"

Lidia looked him in the eyes and said, "Son, what made you turn back? When I heard that it was Radu, I knew you had to be in on this with him. You were inseparable, and he would not have planned such a thing without your knowledge. When I found your wet clothes on the floor in the bedroom my suspicions were confirmed."

Daniel never could lie directly to his mother. He broke down and wept with her. He admitted to his mother that he had been in on the plan to escape from the beginning. He explained how they had found the magazine proving to them that life on the outside was drastically different than life in Romania and how they had been deceived all these years. He told her that as much as he loved his family, he wanted to experience what existed in the West. Romania was a hard

43

place to live. He wanted a better life for the wife and children he hoped to have one day. She asked him why he didn't go through with his plan.

Obviously, he had been in the river with them. He said, "After we got into the water, the waves were awfully high, and they were pushing against us, and I was afraid that I was not a good enough swimmer to make it. Radu said that the waves were good because it would make it almost impossible for their heads to be seen as they crossed. Anyway, at the last minute, I decided it was better to live in Romania than to drown in the Danube and be eaten by fish."

"Oh, son, I think God was watching over you."

He agreed with her, but in his heart, he was wrestling with the possibility that he was wrong regarding his atheism.

"Your father knows. He will have a hard day at work thinking about how he almost lost his only son. He will be anxious to see you when he gets home. This will probably be the longest day of his life, except for the day before we got married." She grinned, and Daniel smiled and hugged her.

"Son, your father and I said that your involvement in this absolutely must not get out."

Daniel agreed and told her how he already was trying to distance himself from Radu by the things he said at Radu's house and in the yard outside in the hearing of others.

"That is good. It is important people believe you. You lied to me last evening about going on a hike with some boy named Pavel."

"Yes, Mother. I was trying to cover up what I did."

"No more lies, son. Promise?"

He promised with his fingers crossed behind his back. He still dreamed of leaving Romania. Later, he very carefully hid away his map and Serbian vocabulary.

As his mother had said, when his father got home there was a lot of hugging. The girls, not knowing anything that took place, were wondering why their father was hugging their brother so much. He had never done that before. Daniel had to retell everything to his father, and his mother was there to make sure she hadn't missed anything.

When he finally went to bed, he thought, "What if there is a God out there watching things on earth?" He also thought of how this event seemed to have drawn him into a closer relationship with his parents. What a tragic way to bring a family closer together. He finally fell into a restful sleep not knowing what tomorrow had in store for him. If he had known, he would not have slept at all.

Lidia kept things quiet to let him get his much-needed sleep. With three girls in the house, that was a chore. When he finally got up, he gulped down some bread with jam and coffee, and headed to town to get the latest news. As he approached the center of town, it was obvious that something was really stirring the people. He quickly learned the Securitate had the two boys' bodies put on display in the town square so people could see what the government does to those who are traitors and try to escape Father Ceausescu (as that tyrant liked to think of himself).

Daniel thought, "Oh boy. I must make an appearance. Since everyone knows of my relationship with Radu, I had better make this the best performance of my life." Only then did it occur to Daniel that Sergiu's involvement in the plot would give him an out. As he entered town, he thought, "Here goes."

Dozens of people were milling around the two open pine boxes. Of course, everyone wanted to make sure they were seen as a disgrace for the two. As he approached, many people who knew him began to ask him if he knew of the plans to escape. He kept answering no to their questions and saying that he was shocked by what had happened.

Approaching the bodies, he sensed the fixed gaze of the Securitate agents on him. He first looked at the body of his best friend. His composure broke when he saw the bullet-ridden, bloody face of Radu! They hadn't even cleaned the blood from his face. Oh, it was horrible! It almost did not look like Radu. "He must have died instantly" was the comforting thought that went through Daniel's mind. "I am glad he didn't feel any pain."

Through the tears that were now freely flowing, he exclaimed loudly, "Radu, Radu, how could you do this to me? We were supposed to be best friends. Last week we talked about working at the shipyard together and living in Orsova with our future families! You didn't plan to work with me at the shipyard at all! You lied to me!"

Then he walked to Sergiu's body. He was horrified to see his bullet-ridden face totally unrecognizable. He blurted out, "Sergiu, you must have been responsible for this. Radu would never have done this by himself. You turned my best friend against me and took him from me! I will never forgive you!"

Then, still teary eyed, Daniel turned to head for home. He hadn't walked more than a few meters when he was grabbed by one of the Securitate agents who witnessed his outbursts. Pulling Daniel by the arm, he said, "Come with me." He was taken to their office. The entire way there, Daniel feared the worst.

The agent shoved him into a seat in the office and began to question him. "Your friends must have been stupid. The waves were so strong that night it would have taken an Olympic swimmer to make it across before the patrol boat returned. It was like shooting ducks." Daniel responded that Sergiu wasn't his friend. At that, one of the officers slapped him hard across the face.

"You must have known of their plan because Radu was your best friend, by your own admission. If you had been loyal to the Regime, you would have told us of his plans."

Under repeated questioning of that nature, Daniel maintained that he knew nothing and that he supposed Sergiu was the one who convinced Radu to try to escape. They slapped him across the face several more times in anger, but Daniel managed to maintain his composure. After what seemed an eternity, they said, "You can go for now, but this is not over! We will meet again!"

Daniel ran all the way home. George was waiting nervously for him. When he saw the blood and bruises on Daniel's face, he yelled for Lidia to get come cloths and cold water from the well. They did the best they could to dress his wounds. His sisters stood wide-eyed, and the youngest, Delia, was crying. After his wounds were dressed and he was given a cup of hot tea, his parents told the girls to go outside and play so Daniel could rehearse all the events of the day. They wanted to know every detail. It was agreed that he had been very lucky to this point. Daniel told them what the agent said about this not being over.

As summer was in full swing and crops needed attention, Daniel busied himself working in the garden and tending the animals. He had not yet gotten a job, so he was obligated to work the family land and help in any way he could around the house. All the time, he thought of Radu and the events leading to his violent death. He repeatedly rehearsed the plans they had for escaping and living together. He also was continually haunted by thoughts about whether or not there was a God who had intervened to save him. If so, why? Radu was no more an unbeliever than he was!

A few days after the attempted escape, there was a knock at the door. George was at work, so Daniel answered. He hardly had the door open when a couple arms reached in and pulled him out of the house. Without explanation or even allowing him to tell the family what was happening, two Securitate Agents whisked him into a car and took him to the police station.

Daniel thought, "It was too much to hope that I was safe from further interrogation."

He was roughly taken inside, thrown into a chair, and told that they had evidence he was involved in the escape plans and had changed his mind at the last moment. Daniel's heart nearly stopped. His first thought was, "How did they find out?" Luckily for him, he held his composure. He thought, "Wait a minute, they are fishing and hoping to trip me up."

He calmly responded that he knew nothing of the escape plans. The officer slapped his face and called him a liar. Again, Daniel insisted he knew nothing of the escape.

"He was your best friend. You expect us to believe you knew nothing? How is that possible?"

"Yes, Radu was my best friend. I don't deny that, but he knew that I don't know how to swim, so why would he have included me in a plan to escape by swimming the Danube? I would think it would have been a risk to include me in his plans if I couldn't take part in the escape." That argument brought a response he had not anticipated.

One of the agents said, "You can't swim? We will see." Daniel was roughly thrown into a car and driven to the dock where the patrol boat was moored. They shoved him into the boat and started out into the Danube.

Daniel realized they planned to throw him overboard to see if he could swim. He had to fake drowning even if it resulted in his death. To swim would assure his death anyway. They would probably kill him on the spot the moment he started to swim. Sure enough, a few meters out he was thrown overboard. As he was entering the water, he cried out in his heart, "God, save me, please!" He took a big breath before going under and stayed down as long as he could, and then thrashed his way to the surface sputtering, taking a big gulp of air and going down again thrashing on the way down. He was surprised when he hit bottom.

They had not taken him as far out as he thought. He waited again for a few seconds and headed to the top, again thrashing all the way and sputtering water. Taking a good breath, he went down a third time. He determined that he must take a chance and stay down this time, hoping the patrolmen would be convinced and come down for him. He waited for what seemed an eternity when one of the patrolmen dived in to retrieve him. Lucky for Daniel, the patrolman found him and pulled him to the top. While coughing as if his lungs had taken in water, Daniel took a mouthful of water that he spewed out.

They were apparently convinced because they pounded on his back as they headed to shore. To keep up the charade, he kept coughing and sputtering. He was shoved back into the car and taken home. They shouted some threats that they would be watching his every move from this point on.

Daniel began to shake uncontrollably from the chill and realization that he had narrowly escaped death. His mother and sisters, anxiously waiting inside, witnessed his arrival and ran out to retrieve him. Lidia immediately wrapped him in a blanket.

When George got home, Daniel relayed the events of the afternoon. George wept and clutched him on his lap on the sofa as if he were a small child. Daniel was embarrassed but enjoyed a level of attention that he had never known before. He could not remember a time in his life when his father had ever held him like this. If there had ever been any doubt regarding the sincerity of his father's love, it evaporated.

Finally, somewhat embarrassed in front of his mother and sisters, he said, "Ok, Dad, now I am sure you love me. At that he jumped up and said, "Wow, I should be interrogated more often. This is great! Are we going to have some cookies and tea too?"

At that, Lidia said, "I think it would be most appropriate." Since it was summer and the girls didn't have school, they all stayed up talking into the wee hours of the night. Daniel was alive, and that was worth celebrating.

Apparently, the Securitate agents believed Daniel's story because he was left alone after this second encounter. Perhaps they felt they had made a sufficient impression on Daniel and the town people to accomplish what they wanted.

And indeed they had, for the talk of the town for weeks was the appearance of the boys in the caskets. The authorities had made the families bury the boys the same day they were viewed, and they were not allowed to do anything to make the boys look presentable for burial. The Securitate agents had nailed the lids on the coffins before they left the square and accompanied the bodies to the gravesite to ensure that their wishes were carried out.

According to the traditions of the Orthodox Church, there would have been a service conducted by the priests, at which time they would pray over them and absolve them of their sins. For the bodies to be immediately buried in their condition after viewing was indeed a travesty to the families, exactly what the authorities wanted. They got maximum mileage from their actions.

CHAPTER 7 ESCAPE PLANS ARE ON THE BACK BURNER

At the end of the summer, Daniel got a job at the shipbuilding plant in town. He continued to live at home with his parents and sisters, and the first thing he purchased with his wages was a bicycle. A car was the furthest thing from his and most everyone's dreams. The bicycle was a real blessing because he could now move about so quickly.

One day Daniel was speeding into town to get some things from the market for his mother. He was a little careless and bumped a girl who was laden down with her purchases. She dropped her bag, so he jumped off the bicycle to help her. It was Veronica, a young woman who had graduated a year before him. Because she was a year ahead of him, he had not paid particular attention to her in the past. Now she had his attention! Their eyes met as he tried to apologize.

She responded, "Oh, it was nothing." They soon realized that the bag she was carrying was ripped. Daniel insisted that she put her things in the basket wired on the back of his bicycle, and he would walk her home before he went shopping.

As they walked, they talked about many things, not the least of which was the subject of Radu. Daniel maintained his cover story with her. He learned she was working at the dress factory in town and living with her parents. That was about it.

As Daniel left her at her home to return to the market, he thought, "I didn't realize how pretty Veronica was; she seems so grown up. She is indeed a woman, a woman who needs a husband."

Back at Veronica's home, her mother, who had met them at the door, asked, "Who is that good-looking young man?" Embarrassed, she told her mother his name. "Why, Veronica, you are blushing." Indeed she was, for at that moment she was thinking that he needs a wife.

When Daniel finally got home with his purchases, Lidia asked what took him so long. "I needed these things to begin supper. Now we won't eat on time, and you know how your father likes to eat on time when he is not working the night shift." Daniel explained about the chance meeting with Veronica and how he was obligated to help her home with her purchases. His mother grinned at him and winked. "Why, Daniel, you're blushing! Does that mean you like this girl?"

"Well," he said, "She is kind of cute, and she is available."

"Are those wedding bells I hear?"

"No, Mother! Our goats are coming home. You hear the bells around their necks." How neat it was that the goats happened to be coming home at that very instant!

They laughed as Daniel went out to put the goats inside the fence and give them water. The goats were a new addition to the family. They were getting very fat from all their foraging. They represented the potential for homemade goat cheese, a favorite of the family and most of the villagers. It was expensive in the markets; now they could make their own.

The summer soon turned into fall. Daniel was busy working at the shipyard and helping around the family farm as much as he could. As small as the farm was, there was much to be done since everything was done by hand. Of course, they had the milk cow to pull the plow for planting and the wagon when they brought in the hay and the crops during the harvest. That old milk cow was a blessing to the family. Milk was not available to purchase, so those lucky enough to have a cow were envied.

She had another calf this year. Once again, the neighbor's bull had been successful. The little calf was the apple of the family's eye, so to speak. He was a handsome little fellow but not destined to be in a beauty contest. He would become food when he grew to full size. However, since they still had the bull from the previous year, this little fellow would get a reprieve for another year.

The hardest work around the farm was cutting the tall grass for the cows, and goats, in the winter. Cutting the thick grass was a hot, sticky job. There were also the insects to contend with. After the grass dried, they would go out to collect it and pile it high on the wagons. The person on top had the easiest job. The one who threw the grass up with a pitchfork had the difficult job. Of course, that was usually Daniel's job while his father stood on the wagon. When they got back to the house, they would weave the hay around a wooden pole planted in the ground and build it up to a height of about three meters (15 ft.). That would hold the hay in place and allow it to dry as the wind blew through. It looked like a giant beehive when completed.

During summers when rain was scarce, the garden needed watering. It was a lengthy and very tiring process, but they had a system worked out. Daniel would crank the water up from the well and pour it into one bucket after another while his mother and sisters would carry the buckets out to water the plants. If Daniel worked hard enough at it, he could keep them busy non-stop until done. It would take about two hours of hard work to water the entire garden.

Halfway through the summer, Daniel brought a great blessing to the family. With his work at the shipyard, he was able to help with the family budget. He purchased a submersible pump and a long hose to bring the water out of the well and to the garden. This was, indeed, a luxury! Most people only dreamed of such a thing.

One thing was for sure, those years of hard work and carrying water caused Daniel to acquire quite a set of biceps that were not unnoticed by a special young lady. Yes, Daniel had been seeing Veronica on a regular basis.

They were developing a close relationship, and everyone was speculating on the outcome. But then Veronica began to act a little strange. Her behavior change seemed to have something to do with her visiting the small Baptist Church Daniel had attended the previous Christmas with John. With his feelings about the Repenters, he was not pleased with her frequent attendance, nor could he understand her sudden interest in attending so regularly. She asked him to come with her. He liked her a lot, but he wasn't sure he liked her that much. Of course, without Radu to chide him, he had considered attending to please her. At the end of the harvest, the little church was having a special service followed by a banquet. Veronica begged Daniel to go with her. He determined that maybe he really did like her enough, and he relented. He escorted Veronica to the bus that would take them to the nearby village.

The moment they stepped into the little church, John ran over to shake his hand and welcome him. He hadn't really seen much of John since the last holiday season. He had a cute girl hanging by his side and he looked happy and well. After a short conversation, the service began. Veronica grabbed his arm and led him to a seat. She was beaming from ear to ear. Daniel hadn't realized how much this meant to her. She really did like him - perhaps love was a more appropriate word to use. He had to admit that he really liked her a lot, too. But there were some concerns he had about his relationship with her. One was her increasing involvement with the Repenters, and the second was that he had not given up his dream of escaping. His thoughts were cut short when the service began with prayer.

This prayer would be beyond what he experienced when he had attended the New Year's Eve service with John. Again, he observed that the pastor and adults all had their eyes closed, but some of the children did not. He decided that since the adults all had their eyes closed, he should do the same.

As the prayer continued, he thought, "Wow, how can someone pray for so long? It seems like the pastor is praying for everyone in the village and every illness that anyone knows about. Will he ever end? The Orthodox never pray in their services, not that I have attended many services. The only prayers in the Orthodox Church are the short prayers the priests read from a prayer book. Those aren't genuine prayers. But this prayer, as long as it is, seems to be

51

genuine and the pastor isn't reading it either! The entire prayer meant nothing if there was no God. But these people surely thought there was a God listening to them!"

Following the prayer, the people began singing. Of course, Daniel didn't know any of the songs, and he had never sung before, except for the national anthem, a song they were required to sing in school on special occasions. So, he just sat and listened to the words like he had done the year before. He caught John looking over at him and smiling. Finally, after several songs Pastor Petrica preached a long message beginning with thanks to God. Daniel listened carefully to hear if he left anything or anyone out of his thanks. When he was finished, Daniel mused to himself, "No, I don't think he did!" Next, Pastor Petrica caused great discomfort for Daniel when he spoke of putting one's faith in Jesus Christ for salvation. This seemed a replay of what he had heard in the New Year's Eve service.

Then, the pastor did something unexpected, when Daniel thought he was finished with the message. The pastor asked if anyone wanted to come to Christ for salvation. Daniel did not understand what he meant, but apparently Veronica did because she raised her hand. The pastor asked her to come forward. He knelt with her in front of the podium, and they prayed together privately. She came back to join him with tears in her eyes and a smile on her face when they finished. The pastor told the little congregation that another soul was brought to the Lord and that Veronica had become a true Christian.

Now that was strange! How could one become a Christian by a prayer? In the Orthodox Church, all that was necessary to become a Christian was to be baptized as a baby and go through a catechism. Veronica had been baptized as a baby and had gone through catechism like everyone else. So, wasn't she already a Christian? Daniel was perplexed. He was not sure he wanted to continue his relationship with Veronica. She had to go and do this strange thing! What would his family and friends think if they knew about this? He certainly was not going to tell.

Following the service, everyone moved on to the meal prepared by church members. Daniel had wanted to leave after the service, but there was no way of getting out of it. John and Veronica insisted that he stay and suggested that they sit with him at his table. As they were eating, John announced to Daniel and Veronica that he and Ioana had become engaged and were to be married around Christmas. Veronica and Daniel congratulated them, and Veronica ran around to hug Ioana and exchange a few private words.

A little later, John said to Daniel, "I would be happy if you would come to my wedding and be one of my groomsmen. Since Veronica is one of Ioana's best friends, she will be a bridesmaid." Daniel didn't know what to say. He felt surrounded. It sounded like they had him almost married to Veronica.

"I will have to think about it."

"Take your time."

When the meal was over and the salutations were given, Veronica and Daniel left arm in arm for the bus stop.

They walked in silence for some time before Veronica said, "Daniel, you are very quiet. What is wrong?"

"Well, what you did today after the message seemed very strange to me."

"What I did was not strange. I repented of my sins and asked Jesus to come into my life as my Lord and Savior. The Bible teaches that this is how a person becomes a true Christian."

"How can you do that when you don't even know if there is a God or that Jesus ever really lived on the earth?"

"But, Daniel, I know that God does exist, and Jesus not only lived on the earth, but He died to save sinners like you and me. The Bible tells us that if we are to have a relationship with God and have eternal life in heaven, we must repent and accept Jesus as our Savior."

"The Orthodox Church teaches us that if we are baptized at eight days of age, we are in the Church, and if we do enough good works, we will be sure of going to heaven when we die. The "last rites" given by the priest gives additional assurance."

"But, Daniel, that is not what the Bible says. We must come to God on His terms. He sent His Son, Jesus, to pay for the sins of the whole world. Salvation is only through faith in Him alone."

"Now I see why everyone calls these people, Repenters. I always wondered why they were called that. I don't think I have to repent. I am not so bad and don't do a lot of the things that other people do. For example, I never get drunk like some of the priests do. In fact, I don't even drink alcohol."

"Oh, but Daniel, have you ever told a lie?"

"Well, of course. Everyone tells a lie now and then when it is necessary."

"There, you admitted that you are a sinner. The Bible says, 'Thou shalt not lie.' If you lie, you are a sinner. That means you need to be saved, too, if you are to go to heaven. Only repentant sinners will be in heaven. Daniel, I really like you a lot. I even think I love you and don't want you to go to hell when you die."

Daniel gulped and did not know what to say. She said she loved him. She is getting serious. The trouble was he was thinking that maybe he loved her, too, but this religious stuff was going to get in the way of their relationship. He didn't really respond to her because he was not sure what to say. He didn't want to hurt her, so he didn't verbalize his thoughts at that point. They walked on silently. When they reached her house, he gave her a little kiss on the cheek and said good night.

53

All the next week Daniel was plagued with the events that had taken place at the little church of the Repenters. The two most perplexing things he had to deal with were the fact that Veronica had become a Repenter, and he had to decide if he would participate in John's marriage to Ioana. He didn't see Veronica at all that week, and he wrestled with the decisions he had before him. Finally, he knew he had to make a decision about the wedding. His decision about Veronica would have to wait until later.

When Daniel went to Veronica's house to discuss the wedding situation, she seemed desperate to see him. Her love for him was becoming very evident. He said, "I don't know what to do about John's wedding. John seems to be the kind of person I would like to be friends with, but I hardly know him, and with him being a Repenter, I just don't know how much I want to be associated with him."

With sorrow in her voice, Veronica said, "Daniel, I am a Repenter too. What about me?"

Boy had he stuck his foot in his mouth! "Well, you are different!"

"How am I different?" And then she began to cry.

Oh, it really hurt him to see her cry. He held her, and after a few moments said, "You're different because I love you! Please don't cry."

She looked up at him with her tears overshadowed by a smile. "Oh, I love you Daniel!"

After a few moments of a wonderful embrace, Daniel said, "Ok, I will be in the wedding if it will make you happy."

"Oh, it will make me happy!"

So that was it. Daniel would be in the wedding. Veronica said, "Come with me to the village to tell John and Ioana!"

John and Ioana were delighted with the news, and John insisted that they stay for tea and cake.

They talked much of their plans to live in the village with his parents until they could build a small house on the back of his father's little plot of land near the garden.

Finally, it was time to get Veronica back to town so he could return to his village. It was getting late, and they would probably be stopped by the night patrol and questioned. Arm in arm, Daniel slowly walked her home from the bus stop. Sure enough, they were stopped and asked what they were up to. They explained why they had gone to the village. As always, there was suspicion. Daniel was so tired of the continual harassment under which they had to live 24 hours a day.

After their little inquisition, they arrived at Veronica's door. They embraced, but this time it was not a little kiss on the cheek but a warm kiss on the lips. And, then one more kiss was necessary for good luck, or so Daniel said as he planted the second kiss. Veronica didn't mind at all. They parted and he headed home.

Before he had gone far, he was stopped by the same night patrolman. This time he said, "I never believed that you didn't know that Radu planned to escape over the Danube. I think you were planning to go but something stopped you. We are keeping an eye on you. Of course, I see you are getting on with Veronica. That would be a lot to leave behind, so maybe you won't try to escape after all."

At that, Daniel just walked away from him and continued home. He thought, "My, how I would love to plant my fist on that patrolman's nose!" As Daniel lay in bed, he thought of his conversation with him. Yes, he would still like to escape. He was plagued constantly with the thought of a better life in the West. And yes, he loved Veronica, but he was not sure his love was enough to keep him here.

Daniel's family had one of the best harvests in many years. The new water pump had allowed the family to water the garden much more often, and the results were evident. Daniel had to work much harder harvesting than previous years because he did not have Radu to help him. Also, as always, he had to assist the family in harvesting potatoes in the government collective farm nearby.

This year Veronica gave the family some help, so there would be no "stealing" of potatoes like in previous years. When Daniel had shared his scheme with Veronica, she clearly told him that it was stealing!

"Our government steals from us, but the Bible says that all government powers are allowed by God, and therefore, we do not have justification for stealing." Though Daniel couldn't agree with her, because of his love for her he declined to continue the practice, at least for this year.

The time of John's and Ioana's wedding finally arrived. On the way to the wedding, Veronica clutched Daniel's arm and talked nonstop with a level of excitement not shared inwardly by Daniel. He tried to give the impression that he was excited, but he was plagued by his previous discussions with her regarding her newfound faith. He simply could not accept her form of Christianity.

Pastor Petrica began the wedding service with a long prayer. It was clear to Daniel that the Repenters didn't do anything without long prayers. As the service continued, Daniel realized that this was going to be an interesting wedding, not like anything he had ever seen in an Orthodox wedding.

In an Orthodox wedding, the Priest reads a short prayer and gives a blessing, while his assistant swings an incense container on a chain so that the smoke fills the air. It seems sort of mystical, but then everything about the Orthodox practices seemed a little mystical. Maybe that is why he never saw any truth in the religion and came to doubt any of the stories in the Bible, or even the existence of God.

Soon after the prayer, there was a long message. Pastor Petrica talked about what the Bible said about marriage and marriage being ordained by God. Then he spoke of the importance of faithfulness to each other. Daniel was surprised to learn that the Bible said so much about marriage.

The thing that really got Daniel's attention was when the Pastor spoke of the importance of a Christian home, where both husband and wife have consecrated themselves in faith to serve the Lord with their lives and raise their children in the fear and admonition of God. Pastor Petrica said a Christian should not even consider marrying a non-Christian. He said it was the clear teaching of the Scriptures.

That hit like a bombshell! Daniel did not have it in mind when he had contemplated marriage to Veronica. He couldn't bring himself to be a Repenter. If that was what Veronica expected, then marriage was not in the cards for them. Perhaps his feelings about Veronica were not strong enough to keep him from trying an escape this coming summer after all.

The vows given to each other mimicked, to some extent, phrases from the Pastor's message. It seemed like the promises being made would be difficult to keep.

Following their introduction as husband and wife, and the important kiss, John and Ioana headed down the aisle to get ready to greet the people as they left. John shook hands with Daniel and whispered, "I suppose you will be doing this soon." Daniel was a little embarrassed but said nothing. He just nodded with uncertainty.

Following the service, a several-course meal went on for about three hours. People wished all kinds of blessings on the bride and groom. Daniel was beginning to feel a little uncomfortable, but since he and Veronica were sitting with the wedding party, he had no choice but wait it out. There were a couple other things in a normal Orthodox wedding absent in this wedding-no dancing or alcohol. These are necessary ingredients for an Orthodox wedding. It was a part of every wedding he ever witnessed.

One thing that did impress him was how much they enjoyed fellowship in the absence of alcohol and dancing. There was no foul language, sexual comments, or loose language. Instead, the conversation always seemed to center around God and the Bible.

When the meal was over, Daniel and Veronica headed home. He was very quiet while she was bubbling over with conversation. Finally, she asked Daniel why he was so quiet.

"Oh, I am just tired, I guess. It has been a long, busy day."

Veronica surmised it was because of her new-found faith, so she decided to confront him. After all, they were in love, or so she thought, so she needed to know what he was really thinking.

"Daniel, is it my faith that is bothering you? You don't understand why Christ is so important to me, do you?"

After a long pause, he responded, "No, I guess I don't. I love you, but we are very different. I don't see things the way you do. I guess the message the pastor gave today has put some doubts in my mind about our relationship. I can't be what you expect in a husband if you are going to be true to the principles the pastor said in his message."

Veronica looked up at him, and he could see the tears streaming down her face in the moonlight. It broke his heart to see her crying. Trying to fight back her tears, she said, "Daniel, I have come to love you deeply, and I feel that I can't live without you. I had so hoped and prayed that you would become a Christian like me so we could get married and have a Christian family. Many in our church, as well, have been praying for you. I felt sure you would accept Christ as I did, but I fear that I have only been dreaming."

"I am sorry Veronica, but I don't see it. Maybe I will someday, but not now." They quietly walked home. When they got to Veronica's front door, Daniel held her hand for a moment, and, fighting back his own tears, said with a faltering voice, "Good night. I will see you later."

Veronica whispered a tear-soaked, "Good night, my love." Those last two words would haunt him many times in the future.

As Daniel walked home, he reached his conclusion. He was going to escape as soon as the weather permitted. He couldn't bear to live without Veronica. He must leave and begin a new life and have a new love. If he left, it would cause her to move on and find another man who thinks the way she does. That evening was the pivotal point for Daniel's future. From that time on, escape would be the only thing on his mind. He would escape the tyranny of Ceausescu.

CHAPTER 8 ESCAPE PLANS ARE A GO!

Veronica was shattered by the loss of Daniel and all the dreams she had for marriage and a family with him. She wondered if she would ever love again. Only time would tell. She could find no comfort at home. Though her mother and father loved her dearly and shared in her sorrow, they could not understand what was taking place or why. Veronica found her main solace in her good friend Ioana. In the days ahead, they would spend a lot of time together.

Daniel's parents shared their son's sorrow, too, but like Veronica's parents, they did not understand what had happened. When they asked him, he would only say that things just didn't work out because they were too different.

Then, one day, Lidia drew Daniel aside and asked if it was Veronica's faith keeping them apart.

"Something like that."

"I don't see why you can't accept her religion if that is all that is necessary for you to be married. Obviously, you love each other deeply. Your father and I and the girls really like Veronica, and we really looked forward to your marriage. Veronica would make such a wonderful daughter-in-law."

"There is more to it than you understand. The Repenters are very different than us, especially me, since I don't believe in God. I don't want to discuss it any further."

Christmas and New Year's Day passed with none of the joy that Veronica and Daniel had anticipated. Both of them had planned to share their joy with one another and their families. Neither Daniel's nor Veronica's families could console their loved one because neither family could understand how Veronica's faith could stand between their love. Had they heard the pivotal message that caused the chasm, they might have had some level of understanding.

Winter turned into spring as Daniel kept busy with his job and helping the family. With his resolve to escape, Daniel wanted to help them as much as he could and spend as much time with his family as possible. He built a small addition to the animal shed. With the addition of goats, the last winter had been awfully uncomfortable for the livestock in a shed originally built for two cows.

Daniel was not very Romanian, with respect to how he treated the livestock. Most Romanians cared little about their animals and saw them only as a means of food or other benefit. From the time he was a child, he was always concerned about them and cared for them as pets. That was why it was difficult for him when the time came to kill one of them for food. He felt that the least he could do for a condemned pet was to make them comfortable.

Having had a whole year more to plan, Daniel felt he was as ready as he would ever be to try his escape with the arrival of warm weather. He just needed the right conditions: a dark night with a calm river. Several things were different this time. He had perfected the map he would take with him, had done considerable study of the language, and had a waterproof bag. He could not be absolutely sure it was waterproof until it was tested under real conditions.

He had purchased the zippered vinyl pouch and lined the seams with beeswax inside and out. Before leaving, he would smother the wax over the zipper and then put industrial tape, taken from the shipyard, over the waxed zipper and seams. He had also acquired some strong twine from the shipyard and heavy black grease to put over his face and neck. He already had black hair, and he was going to wear a black shirt he had purchased for the occasion.

On a Thursday afternoon, his day off, he rode his bicycle into town. As he looked across the lake, he noticed the patrol boat was moored at the ship-building yard where he worked. He wondered if something was wrong with the boat. It would be dark tonight and the weather was calm. This would be a perfect night if the boat was not operating.

He needed an excuse to ride his bicycle and find out what was going on with the patrol boat. He thought, "I will use the excuse that I want to see Mitruti and ask if he wants to go fishing with me tonight."

Arriving at the guard post entrance, the guard asked, "Do you love this place that much?"

"Yes, I miss it dearly. Actually, I want to see if Mitruti wants to go fishing when he is done working. The perch are spawning and are easier to catch."

"I have been instructed not to let anyone in tonight. There is a problem with the patrol boat. They have to rebuild the engine and get it going. I don't think Mitruti, or any of the others in his group, will be going home until the boat is repaired."

"Well, I guess that is my answer. I fish by myself tonight." He got on his bike and slowly meandered along, yelling over his shoulder, "I will see you tomorrow." He wanted to race home, like his heart was doing, but he had to appear completely calm as he rode away.

Once out of the guard's sight, Daniel rode like never before. This was a miracle. With the patrol boat down, his escape was almost assured. He quickly bought a few items at the little store in town to put in his bag. Then he hurried home and put the provisions he had just purchased with his other things in the new addition to the shed. He had built a secret compartment in the loft so he could hide the things he would take when he escaped. That had been one of his motives in building the addition. The hiding place in the shed he had built the previous year was not as safe as he felt was necessary. He had camouflaged the new compartment so well that no one would be able to find it.

Since it would not be dark for a while, he went about his chores as if he didn't have a care in the world. When darkness approached, his heart started racing again. He was going to do what he had dreamed of doing for the past two years. Though he loved his family, they would get over his escape in time. Besides, he firmly believed he would see them again. After he had citizenship in Germany, he hoped that he would be able to make enough money to purchase their freedom as others had done in the past. He also hoped for the day that the Ceausescu Regime would collapse. It didn't seem possible, but all Romanians hoped for it.

His heart remained broken for Veronica. He had seen her a few times briefly over the past few months and knew he still loved her. He tried to convince himself that his leaving would be better for both of them.

Daniel's preparation included a note to his parents and a note for them to give Veronica saying things he could not tell her in person. Like the first escape attempt, he decided to put the notes under his pillow to be found after he was gone. It was time! He went to fetch the notes and took them to his bedroom to read one last time, as if somehow the notes would contain the emotions he felt at that moment. He was choked up to the point of tears.

Dear Mom and Dad,

I love both of you and my sisters more than words could ever express. You have been good parents to me, and I probably deserved all the beatings I got over the years. I just cannot continue to live under the present regime. I know life is better in the West. I am headed for Germany, and I am sure I will get asylum there. I have planned my escape well. By the time you read this letter, I hope to be in Serbia and on my way. I have a map and provisions to get me by until I can find other food. Just in case there is a God, say a prayer for me. As soon as I get citizenship in Germany and earn some money, I will try to purchase your freedom. Of course, if the political system should change, perhaps I could make a visit. I hope so much that the present regime will collapse. If I thought it would be soon, I would wait for better times. Please take the other note to Veronica. I guess you will know from reading it how I feel about her. It says things I could not say to her in person. Goodbye. I love you very much!

Daniel

Dear Veronica,

As you now know, I am no longer in Romania, or, I should say, I hope I am safely out of the country. I began to think of escaping two years ago and made plans to leave with Radu. At the last minute, I decided it was too risky, and, as you know, that was a wise decision since Radu was killed in the attempt. I feel I am much better prepared than we were at that time. Only my parents knew of my planned escape with Radu, so you must keep this a secret. When I began to fall in love with you, my plans faded away. I wanted to marry you and have a big family. But I didn't understand your faith at first. As we became more involved, I realized I could not meet your expectations. I knew it wouldn't work out for us. I don't even know if there is a God, so I am a long way from where you are. I can't imagine ever believing as you do. I hope you understand why I had to end our relationship. I love you too much to hurt you any further. My leaving is better for both of us. You need to get on with your life and find another man to love you as I do. You don't know how hard it is for me to ask you to give yourself to another because I feel a jealous love for you. But you must! I also must move on and find a new life and a new love. At this point, I can't imagine loving another as I have loved you. Please pray for me to your God, and if He exists, I hope He will answer your every prayer. I hope one day to return for a visit. I will probably find you happily married with a house full of children.

Forever yours my love! Daniel

After putting the letters under his pillow and wiping his eyes, he got up his courage and walked into the kitchen. "Mother I am going for a walk. Do we have any snacks around here?"

"There are some cookies in the pantry. You can finish them off."

In order not to give a hint of his plans, he said, "Oh, do I have to eat all of them?"

"Yes, that is punishment for being such a good son."

"See you later."

"Don't be out too late." (Little did she know how much later it would be.)

Daniel stuffed the cookies into his pocket, thankful for the burst of energy they would give. Food would be scarce after he got over the river. He went into the shed to retrieve his supplies and was off through the garden into the woods. He had made this trip several times, both during the day and at night, so he would be able to find his way quickly in the dark. From his vantage point, he was assured that the patrol boat would not be a problem. He could see men working with spotlights in the engine compartment.

By the time he reached the river, his eyes were bathed in tears at the thought of how much he would miss his family and his dear Veronica. But then, she was no longer his. Would she miss him as much? Well, this was best for her, too, because he was no longer hers either!

He took off his shirt, trousers, shoes, and socks and put them in his travel sack. Then he put on his black shirt. He hated that all his clothing and blanket would be wet. He figured with the hot weather they were having, he would lay low to spread his clothing and shoes to dry once he got over the river.

He smeared the dark grease all over his face and neck. Getting that grease off would be a chore, but he had a precious bar of soap in the waterproof bag for that purpose. How he hoped the waterproof bag would stay dry. As he slipped into the water, he muttered under his breath, "God, if you really exist, will you help me to get across?" The water was colder than he had expected, but it was fairly calm, almost too calm. He would have to be careful not to stir the water too much and draw attention to those manning the spotlights.

Before proceeding, he counted the seconds between spotlight passes would converge on the place he was crossing. The lights shined over his crossing point only for a moment, so he should be ok. With his distance from the towers, he didn't think he could be seen with his face covered with grease. Just to be safe, he planned to remain still and duck just under the surface as the light passed. He would be able to see the light through the water when it passed. Then he would raise his head above the surface and continue across.

The first couple passes weren't a problem. On the third pass he was a little slow at stopping and ducking, and must have caused some movement of the water because as the light passed, it immediately swung back. He held his breath for what seemed like an eternity. The lights from the two towers kept moving about over the area in which he was submerged. To come up now would be certain death.

Finally, the tower personnel were satisfied that no one was there. He was able to raise his face in time to catch a life-saving breath. From that point on, he was much more careful. Little by little he inched his way to the Serbian side. It took him a half hour to make the crossing. What elation when he reached the other side and nestled under some overhanging branches to rest for a while until his heart stopped racing! The spotlights didn't reach where he was hiding. He said softly, "If you exist, God, thank you for safety on this leg of the journey."

After about ten minutes savoring his success, he crawled up the bank, grabbing tree roots to pull himself up. He dropped his bag with all the clothing and survival gear. Luckily, the handle hooked on a root. As he reached down to retrieve it, he said, "God, thank you for not letting my bag fall in the river. I might not have been able to retrieve it before it sank."

In the darkness, he stumbled about trying to find a place to keep him hidden while he slept. He had studied this tract of land several times in preparation for the trip across and had never seen anyone near the river, but he wasn't taking any chances. He finally found a clump of bushes around a large tree. He felt around for a surface that felt a little comfortable. The first thing he did was to check his waterproof pouch. Yes, it had remained dry. He said yet again, "God, thank you for keeping my pouch dry." He felt so silly saying that.

Even though his blanket and all his clothing were soaked, he found it more comfortable to be wrapped in the blanket rather than lie against the elements. The blanket seemed to keep some of his body heat in. Once his adrenalin subsided, he fell asleep.

Sometime during the night, he had a nightmare that the patrol boat was after him, and he awoke yelling, "Don't shoot, don't shoot!" As he came to his senses, he realized the patrol boat was back in service. It was just across from him, only a few dozen meters away, and was shining its spotlight in his direction. He panicked. Perhaps, in his subconscious state, he had heard the boat which brought on the nightmare. Apparently, the men in the boat heard something, and cut their engines, shining their light in his direction. After a few moments, they started their engines and continued on their way.

Daniel couldn't believe it. He managed to escape successfully and then almost divulged his presence because of a nightmare. As far as he knew, he had never done that before. But he had never escaped from Ceausescu's Regime before, either.

He decided to move farther from the river. He walked for about an hour, and finding another spot to rest, he fell asleep, again shivering in the cool of the night. He awoke at the crack of dawn. It looked like it would be a sunny day. He moved to a high knoll using the trees and bushes as a shield so he could get a lay of the land. From his vantage point, he could see the Danube and the city of Turnu-Severin, which was about 24 kilometers east of Orsova. He could see a considerable distance south, west and north. He was safe. There did not seem to be any civilization around the proximity of where he was hiding. Perhaps a kilometer away he saw a shepherd with some sheep and goats. That was all.

He chose a particularly sunny, but somewhat private, spot and laid out all of his clothing, his raincoat, and his blanket. He laid unclothed on the grass so all his clothing would have equal opportunity to dry. He laughed at the thought of what he was doing, but he was free. Well, not yet, but being free from Ceausescu's Regime was a freedom in itself. Again, he fell asleep, only to wake up feeling like he was being roasted. He felt really rested and ready to go. All his clothing and blanket were starchy dry. He quickly dressed and decided to move west, using the river as his guide.

He knew there were a couple of large villages many kilometers ahead. He had seen them when he had ridden a bus along the road on the other side of the Danube toward Pojejena to visit his cousin. He would have to be careful circling these villages. In the area of Pojejena, the Danube turned rather sharply northwest toward Belgrade, the capital of Serbia, one of the six nations in the confederacy known as Yugoslavia. He would continue to keep the Danube in sight, if possible, until it reached Belgrade. He would have to skirt the city to the southwest and then move northwest again toward Austria. He would try to stay in the mountains as much as possible, but his one concern was the possibility of encountering a wild bear or boar. He had been told they were in the mountains of Serbia like in the Romanian mountains. This possibility meant that he needed to keep as close to civilization as possible, but that carried a greater risk of being detected.

He had no protection other than a rather straight and strong branch he found. With his knife, he carved a long, sharp point on one end. He hoped that he would be able to defend himself if attacked by an animal.

After some hours of walking, he figured he had traveled about eight kilometers and felt the need to rest. He had not been walking on any man-made roads or paths, and it was rough on his feet and legs.

He broke into his food pouch for the first time and ate a little cheese and a piece of candy to get some energy. He crossed a little stream and took time for a long drink. He knew that the water might not be as pure as it looked, but beggars can't be choosy. He filled his water container and found what appeared to be a safe place to sleep for the night. He had wanted no moonlight for his crossing of the Danube, but now he wished for the comfort of some light.

The next morning, he was up at sunrise again. All was quiet as he moved along. The only sounds were the crackling of twigs and branches under his feet and the swishing sound his legs and feet made against the dry grass and weeds. He decided to seek the highest point in the region to get his bearings. He could not see the Danube from this point, a fact that worried him. Perhaps he was moving in too much of a western direction. He changed to a more northerly direction to regain sight of the Danube, his only sure landmark until the river turns northwest toward Budapest and Prague.

After a couple of hours, he came over a knoll, and there was the familiar Danube and the first large village he had seen on his trips to Pojejena. He was making good progress. He now changed his direction more westward to skirt the village and then traveled northward the remainder of the day where he could clearly keep the Danube in sight. It gave him a measure of comfort being able to see the homeland he had just left.

CHAPTER 9 GREAT SORROW IN ROMANIA

Back in Romania, when Daniel didn't return home, his parents knew that their son was gone. Lidia went to his bedroom. She lifted the pillow, found the note, and not wanting the girls to know yet, called to George. When he entered the room, Lidia told him Daniel was gone. "I haven't heard any gunshots tonight. Do you think that means he got over the river safely?"

"I heard the patrol boat had been in for repairs for several hours. Daniel must have known that and chose this as the time to leave. Somehow, I knew that he would leave one day. When he broke up with Veronica, I saw a change in him. She was holding him home until they parted. I am not surprised."

They sat on the edge of Daniel's bed and began to read his note. About halfway through, they wept. They knew their son loved them, but he had never said such tender things before. For a long time, they held each other closely. Their hearts were broken. They felt a loss they couldn't bear.

Lidia suggested they read the letter Daniel had written to Veronica. As they read, both of them wept again. "Oh, such love he had for her. Oh, why couldn't he have married her? I don't understand what would have kept such love apart."

"George, did you note that Daniel asked Veronica to pray for him? That seems strange since he has adamantly declared his atheism in the past. He did note in a previous conversation how the Repenters prayed long prayers from their hearts and not from a prayer book like the priests use. Perhaps that is why Daniel didn't ask us to pray for him. How terrible, at a time like this, to not know how to pray for our son! I must go to Orsova tomorrow to see Veronica and take this letter to her. I have to know what it is about her faith that pushed him away." George agreed with her.

The three girls came in to find out why their parents were crying. When they learned that their brother was gone, they, too, wept for a long time.

George did not tell them about the notes or where he had gone. If the girls knew of Daniel's escape, he feared that their youthfulness would not allow them to maintain confidentiality. Daniel's absence would be noted by authorities when he didn't show up for work. The family would certainly be interrogated.

Their safety as a family could be compromised if any member of the family did not use the utmost care in responding to inquiries about Daniel's whereabouts. There was the danger of possible physical abuse to George. Thankfully, the female gender was usually not subjected to physical abuse in questioning techniques.

Maria, the oldest and in her second year in high school, cried the least. She had become somewhat politically astute and understood what was wrong with their government. After the younger girls had vacated the room, Maria said to George, "I bet Daniel escaped over the Danube. I will miss him greatly, but good for him. He will have a better life. He won't forget us! I know that he will come to visit us as soon as possible. I am sorry, but I am proud of him for having the courage to do this."

"I have to agree with you, but I will miss him greatly around the farm. He was such a wonderful help and hard worker, but I am proud of him, too, and I know that his love for us will bring him home again. However, we may have to wait a long, long time."

Trusting Maria's level of maturity, Lidia and George shared the notes with her. She understood well the necessity of not acknowledging his escape.

In order to prepare for a united defense, George, Lidia, and Maria concocted the idea that perhaps Daniel was so disappointed at Radu's death that he wanted to get away from Orsova and start a new life somewhere else in the country.

Of course, when Daniel didn't show up elsewhere in the country, the future could still contain some manner of retribution. Worse yet, if Daniel was to be caught in Serbia and returned to Romania, he would be killed, and they would pay a severe price, possibly death.

If there was ever the need for knowing how to pray, this was it! Unfortunately, at this point, prayer was not a part of their lifestyle.

The next morning, Lidia headed for Veronica's apartment, hoping that she would be there. She came to the door and was shocked to see Lidia looking up at her with tears in her eyes. "Has something happened to Daniel?" At that, Lidia broke down.

"Daniel escaped over the Danube last night. He left a note for you and one for us. I confess that we read his letter to you, too. I hope you won't be angry with us."

Veronica beckoned her to enter. "Please come in where we can talk." Without further word, Lidia handed the letter to Veronica, who sat down and slowly read the letter from her beloved Daniel. She read it a second time to make sure she had not missed a single word.

She cried silently and then smiled. "So then, he really loves me as much as I love him. I will never love anyone like I love Daniel. His letter bids me to find someone else to love, but I don't want anyone else. I want Daniel, and I will wait until he comes back."

"But we do not know if or when he will ever come back. What if he finds another to love?"

"But he won't love another. I am sure of that after reading this letter."

"For your sake, I hope you are right."

They spoke of Daniel's decision and how he had almost made an attempt to leave with his friend. Veronica assured Lidia that the Lord was directing his life. Veronica had not ceased to pray for him every day since their parting. Lidia said she wished she had the same confidence in God that Veronica had.

She then asked a question that was to be the most important question of her life, though she did not know it at that moment.

"What is it about your faith that caused my son to break his relationship with you when he loves you so much? I cannot understand what could possibly stand between such love!"

Veronica paused. "This will take some time. Are you able to stay?"

"Oh yes, please tell me!"

"Not so long ago, I was like most Orthodox Romanians. I considered myself to be a good person. I followed the traditions of the Orthodox Church. Perhaps I was even more zealous than most. Not only did I observe all holidays, take alms to the church, burn candles for the dead, and go to confession on a regular basis, but I also attended the services almost every Sunday. However, I had no peace in my heart. I did not feel close to God. I even doubted that He really existed."

"I thought, if we are the result of evolution over millions of years, like we are taught in school, and even in the Church, where would God fit in all this? When I told the priest of my doubts and questions, his response was that I only needed to trust the Church and I would be ok. He said that my baptism into the Church assured that I would go to heaven. When I asked him how we knew there was a heaven, he said we just needed to believe there was a heaven. His response did not give me much assurance."

"Then one day I met Ioana, a Repenter. I had always despised Repenters because we were taught that they were heretics with a strange doctrine. Ioana was so respectful to me, and yet, I laughed at her and cast her off. I felt I had honored the Church with my response. Later, as I thought about her, I began to feel guilty. I know now that it was the Lord bringing conviction to my heart. I became so overcome with guilt I sought her out in her village. Though I expected she would not want to see me, she graciously invited me into her home. I asked her a question almost like you have just asked me. It was the most important question I have ever asked anyone: What makes the Repenters different than the Orthodox? That question began a process of changing my life, though it took me some months to make the decision that would finalize the change."

"Ioana told me Repenters trusted what the Bible, God's Word, taught, and not the Church and the traditions of men. I told her we believed the Bible in the Orthodox Church. She asked me if I had ever read the Bible. I told her no and that we were told to let the Church interpret the Bible for us. She told me that was my problem. She said if I read the Bible and believed it, I would very quickly see that the Orthodox Church was not really founded on the Bible, but rather a thousand years of traditions. You can imagine my shock and even my disbelief. She challenged me to read the book of John in the New Testament. Of course, I didn't know what the book of John was. I confess I was more than a little embarrassed, but told her I would think about it. She asked for my Bible and showed me where it was."

"Then, she invited me to go to church with her the next Sunday. You can imagine my initial response to her invitation. Me go to a Repenter's church? What would my friends say? She simply asked, "What is more important, pleasing your friends and going to hell or pleasing God and going to heaven?" That question made me angry. Who was she to tell me I would not go to heaven? The priest told me I would go to heaven if I kept the traditions of the Church. I told her I would think about it and left. All the way back home, I kept arguing to myself that I was right, and she was wrong."

"During the entire week, I was miserable. I kept thinking if I was right, why was I so unhappy and unsure of my faith, and she seemed so happy and confident in her faith? When Sunday came, I determined to go to my church like I always did to seek confirmation that the Orthodox Church was indeed right. I burned some candles for the dead, made the sign of the cross several times, once for me, once for my mother, and once for my father, and entered the church. I made the sign of the cross to each saint depicted on the walls. The priest came out and the cantor followed, shaking his incense container. The priest read from a prayer book, and we repeated the same prayer. He said a few things about obedience to the Church and the service was over."

"I left feeling empty, as always. I determined that I would visit the church of the Repenters with Ioana the next Sunday. I swallowed my pride, took the bus to the village, and told Ioana that I would go with her. I was scared to death! What would I find? On Sunday when we got to the church, she proudly introduced me to her friends who all made me feel so welcome."

"After a while, the Pastor came in and Ioana introduced me to him. He was just an ordinary-looking man, but he had such a big, warm smile. He wasn't wearing a robe or any of the other apparel that Orthodox priests wore. There was no incense, no pictures of saints or any icons anywhere in the church. The walls were just painted white, and there was a simple little cross behind where the Pastor spoke. It didn't feel like a church."

"Then the Pastor led the church in a prayer. I looked around and everyone had their eyes closed, except for some of the little children. The Pastor was not reading his prayer. It seemed to come from his heart. Some of the people were saying amen. I guessed that meant they agreed with his prayer. I had never heard such a long prayer in my life. Afterwards, they sang several songs. They actually acted like they were enjoying themselves. There was a little choir that sang a special song. I had never heard such singing."

"After the singing, the Pastor preached a message from the Bible for an hour. I remember thinking, will this ever end? The total service lasted over two hours. The Orthodox service is always over in less than a half hour. I had never heard before the things the pastor said. He said that we were sinners who needed to repent for salvation. Jesus had died to pay for our sins, and we were saved by trusting in Him instead of a church or baptism. That was exactly opposite of what the Orthodox Church tells us. Well, I left that service, not convinced yet, but sure that I needed to hear more. Each Sunday I would return, and I even began to attend the evening services."

"During this time, I met Daniel, and we began to see each other. I asked him to go to church with me. He didn't want to, but he came one Sunday to please me. Strangely enough, that was the Sunday I went forward to accept Christ as my Savior. I know Daniel didn't understand what had just taken place. I didn't fully understand myself. But I felt the weight of my sin and guilt lifted. I began to read the Bible every day, and I soon realized that as a Christian, I should not marry a non-Christian. I began praying for Daniel to make the decision I had made, so we could marry and have a proper Christian home. He simply could not see what the Lord enabled me to see. He kept telling me that he was not sure there was even a God. That was when we parted. Well, there you have it in a nutshell."

Lidia just sat in silence for a few moments. "You say you became a Christian. I don't understand. We Orthodox are already Christians."

"Yes, I thought that, too! But I realized the Bible teaches that we become a Christian by accepting Jesus Christ alone by faith for our hope of heaven. No church can save you. Baptism does not save you. I am sorry Lidia, but if you do not repent and come to Christ as your personal Savior, you are not a Christian. That is what the Bible teaches, and the Bible must be the basis of our faith."

"Now I understand why Daniel felt it necessary to break his relationship with you. So, what you are telling me is that if Daniel had done what you did, you could have married him, and he would never have left Romania? I wish he had done that so I would have my son and you as my daughter-in law."

"But, what about you?" You need to be a Christian too!"

"Oh, I am not ready for that. All my life I have been Orthodox, and all my family and friends are Orthodox. They would leave me if I became a Repenter. I don't think you understand what you are asking of me."

"I am not as old as you are, but I DO understand what I am asking you to do! It cost me my former friends and my only true love. But I now have new friends who share the same joy I have. All I need now is my true love. I will continue to pray that somehow the Lord will reach him wherever he ends up and bring him back to me as a Christian to share his life with me."

"For your sake and my sake, I hope it will happen. I think you should pray for me, too."

"Oh, I have already been praying for you and will continue until you see what I saw." With that, they said goodbye and Lidia departed.

CHAPTER 10 EVADING CAPTURE

Daniel could not have imagined the conversation that had taken place between Veronica and his mother while he was carefully making his way through the Serbian countryside. Having traversed around the village of Milanovac, he moved farther northwest, always trying to keep the Danube in sight as his marker. He also skirted the villages of Dobra and Golubac (with the stone quarry). The quarry was much larger that it appeared from the Romanian side.

His food was running out rapidly, and Daniel knew he was going to have to take a risk to obtain food. On the afternoon of the third day, Daniel had reached a point where the Danube made the bend in a westerly direction toward Belgrade. The ancient Roman Ruins were at the bend in the river. They also looked so much larger. Opposite the ruins on the Romanian side were the villages of Pescari, Moldova Veche, Moldova Noua, and Pojejena, where his cousin lived. He was amazed to see all those familiar landmarks from such an elevated vantage point. He sat down and looked for a long time before moving forward in his journey.

This would be the last view of his home country for a long time. He wept for a while as he thought of his family and Veronica, his Veronica. But, no, she was not his. He had lost her because he couldn't accept her faith. She would have to belong to another. He took a deep breath and said out loud, "There is no turning back. I must be on my way and make some distance before dark."

Soon it was too dark to continue safely. He spent the night overlooking the lights in the villages he had identified a few hours before. He slept restlessly that evening, awaking several times to ponder his future. Finally, he saw only a few lights in the distance. He thought, "Those lucky people are all snuggled in bed while I am out here on the damp ground in a blanket." But he was very thankful for that blanket in the cool early morning hours!

The next morning, he was up at sunrise and continued in a westerly direction. Several times he was almost seen by villagers who were foraging for berries or mushrooms. He had to be careful not to be seen! He had found and eaten some berries himself, but they didn't fill his need for more substantial food. He continued plodding along until dusk, wondering where he should spend the night and what he could do for food. Just when he thought he would experience another evening without food, he saw a lonely farm nestled in a shallow valley with a garden. A garden meant food! Oh, how he needed food! He carefully made his way to the little garden behind the house and rested behind some bushes where he could not be seen from the house.

The little trail of smoke from the chimney attested to the fact the evening meal was in progress. How he would like a bowl of soup and a piece of bread! Soon he smelled the evidence of what he saw in the smoke. Well, the soup would have to wait. For now, some fresh vegetables would do. Daniel carefully surveyed the little garden, identifying what he hoped to retrieve when darkness set in. He didn't see or hear a dog, so he thought he would be undetected.

Soon it was dark, and Daniel carefully slid down into the garden. With help from the moon, he found tomatoes and cucumbers. He filled his pouch full and began to move out of the garden when, out of nowhere, a dog appeared and began barking. Startled, Daniel froze for a moment, but as the back light came on, he decided to leave faster than he had entered. The dog followed at some distance, barking all the while. He ducked behind a clump of bushes as the door opened and the form of a man appeared with a flashlight. He shined it toward the garden, and seeing no one, called his dog back. The dog headed back to the house, stopping often to look back as if to say, "I know you are out there, you thief."

"A thief I am," Daniel thought, "But I have no choice. I need food to continue on my way." As he stumbled through the moonlit darkness, he rubbed the dirt from a cucumber onto his sleeve and enjoyed it like he had never enjoyed a cucumber before. He felt the same way about the tomatoes he savagely consumed!

Daniel moved further into the woods, wanting to put distance between him and the house before resting for the night. As yet, he had not considered a fire. The matches in his pouch were beckoning, but he dared not risk detection.

Daniel had a restless night, dreaming he was found by the dog that barked from the garden he had pillaged. He awoke with a start and sighed when he realized it was only a dream. He fell asleep again wrapped in his blanket. At the crack of dawn, he woke up again, cleaned the dirt off a cucumber and tomato, and had breakfast. Oh, would a cup of coffee be a welcome treat. He moved on, trying to keep the Danube in sight. He was thankful that he was at an elevation, most of the time that allowed him to survey his surroundings and detect any possible danger. He wished that this could be the topography he would find the whole way to the Austrian border for safety's sake, but he knew that would not be.

Later that day it began to rain. Daniel was so thankful for the raincoat he had brought along. Without it, he would have been drenched again, and miserable. He could not believe he almost left it home because it was so bulky and had taken so much room in his travel bag. He waited out the storm, crouched under some bushes shielding him from most of the rain and the cool wind that came with it. Finally, the sun broke out and he moved on. Wondering how far he had gone, he looked at his map to figure out his location. The map didn't indicate much civilization where he thought he was. He decided he probably had not gone as far as he had hoped when he began that morning.

Daniel continued walking a couple more uneventful days before he saw any signs of life. In one sense, he was thankful for that, and yet, he had such a feeling of loneliness. It was bad enough to be in another country, but to not be around people was disconcerting. He was also losing track of time. How many days had it been since the night he crossed the Danube? He sat down to rest and determined he had been walking for seven days. He said out loud, but not too loud, "So today is the first week's anniversary of my escape, my liberation. I should celebrate. Aha, I still have a couple of the candies I brought along for a special occasion. I guess this really is a special occasion!" As he sat eating his candy, he wondered what Veronica's response had been to his letter. He imagined her in church telling Ioana and John that he had left. He wondered about their response. "They probably feel sorry for this old sinner. They are probably praying for me. They pray for everyone else. Why not include me?"

Indeed, the Sunday morning after he left, Veronica went to her little church with a heavy heart. When would she see Daniel again? Would he, indeed, keep himself for her as she hoped? Being sure of their confidentiality, Veronica told John and Ioana about Daniel's escape and shared his letter with Ioana. As she read it, they cried together.

"Such a love can't end! God has to bring him back! I will pray every day that he will find God in his journey and return to you, to take you as his bride."

"Yes, that is my prayer too. I will never love another, so he must come back to me!"

They did not dare to mention Daniel's escape, though they wanted dearly to have the church pray on his behalf. Veronica also shared her conversation with Lidia and asked Ioana to pray that Lidia would continue to come with her to church and give her heart to Christ.

Back in her village, Lidia spent that Sunday in serious contemplation of the things Veronica had said to her. She had almost decided to visit the little Repenters' church where Veronica attended, but she still was not ready to risk a break with her faith.

CHAPTER 11 AN ESCAPE HAVEN

Daniel spent the one-week anniversary of his escape making good time since the forestation was not as dense. In late afternoon, as Daniel wondered where he would spend the evening, he came upon a small village. There were people outside the nearest house talking loudly and laughing. He thought for a moment that they were speaking in Romanian. That could not be, but yes, they were speaking Romanian! His heart jumped. "Do I dare approach them? Yes, I must. I hope they will receive me. I must take the chance."

As he walked forward, one of the old men saw him and, after a moment, spoke to him. In response to Daniel's question, he said, "Yes, we are Romanians." Daniel ran toward them with his heart almost beating out of his chest. Without thinking, he hugged the man. The old man, Mihai, sensing his emotional state, hugged him back. Then he looked Daniel in the eye. "You have escaped from that old scoundrel, Ceausescu, haven't you?"

"How did you know?"

"Look at you. You are a mess! Only a Romanian on the run would look like you."

By this time everyone had gathered around him and were asking so many questions he couldn't keep up with them. Mihai said, "Let the boy alone for now. He needs a bath and a change of clothes. After that we will eat and talk." He instructed his wife to heat some water for a bath.

Soon he was in a tub of warm water. "This is almost heaven. There I go again talking about heaven." After his bath, Daniel sat down to eat with his new-found friends. He was in for another surprise. They prayed before the meal. Only Repenters would do that. He asked them what their faith was, and they said that they were Baptists. "Baptists are what we call Repenters in Romania. I am familiar with the little Baptist Church in a small village near Orsova." Not wanting to be drawn into discussion, he quickly changed the subject.

He learned that this was a small Romanian village fairly close to the town of Barajevo. Mihai gave Daniel some of the history of their people.

"Our people had been working here as loggers when the Communists took control after World War II. I was a young man then. We had no way to return to Romania, and after Ceausescu took over the country, we were happy to stay where we were. Our President Tito was never a tyrant like Ceausescu. He was friendly with the West and had received money from America to help support his country as a buffer state against the Soviets. His policies assured us quite a measure of freedom."

"Daniel, you are safe in our village and your presence will not be divulged. Being on the path toward Austria, we have helped more than one Romanian refugee on his way to freedom. In fact, about a year ago, a young fellow by the name of Eugene came through our village just like you have. He spent a couple of days before moving on."

"Then he did make it. He was from Orsova, and many wondered if he had made his escape."

"Well, he made it safely as far as our village. I hope he made it all the way. Since we heard of nothing in the news, we assume he made it over the border to Austria. Who knows, maybe you will meet him somewhere over there."

They talked well into the evening about life in Romania and Serbia, the largest of the six countries in the Yugoslav confederation. Daniel told them about Radu's and Sergiu's attempted escape and how they were killed. He also mentioned the magazine he had seen and that had caused him so much dissatisfaction with Romania. He asked them what they knew about life in the West. Again, the old man responded to some of Daniel's questions.

"Many Americans and Western Europeans come to Belgrade on tours. These tours also go to Budapest, Hungary and Prague, Czechoslovakia. We understand these three countries also have much better conditions than any of the other Communist Bloc countries. The revolutions that took place in Budapest in the '50s and in Prague in the '60s caused the Communist regimes to modify their level of control. They all have a considerable number of privately-owned businesses like we have. Also, some of the stores in Belgrade sell many products made in the West."

"In Romania, we have been led to believe that life in all of the Soviet-controlled countries was the same."

"We have seen many pictures from Western Europe and America. Their societies are clearly advanced far beyond the Soviet controlled countries"

Mihai, who was obviously the patriarch of the small clan, finally changed the discussion on politics and asked Daniel about his faith.

"Well, my family is Orthodox like most everyone, but I don't believe in God. We were taught in school that all life on earth was the result of evolutionary chance over millions of years and there is no God. It makes sense to me. Besides, I don't think many Orthodox really believe in God either. Most of the people don't go to the church, except maybe at Christmas and Easter. It is a cultural thing, I think. Religion evolved with the human race, and since science has proven evolution, the human race will evolve beyond religion. Anyway, that is what we were taught in school."

"You mentioned that you were familiar with the Baptists near your home. How is it that you are familiar with them?"

"Well, I used to date a girl who became a Repenter. That is why I stopped seeing her. I didn't fit in with her beliefs." He got a lump in his throat as he shared this information.

"We choose to believe the Bible instead of the lies of the atheist evolutionists. We do not believe that science proves evolution. The problem with the evolutionist is that he does not want to obey God, so he tries to prove God does not exist. The Bible was in existence long before Darwin and Communism."

"How do you know these things anyway?"

"Oh, I have a nephew who is a pastor and received his theological training in the West."

Sensing that maybe Daniel was uncomfortable with the discussion, he trailed off by saying, "I will pray that you will come to the Lord one day in your new life, wherever you end up."

Daniel thought, "Repenters are the same regardless of where they are. They are always talking about prayer. One thing is certain; they really don't believe their Bible is a book of fables as we were taught in school. What if evolution is untrue, as Mihai believes? That would mean I gave up the woman I love for a lie."

That thought sobered his countenance so much that Mihai asked if something was wrong.

Daniel responded, "No. I was just thinking that if you are right about evolution, it means I gave up the woman I loved for a lie." As the words left his mouth, he thought, "I can't believe I told that to a stranger, but he seems more like a father than a stranger."

"I am sorry, son."

The conversation turned to some political discussions, which Daniel found to be very enlightening. Romanians were really kept in the dark about many things. He could understand why. If they knew the things he was hearing, they would revolt. No wonder Ceausescu maintained such control. He knows that if the people knew the truth about life in the West, he would not be able to hold them in such conditions.

Daniel was given a comfortable bed to sleep in, and he had the most restful sleep in over a week. He awoke long after the villagers had left for their fields and chores. When he got up, Mihai said, "Well there, our visitor is up. We knew you needed your sleep, so we left you alone. Come and have some breakfast." He was served eggs, potatoes, tomatoes, bread, and coffee. Truly, this was a king's meal! He was encouraged to eat all that he wanted, and he did. This was all like a dream. Here he was in a foreign country with his own people. He hoped that he would find Romanians in Germany.

Following the meal, Mihai, who was too old to do much manual labor, said, "Son, have a seat and let's talk of your plans so we can see how we can help you."

"My only plan is to get to Germany. Because my family is German, I am sure I will be allowed to get citizenship. I just know I must get into Austria to get asylum and then I can make my way to Germany. I borrowed a map from a family of Serbians and traced the map so that I would have a guide. The map is very old, so I am not sure how accurate it is. Perhaps you could look at it and show me how I should go to keep from being caught. Food is another problem for me. I had to steal some vegetables a few days ago and was almost seen."

"I will have my son look at the map. My eyesight is not so good anymore, and he knows the country better than me. I have spent most of my life around the farm, but he travels considerable distances selling wood that we cut in the forest. I was discussing your situation with him. If you are willing to wait for a few days and help around the farm, you can go with him on the lumber wagon. He has to make another trip near Belgrade. That will save you a lot of walking, and he can help you get around the city. The Belgrade area is the most dangerous part of the trip for you. Most people would help you because they know how bad the regime is in Romania. But there are some who would turn in their mother for money or favors. To be sent back to Romania would be certain death. The authorities would love to use you as an example to scare others from doing the same."

"From Belgrade, it will take you approximately one day to cross into Croatia. Once through Croatia, you will have to cross a small strip of Slovenia, which borders Austria. I would guess that the total time it will take you from Belgrade would be the same amount of time it has taken you to get this far. That is, if you can keep moving rapidly and the weather permits."

"When I get to the border with Austria, what kind of barrier will I find?"

"I have been told there are two fences with a meter of ground between them that you will have to cut through. You will need metal cutters. I understand the fences aren't patrolled very diligently. Many of our governmental authorities do not seem to be terribly concerned about those passing through to freedom from Romania. I think most of them probably have a distain for Ceausescu. They understand how difficult life is for Romanians."

"We don't have too many people wanting to leave. Our government has been reasonably fair since Tito refused to implement dictates from Moscow. In fact, Tito refused to attend any of the summit meetings of the Communist leaders, because he would be killed for his refusal to meet the wishes of Moscow.

"When threatened, he basically welcomed them to come over and try to make us obey their dictates. He was a tough leader and did not easily scare. He reminded Moscow of World War II when the Yugoslav soldiers were considered among the most fearsome. We have the benefit of mountains they would have to traverse. Romania would not be compliant to an invasion from Russia to get to the Yugoslav border." Since he died in 1980, the government has carried forth the same type of control."

"Possibly our greatest strength is our relationship with Western Europe, and particularly, the United States. I think they would intervene if Russia were to invade. So you see, within the Communist Bloc, we are one of the most desirable countries in which to live. You haven't seen much of Serbia yet, but as you get closer to Belgrade, you will see that our economy and lifestyle is far, far above Romania and many of the other Soviet Bloc countries. But that is enough boasting about Serbia and Yugoslavia. You are not planning to live here, so I don't have to sell you on our country. Tell me, what are you carrying with you for the trip?"

"Well, I don't have much. I couldn't take much over the Danube. As you have seen, I have a blanket, rubber raincoat, and one change of clothes. In my bag, I have a knife, fork, spoon, and a metal plate. Then there is my self-made spear. That is it. I don't have anything to cook with. Oh yes, I have some matches, but I have been afraid to have a fire for fear of being seen."

"I think you are wise not to have a fire unless you are absolutely sure that no one is around. You just never know. I do think we can help you. There are some things that you should have in addition to what you were able to bring with you. I would say you need a machete. Your knife won't help you much if you have to cut your way through brush. Also, it will help you for protection against wild animals along with your spear. From time to time, we have problems with bears, but our biggest problem is wild boars. Of course, if you are confronted with any, your best bet is not to try to make a meal out of them because they may make a meal out of you instead. The boars are ruthless and usually travel in packs. So if you see one, you need to get out of there, because there will be others nearby. Attack one and you have attacked all of them. Even with a machete, you are no match for them."

"Oh, I know about wild boars. We have had problems in our area from time to time, too. They will come down to the foothills from the mountains and make a meal of our gardens. When we have a problem, we get our neighbors as reinforcements to go after them. If you can kill one, they taste pretty good."

"Next, you will need a metal pot in the event you are in a position to cook. Or, you could use it for picking berries, etc. You need a flashlight with good batteries, and you should have a jacket. As you approach Austria, the evenings will get very cool because of the increased elevation. Of course, you need food provisions, so you don't have to risk getting caught looking for food. All of these things we will provide for one of our own."

"I don't know how to thank you for this help. I am not sure how I would have made it on my own."

"That is ok my boy. We helped that Eugene fellow too! He wasn't any better prepared than you. Of course, son, the best thing we can do is pray for you. Our God can help you. It sounds like He has been helping you a lot already. I believe your finding us was of the Lord."

"I don't know what to say. Like I said before, I don't think that I believe in God."

"The Good Book teaches that we are to sow the Word. That is all I am doing. God will do the rest in His good time. Just keep an open mind and listen to counsel from those that have experienced these things."

Later, as he thought about his discussion with Mihai, Daniel pondered regarding his comment that he didn't think he believed in God. Several months back, he would have said resolutely he did not believe in God. He had to admit he wasn't as sure of his atheism as before. In addition to Veronica and her little church, his time with these Repenters had definitely given him food for thought.

It was noon already, and other villagers were filing back to their homes for lunch and a rest. Mihai said to his son, "Virgil, I have been talking here with Daniel about his trip. I told him that if he is willing to help around the house for a few days, he could go with you on your trip to sell wood near Belgrade. It should be safe to take him along since you have been a familiar site these past years. You could give him directions from there to the border with Croatia. I can't read his map of Yugoslavia because of my bad eyesight. You could tell him how current it is and give some pointers to him. He needs some other provisions that we can provide. I have made a list of the items he will need. As with Eugene, Daniel didn't bring much for the trip."

"That is fine with me. Daniel, I see this as a ministry for me to help people escape oppression. As you know, you aren't the first, nor will you probably be the last, person we will help. Our location is just about directly in the path of anyone heading for the Austrian border from Romania. There are others in surrounding villages who are also sympathetic with Romania's plight and who are aware of the help we are giving escapees."

"In preparation, I designed my lumber wagon with a small enclosure in the middle of the wagon with access from underneath. In the event we encounter potential problems with authorities or any other hostile persons, you can jump under the wagon, remove the small boards, climb inside, and replace the boards making the bottom look perfectly normal. With the heavy logs piled all around, no one would ever suspect such a hiding place. I think it is rather ingenious, if I say so myself."

"As dad said, if you are willing to help around here, there is plenty to do. We are so busy cutting wood to take to market that sometimes the necessary repairs around here don't get done. As you can see, my father is not the man he used to be. We want to keep him around as long as possible, so we don't work him too hard."

He winked at his father, who nodded, acknowledging the comments as true.

"I would be more than willing to help around the farm. I am a good worker and besides, I have to find some way to repay your kindness. I am not sure what I would have done without your help."

Virgil's mother told them to come to the table while the food was hot. As they gathered around, Virgil led the family in prayer for the food and for bringing Daniel into their midst. Daniel was humbled that they were praying for him again. He didn't deserve such consideration. He continued to marvel at their confidence in their faith.

Following lunch, Virgil pulled out a Bible and read a portion of Scripture, which seemed to be aimed at Daniel. He read about the sinful nature of man and how God had provided Jesus as the Savior of men if they would put their trust in Him. He would later remember that passage as being from the first three chapters of the book of John.

Following the reading, they had prayer, and once again, prayed that Daniel would be led to the truth. Daniel thought, "I need to get away from these people. They are almost persuading me to accept their faith."

The next four days seemed to go slowly since Daniel was so anxious to be on his way to freedom. He worked harder than he had ever worked before to show his appreciation for what these people had done for him and were going to do for him to help assure his successful journey to Austria. At the end of the time, he was lavished with praise for all the repairs he had accomplished. He had built a new fence around the animal pen and put a new roof on the animal shed. Wood was not a problem because wood was the business the villagers were in. They already had it prepared for the repairs. They simply needed the capable help to get the work done. Daniel's experience with building his father's sheds sure came in handy for the tasks at hand. For these four days, Daniel was a captive audience to the Gospel. His hard shell was softening.

Mihai presented Daniel with the provisions he would need. In addition to the things already promised, he decided Daniel should leave his light-colored blanket behind and exchange with one that was a dark color to blend in with forest surroundings as a camouflage. He was also given a small Bible to read. Though it would be extra baggage when he already had so much to carry, he dared not refuse it. Besides, in his spare time, perhaps it would be interesting to read.

Finally, it was time to proceed on to Belgrade with the load of lumber. Virgil, his young son, and Daniel took off, with blessings in the form of a special time of prayer for the success of the lumber sale and Daniel's trip to Austria. Their confidence gave him assurance that he would be successful.

CHAPTER 12 JOURNEY TOWARD BELGRADE WITH A CLOSE CALL

The first two days of their journey went without incident. They were still in, basically, an undeveloped part of the country, so there was no meeting with any government authorities or police. On the third day, they were approaching a main highway leading into the Belgrade metropolitan area. This road went to the west and crossed the Sava River. Seeing some commotion ahead, Virgil suggested that Daniel climb into the special hiding place. He didn't need any encouragement to move quickly with his things.

As they approached the highway, Virgil breathed a prayer of thanks to the Lord for his wisdom in having Daniel hide. He told his son not to say anything. The police were stopping every vehicle and searching them. As it turned out, they were looking for a fugitive prisoner. Though they were not looking for political escapees, they would have gladly taken Daniel as satisfaction for their efforts. After asking to see Virgil's passport and papers of permission to travel and making a cursory look at his load, he was waved on. With a sigh of relief, Virgil nodded to the officer and snapped his whip to get his team moving ahead. He determined that Daniel should remain in his hiding place until they crossed the river. They would camp near the outskirts of Belgrade, at the edge of the forest that would hopefully provide Daniel the safety he needed to get past the Belgrade metropolitan area and on to the Croatian region of Yugoslavia. After a quick meal, Daniel would be sent on his way.

Daniel was most thankful when they finally arrived at their resting place for the night. He was feeling nauseous from being cooped up in darkness and with extreme heat. His blanket had provided some padding on the hard boards, but it was anything but comfortable.

Virgil made a fire and put on some soup and coffee. This was the last hot meal Daniel would have on his journey to the Austrian border. He would not have the courage to have a fire, for fear of being found.

As they talked about the help provided by Virgil, Daniel noted that he would have had a difficult time crossing the Sava River, as it was close to the width of the Danube. To swim would have been difficult, and to cross the busy bridge in the open would have been very dangerous.

After eating, Virgil gave Daniel some final instructions and warnings and sent him off into the night. Though anxious to be on his way, Daniel had an empty feeling in the pit of his stomach. He would miss these Repenters. He was made to feel like part of the family, and he had felt such safety in their presence. Would he ever see them again? He was glad for the darkness, which hid tears as he hugged Virgil and his son whispering "goodbye."

As he entered the darkness of the forest, he heard Virgil's parting words, "God be with you, son." There was almost a comfort in those parting words. Perhaps God really was there and would be with him and protect him.

As instructed, Daniel was to travel all night, staying fairly close to the highway going west from Belgrade. This way, he saw lights of the city and passing cars sufficient to provide him a continuous landmark by which to travel. By morning, he had passed the Belgrade metropolitan area into what appeared to be wilderness. He was still near the highway, which went in a northwesterly direction for a while according to his map, so he knew he was going in the right direction.

As the new day dawned, he decided to find a safe place to sleep. Finally, he spied a small ravine between a couple trees with an eroded area under one of the trees with exposed roots. Minus the thorn bushes, it reminded him of where he and Radu had hidden the magazine. He moved leaves and twigs about to make somewhat of an enclosure. He settled in with his raincoat under him, his blanket over him, and his bag as a pillow. Unless someone came directly upon him, he was safe from sight. He slept restfully all day.

He awoke in the afternoon, and peeking out from his position, saw no one. He left his security and looked around to get his bearings from the location of the sun. He then consulted his map. He thought he knew approximately where he was. He ate some of his provisions and lay down again to sleep. He would need full strength to walk all night again.

He awoke as dusk was setting in, and he looked out from the ravine again. All was clear. He ate some dried jerky, packed his few provisions, and launched out. He was getting a much earlier start than the previous evening, so he thought he should make very good progress. Soon the darkness enclosed him. It was more difficult this night because he didn't have the lights of the city and busy highway to guide him. He wasn't making the progress he had expected. He had no problem using the sun as a directional guide, but not so with the moon. Besides, the heavy forestation didn't provide much light from the moon. In the middle of the night, Daniel was feeling weary and would love to have stopped for a long rest. But he couldn't afford such a luxury. He had to keep going.

His heart raced as he thought of how far he had come since he crossed the Danube. How many days had it been? He tried to count the days, but he wasn't sure. They seemed to run together, and yet it seemed a long time ago. He had a lot of time to think.

Thoughts of Veronica flooded his mind such as the last wonderful kiss he and she had shared. Oh, how he loved and missed her, especially now in his loneliness. He wondered what she was doing and, again, how she had responded to his letter. Even though it suggested that she forget him and move on, his heart broke at the thought of her being in the arms of another man.

His thoughts moved on to his dear family. He had taken them for granted and hadn't realized until now just how much he really loved them. So many questions flooded his mind. When would he see them again? It might be many years. He tried to imagine what his sisters would look like years from now. Would he come home to find them grown up and married? Would his parents still be living when he was able to return?

What occupied his thoughts more than Veronica and his family, however, were the Repenters he had been with. In those several days, the beliefs he had clung to so tenaciously had been turned upside down with questions. Was it possible that he had been totally wrong about the existence of God and the origin of life?

He was startled out of his day, or rather, night dreaming. There was something ahead of him moving along with heavy footsteps. He stopped and quietly dropped to his knees. Whatever it was had probably heard him, too. It sounded like it was moving in his direction. He quickly opened his bag and fumbled around for the flashlight. He hated to use the light if it was a person, but what if it was an animal? Finding the light, he took the machete in hand and breathed out, "Here goes." He shined the flashlight in the direction of the sound, and to his dismay, it was a large bear that seemed as startled by the light as Daniel was in seeing the bear. For a moment, both sat quietly looking in each other's direction.

Daniel felt around for something to throw while keeping the light squarely fixed on the bear. It stood up as if to display confidence. Daniel found a large rock, and with shaking hand, he picked it up and threw it at the bear, yelling at the same time. To his surprise, the rock hit the bear in the chest. The bear was equally shocked. Who knows how the mind of a bear works? If he thinks like a human, he might say, "I don't know what it is, but it has a light, makes loud noises, and throws things. I better get out of here!" Whether or not the bear thought anything like that, it took off running as Daniel threw another rock after it and yelled again.

If Daniel had been feeling weary, the adrenalin pumping through his body cured that problem for the remainder of the night. He decided to keep the flashlight in a state of readiness in his pocket; he also decided he would carry his machete and spear in one hand and his bag in the other. Imagining himself a

84

great hunter made him feel safe with the machete. No bear had better mess with him!

He experienced no more excitement after that. As dawn approached, Daniel realized he was exhausted. It was time to find a place to sleep again. But first, he wanted to get a fix on his location. As the sun peeked over the horizon, shaded by the trees, Daniel looked for a place with some altitude so he could see his surroundings. About a kilometer away, he saw a protrusion of rock. As he approached, to his delight, there was a patch of wild blackberries. They were tart, but he enjoyed them nevertheless. He ate them like there was no tomorrow, but tomorrow would come, and he would be sorry he had eaten so many.

After his feast, he climbed the rock to view his surroundings. "Wow, there is Belgrade. I have really come a great distance after all." He checked his map again and determined he was still going in the right general direction and would soon cross over into Croatia. When the sun set, he would have a better idea of a true westerly direction. Before that happened, he needed to get some sleep.

Daniel found a sheltered area in the rocks that was perfect. He had a good vantage point, and if anyone approached the area, he would never be seen, unless someone climbed the rock as he had done. "I am very safe here as long as I don't snore." His mother had always told him that he snored when he slept on his back, so he was careful to lie on his stomach.

Feeling very safe, Daniel fell into restful sleep and didn't wake until the sun was well past high noon. He ate a small lunch and drank the last of the water in his small bottle. He would have to find a stream soon to fill his bottle again. He hadn't seen any water the whole previous day, so he was a little concerned.

Even though it would be a few hours before dusk, Daniel felt secure to travel for the day. He had about four or five more hours of daylight, so combined with the night, he could get in about twelve hours of travel time. He trudged along for several hours, and as dusk was approaching, he came upon something he had not seen for some time, a village. It looked to be a fairly large village from the number of houses he could see. There were probably more houses beyond his sight. It would take some time to skirt the village, as it seemed to be directly in his path.

He found cover in some bushes and pulled out his map. To the northwest of Belgrade, the map showed a couple of large villages. Perhaps this was one of them. If he could identify this village, it would be a perfect confirmation of the direction he was taking. But how was he to know? He would have to find a sign, but that would require him to leave his cover which could be dangerous. He decided to stay where he was until dark. He would have to use the flashlight to read any signs, and that risked detection, but decided he would have to take the chance.

He also needed water and had not come upon any streams along the way. He was getting thirsty. There was a well in the back yard of the house closest to him. Perhaps, after dark, he could quietly drop the bucket in the well and pull up some water to fill his bottle. If he could drink enough at the well, he could save all the water in the bottle for the following day's travels. If the incident with the bear provided an adrenalin rush, it was nothing compared with what was coming!

Amid the sound of children playing and dogs barking, dusk came and soon there was silence and lights going on throughout the village like stars in the night. "What a difference," Daniel thought. These Serbians were very fortunate. Their government didn't shut their power off at night like at home, when dusk brought thick darkness except for any light provided by the moon. Daniel waited until there was total darkness.

Placing the flashlight in his pocket for quick and easy retrieval, Daniel crept down toward the road. In the small amount of moonlight, he could not see a sign. Perhaps he was too close to the village and the sign was farther back on the road. He began walking away from the village, hoping to stumble upon a sign. The farther the sign was from the village, the safer he was. Likely no one would see his flashlight for the few moments he would need it.

He stopped when he thought he saw one. He hurried forward and drew his flashlight out. He made note of the name Vinkovci and turned off his light. He was no longer in Serbia. This village on his map was in Croatia. He had gone farther than he thought.

Feeling proud of himself, he stuffed the light in his pocket and was about to step forward when a voice barked out, "Stop! Who are you?" He wanted to run, but his legs wouldn't let him. He had studied enough of the Serbian language that he understood those words. "If I run and this is the police, I will be shot trying to run away."

He slowly turned to confront the face behind the voice, but it was shielded by a blinding light. Daniel could see nothing, and fear gripped him. It must have shown, for the man said in Serbian, "Don't be afraid." The light was lowered so Daniel could see the form of a large man, perhaps in his '40s. Daniel tried to explain, and the man said, "Ah, a Romanian."

Daniel blurted out, "Da, Da", meaning yes, yes, in Romanian. The man beckoned him to follow, but Daniel beckoned toward his belongings. The man seemed to understand him and walked with him to retrieve them.

He was taken a short distance into the village and beckoned into a house facing the road. As they entered, Daniel was petrified. He thought, "I am finished! I will be turned over to the authorities after making it this far." The man beckoned for Daniel to sit, and then he called out for his wife, Rosa, and their two children. The man blurted out, "Romanian."

86

Daniel must have shown fear because, as she approached with a smile on her face, she said, "Calm down young man. You are safe with us."

He blurted out a phrase he had learned from the Repenters, "Slava Domnului," which means "Praise God!"

"Oh, a Christian," to which he quickly corrected her. No, he had learned the phrase from some Repenters he had known in Romania. She said she was not familiar with the term "repenter". Daniel explained that was what people were called in Romania who believed they had to repent to become a Christian. She just shrugged her shoulders.

With Rosa's limited knowledge of Romanian and his limited knowledge of Serbian, they managed to carry on quite a conversation. He learned she had some Romanian relatives, so had picked up some of the language. Even though they were in Croatia, they were Serbians. It was not unusual at the borders of the countries making up Yugoslavia for people to overlap in their ethnicity.

Daniel explained that he had escaped from Romania over two weeks earlier and was headed for the Austrian border. He explained how he had studied the Serbian language for just such an occasion as this. He was assured of safety with them but was told he was lucky it wasn't one of the other villagers who found him. He might have been turned over to the authorities for a reward.

Rosa and her husband, Bundi, said he could spend the night, but it was dangerous to do so if neighbors found out. Daniel responded that he couldn't stay anyway because he was traveling only by night. He showed them his map, and they verified the location of the village on the map and showed him where they thought the best place was to cross into Slovenia and on to the border with Austria.

Daniel asked how far he was from Austria. Bundi thought he had at least three or four days of travel if he didn't run into any trouble along the way.

He was given some hot soup, bread, and coffee. When he asked to fill his bottle with water, they insisted he take a second bottle because he would have difficulty finding water along the route. Daniel told them he really needed to be on his way. Bundi agreed and told him he would guide him around the village so he would, hopefully, not encounter anyone else.

Thanking Rosa and saying goodbye, he followed Bundi out into the road where they retraced their steps back out of the village. Then they cut up into the forest. Daniel was led around the village and pointed in the right direction. They shook hands vigorously for a moment, and Bundi turned away leaving Daniel looking after him. Without apology, Daniel quietly said, "Slava Domnului".

CHAPTER 13 ANOTHER CLOSE CALL

Daniel started out once again. "I was lucky this time, but I must be more careful. I cannot afford to make any mistakes, and I am getting so close, only three or four days if I keep up this pace!"

He traveled all night, staying close to the road, for he was told that the road went several kilometers in the direction he needed to go. The man told him the landmark he should look for, where he was to turn straight west. There would be a fork in the road, and he would follow the left branch. It was not really a road and went on only a short distance. It was an old loggers' spur used in the past. Once past that spur, he was in uninhabited forest for about 15 kilometers (10 miles). He would pass a couple of villages, so he would want to take care to skirt them.

He continued on into the night, wondering if he had missed the fork in the road. How could he have missed it? It goes to the left and he had been walking on the left side of the road. He was no longer sure he was going the right way, when, all of a sudden, there was the fork! He could faintly make it out in the moonlight. Most of the trees in the area had been cut down, giving a view of the area.

Even though it was quiet, and no one was around, for some reason, Daniel sensed he should not continue in a straight path. He would be out in the open. Instead, he made a sharp turn to the left into the forest.

He soon realized that his 6th sense was correct. As he was walking along, he saw a small flash of light to his right. He dropped quietly to the ground and lay on his stomach without moving. He suspected that someone was lighting a cigarette. He kept his eyes fixed on the spot and waited. At times he thought he heard low talking. He wished he had gone further to the left before turning north. He was much closer to the source of that light than he wanted to be.

His adrenalin was pumping, and he had an urge to get up and move farther away, but now he could hear talking. Obviously, there was more than one person out there. If he moved, they might hear him. He was surprised they had not already heard him. Sunrise was a long way off, so he would not risk anything for the sake of time.

He waited for what seemed to be a long time and nothing happened, though he would occasionally see several little flashes of light and occasional talking. He surmised that there must be more than two men.

Awhile later, he heard something or someone about fifty meters directly ahead of him emerging from the forest, the very area he would have headed had he moved. Two men came into view with a dog on a leash. Was he in trouble? Instead of coming further toward him, they announced their arrival in low tones and crossed to join the others. Now there must be at least one dog and four or five men.

Could it be that they were looking for the escaped criminal who was being sought a couple days back when he had to hide in Virgil's logging wagon? It really didn't make any difference if he was caught. Even if they were there looking for a criminal, he would make a good consolation prize to justify their efforts. There was no leaving. He had to remain where he was and not make a sound. The keen hearing of a dog would put him in peril!

He wondered what he would do if the men stayed there all night? What if this was a permanent patrol station relieved by others for round the clock surveillance? There was an abundance of leaves and brush around him, and he was far enough inside the edge of the woods that he would not be seen unless someone approached.

He decided to carefully take the blanket out of his pouch and spread it over himself in case he had to remain there during the day. The thought of that almost panicked him, but very slowly, quietly, and carefully, he took the blanket out and spread it over himself, including his head, leaving enough room to keep his eyes fixed on the location of the men and dog. More time went by. He could still hear low talking and an occasional laugh. The dog seemed to be asleep, for which he was thankful.

Finally, dawn approached, and Daniel's worse dream seemed to be coming true. He was in trouble. As the sun was peering over the horizon, he heard the sound of an approaching truck from the other fork in the road he had passed. It stopped in front of the clearing, and not more than 50 meters (165 ft.) from him. The passenger in the truck shouted a command, and five men and one dog approached the truck carrying their folded chairs. They were talking with the driver and his passenger. Daniel couldn't understand what they were saying, but the men were pointing toward the west where the two men and dog had come from and moving their arms in a sweeping motion. Daniel speculated that they may have been pointing out the area they had searched. The passenger gave a command and a sweeping motion, and the soldiers and dog jumped up into the back of the truck.

The truck turned around and returned in the direction it had come from. Daniel did not move for a few minutes. It was light enough for him to see into the trees where the men had spent the night. There was nothing there, no equipment, chairs, or anything. It had apparently been a temporary surveillance point.

Now he could see quite clearly into the surrounding forest. "Just in case they send another truck out here, I had better get out quickly." He stuffed the blanket in his bag and took off running deep into the forest. He ran for some time before stopping to catch his breath. That was a close call. Perhaps the prayers of the Repenters were working.

CHAPTER 14 THE JOURNEY TO FREEDOM CONTINUES

After moving a lot farther into the forest, exhausted from running and lack of sleep, he knew he needed to stop. He searched until he found a large fallen tree that provided cover, at least from one direction. He drank some of his rapidly depleting water and ate a little food. Then he wrapped himself in his life-saving blanket and fell off into a deep sleep.

When he finally awoke, it was late afternoon. He carefully surveyed the area. Determining that all was safe, he stuffed the blanket into his bag again and started off. Up to this point, he had a landmark to assure his directions were correct. First, there was the Danube River. Then after being dropped off by Virgil, he had the road. Now he had nothing. He only had the sun, which was already setting. Though the forest was fairly dense, he could still make out where the sun was when he came to less dense areas. He corrected himself so he was once again traveling in a northwest direction. He assumed that he may have been running due west when he originally took off deeper into the forest.

Having rested, he was ready to walk the remainder of the day, believing he was deep enough in the woods to not be seen. He thought that if he walked until sunrise, he could get in about fourteen hours. If he picked up his pace, he could make even better time than he had been making. That seemed possible, since the terrain was much more level than where he had come from, and the trees and brush were thinner.

He continued through the night, and as dawn was approaching, he realized the forest was thinning even more. Had he cleared the forest? That would mean he would lose his cover. Soon he was at the edge of the forest, and he could see a village ahead with a few puffs of smoke spiraling from chimneys, indicating that breakfast was on the same stove. He had to determine where he was. To the right he saw a road and decided to look for the village sign. As he approached the road, he heard a motor and instinctively dropped to the ground. It was a bus. "Aha, there is a lighted name plate on the front of the bus." He made note and lay flat as the bus passed by. It said Varazdin.

When it was far enough ahead of him, he jumped up and ran back to the edge of the forest for cover while he pulled out the map that had been updated by Virgil. He was very pleased because he was getting close to the border of Slovenia. That meant he had to be within 50 kilometers of the Austrian border. Exhausted from 14 hours of walking nonstop, he decided to retreat into the forest to find a secluded spot to sleep. This close to the border, he would travel only by cover of darkness. He found a dense clump of bushes in a clearing and chose that for his bed.

A short while later he was awakened out of a deep sleep. He jumped up to realize that it was a light rain, but he was wet since he was not sleeping with his raincoat on. He quickly pulled it out and put it over his wet clothing. The problem was the color of the coat. It was yellow.

As long as he stayed in the forest under cover, he was ok. He tried to sleep sitting up against a tree. He dozed a little, but his legs and feet were soon drenched, and with the discomfort, he could not get the sleep he really needed. By the end of the day, he was feeling quite miserable. Oh, what he wouldn't give for warm clothes and a fire! That was wishful thinking, indeed. So, he just sat there with a fairly dry upper body and soaked lower body. He laughed to himself as he thought, "Well, it could be worse. I could be totally wet!"

Finally, the sun began to set. Before losing all light, he pulled out his map, which had been sheltered inside his raincoat. He determined that he should go around the village of Varazdin to the left, head due west toward Maribor in Slovenia, and then strait on to the Austrian border. Now that he was so close to the border, he began to worry about what he would find. Would it be a thick wire fence (like the old Repenter thought), concrete, or both? Would there be guard towers, and if so, how close together? Is there any cover from trees or bushes? Finally, he thought to himself, "Well, there is no sense in worrying about it. I will be there soon enough and then I will know."

As soon as it was completely dark, he moved from cover of the forest and began to walk around the village, making sure to stay far enough away so dogs would not see or hear him. He used the lights in the village houses as a guide. In about thirty minutes he was around the village. If his map was correct, there would not be any other villages between him and Maribor. His adrenalin kicked in and he picked up his pace considerably. He was out of the forested area and the terrain was quite flat at this point. It had continued to rain. His fast pace was creating heat to compensate for the cold, wet clothing and shoes.

Occasionally, there was a break in the rain clouds, allowing the moon to shine through and help him with his travel. He could only hope that he was still going in the right direction. Then, it began to rain heavily. "Oh great, I really needed this!"

All of a sudden, rather abruptly, he was entering another forested area. That would slow him down. He entered carefully and began the process of picking his way through the trees. At least it wasn't dense like before. The drawback was that he had moonlight before. Now, because of the rain, he had virtually no natural light. He continued like this all night, with intermittent rain to continue his chilled misery.

At sunrise, he found a clump of bushes in which to sleep. Though he was wet, cold, and miserable, he wrapped himself in his blanket and slept for several hours. When he awoke, he finished what little food he had left. The rain had stopped, and since it wasn't safe to travel until evening, Daniel decided to look at the Bible the Repenters had given him. It naturally fell open to the third chapter of John.

A book marker had been placed there and verse sixteen was underlined. Out of curiosity he read, "For God so loved the world, that He gave His only Begotten Son, that whosoever believeth in Him should not perish but have everlasting life." He recognized that verse. The old man in the village, Veronica, and her pastor had quoted that verse. It was no accident that the Bible opened to this place. He decided to read the entire chapter. He had never heard such things before, so he kept reading until he realized it was time to think about moving on. He decided he would read more in the future.

Darkness soon enshrouded him as he continued on through the forest. Sometime in the early morning hours, the forest began to thin out again, and soon he was in an area with spotty tree coverage and bushes. Ahead was a village. Was it Maribor? It must be. He determined to circle the village to the left. It was still early enough that he was probably safe from detection. Once he was far enough beyond the village, he determined to find a place to sleep for the day.

He was still drenched and cold, just plain miserable! Finding an area surrounded by bushes, Daniel took off the raincoat and wrapped himself in his blanket, covered himself with the raincoat and fell asleep. He awoke after several hours and decided to continue, even though it was still daylight. Adrenalin was kicking in. He had to be near the border, and he determined to continue until he reached it. At least the rain had stopped, allowing his clothes to slowly dry as he walked along.

By the middle of the night, the trees began to thin out, making traveling much easier. There was a break in the clouds and Daniel was startled to see a tall guard tower about 100 meters (325 ft.) to his left. He dropped behind a very small bush for cover. Instantaneously, he realized he must be at the border. He ripped off his raincoat because of its light color, turned it inside out and shoved it under the bush. He wouldn't need it now that he was at the border.

He hadn't seen a tower to the right, so he surmised that was the direction he should go. He began to run back toward the tree cover. Just as he entered the trees, a spotlight shined in his direction and instinctively, he dropped prostrate on the ground. The light moved about the area for a minute or so. People in the tower must have thought they had seen something. They had! That was pretty close! After lying low for several minutes, Daniel crawled back into the tree cover and moved to his right another one hundred meters or so and then came out for a look in the occasional light.

Aha, there was another tower about 100 meters to the right. He calculated the distance between the towers to be about 300 meters. Pacing back to what he thought was about a mid-point between the towers, he ventured out of the trees on his hands and knees. Daniel was very thankful for the cloud cover and hoped it would continue. As he looked up, it didn't appear that there would be any breaks for the moon to show through for a few minutes. A moon-lit night would have made escape impossible that evening.

He took the wire cutters out of his bag and tied the bag under his stomach with the rope he had been using for that purpose. He would be able to run on all fours close to the ground and, hopefully, not draw any attention. He could also drop to the ground instantly if necessary. He put the cutters in his pants pocket and began to run on all fours across the opening. The big question was how far ahead the fence was and what type of fence it was. It seemed like a long distance, and he was getting very tired crawling this way.

After about 50 meters, he came to an abrupt stop against what appeared to be a steel fence. He felt along with his hands and wondered if he would have been better off to remain in the forest until light so he could see the towers and fence and know exactly what he was up against. Then he could have crossed the next evening. But he might not have had the cloud cover. He was here now and had to make haste before someone decided to turn on the spotlights. He was surprised they hadn't done so yet. Maybe they were giving him a fighting chance. His dark blanket had protected him before, and maybe it would again.

He pulled it out and spread it over himself and his bag. It looked like perhaps there were two fences about a meter apart. He began to cut through the wire of the first fence. The cutters worked well. He cut an opening in the outer fencing, bending the sharp wires aside. He crawled partway in to see if he could touch the other fence. He could. Was this all there was between him and freedom?

He was about to crawl through the opening to start cutting the other fencing when the spotlights from both towers came on and began to pan the area. Daniel pulled the blanket over his head and lay flat. There was enough distance between the towers that the lights were not strong enough to disclose him or the opening he had made. They were strong enough to pick up movement, but who was moving?

After about a minute of panning, the lights went off. He decided, just in case there was some deceit in their methodology, to remain motionless under the blanket. Sure enough both lights came on simultaneously a few seconds later and did a quick pan over the area again. "Tricky", Daniel thought. After a few moments, he quickly crawled through the first opening and feverishly began cutting the wires in the second fence. He decided he didn't have time to be neat and precise. He had to get through before the lights were turned on again. He would be trapped like an animal between the two fences. After some minutes he had an opening. It wasn't as big as he thought it would be. But he would be able to get through if he was careful.

He turned around and started to crawl back through the first opening to retrieve his worldly possessions. At that point, the spotlights went on and panned toward him. He spun around without having retrieved his things and dived through the second opening as gun fire began. Because the opening was so small, he ripped his clothing and received two cuts on his back from the exposed wires. The wounds were painful, but he was alive. "Forget the bag", he thought, as he leaped to his feet and ran into the darkness, not knowing if he was over the border or not. He tripped and fell flat on his face.

CHAPTER 15 FREEDOM AT LAST

As Daniel got up, he was looking into two flashlights. In a panic, he raised both arms and said in German, "Don't shoot, don't shoot."

The men responded in a German dialect. "Welcome to Austria."

Daniel blurted out, "Thank God. I made it. I am free!"

One of the men said, "Yes, you are free, young, man. Come with us. You are a sight to see! You have been injured. We need to get that taken care of."

They walked a short distance to a small building. Herman went for a first aid kit, while Heinrich asked Daniel if he would like a cup of coffee. "Da, da!" Even that simple gesture was a new experience for Daniel. He had never seen an electric coffee brewer, and there was a bowl of sugar packets and a bowl of little disposable cream containers. This was a new way to enjoy a cup of coffee.

While he drank his coffee, Herman cleaned Daniel's cuts and dressed them. Heinrich retrieved a form from a desk drawer and began to ask Daniel questions. Daniel had his Romanian identification papers in his pocket. They would verify the facts that Daniel gave to them regarding who he was, where he was born, when he was born, and where he lived before his escape.

After completing the form, Heinrich phoned headquarters to tell the officials that they had another escapee. He jokingly said, "We have another hole in the fence to patch up."

Herman responded, "If it was my decision, I wouldn't repair the hole. It would be easier for others to get through the fence. But our agreement with the Yugoslavs is to assist them in preventing escapes as much as possible. I am not so sure that they really want to stop people from crossing the border. I am not even sure how seriously they were trying to shoot you. They have to make it look good. I think the Yugoslavs detest Ceausescu as much as everyone else. If the Border Control was really sincere, they would shine the lights much more often than they do. Of course, from time to time, they catch and return escapees to appear to fulfill their promises to the Ceausescu Regime."

"Do many people cross the border?"

"There have been a few, especially when the weather is warm."

Daniel asked if they kept a record of people who cross the border.

"Yes, we do."

Daniel asked if a Eugene had crossed about a year ago. Heinrich looked through the journal for the previous year and said, "Yes, here is his name."
Did you meet him?"

"No, we didn't have the pleasure."

"Everyone had hoped that he made it. I did not know him, but he was from the town close to my village. He was one of the reasons I began to think of escaping with my best friend, Radu and another fellow, Sergiu."

Herman responded, "Why are they not with you?"

"One evening a little over a year ago, after much planning, we were planning to swim over the Danube. It was very choppy due to a coming storm. Radu said it was a blessing because it would make it very difficult for the tower lights to spot us. The problem is that I am not such a good swimmer, and I didn't think I could endure against the waves, so I returned to shore. As I was going back through the woods toward my home, I heard gunshots and the motors of the patrol boat that frequented our area."

"We had timed the boat trips, but apparently the guys had not made it across when it returned. Had I continued on, I would not be here!"

"The terrible thing was that the Securitate displayed their bodies in town and insisted everyone come to see what happens to those who try to escape. It was horrible! Their faces were riddled with bullet holes and covered in blood. They made the families bury them in that condition."

Heinrich proclaimed, "Well, Daniel, I am glad that you turned back."

"Me too!"

"Perhaps you will meet Eugene someday. For now, why don't you sleep? When we end our shift, we will take you to our Visa Processing Center. You will need visa papers authorizing asylum while you determine who will give you a permanent resident visa, and you should have some additional medical attention for your wounds."

"Can't I live in Germany if I want?"

"I don't see why Germany wouldn't give you a visa since you are of German heritage. But you should consider Austria since you are already here. We speak essentially the same language. Our country is more beautiful, and we have Vienna and Salzburg, two of the most beautiful and historic cities in Europe. These cities were the home of many of the great composers. Musical history comes alive in these two cities. You must visit them while you are making your decision. Obviously, I am partial to my country, but that is the way it should be. A person should love his home country."

"I love my family and a woman I shall never have, but I don't love Romania. It is a terrible country. I wish I had never been born there. I will never live there again. I hope to visit someday after I get my German citizenship, but I will never live there again, even if the present regime changes."

Daniel had never heard the phrase often quoted in the Christian community, "never say never!"

Heinrich said, "Pardon me for asking, but I am curious about the woman you loved and left behind. You say that you will never have her. Why is that?"

"Well, her religious faith is very strong, and I do not believe in God, so she could not marry me."

"Then, why did you say, "thank God, I am free," when we welcomed you to Austria? Maybe you really do believe in God after all."

Daniel was caught off guard by that question and responded, "I don't know, maybe I do a little."

Herman beckoned him to a room with a bed and said, "You have had a busy day. Why don't you sleep for a while?"

Daniel first went to the bathroom. When he returned, he said, "Wow, such a bathroom! I could enjoy sitting there for a while. It is so large and clean, and everything works. We don't have anything like this in my village. We all have outdoor buildings. In the winter you don't take much time doing your business or you freeze to death. Even bathrooms in the apartments are nothing like this. Most of the time the water doesn't work, and you have to flush the toilet with a bucket of water. That is, if you have working water."

"In Orsova, the town near my village, the authorities are always turning water off without warning the people why or when they will turn it on again. You can imagine the problems with toilets. When the people have water, they fill their bathtubs so they will have water for toilets and to wash."

Heinrich replied, "Actually, we have many outdoor toilets yet in Austria in the small villages, but they are rapidly disappearing."

Before heading to bed, Daniel asked what day of the week it was. He thought it was Saturday, but the officer said it was Sunday. He had lost a day somewhere. As he lay down, he had too much on his mind to sleep. After all, he had been free for only about two hours. How could he sleep at such a historic moment in his life? The clock on the wall said it was 2:14 a.m., so he had entered Austria just after midnight. Austria was one hour ahead of Romania, so it was 1:14 a.m. there.

He wondered if Veronica and the Repenters who helped him in Serbia would be praying for him in the morning service as they promised. He thought about Veronica for a long time. Then, he thought about the question Heinrich had asked him. Why did he say, "thank God, I am free?" Maybe he did believe a little. "I had some close calls and met some people who helped me get here. Was all of that luck or was there a Higher Power looking out for me? Veronica and the Repenters in Serbia sure believed that God would watch over me. Perhaps, sometime in the future, I will have to consider these things again." With that thought, he lost the battle to stay awake and fell into a deep sleep.

CHAPTER 16 BACK IN ROMANIA

Back in Romania, after reading the letter Daniel had written to her, Veronica remained convinced that Daniel would be hers to have and to love one day.

She had prayed, "Oh Lord, you know I love Daniel with all my heart, and he loves me. You have promised that anything we ask in Your name for Your glory will be ours. I am asking that You save Daniel, keep him for me, and bring him back to me. I will be patient and wait on Your time. Amen."

Daniel could never have imagined, in his wildest dreams, that on this very Sunday morning his mother would attend church with Veronica. Following her visit with Veronica, she had come under conviction of the Holy Spirit. She had been miserable the entire week. She realized she was looking selfishly at herself and the persecution she would experience if she became a Repenter.

Here was Veronica, willing to give up her friends, and even her Daniel, for the sake of her faith. Early that morning as she was getting dressed, she thought, "I suppose all the Repenters have had to give up friends and maybe even some family to believe in God the way they do. Such faith makes me envious."

Veronica was overcome with joy when Lidia had come to her home a few hours earlier to tell her she would go to church with her. She had been thinking all along that if God brought Daniel to her as she was pleading, that would mean Lidia would be her mother-in-law. It would not be enough for Daniel to accept Christ. His whole family needed to come to Christ. Was this the beginning of God's answer to her prayers?

Veronica and Lidia had something in common: someone they both loved. There was already a bond developing between them.

Veronica was at the bus stop waiting for Lidia early the next morning. She couldn't wait to see if Lidia would actually come. She had often invited others and received promises that never materialized. But this morning, she was not to be disappointed! At a distance, she could see Lidia walking toward her.

Veronica greeted her with a hug and kiss on both cheeks showing her joy in having Lidia accompany her to church. Lidia was very quiet during the bus trip to the village. She was thinking of the significance of this trip and mulling over in her mind thoughts she had struggled with all week. From the time Veronica began to witness to her, Lidia had been thinking over the same types of questions that Daniel had been tossing around. The Orthodox didn't believe repentance was necessary because they were baptized into the Church. This rite made them Christians, or so they thought. But if Veronica and her church were correct, the Orthodox didn't become Christians by baptism, membership, doing alms or any other good works. How could the Orthodox Church be so wrong after 1000 years?

This would mean that her entire belief system was wrong and had been her entire life. And this would be the same for the untold millions who had lived and died in the Orthodox Church. According to Veronica, it is the Bible that says they are wrong, not her church. As bad as all that was, according to the Repenters, if one didn't repent and ask Jesus to save them, they would go to hell!

What about her dear mother who died a few years ago? She was a devout Orthodox and was sure her baptism and alms would gain her eternal life, if there was a heaven. The existence of a heaven was something that she and other Orthodox members sometimes questioned. If there is no heaven, that was the end for her mother. In fact, death on earth would be the end for everyone. Therefore, ultimately life would have no meaning, and there would be no basis for morality.

"These Repenters seem to have none of the doubts that I have had. They are so sure of their faith! How do they develop convictions that allow them to take the criticisms so often levied against them?"

Her thoughts were interrupted as the bus arrived in the little village. Those thoughts and questions would often be replayed as she struggled with her decision to accept the faith of the Repenters.

When Veronica and Lidia arrived at the little church, the morning greetings were so extensive that the service started late. Every single person had to personally greet her, including the pastor. After the traditional singing, prayer time began. When Veronica prayed, without divulging any specifics, she prayed for Daniel to be saved. Then she prayed that Lidia would be able to understand her need for the Savior. Lidia would have been embarrassed if she had not known Veronica's sincerity.

As the prayer time continued, not unlike Daniel a year before, Lidia thought, "These Repenters pray for just about everything and everyone, don't they? And their prayers aren't from prayer books like the short prayers of our priests. The people in the Orthodox Church would never think of praying out loud. They certainly wouldn't be praying that people would repent and be saved."

Though Pastor Petrica did not know Lidia would be in the service that morning, Lidia thought the message seemed to be aimed directly at her. She resisted letting go to do what her heart was telling her to do. On the way home following the service, Lidia peppered Veronica with question after question.

CHAPTER 17 ON TO THE REFUGEE PROCESSING CENTER IN VIENNE, AUSTRIA

While Veronica and Lidia were in church, Daniel would be in the process of filling out the paperwork for a temporary visa.

Daniel was very alert to all the new things he was experiencing. As Herman was taking him to the main center for processing aliens, his immediate observation was there were no police checks along the way. The roads were wonderful, compared to roads in Romania and Yugoslavia. The houses were beautiful with flowers growing in window boxes. There was green grass in front of the houses, and there were no farm animals in the yards surrounding the houses. The cars on the roads all looked like new to him in comparison to most Romanian and Yugoslav cars.

What was this "air conditioning" in the car? Daniel could never have imagined such a thing in a house, let alone a car. When they arrived at the processing center, the door opened automatically as they approached. Daniel looked around to see who had opened the door. "Now, that is strange", he thought. Once inside, he observed a large metal machine people were drinking water from. "Can I do that, too?"

"Sure," said Herman. "You can drink as much as you want. It is free."

After a long drink, Daniel thought, "Wow, it is cold." The only cold water he had ever tasted came out of natural springs, and even then, it wasn't this cold.

He observed a worker typing on something that looked like what he had seen in the magazine. Herman explained what a computer was.

"I wondered when I saw pictures because it looked similar to a typewriter, but a computer in Romania means a machine that adds and subtracts."

"I rather suspect you will be seeing a lot of technology you have never seen before."

At that, Herman said, "Daniel, you are in good hands now. It has been nice meeting you. We will probably never meet again, so I wish you the best as you make decisions regarding your future."

Daniel thanked him and told him that he would never forget his experiences with him and Heinrich. He concluded with a hearty handshake and kiss on the check.

After an hour or so of questioning, signing forms and getting his picture taken for the temporary visa, someone explained to him the rules he must live under and what his responsibilities were until he was accepted by the country that would give him a permanent entrance visa. In the meantime, he was given a month to make inquiries and decisions. The government of Austria would give him a place to stay in a youth hostel in Vienna.

When asked if he had any questions, he responded, "Do you know Eugene Popescu?"

"Oh, you know Eugene, do you?"

"No, I just heard of him. He lived close to where I lived, and I heard he escaped about a year ago."

"Well, he decided to immigrate to Austria, and he is still living in Vienna in the same hostel where you will be staying. He is in room 27, and you will be in room 33. Here is a map of the city showing where the hostel is located. They serve meals there for a very reasonable price. That would be the best place to eat. You can take these papers to the office over there, where they will give you Austrian currency and a bus ticket to Vienna. The bus will leave in about two hours. You won't want to miss it. I am sure Eugene will be happy to show you around."

Daniel thanked her and moved on.

The lady in the next office smiled and handed him an envelope with cash. She told him that each week he would need to go to the address on the card she gave him to pick up his allotted money for the next week. She explained that was all the money he would receive per week, so be careful how he spent it. She also gave him a voucher to get some basic clothing at a store near the youth hostel. "Good luck, Daniel."

Daniel had almost two hours to walk around before the bus arrived. There was a wall with many pictures of life in Austria. Daniel was quite captivated by the pictures. He found out he could understand fairly well the captions under each. He felt very secure with his ability to communicate. He thought it would be more difficult, but his excellent knowledge of the German language was a great help. Finally, it was time to board the bus. It was air conditioned like the car and had music playing. "Now, this is living!"

As anyone who has traveled in Vienna would understand, Daniel was virtually in a trance as the bus traveled right through town and past St. Stephen's church. The bus stopped in front of the youth hostel and Daniel stepped off. He did a 360 degree turn to take everything in. He thought he had seen some impressive churches in Romania, but they were nothing compared to St. Stephen's Church.

He stepped into the hostel and a clerk behind the counter asked if she could help him. He showed her his papers, and she called someone to take him to his room. She explained that the cafeteria would be open for another hour. He thanked her and followed the attendant to his room. The door was opened, and he was given the key.

Though the room was modestly furnished compared to what he would experience later, at this point he was impressed. He even had his own bathroom, and everything worked like the bathrooms in the Border Control and Visa Processing Centers. If only his mother and father could see this, they would understand why he left Romania. He looked into the large mirror and said out loud, "Hi there, Mr. Free Man!" A free man was not all he saw. His clothes were anything but presentable. He was a mess!

He pulled out the vouchers he had for clothing and went to the front desk to ask where he was to go for his new clothing. He was instructed to walk only a couple doors down from the hostel, but was admonished to do so quickly if he wanted to eat in the cafeteria. He hurriedly made his way to the clothing outlet. He had never seen so much clothing in his life in one place. With assistance from the clerk, a very attractive and single young lady, he chose the three outfits of clothing allowed with the vouchers, some underwear, socks, one pair of shoes, and a light jacket. He thanked the clerk with one last admiring look, and hurried back to the hostel. "Wow, she is cute!" For a fleeting moment, he thought of his beloved Veronica.

His thoughts wandered off as he entered the hostel and made his way to his room. He would have to take a shower quickly and put on one of his new outfits. There was no way he could go to the cafeteria looking like he did. He had less than a half hour to get there before they closed, and he was famished. He undressed and stepped into the shower. This would be a new experience for him. He had never had a shower in his life. He reached for the knob and said, "Here goes." Here goes was right! As he turned on the first knob, ice cold water spurted out and he jumped out of the shower. He turned the water off and then noticed the second knob. "Maybe this is the one I want." He turned it on, and lukewarm water came out. "That is better," he thought as he stepped back into the shower, leaving a puddle of water on the floor. As he was relishing the warm water, all of a sudden, the water turned hot, and again he jumped out of the shower. "Wow, talk about extremes! You dummy, you are supposed to turn both of the knobs to get the right temperature." A moment later, using his great technical skills, he was taking the first wonderful shower of his life. He wanted to spend a long time enjoying this new experience, but his stomach reminded him of more important things.

He quickly jumped out, dried, dressed, and headed for the cafeteria. He barely made it before they closed the door. He was in for another surprise. As he entered the line and took a tray, napkin, and silverware, he saw an assortment of foods like he had never seen in his life. Not recognizing some of the items, he just reached for a sandwich, a salad, and something that looked good for dessert. A moment later he was standing before a machine that dispensed soft drinks. He stood there looking at the machine, wondering what he was supposed to do. The cashier was watching him with interest.

Finally, she said to him, "Haven't you seen one of those before?"

"No, I just got here."

"I bet you are one of the lucky ones who escaped the Iron Curtain. Welcome to the free world. Take a glass, and if you want ice, push the glass under the middle metal lever." He did so, and jumped when ice fell into his glass. It was fully filled!

She laughed. "You will get the hang of it. Pour some of the ice out on the grid. There you go. Now choose the drink you want."

He said he didn't know what he wanted.

"Why not try Coke? That is a real favorite. It comes from America. You can try others in the future."

"Well, if it is from America, I bet it will be good." He filled his glass, paid the clerk, and chose a table to sit at. Most of the tables were empty by this time, so he ate in silence.

When he finished eating, he asked a worker who was putting food away where he was to put his tray and dishes. She pointed to a conveyer belt. He placed the tray on it, and it started to move. He watched the tray disappear into an opening in the wall. He asked the worker, "Where did the tray go?"

She laughed again. "It went back to the kitchen where another worker is washing dishes. You are the last person, and he was waiting for your tray so he could finish the dishes for the night."

"How did that thing know to take the tray back there?"

"There is an electronic sensor under the conveyor belt that turns on when it senses the weight of a tray."

"Oh, I see." He really didn't understand at that point. He left the cafeteria, thinking that every time he turned around, there was something new. Certainly, he should not be surprised about anything in the West!

Feeling full and clean, he decided to see if Eugene was in his room. After getting no response, he went for a walk to see what other new experiences awaited him. As he stepped into the street, he noticed how happy everyone seemed to be. He looked in shop windows, seeing things he had never seen before in an abundance he could not imagine. He headed toward St. Stephen's Church.

Suddenly, a man dressed in strange clothes approached him and asked him if he wanted to buy a ticket for the Mozart Concert that evening.

"What is a Mozart Concert?"

"Oh. You must be new to our city." He explained that he was selling tickets to the concert that was being performed that evening. He told Daniel that the

Mozart Symphony Orchestra performed every evening and that he was one of the members.

"Why are you dressed like that?"

The man laughed. "This is the way the musicians dressed in the time of Mozart."

Daniel asked how much it was for a ticket and the man told him it was $20.00.

"Oh, I can't afford that!"

The man left saying, "I am sorry," as he approached another potential customer.

Daniel approached the church and entered. He realized it was a Catholic Church. He had never been in a Catholic Church before. The interior was incredible! It must have taken a long time to build. There was a service going on, and a priest was talking while another man was swinging an incense container on a chain, just like in the Orthodox Church at home. The people were making signs of the cross when they entered. He was thinking that the service didn't seem much different than an Orthodox service.

He then observed that the priest was talking in Latin. He knew it was Latin because the Romanian language was Latin-based. But it was different enough from the Romanian that he couldn't understand much of anything the priest was saying. He wondered if the people could understand. At least in Romania, the priest conducted the service in the Romanian language so the people could understand.

After some time, he departed and continued his trek toward the hostel, watching the people passing by. Most of the shops were closed by now, so he could only look in the windows. But that was interesting enough.

CHAPTER 18 DANIEL MAKES A FRIEND

Daniel found his way back to the hostel. This had been the most interesting day of his life. He went to room number 27 and knocked on the door. A few moments later the door opened, and Daniel said, "Buna Seara" (Good evening).

The young man's eyes lit up as he exclaimed, "A Romanian!"

"Yes. Are you Eugene?"

"Yes. Please come in. How do you know my name?"

Daniel then explained how. They talked for hours, sharing their escape stories and talking about everything under the sun, but mostly about life in Austria compared to life in Romania. There was so much to experience! Their escape stories were quite similar, except when Eugene had crossed, the lights were not operating. He had missed the excitement that Daniel had when he crossed. Eugene explained how he decided to live in Austria and had gotten a permanent visa. He had a job and was in the process of fulfilling requirements for citizenship.

After some time, Eugene suggested that they go out for coffee.

"At this time of night?"

"This isn't Romania. We have coffee shops and pubs open all night."

They stepped out onto the street.

"No, this is not Romania!" Streetlights shined brightly and many people were passing by in small numbers. It was not like the total darkness back at home!

They went into a quaint and very European little espresso coffee shop. Eugene said, "Let me buy. You are going to find out what real European coffee tastes like." The waitress brought their purchase to the table, and Daniel learned that, indeed, those little cups packed a wallop!

They talked for a couple more hours regarding life in the West. Eugene had been in Austria long enough to have gained much knowledge regarding life in the West and the technological advances that had so distinguished free countries from the Communist Bloc countries. Eugene seemed to be an endless encyclopedia of information, which Daniel tapped continually.

They retired for the evening with Eugene's promise to take Daniel on a tour of the city the next day. It was his day off. Daniel lay in his bed for a long time before falling asleep. Perhaps the caffeine from the strong cup of coffee was contributing to his inability to sleep, but the sights of the day and his discussions with Eugene were enough to keep him awake.

A knock at the door interrupted his much-needed sleep. He jumped up, put his trousers on, and opened the door. It was Eugene. He jumped inside the room and said, "Let's go! There is a lot to see today!"

Yawning, Daniel got dressed while Eugene talked on about what they were going to see. Daniel asked Eugene if the cafeteria was open.

"No, it's too late for that. We can get some coffee and a donut."

"What is a donut?"

"It is an American food served in a new American donut shop franchise."

"What is a franchise?"

"It is a term for companies that grow rapidly by selling the right to merchandise their goods to people with financial resources. Eating establishments will often grow this way. Many American companies are now doing business by selling franchises to Western Europeans.

They stepped out onto the busy sidewalk and made their way to the donut shop. It was full, so they sat at the counter on some stools. Daniel spun around a couple of times and then felt foolish as he realized other people were looking at him. Never having seen a donut before, he just picked one that had pink frosting. The coffee was served in a large mug much bigger than the cups used in Romania, or even at the shop the night before. He remarked to Eugene about the size of the cups.

Eugene explained that he would notice that this coffee wasn't as strong as Romanian coffee or the traditional European espresso coffees such as they had the previous evening. Americans drink a lot of coffee. "If their coffee was as strong as European coffee, they probably wouldn't drink as much. This is also probably why many Americans drink their coffee without sugar or cream."

Soon, they were back out on the street. Eugene explained how they could buy a bus pass for the day that would allow them to use any bus to go wherever they wanted. Since Daniel had already been in St. Stephen's Church, they passed that by on the tour. First, they went to the Musikverein, which was used for plays and musical performances. It was famous and very old according to Eugene. Next, they went to the Mozart Orchestra Hall where the Mozart concerts were performed. Third, there was another large orchestra hall where other symphonies were performed.

"This is sure a city of music," Daniel exclaimed, as they went out and caught the bus to go to several museums. There was a history museum, a music museum, and an art museum. By the end of the day, Daniel was worn out. There was much more to see, but there would be other days.

As they walked from the bus stop to the youth hostel, Eugene said, "My favorite city is Salzburg. I don't work on Sundays. Let's hop a late bus on

Saturday evening after I get off work and go there. I know a cheap hostel that we can stay in. We can tour the city all day and then take a late bus back to Vienna."

"I am not sure if I can afford to do that."

"Look, it will be on me this time. I have a good job and can afford it. I want you to see the city because I think you will like it as much as I do. I haven't been there for a few months, so this will be a treat for me as well."

They walked into the hostel and headed straight for the cafeteria. They were both famished after such a rigorous day of sightseeing. Daniel decided to try another soft drink and some different food. There was so much to experience! Eugene suggested that they go to the TV room and relax for a while. When they got there, they found it empty, so they had their choice of what they would watch. Eugene grabbed the remote and plopped down.

"Daniel, what do you want to watch?"

As he started flicking through the channels, Daniel said, "I can't believe it!"

"You can't believe what?"

"We only had one channel in Romania, and it was only on for a few hours, with mostly political stuff about how great Ceausescu and the Communist system is."

"I am sorry. I forgot. This isn't Romania. We have what is called cable TV in the city now. There are channels from America and other European countries. Over 30 channels must be available." They decided on an American western with John Wayne.

The next four days while Eugene was working, Daniel just walked around the city taking everything in. He would anxiously wait for Eugene to return from work. They would eat the evening meal together and just talk. Daniel wondered what he would have done without Eugene's help. He was really becoming a good friend. Daniel couldn't wait until Saturday evening. Eugene had talked about Salzburg so much, that Daniel had great expectations.

When Saturday evening came, Eugene suggested they go to another franchised American restaurant, and then catch the early evening bus. So, Daniel was in for yet another pleasant surprise. He had never had a hamburger. They had milk shakes for dessert. Daniel could not say enough about what a treat that was! After eating, he decided right then and there that he liked America.

They walked over to the bus terminal and in half an hour were on their way to Salzburg. The trip out of the city was as exciting for him as the trip coming in nearly a week ago. This week in the city had been almost like a dream. Once outside the city, there was just the beautiful countryside and the beautiful horizon with the setting of the sun. They arrived in Salzburg about 10:00 in the evening. They made their way to the hostel, finding accommodations as Eugene had assured him. They shared the same room and fell into their beds for a much-needed rest before the full day that Eugene had planned for them.

The next morning, they were up at the crack of dawn. They went to a coffee shop that Eugene was familiar with and had a traditional cup of European coffee and a tart to start the day off. While they ate, Eugene mentioned all the places they would try to see. There was the castle above the city, the two homes of Mozart, two beautiful churches, and the cemetery used by the Americans when they filmed The Sound of Music. There were shops to see, street musicians, and painters selling their wares.

"So Daniel," Eugene exclaimed after finishing their small meal. "What shall we see first?" As they entered the street, there was the giant castle overlooking the plaza.

"I want to see the castle."

"Do you want to walk up and take the incline down, or vice versa?" Before Daniel could answer, he said, "Let's take the incline first, so you can see the entire city on the way up. It is neat!" Daniel had never been on an incline, so he readily agreed to Eugene's plan. What a view!

As they started their tour of the castle, Eugene began to tell him the interesting history.

"The castle was first constructed in 1077 by an Archbishop of the Catholic Church, and its present size and construction began in the mid-1400s. It is one of the largest castles built in any European country. It could provide safety to the people of the city any time they were attacked by enemies. They had dug through the rock to reach the water table hundreds of feet below the castle. With enough food provisions, they could wait out an enemy for a long of time."

"When Napoleon was conquering Europe, he brought siege to the city of Salzburg. As before, the people ascended into the castle, and Napoleon was unable to scale the walls. In fact, this is the only castle in Europe that had never been taken by military force in ancient times. After months of unsuccessful attempts, Napoleon issued an ultimatum. He was going to continue his conquest of Europe but would leave a contingency of troops behind. When the people eventually ran out of food and left the castle, they would be slaughtered to the last man, woman, and child. After consideration, the people surrendered the castle."

Daniel marveled at the size of the fortress. It was truly a monument to man's ingenuity. "I thought Bran Castle (Dracula's castle) was a big deal, but compared to this, it is nothing."

"In terms of size and defensibility, you are right, Daniel, but Dracula's castle carries a real historical significance because it was there that Dracula (Vlad Dracul III, Prince of Wallachia) was kept prisoner for a couple months before being put to death by a usurper to his position."

"He helped stop the Muslim invasion of Wallachia, present day Romania, in the mid-1400s. To Romanians, this is a monument that has real significance in our past."

"You do have a point there, Eugene."

After the tour was complete, Eugene and Daniel walked the somewhat serpentine foot path back down to the street level where the area was alive with people. Many vendors were selling their wares. There were exotic foods, potteries, clothing, handmade clothes of all kinds, and more. Daniel was keeping an ear out for different languages.

It was obvious from observing the physical features and clothing of the people that people from all continents were visiting for business or pleasure.

Next, they went to the cemetery filmed in the American movie, The Sound of Music. From there, they visited two ornate Catholic churches that were centuries old.

Daniel asked Eugene why there were no Orthodox Churches.

"I am no historian, but it was something about the split of the Roman Empire a thousand years ago or so. The Eastern part of the empire, called the Byzantine Empire, came under a Patriarch, the equivalent of the Pope. The western branch continued under the Pope and remained Catholic. Austria was in the western branch of the empire. Because of the Reformation, there are many Lutheran churches here as well. Of course, the whole religion thing is of no interest to me since I am an Atheist."

At that, Daniel piped up. "I don't believe in God, either. I guess we have more in common than I thought. It is good to know that there are other intelligent people around. I have had some exposure to the Repenters, and they are serious about their faith, but I think they believe in someone who doesn't exist."

"Yes, I saw the same thing in the Serbian Repenters who helped us. I almost wished that I could share their faith because they were so certain, but it doesn't stand to reason. We were clearly taught in school that science has proven evolution to be true. The idea of some God being over the whole universe doesn't make sense to me. Both positions can't be right."

That settled the issue for the time being as they continued on in their tour of the city.

In early afternoon, they stopped at a small restaurant to buy something to eat. The prices seemed particularly high, so they didn't get much. Eugene said, "It must be the foreigners running the prices up. Shop owners know that they can charge more, and the rich foreigners will pay. But there is one problem; we aren't rich."

"You can say that again."

They stopped for a while to listen to a couple small groups playing classical music. People were dropping money onto a blanket. Daniel felt a little guilty because, even though he enjoyed the music, he couldn't afford to contribute a tip. Next, they watched artists painting and sketching scenes of the town that they would then offer for sale. The prices seemed reasonable, but again, Daniel was in no position to buy any souvenirs. Besides, where would he put them, not knowing where he would live and what his accommodations would be in the future?

CHAPTER 19 BACK IN ROMANIA AGAIN

While Daniel was confirming his atheism with Eugene and touring Salzburg, Veronica sat next to Lidia for the second Sunday in a row. Lidia was coming close to confirming her faith in the God of the Bible. She had been reading the books of John and Romans at the encouragement of Veronica. Never had she read the Bible, and never had she been so challenged to see herself as God sees her.

"Veronica, I have read the two books of the Bible as you suggested. I guess I have never seen Christ in His glory as the Son of God like the Bible makes so clear. I know that was exactly what you told me, but I didn't want to believe you."

"Lidia, you are beginning to see why we keep quoting the Bible. If something is not taught in the Bible, then it is something added to the faith by men."

Lidia determined she must follow Veronica's advice in her quest for truth. So far, everything she told her seemed to be exactly true.

That Sunday, the pastor told the congregation he felt compelled of the Spirit to pray earnestly for Daniel's salvation. Of course, the little church knew nothing of Daniel's escape, so there was no prayer for his safety. But Veronica kept that prayer in her heart. Perhaps God's Spirit compelled Pastor Petrica to pray for Daniel at that moment, because hundreds of miles away Daniel was celebrating his belief in atheism with Eugene.

On their way home, Veronica asked Lidia, "What do you think about Pastor Petrica's message today regarding the necessity of putting faith in Christ alone?" She paused for a while, but Veronica patiently waited.

"I am almost persuaded."

"I pray that your 'almost persuaded' won't be like that of King Agrippa in the Book of Acts after he heard Paul preach to him about Christ. King Agrippa said, 'Almost I am persuaded.' As far as we know, he was never persuaded and is in hell today with all who have rejected Christ. I pray that you will continue pursuing the truth."

"Oh, I will!"

The two of them walked along in silence for a while toward the bus stop.

The silence was broken by Lidia when she said, "You talk of hell like it is a real permanent place."

"The Bible teaches us that it is eternal. Pastor told us recently that hell is mentioned more times than heaven in the Bible."

"Don't you think God will take into consideration how serious people were in their faith, even if they were wrong? My mother was a very devout Orthodox believer and would always tell us to stay away from the Repenters because they did not know what they were talking about. I remember one time when a Repenter tried to talk with her, mother laughed at her and told her to leave and not come back. That is how serious she was about defending her faith. Certainly, God would be pleased with her seriousness. After all, she believed in God. I can't bear the thought of my mother being in hell."

"I know what you mean. My mother and father have rejected my attempts to get them to consider what the Bible says. If they die without Christ, they will go to hell, too! You see, in the first chapter of Romans, God says that men are without excuse, because they should have enough evidence to tell them they are sinners and in need of someone to pay for their sins. When people believe they are ok, because of their sin nature, it is easy for them to willingly reject investigating their real condition."

"Repenters have been around all my life, and I not only rejected them, but made fun of them. Even the name they give us signifies what we should know in our hearts is necessary to please God. For example, I found it easy to sin and convince myself that it was really ok to sin because I was baptized into the church. I think down in my heart I knew that my life was not pleasing to God, but it was so easy to overlook my obvious condition and pretend like everything was ok."

Lidia admitted that there were times when she sinned and knew she was wrong before God, but she could very easily convince herself that she was really ok too, because she was baptized into the church and had nothing to worry about. She was very quiet on the bus trip home. Veronica decided to leave her to her soul searching.

CHAPTER 20 BACK AT VIENNE AND DECISION TIME

Back in Salzburg, following their noon snack and after enjoying the street artists and musicians for a while, Eugene suggested they go to Mozart's childhood home and see the pianos that he played and some of the music he wrote at a young age. Off they went to the multi-story house where he lived during his childhood. It was right in the middle of the present shopping district – a tall, narrow yellow building. It was an obvious attraction because a steady flow of people was going in and out. Daniel found it to be very interesting, though he had never really had much exposure to classical music. At home, he was into Romanian folk music.

Eugene reminded him that he wouldn't find much Romanian folk music in Germany and that he should consider the merits of classical music.

"If you say!"

From Mozart's childhood home, they crossed the river and headed up the hill toward a house Mozart lived in as an adult. It also contained several instruments and early pianos that he played while he was writing music.

They got back to the center of the city and had time for a coffee before catching the bus for the three-hour trip back to Vienna. It had been a tiring day, but overall, very rewarding for both of them.

When they arrived at the hostel, Daniel fell into his bed and slept so late that he missed breakfast. He mused that he wouldn't starve by missing a meal. He had already eaten far more than he would have eaten in Romania during the same period of time. "This would be a great life," he thought as he got up and took a shower. Taking a shower was already normal. Daniel adapted to his new life quickly. By this time, the newness was wearing off on just about everything he had experienced. Nothing surprised him anymore. He was surrounded by the things he had seen in the magazine and so much more. It is strange that the things he longed for didn't seem as alluring now.

He decided to go out for a morning walk. A couple blocks from the center of town he settled onto a park bench. Some young men and women were coming his way and handing something to the people they passed. One young man strode right up to Daniel and asked him a question in English. Daniel just shook his head. The young man yelled back to one of the others who came over. In broken German, the young man introduced himself as a college student on a mission trip from a Baptist Bible College in Minnesota. He and his companions were passing out Christian literature.

He handed a religious brochure to Daniel, who took it and asked, "Are you Baptist Repenters?"

The young man who introduced himself as Stephen said, "Well, we are Baptists. I haven't heard of us called Repenters, though the Bible clearly teaches about how men everywhere need to repent and turn to Christ instead of organized religion for forgiveness of sins and eternal life in heaven. You are familiar with Baptists, then?"

"There is a small Baptist church in a village near my home in Romania, but we call them Repenters. I guess it is because the Orthodox don't like the idea of repentance. I dated a girl for a while who is a Repenter."

"Well, Daniel, what do you think about the Baptist faith?" Daniel was embarrassed to tell him he considered himself an atheist. "Promise me you will read this brochure and give serious consideration to what it says." Then, Stephen asked Daniel if he was on a vacation.

"No, I just escaped from Romania through Yugoslavia about three weeks ago. My family is German, which is why we can talk together. I doubt that you would know any Romanian."

"That's incredible!" Stephen called the rest of the group over to meet Daniel and hear his story. They were all mesmerized with him and had dozens of questions.

"Where are you planning to live?"

"My goal has been to live in Germany because of my heritage, but a Romanian friend who also escaped from my area is living here in Vienna and is trying to convince me to stay in Austria."

After quite some time, Stephen told Daniel they had to move on. He handed him a card with the Baptist Bible College name and address on it. It included Stephen's full name and phone number.

"If you ever get to America, call me. God bless you!"

Daniel sat down and began to read the brochure carefully. He had never read any religious materials in German. There were some of the same claims Veronica made regarding her faith, including some of the same Bible verses she, her pastor, and the Repenters in Serbia had quoted to him. He couldn't seem to get away from the Repenters or their message. After reading and considering the material, he sat back and began to think about all of the dangers and near tragedies he experienced in the process of his escape. As he reviewed all of these experiences, it turned out to be a painful process. His doubts kept gnawing at him.

What about those times he sought God's help with the caveat "if He existed"? If he really did not believe in the existence of God, then why would he allow himself to ask for His help in time of need? What about his exclamation, "Slava Domnului"? Even Herman and Heinrich had noted this. Was it possible that God did exist and that He was protecting him until he would come to his senses and acknowledge Him? Veronica and the Repenters in Serbia were praying this in his stead!

Again, he thought, as so many times before and somewhat painfully, that if God existed and Veronica's faith was true, he had given up the only one he had ever loved, aside from his family. He needed to think about something else to get this out of his mind. "Besides," he mused, trying to console himself over the loss of Veronica, "If I had stayed for Veronica, I wouldn't be here enjoying freedom and all of this good life. Veronica will find another, and I am free to go on with my life of freedom."

Daniel decided to go to a local library he had seen to investigate Germany and the United States. He always assumed he would quite naturally go to Germany because that was where his ancestral roots were. But it seemed like every time he turned around, he saw progress attributable to the United States. He began to doubt that he really wanted to immigrate to Germany.

Perhaps he should try to go to the America instead. He first picked up an atlas and pulled from his pocket the card Stephen had given him. He was going to find out where the students were from. He found Minnesota and the location of the college. It was in the middle of the country. What a large country! He found some books about U.S. History and the things that had made it so great. He found it interesting that some of the writers claimed America to have been founded on biblical principles. That would be totally contrary to the philosophy of Communism. He read that Baptists had played a significant role in the establishment of the country. Twice America had helped save Europe from German attempts at world dominion and had kept the Soviet Union at bay for these past 40+ years.

"My, how ignorant I am about world history! Certainly, Communism was sustained by lying to the citizens of the countries under the domination of this philosophy. Obviously, Communism has utterly failed. One day of freedom in the West is sufficient proof of that. A country that had such an impact for freedom in the world must be an incredible place to live."

One of the librarians came to him and explained that the library was closing, and he would have to leave. Was it that late? He had missed lunch, and it was time for the evening meal. He walked back to the youth hostel while his heart raced. He had made his decision. He must try to go to America!

When he got to his room, Eugene was knocking on his door. "Oh, there you are. Where have you been?"

"I have been at the library much of the day."

As they headed for the cafeteria, Daniel couldn't wait to tell Eugene the things he had learned about America.

Having gotten a tray of food, they sat down, and the flood of information began to pour out of Daniel. He had hardly eaten a bite in his haste to tell Eugene what he had learned. Finally, Eugene said, "Hey man, eat your food, and we can go crash while you get this out of your system."

"Ok. I will finish, but I don't think I will get this out of my system! I want to immigrate to America. It is final. I must get to America!"

"You are kidding!"

"No, I am not!"

"You can't make such an important decision in one day."

"Oh, yes I can, and I did!"

Eugene gazed at him with amazement. He really was serious about his decision!

They talked on in the lounge of the hostel for hours. Daniel proved himself to have soaked up information about America like a sponge. As they departed to their rooms for the evening, Eugene accused Daniel of becoming an American encyclopedia, which brought a laugh from both of them.

CHAPTER 21 PURSUING A VISA TO AMERICA

The next morning, Daniel and Eugene had breakfast together. Daniel announced that he was headed for the library. Eugene didn't have that privilege and headed for work.

Daniel spent the whole day there again, though this time he took out time for lunch. His heart raced as he read on about life in America and viewed hundreds of pictures. To his surprise, he found the American Declaration of Independence and the entire Constitution translated into German. He began to read it and became so captivated that he read the entire document. He couldn't believe what he read. It only convinced him that he wanted to go to America.

The many references to God utterly amazed him. If there was no God, how could such an amazing and powerful nation be founded on Someone who didn't exist? What did they know that he didn't know? Perhaps the Repenters were, indeed, correct in their beliefs.

Against his better judgment, he said in his heart, "God, if You exist, will You please let me get to America?" That evening he met Eugene for dinner, and once again, he was a flood of information. He told Eugene that he was planning to go to the American Embassy the next day to try for a visa. It was settled.

Daniel and Eugene had breakfast together again, and Daniel could hardly eat for his excitement. Eugene wished him luck and told him not to get his hopes up too high, because he very likely would not be granted a visa. America was where everyone wanted to go, and most were being rejected. He reminded Daniel that he had no skills to market in America, but Daniel was not to be thwarted or discouraged in his quest.

Eugene took a bus to work, and Daniel took a bus to the American Embassy. His heart pounded against his chest at the thought that when entering the Embassy, he was standing on American territory, politically. He gained entry and headed for the counter labeled, "Visas to America". When it was his turn, a lady asked him what she could do for him.

"I want to go to America."

"Doesn't everyone?" She gave him an application to fill out with the instruction to return to the line when he was finished, and they would set up an interview. He quickly took a seat and labored over the questions. He wasn't sure about some of the questions and bothered others around him for help on those he didn't understand.

Finally, after what seemed forever, he jumped up to stand in line again. When it was his turn, he handed the form over to the clerk. After perusing the answers and clarifying a few points, she told him she would set up an interview for the next day. Did she really say the next day? He wondered if he could wait that long. Did he have a chance? He took the card with the time on it, stuffed it carefully into his pocket and thanked the lady.

His feet hardly touched the ground as he made his way back to the hostel just in time to have lunch. He spent the afternoon in the library. As per his custom, Daniel met Eugene for dinner. He talked Eugene's ears off about the day's activities. Eugene again warned him not to get his hopes up.

Daniel asked Eugene if he would go to a movie with him at the theatre nearby. There was an American movie showing. He had never seen a movie at a theatre, and besides, he needed to start preparing for life in America. Obviously, Eugene's warnings were falling on deaf ears. Nevertheless, he agreed to see the film with Daniel. A recent American western was showing with subtitles in Austrian. After seeing his first western at the hostel on television, Daniel was mesmerized at the thought of the Old West in America. He was particularly impressed with John Wayne.

Daniel did not sleep much that night and was up at the crack of dawn. He took a shower, combed his hair carefully, and put on his best outfit in preparation for his interview. He headed for the cafeteria and breakfast. In his haste, he spilled juice on his trousers. One would have thought he had lost his best friend. He even had tears in his eyes as he hastened back to his room to put on his second best. He headed for the embassy less confident than he had been earlier. After all, he wanted to make the best impression possible. He presented himself as available for his appointment, even though he was two hours early. Daniel proved that two hours could feel like four hours. Finally, it was his turn to enter the small cubicle for his interview with the Assistant Ambassador, Mrs. Johnson. Many of the questions asked were already on the application form he had filled out.

Hadn't she read his application?

As the interview progressed, the thing that gave him the most encouragement regarding his chances of obtaining a visa was his responses to questions regarding what he knew about the government of the United States. Mrs. Johnson seemed impressed. She asked him where he had acquired his knowledge of the Declaration of Independence and the United States Constitution. He responded by saying he had found them translated into German in the library. That seemed to please Mrs. Johnson very much.

She asked Daniel what he was most impressed with in the Declaration of Independence. He answered that he was amazed by the references to God. That was completely opposite to the government documents of Communist Romania. Then a similar question was asked regarding the Constitution. Without hesitation, Daniel said how much he was impressed with the Bill of Rights. He could not imagine a country that would care so much about the rights of the people. In Romania, the people had no rights. The government had all the rights, and the people had no recourse about anything. If they resisted, they might disappear in the middle of the night.

When asked what he wanted to do if he got a visa, without hesitation he said he wanted to go to college or learn a trade. He didn't want to be an ordinary person. He would owe it to America to earn his right to be there. He wanted to earn a good wage so he could afford to buy his parents' and sisters' freedom someday. Daniel then told Mrs. Johnson about meeting the students from the Baptist Bible College in Minnesota and the card that Stephen had given to him. Perhaps he would go to college there.

Soon the interview was over, and his picture was taken. He was told to return in 7 days to learn the decision. Daniel thanked Mrs. Johnson and left the embassy.

Daniel felt that he had made a good impression. Mrs. Johnson seemed impressed with his escape from Romania and the fact that he had already read the Declaration of Independence and the U.S. Constitution. He went to the hostel to wait for Eugene.

As always, Daniel controlled the conversation at the dinner table. When he rehearsed all the questions and his answers, Eugene noted that his response regarding the Declaration of Independence and Constitution were winning responses, in his opinion. He also thought that the fact his picture was taken was positive. If they didn't think he was a worthy consideration for a visa, why would they take a picture of him? Daniel was greatly pleased with Eugene's assessment of his interview. Now he would spend the longest 7 days of his life waiting for the most important decision in his life, next to his decision to escape from Romania. Little did Daniel realize that a greater decision was yet in his future.

The next Sunday was just any ordinary Sunday for Daniel, except for his continued anticipation of the response that would set the course of his life in ways he could never have anticipated.

CHAPTER 22 JOY IN ROMANIA

It was no ordinary Sunday in Veronica's little church. After a miserable week of deep conviction regarding her sins, Lidia met with Veronica and caught the bus to the Repenters' church. Lidia was very quiet all the way to the village. Veronica had prayed earnestly for her salvation the entire week and took this time of silence to implore the Lord to make this the day that Lidia would put her trust in Him. The walk to the village was filled with anticipation.

The service began as normal with prayer for the many needs of the people, including, as always, Daniel. The pastor prayed that this day someone in their midst would surrender to the knocking of the Lord on their heart's door. Before he could finish his prayer, Lidia began to weep. The pastor asked the people to continue in silent prayer as he left the pulpit to approach her. He asked her if she was ready to accept Christ as her Savior.

Through her tears, she said, "Yes, I am ready now." He asked Veronica to accompany him outside the church where there was a bench and privacy with the surrounding bushes.

That morning, while Daniel was wringing his hands regarding his upcoming life-altering decision, his mother's hands were resting in Veronica's as she prayed to accept Christ as Savior.

As they entered the back door of the church all eyes were upon them. The people broke out in smiles, and one of them said, "I think it is time to sing praises to our God." What a song service it was! Veronica asked if she could sing a special song on the spot to share her joy in the salvation of Lidia. She thought, with the great confidence she had in Daniel's return to her, "Praise God, my future mother-in-law has been saved. Now we must pray my future father-in-law and sisters-in-law into the Kingdom of God."

Lidia had listened to every word of the sermon that morning, realizing the day would change her life forever and test her faith when her friends found out. She wondered what her husband would say. Did she dare tell him? How would she tell her girls? Marie, the one in high school, would be the most affected. She had developed friendships with other students who would most assuredly, taunt, if not reject her.

On the bus home, she shared those fears with Veronica, who understood well the price to be associated with Repenters, especially with children who can be crueler than adults. She promised to uphold the family with prayer and offered to talk with the girls regarding their mother's decision. Lidia said she would like that. Perhaps sometime she could talk with George about his wife's decision. Veronica told Lidia that the best way to influence her family for the Lord was to grow in her Christian life, so they would see a difference.

CHAPTER 23 JOY IN AUSTRIA

Seven days had finally passed, and it was time for Daniel to learn the decision of the American Ambassador. He dressed his best and headed for the US Embassy, desiring to be the first to enter. He had no appetite, so had skipped breakfast. When he entered and climbed the stairs, his legs felt like rubber. Being the first person to enter the waiting room, he caught the eye of Mrs. Johnson, who was just coming out of her office. She smiled at him, walked over with her hand extended, and said, "Hello, Daniel. Welcome to America." Did he hear what he thought he heard? The handshake confirmed it.

Through moist eyes, he said, "Really?"

"Really! Let's discuss what we must do next. Normally you would have to come up with your own plane fare and find someone to sponsor you, but we have an interesting situation. There is a Romanian Baptist Church in Chicago, Illinois, that has contacted us and offered to sponsor any Romanian youths who have escaped into Austria. They will pay for your ticket, meet you at the airport, provide you a place to stay, and find a job for you. How does that sound, Daniel?"

"I don't know what to say."

"I think, if I was you, I would thank God."

"I will."

This time it wasn't a slip of the tongue. He knew he was going to have to face up to his beliefs about God, especially since Repenters were the ones who were going to bring him to America. It was becoming abundantly clear that Repenters would continue to have a real impact on his life.

Mrs. Johnson told Daniel she would contact the church in Chicago and work out the details. She told him to come back in a week, and she would have all of the arrangements. He thanked her, not wanting to let go of her hand. At that moment, she was his heroine. As he left the Embassy and passed the guards, he said, "I am going to America!"

They responded with a big smile, "Welcome."

"Less than a month ago I heard 'Welcome to Austria.' Now I am hearing 'Welcome to America.' I think I like the second welcome better."

Later that day, he sat on a bench outside the hostel waiting to tell Eugene his good news. As Eugene approached, he knew the answer without even asking. Daniel was beaming from ear to ear.

He walked up, reached out for his hand and said, "I wanted you to stay in Austria, but I am happy for you if this is what you want. Who knows? I may wish that was my destination. You won't forget me now, will you?" They laughed together and Eugene said, "Let's go eat and hear in detail how your day went."

The next day, Daniel was too anxious to stay in the hostel. He spent the entire day in the library trying to learn everything he could about America. That evening, noting Daniel's anxiety, Eugene told him that he was useless. They laughed together. A week later, Daniel was up at the crack of dawn. That was not difficult since he had hardly slept. He arrived at the embassy before it opened and paced the sidewalk like a caged animal.

Once inside the entrance, Daniel met briefly with another of the embassy officials who gave him his Immigration Visa and a packet of pertinent papers that explained his responsibilities after getting established. He was given a one-way ticket to O'Hara Field in Chicago, Illinois, for departure the next Friday. The idea of a one-way ticket increased his confidence regarding the future. John Enescu would pick him up at the airport. This was it. He really was going to America to begin a new life!

That evening, the two friends went out on the town till the wee hours of the morning. Both of them talked about their future plans, including the hope of marriage and family. Eugene had a female friend where he worked. Though they had not actually dated, Eugene was hoping a relationship might develop.

As Daniel bragged of his plans, it was difficult for him to talk of finding a wife. He could not get Veronica out of his mind. Though Daniel had enough caffeine that evening to keep many men wide awake, his exhaustion rendered him a restful sleep well into Saturday morning. He woke up long after the breakfast hour.

He dressed and knocked on Eugene's door. He, too, had slept in. They decided to go out again for coffee and donuts. Daniel asked Eugene to accompany him that weekend to see more sights in Vienna. It was an incredible city, and he didn't know if he would ever come back, so he wanted as many memories of the cities as possible. He also wanted as many memories as possible with Eugene.

Each evening they went out to drink coffee and talk well into the night. Even though Eugene had to get up early for work, he sacrificed his sleep for the last fleeting days with Daniel. He, too, thought their parting might be permanent, if not far into the unknown future.

They had become very good friends and promised each other to communicate on a regular basis. Daniel wrote down all the information he needed to keep in touch with Eugene and gave him the address of the church in Chicago. When Daniel was ready to leave for the airport on Friday morning, the two young men embraced each other with tears in their eyes. Eugene headed off to work, and Daniel stepped onto the airport bus.

CHAPTER 24 DESTINATION AMERICA

Daniel had never been at an airport. When he got to the gate and saw the size of the plane, he couldn't believe his eyes. He thought, "How in the world do they get that thing off the ground? Well, it was probably made in America, so I am sure it will fly." As he clipped on the seat belt and saw the door to the plane close, he said, "Thank God."

The plane lifted off the ground on the way to Heathrow Airport in England, where he would take another plane to Chicago. He was in the middle seat on the left side of the plane. The Austrian and Swiss Alps to the left were an awesome sight to Daniel. He was trying to see the ground below and was practically in the lap of the man in the window seat.

The man, speaking in German, said "Is this your first flight?"

"Yes, yes, it is!"

"Here, let's change seats so you can see better, and I can do some reading. By the way, my name is Bob, and I am a journalist returning to Chicago."

"My name is Daniel."

They exchanged seats and Daniel kept an eye out the window as they began a conversation. Daniel asked him what a journalist was and why he was in Austria. He explained that he had come to Austria to see his family and to cover a story of interest about Austria's trade with Yugoslavia, Hungary, and Czechoslovakia. He had immigrated to America many years ago. Then he asked Daniel where he was going. Daniel explained how he came to be on the flight.

Bob was no longer interested in reading. He asked Daniel if he could record their interview. "I guess so." Then Bob pulled out a small device not much bigger than a package of cigarettes and began to speak into it.

Daniel asked, "What is that?"

Bob explained that it was a small voice recorder. He played back what he had just spoken, and Daniel said, "I don't believe it! I have never seen anything like that before! I have never heard my voice before! Can I hear it again?"

Bob said he could hear it as many times as he wanted. He noted that perhaps he would write a story for his newspaper in Chicago. Taking many notes in his recorder, he questioned Daniel the entire trip. Daniel felt very important as he told him about life in Romania and his escape. The journalist told Daniel to stick with him when they got off the plane, and he would make sure that Daniel got to the correct gate for Chicago.

When they landed, Bob took Daniel for a sandwich and a drink. They had a couple hours before the next flight, and the meal wouldn't be served for an hour or more after taking off. As they ate, Bob continued to question Daniel.

"I hope you don't mind the questions. It is just that I have never met anyone who had escaped from the Iron Curtain. For me, this will make an incredible story. You will have to keep an eye on the Tribune to see if my article makes it into the paper. I am sure the editor will approve an article of this nature. There has been much discussion in recent months about the Soviet system. Many think Communism in Eastern Europe will collapse."

"That would be wonderful, but I don't think it will ever happen."

When they reached the gate for the flight to Chicago, Bob gave Daniel his business card and told him to feel free to call him if he needed anything. "I will be in First Class so we may not see each other again. Good luck young man. By the way, don't forget to check the Tribune next week for my article."

The next plane was much larger than the first. Daniel simply couldn't comprehend the size. This flight had a large TV screen in front of each block of seats. Daniel couldn't believe there would be TV on an airplane. He was not so lucky on this trip. The people around him all spoke English. When the other passengers tried to talk with him, he could only smile and shrug his shoulders. He very quickly realized that he was in a hostile language environment. He panicked at the thought. When the stewardess brought the drink cart, and later the meal cart, he was in luck, because she spoke German as well as English. Sensing how intimidated Daniel was, the stewardess returned after distributing the meal. She talked with him, answering many of his questions regarding the plane, the altitude, and the speed, etc.

Daniel asked her how it was that she spoke German on a plane going from England to the United States.

She said, "The airlines try to hire stewardesses for transatlantic flights who are bi-lingual because often there are passengers speaking other languages, such as you. We are able to provide help to those that do not speak English. I have been able to help a family in the back of the plane that also speaks German. We have another stewardess on this plane who speaks French and one speaking Russian."

This conversation provided comfort to Daniel. He didn't feel quite so isolated.

When the TV came on with a movie, he was once again reminded that he was on his way to a culture he really didn't know and a language that he couldn't speak. He could only watch the movie and guess what the plot was as the drama unfolded. The American movies he saw in Vienna had an Austrian subscript, but this one didn't. Chills went through him for a moment at the thought of getting off the plane. How would he know where to go? How would he know the man coming for him?

After about eight- and one-half hours, they came in for the landing. It was strange! He looked at his watch. According to the time, it should have been dark. However, the sky was completely light as in the morning when they left. He wondered how this could be.

After the plane reached the gate, Daniel decided he would be safe if he just followed everyone else. After some distance, they came into the Passport-Customs area. Daniel thought he was really lucky, because the woman behind the glass spoke German. It had not occurred to him that the people working in the Foreign Passport line would have to be multi-lingual in order to ask questions of foreigners. The lady took his passport and U.S. Visa, made some notations, asked him some questions, and handed his papers back with "Welcome to America, young man." She beckoned him on.

Now what? He watched others. They were turning to the left, so he turned to the left. They all headed to a round devise that had luggage going around and people were taking their luggage off. He had only his carry-on bag with what little he owned in the whole world: a couple changes of clothing and a few personal items.

CHAPTER 25 NEW LIFE IN AMERICA

He noticed where people were going after they received their luggage, so he followed. Not having any luggage, he was allowed to proceed. After passing through a long hallway, he entered a large area where a great many people were waiting for passengers. All he heard was English. A feeling of fear flooded over him. "What am I doing? I could have stayed in Austria with Eugene. At least a German dialect was spoken there." At that moment of doubt, as he was scanning the crowd, he saw a man holding a sign with the words "Daniel from Romania" written on it. His heart leaped! "That's me!"

The man holding the sign was smiling as Daniel headed straight for him. Daniel said expectantly, "John Enescu?" "Ba da" (for sure), he answered. Oh, how good those two words sounded to Daniel as he reached out to shake hands and give the traditional Romanian kiss on John's cheeks while receiving the same from John. He was speaking in his national tongue. How comforting this was!

As they departed, Daniel realized that O'Hare Airport was even bigger than Heathrow Airport in London. "Everything must be bigger in America."

Now that he was safe in the hands of a countryman, his lack of sleep hit him like a brick. The only thing keeping him awake was his excitement. They drove for an hour through more traffic than he had ever imagined. It seemed like an endless city. Finally, they arrived at a multi-story building and pulled into the driveway.

John said, "This is my home. I have an apartment upstairs that I use for Romanian immigrants to stay in while they are getting established in their new life. We have a bed waiting for you." It was beginning to get dark, which served as a sedative to Daniel. He was ready for bed. He met John's wife, Mary, who had a snack for him.

Finishing the snack, he was ushered to his new surroundings: a small apartment with a small bedroom, bathroom, and kitchen combined with an eating area. Mary said, "You get up when you want. I won't expect to see you before noon tomorrow. Just come on down when you awake, and you can have lunch. John will leave for work early in the morning and will be home in the evening. Then we can review everything with you." As soon as his head hit the pillow, he was asleep. And, indeed, he was out until close to noon the following day.

For a few seconds after Daniel awoke, he was disoriented. Then he remembered he was in America. He slept so soundly that he had not even dreamed. He went down to John's residence and knocked on the door.

Mary responded, "Well, you are finally up. Did you have a good sleep?" He nodded affirmatively. "You must be starved. Come into the kitchen. I have a Romanian meal prepared for you as a welcome to America." She gave him a bowl of traditional noodle soup (supa), salad with meat and various vegetable ingredients (salata de bif), and cabbage rolls (sarmale). He hadn't had such a Romanian meal since the last holiday. It was wonderful! Mary noticed that Daniel didn't pray before eating. She would leave any discussion about spiritual things to her husband.

In the living room, Daniel and Mary talked all afternoon about Romania, his escape, and his month in Austria. He learned that John had escaped through Hungary several years before and immigrated to America. They had no children, so it was decided that Mary could make it by living with her parents and helping on their farm until her freedom could be bought. It was a long time before she knew if John had made it out alive. John had tried to write her several times, but the letters were never delivered, probably out of spite.

"I know John will want to hear every detail of your escape, and I will let him tell you about his. It is a very different story than yours."

The thing that so impressed Daniel was that John was nearly the age of 50 when he made his escape.

They then discussed many things about life in America. One question Daniel had was how it could still be light outside when he landed in the middle of the night. She explained to him that Romania is 8 time zones ahead of Chicago. He had a little difficulty assimilating the concept, but as she showed him a globe of the world and explained the rotation of the earth revolving around the sun, he finally got it. Their conversation was interrupted by the arrival of John.

They had more supa, salata de bif, and sarmale. These foods were a treat for John as well. A Romanian can never get enough of these dishes. Following the meal and small talk, John said, "Let's retire to the living room, have a cup of coffee, and talk. I am anxious to hear of your escape, and I will tell you how I escaped."

Mary brought some coffee to the men. When asked if he wanted sugar or milk in his coffee, Daniel proudly declined, saying that he had learned to drink coffee black just like Americans while he was in Austria. John reached out for the milk and sugar, acknowledging that he didn't like coffee without these condiments.

Daniel relayed in detail how he and Radu had planned to escape, how they had found a magazine from the West that had been smuggled into the country, how they hid it and secretly viewed it, and how they had planned their escape. He shared how Sergiu had blackmailed them into getting in on their escape, how Daniel had backed out of their escape, and how Radu and Sergiu were killed trying to cross the Danube.

He then rehearsed all the details of his escape a year later. After hearing the complete story, John soberly said, "Daniel, as you have relayed the account of your escape, I cannot but believe that God was very much involved, and that He has a purpose for your life." Daniel was somewhat taken back by John's comments. Not knowing how to respond, he just nodded.

CHAPTER 26 ANOTHER ESCAPE STORY

John asked Mary for more coffee and then began to relay his story.

"I, too, had reached the point that I was willing to risk losing my life and my wife to get out from under Ceausescu's tyrannical regime. Since we had no children, I felt that Mary could live without me, and if I should be killed, she could remarry. My escape was for both of us. If I got out, I was confident that I could buy her freedom. I had learned that with Romanian officials, money could buy anything. I, too, had lost a close friend in an escape attempt, which only encouraged me to prove I could do it."

"I lived in the northern part of Romania (Transylvania). From where I lived, my escape had to be over land, which carried additional risks. I had prepared to leave in the winter because the border was not guarded as closely as in the warm months. Because the cold weather was difficult on the border patrol guards, the guard stations were moved further apart so not as many men had to be out. That was a benefit to a prospective escapee. Unfortunately, they still had German Shepherds to assist them."

"I had taken very little provisions with me. I worked on my escape route for a long time, selecting an escape path that was approximately halfway between two guard posts, where the surface of the land leading up to the fence was irregular with a shallow gulley. Though it was no deeper than about 30 centimeters (15 in.), by sliding on my stomach in the snow, I was virtually out of sight."

"With the possibility of snow, it had been overcast on the day I chose to flee. I had counted on those conditions to continue into the evening when I planned to cross. I wore a light-colored sweater and a dark-colored coat. Although there was snow on the ground, I figured the overcast night would protect me. However, while I was in the very process of crawling on my belly, the cloud cover broke open and the moon partly showed through. I was perhaps 30 meters (100 ft.) from the fence. I froze. I could see the two guards, one to the left and one to the right. Each, with his dog, was sitting by a wood fire, trying to stay warm. The dogs were lying next to the fires, and I thought they would surely hear the beating of my heart."

"I laid there for a few minutes, earnestly praying for God's wisdom and help. I determined that I had to shed my dark coat since my sweater was light colored.

Knowing how dangerous it was, I nevertheless carefully rolled over onto my back, unzipped my coat and slid forward on my back to shed the coat, leaving it behind. I rolled back on my stomach and inched my way to the fence. By the time I reached the fence, the sky closed up and the cover of darkness resumed. I was very cold now, having been lying in the snow so long. How I had wished for my coat!"

"I carefully cut the wire fencing with a pair of wire cutters I had taken from the factory where I worked. I muffled each cut with a towel I had brought along for that purpose. Finally, I was able to slide through. At one point, my sweater got caught on the fencing, but with care, I freed myself."

"Even though I was on the Hungarian side of the fence, I continued on my belly for some distance, and then got up on all fours until I was sufficiently far enough that I could get up and run. I knew that even though I was on the Hungarian side, the guards would have no problem shooting across the fence to stop me from escaping. I had escaped, but without a winter coat."

"There were no Hungarian guards on the other side. There was no danger of Hungarians wanting to escape into Romania, and apparently they were not concerned about Romanians escaping into Hungary."

"I had determined to make it to Szeged, a large city in southern Hungary about 30 kilometers (20 miles) away. I figured that if I ran the whole distance with intermittent stops to rest, I could make it by dawn. It would help me to keep warm if I ran, too. I set out running. A major road stretched toward Szeged, so that would be my point of reference the entire way."

"There was virtually no traffic on that cold winter night, so I decided to risk running on the side of the road. When I heard a car coming, I would move into the weeds on the side of the road and drop to my stomach. When the vehicle passed, I would come out and continue. I didn't know how I made it at my age without a heart attack, but I did! God was clearly with me. As I got to the outskirts of the city, I had to find cover because the sun was about to peer over the horizon. I was chilled to the bone!"

"I picked out a small farm that had a couple small sheds. I hoped to be shielded and yet catch the rising sun to try to warm me. I didn't know how I would make it without a winter coat, but if I hadn't shed my coat, I might well not have made it at all. In that case, I wouldn't have needed a coat anyway. I found a perfect spot on the south side of a chicken coop. I was shivering when I heard footsteps. I had no place to go and no time to do it. The farmer coming around the corner saw me. I put my finger to my lips to indicate, "Please don't say anything.""

"The man calmly went about his business, and then he signaled with his hands to stay put. He turned around with the eggs he had collected and calmly walked back to his house. I wondered if I was going to be turned in, but I didn't think the man would have completed his chores and given me a hand signal if that was his plan. So, I waited. In about 20 minutes, the man came out with a container of food for his chickens."

"When he arrived at the chicken coop, he quickly pulled out a container of hot soup and bread. Looking around to assure no one was watching, he beckoned me to step into the other shed filled with equipment and some bales of hay. He carved out a place for me to lie in the hay and covered me with more hay for warmth. I had the benefit of knowing a fair amount of Hungarian. Because Transylvania was once part of Hungary, many Hungarians lived in my area. I had gone to school with many and learned some of the language in the street, so I was able to converse with him. The man told me to wait there until nightfall before moving on."

"Seeing I didn't have a coat, he came out at dusk, so he would not be seen by his neighbors. He brought an old coat and some more hot soup and bread for immediate consumption. He had a small sack of bread and cheese for me to take. He had also made a rough map of the city of Szeged and showed how I could best skirt the city. He warned me that some people would turn me in for favors if caught."

"I thanked the man, hugged him, and slipped out. I was on my way since dusk had turned to darkness, and I was thankful for a moonless light. Though it made my way more difficult, the tradeoff for protection was worth it. I was glad that I had brought a flashlight with me because I would have to consult his map from time to time. I continued moving around the perimeter of the city as quickly as I could, thankful for the Good Samaritan who had hidden me, fed me, and given me a coat and the hand-made map."

"Moving rapidly as I did in the previous evening, I was able to completely circle the city. A couple of times, barking dogs and car lights threatened to disclose my position. Under normal circumstances, I would not have drawn attention to myself, but a man moving about in the middle of the night was not normal."

"It took me over two weeks to get to the Austrian border. I had a couple of close calls. One night as I was moving through the countryside, a dog started to bark. A moment later a spotlight began to sweep the field. I dropped to the ground. I could see through the weeds that I had come upon a military post. I laid there for some time and then crawled on all fours for some distance before raising my head to look around. Seeing no one, I made a big circle around the military post. Another major challenge was to get across the Danube River on a heavily traveled bridge. I had to wait until the wee hours of the morning when I saw no auto lights and ran as fast as I could to cross the bridge. I barely made it before a car approached."

"I would try to hide out during the day in places that would allow me to catch morning and high noon sun. I confess that on one occasion, I stole a large blanket I saw on a line. Quite possibly that blanket was responsible for me not being too cold to continue. As I approached a remote village, I was so hungry that I decided to knock on the door of a family near where I had spent the day resting. I saw the man and his wife working about the yard and feeding their livestock. They appeared to be people who might help me, so I approached their door at dusk because I could get away under cover of darkness if their response was not good."

"They opened the door with reticence. I quickly explained that I had escaped from Romania and was headed for Austria and that I was terribly hungry, having eaten almost nothing for a couple days. I implored them to help me. To my surprise, they were very kind, and not only fed me hot soup, bread, and coffee, but also packed me enough bread and cheese to keep me for 2 or 3 days. I thanked them and left, once again thanking God for His provision."

"When I neared the border, I had another close call. I had selected my crossing point between two guard towers because of the number of bushes in the area. As I was crawling toward the fence, something prompted me to pause. As I proceeded, I felt something in front of my hand. I took off my glove and reached up. It was a wire, probably a trip wire to signal my presence. It was about 30 centimeters (15 inches) high. I carefully climbed over it. After that, I proceeded with my glove off, feeling ahead for other trip wires. I found another one only a couple meters from the fence. I prayed the whole way. When I reached my destination, I found a double fence, just as you did. I cut my way through both fences without incident."

"Once on the other side, I had not gone far before I, too, was facing flashlights. I put up my hands, pleading, "Don't shoot. I am a Romanian escapee." Their response was "Welcome to Austria." At least that was what I thought they said. I knew a smattering of German from growing up near a couple of German Romanian families. I was taken to Vienna and received a ticket to Chicago from the Romanian Baptist Church that brought you over. It seems that we had several similar experiences."

"Prior to arriving in America, I had practiced the Orthodox faith somewhat, but without a real relationship with Christ. Like most of our people, I just assumed that if there was a God, I would be covered, since I was baptized and occasionally attended services during the holidays."

"Even though I was not sure there was a God, I found myself continually calling out for His help. As I think about it, to have essentially ignored Him all my life and then continually call upon Him for help was almost a mockery, for which I was ashamed."

"Under Pastor Virgil's preaching and patience, I finally confessed Jesus as my Savior and only hope for eternal life. After joining the church, a member loaned me enough money to purchase Mary's freedom."

"She, too, eventually understood that faith in Christ only would meet her need for salvation and eternal life."

Having shared his personal salvation experience, John wanted to know where Daniel was in his relationship with God.

CHAPTER 27 WHAT TO EXPECT NEXT

Having been tipped off by Mary that Daniel was probably not a Christian, John said, "God works differently with people under different situations, doesn't He?"

"I suppose so."

Getting right to the point, John asked, "Have you ever repented of your sins and accepted God's free gift of salvation?"

"No, I am not a Repenter."

"I would like to talk with you about this in the future."

Daniel nodded acceptance. The Repenters have him surrounded this time with no escape.

"Let's talk about what I can do for you as I have for other Romanians that have escaped and come to Chicago. Being thankful to the Lord for His grace in allowing me to escape and start a business installing hard wood floors, I believe God would have me use my business as a ministry to others. I am the one who provided the money to our church to bring you to Chicago. I don't tell you this for praise, but I want you to know the depth of my faith with the hope that you will one day come to faith in our great God, too!"

"I will provide you a job and teach you a trade that will enable you to earn a good living. I will require you to pay a reasonable rent for the accommodations I provide. If you desire, you may eat with us as well, for a monthly fee. When you are ready to move on, you will be free to go. All of this must be within the scope of the requirements of the Department of Immigration. At this point, I am documented with the Department of Immigration as your sponsor. Accordingly, I am required to report your activities to them on a regular basis while you accomplish the various steps in the process of receiving citizenship. How does that sound?"

"It is more than fair, and I am very grateful for the opportunity to learn a trade, though I have been thinking about the possibility of going to college after meeting a student, Stephen, in Vienna. He was from a Baptist Bible college in Minnesota. But then, why would I want to go to a Bible College since I am not a Repenter? When I learn the language, at least I would like to call him and tell him that I made it to America. The idea of working with wood greatly interests me. I built a shed for my father before my escape."

"Great! You should rest and get accustomed to your new neighborhood for several days. You can begin working next Monday. You will ride with me. That way you will not need to have a car for some time. You will begin learning English on the job. Since all my employees are Romanians, you should learn our language quite effectively. As we are working, feel free to ask questions about the language so long as you continue working in the process. My wife will give you grammar lessons in evenings, as you desire. You will be surprised how quickly you will learn the language. Though some would probably disagree with me, I personally think that English is a relatively easy language to learn."

"The most difficult thing about English is the irregularity in spelling of words. For example, there are many words pronounced exactly the same but spelled differently, and, of course, have different meanings. This is more than compensated for because verbs are not conjugated as they are in Romanian. Once you learn a verb, the form does not change, regardless of who is doing the action. Also, unlike the Romanian language, in almost all cases we simply add the letter "s" to a noun to make it plural. The use of pronouns is another significant difference. Because Romanian nouns are masculine, feminine, or neuter the number of pronouns is two to three times more than in English. You will soon see what I mean."

"Since my wife and I are very much involved in our local church, you should know some things about it. Because it is a Romanian Baptist Church, most of our members are Romanians. They come from all over Chicago. The term "Repenter" is not used to describe Evangelical Christians in America. That is only a term of derision in Romania. The Bible clearly teaches that true salvation results only when we recognize we are sinners and repent of our sin, asking the Lord to forgive our sins for Jesus' sake. Therefore, we are not ashamed of the concept of repentance. God receives all of the credit for our salvation. Those who are bothered by the term suffer from pride, and pride is the sin behind every other sin. Pride sends people to hell!"

"Pastor Virgil says our doctrine is somewhat different from that in our Romanian Baptist Union churches. We accept the doctrinal position of Baptists in America. Pastor Virgil says that the doctrine of the Baptist Union in Romania changed from what it had been when the missionaries first came into our country in the early 1900s. Since you have no background with Romanian Baptist beliefs, this will not be a problem for you if you should decide to follow our faith. Perhaps I should say when you accept our faith, because I am convinced that God is working in you and has a plan for you."

"We have been criticized for having our services in Romanian, but we have found it a way to keep our identity and culture alive until our people reach the point of learning the language and being comfortable with American culture. The problem we have, though, is that some of our older members have really never learned the language or stepped out of our Romanian culture. So, we have benefits and disadvantages in our system."

"You certainly are not required to attend, but we hope you will consider regular attendance with us. Doing so will allow you to understand the Gospel and prepare you to accept Christ as your Savior with understanding and true faith. You will also find it such a blessing to be surrounded by your countrymen. We will be going to church tomorrow evening for the Wednesday service at 7:00. I hope you will be going with us."

The next day, Daniel ventured out and walked around the area. It was an old neighborhood, nothing like the pictures he had seen of large homes in suburbia, but even this old residential area far surpassed anything he had seen for common people in Romania. After some time, he went back full of questions for Mary. She gave him some history of Chicago and the area in which they lived. She explained that in the suburbs living conditions were much better, but they were much more expensive. She explained that it takes immigrants from other countries a great deal of time to afford living in the suburbs. The elderly will never accomplish that level of living unless they live with their children.

"Daniel, I hope you will find that real joy is not in having all the material things that are available. Those who come from poverty such as we experienced in Romania find this a very difficult concept. I will be honest with you. We struggled with this for a while after arriving in America. But now we consider ourselves to be living in luxury by comparison. We are plenty comfortable and could afford to move into the suburbs, but we are satisfied to remain here and serve in our church. We praise God for the ministry He has allowed us to have. We have learned that real joy is found in the freedom to practice our faith with so many brothers and sisters in the church. You know, this is a spiritual thing. Only those who have found Jesus Christ as their Savior and have joy in Him are able to conquer lusts of the flesh."

"There I go again! I guess I have been preaching! John told me not to preach to you. He says that sometimes my zeal for our faith creates pressure on those with whom I speak. I am sorry if I have been too pushy."

"No, that's ok. I have been struggling with what I really believe since I was first confronted by Repenters, I mean Baptists. First, there was Veronica and those in her little village church. Then, I heard Pastor Petrica's messages. Next, I became acquainted with the Repenters, I mean Baptists, in Serbia who I think are most responsible for my ability to escape. Their faith and that of Veronica and her church seems so real to them! They prayed for just about everything and everyone, including me."

"That has plagued me. I had too many close calls in my escape. Now here I am, talking with you, and hearing you explain your strong beliefs. Veronica told me that some 40 people wrote the Bible over a period of some 1,600 hundred years, and there is no disagreement in what they teach. How could that many people be wrong in what they wrote? She said the Bible totally supports your beliefs. I must admit that I am really struggling with the choice that I must make."

"Daniel, I appreciate your honesty. I hardly know you, and yet you have had the courage to share your spiritual struggle with me. Thank you for your trust! Indeed, John and I are praying for you and your decision! I am confident that you will make the correct choice."

Daniel agreed to attend church with John and Mary that evening, to which Mary exclaimed, "Thank you, Daniel, and thank you, Lord!

John arrived home later than normal, so Mary had no opportunity to share the conversation she had with Daniel but noted that he was going to accompany them to church. John smiled with a wink to Mary. They had a quick meal and headed off to church, located only a few blocks from their house.

Daniel was anxious to meet other Romanians. As they entered the church, Pastor Virgil was the first one to greet him. Other members quickly surrounded him, welcoming him to America and to their church.

He was not unaware that there were several very attractive girls in the church not wearing wedding rings. "Wow, I think I could get to like this church!"

The service was just like the Sunday services he attended in Romania. Pastor Virgil began with prayer. They continued by singing several songs. Prayer requests were shared. John reminded them to pray for Romania, that God would break down the Iron Curtain and free them and the other Eastern European countries. Daniel was impressed with the number of requests for the salvation of family members in America and Romania. Following the requests, the pastor asked several of the members, including John, to lead in prayer. When John prayed, he asked the Lord to make Himself very real to their new Romanian friend.

"Oh, great, now everyone knows that I am not a Repenter."

After prayer, Pastor Virgil brought a message on the necessity of personal faith in Christ. There was no doubt in Daniel's mind that the message was aimed at him.

Following the service, a time of fellowship in the basement of the church welcomed him to America. What a surprise! They did this for him? Many of the people came to him and told him they would be praying for him to become a Christian.

"Wow, they get right to the point, don't they? I need to seriously consider the claims of these Repenters. They may not have to pray for me very long."

In Romania, 8 hours before, Veronica's little church had their Wednesday service, and as usual, had prayed for him. Only this time, his mother was a part of that prayer service. She was rejoicing in her newly found faith and was now personally praying for her son. How pleased she would have been to know that a few hours later in America, her son would be in a church service hearing the Gospel!

Of course, how surprised Daniel would have been to learn his mother was now a Repenter. She had even brought her oldest daughter, Mary, with her, somewhat against her will. Lidia felt her daughters should learn of their mother's new faith. The Pastor said her husband and daughters were her mission field. The thought of going to heaven without her family caused her to have a great burden for them.

CHAPTER 28 NEW LIFE IN MORE THAN ONE WAY IN AMERICA

Daniel spent the next couple days venturing ever further from his adopted home and entering stores to look around at all that contributed to life in America. Many little shops were in the area of his new home, so one can imagine his surprise when he saw a large shopping center for the first time.

On Saturday morning after breakfast, John announced, "Daniel, it's time for you to get exposed to more than our little neighborhood. We will drive out to the suburbs where we are laying some wood floors in several new houses. We will take you to one of our shopping centers and have lunch at our favorite hamburger restaurant. You are going to experience a real hamburger and the best milk shake in the world."

Mary gathered a few things together, and soon they were off.

As they headed west on the Eisenhower Expressway, it seemed to Daniel that things didn't look any different than what he saw on the Kennedy Expressway coming in from the airport. But as they crossed the North–South Tri-State Tollway, he quickly noticed a change in the scenery. Instead of older multi story buildings and houses in very close proximity to each other, he observed everything looking much newer and more modern. There were many trees and open areas with beautiful grass.

After a 10-minute drive on the I-88 expressway, Daniel was speechless while passing through some of the most expensive real estate in northern Illinois. The many shopping centers, office complexes and homes reflected a level of opulence that was too much for Daniel to filter. He was so overwhelmed that all he could say was, "Wow!" By the time they arrived at their destination in a housing complex of homes approaching a million dollars or more, John and Mary were almost feeling guilty as they tried to imagine how Daniel was processing what he was seeing. It took Daniel's response to remind them how much God had really blessed America!

Daniel could not believe his eyes! "These houses are all palaces! Who will live here?"

"Oh, this is not the way most Americans live. These houses are being built for very wealthy Americans, people who have high corporate positions in their companies."

John thought it was time to change the subject. "We usually don't work on Saturdays, but the general contractor has promised the buyer that the floors will be finished by the end of this next week. We're headed for the house where you will begin working on Monday. I want you to meet the fellows who will be working with you."

As they entered the house, John's crew was at the door to greet them. Cristi was introduced as the foreman on the job. He also met Eli and Iacov. John explained that Daniel was the man they had been waiting for from Romania. The men were so excited to meet Daniel and were dying to learn firsthand of his escape and the condition of life in Romania at that time. John realized it was time for an extended break so the men could exhaust their curiosity. Daniel was in "story teller's heaven" as he gave the details of his escape.

A half hour later, Cristi said, "Well, fellows, we have some flooring to put down. We can learn more beginning Monday, as long as we can talk and work at the same time."

The men returned to work and as John, Mary, and Daniel left, they heard the men excitedly discussing their interpretation of all that Daniel had said regarding the conditions in Romania. For them, Monday could not come soon enough.

John took Daniel to see the house next door that had just been completed. Daniel was absolutely amazed. "These floors are beautiful. I never would have believed that such quality work was possible. I sure hope I can learn to lay floors this well."

John assured him that before long he would acquire the necessary skills. "I remember when those men said the same thing to me, and now look at the work they are accomplishing."

John sensed a level of shame as Daniel commented on the difference between what he had just seen and Romanian craftsmanship. "Daniel, remember what you have seen is a combination of skill and quality of the wood products available." Daniel agreed that even the greatest skill available in Romania could not result in the quality floors he had seen because of the poor-quality flooring materials available.

Following a tour of the houses, John, Mary, and Daniel went to a nearby Super Wal-Mart. Daniel was speechless! They walked throughout the store while Mary put things in her cart. Daniel had seen some impressive stores in Vienna, but nothing like this. He was overwhelmed with the selections available for every type of product. It seemed that anything someone could imagine was available.

When they went through the toy section, he was truly in shock! He commented that the children in Romania had nothing and needed to use their imaginations. An old tire and a stick would make great fun in his village. But here were endless shelves of toys and games leaving nothing to the imagination. "American children must be spoiled!"

Mary responded, "Yes, this is a very big problem in America. We have so much that children don't appreciate what they have; they want more and more! They are quickly dissatisfied with what they have when new technology comes out. When their friends get something new, they have to have it too! They are never satisfied! And their parents will do everything they can to meet these desires!"

"I am thankful that John and I are not trying to raise children in this opulence. I feel for parents trying to raise children. Christians are also caught up in materialism. We lose many of our children to the world because of the abundance of things. They forsake the faith of their parents to achieve more in this life."

"I can certainly understand how this would be a problem. I hope to be married and have children one day, and this prospect is a little scary."

They went to the restaurant that John had mentioned. The smell as they entered had real drawing power. John decided to order for Daniel and see if he thought it was a good choice.

When the waitress brought the double cheeseburger, large plate of fries, and large chocolate milk shake with whipped cream and a cherry on top and placed everything in front of him, he simply exclaimed, "Wow! Thanks!"

After they were served, John said, "Let us give thanks." Daniel was embarrassed. They weren't going to pray in the restaurant where everyone could see them, were they? He closed his eyes and when the prayer was over, he was afraid to look around for fear that others would be staring at them. It was bad enough that they prayed, but it was done in Romanian for his benefit, which would certainly get the attention of English-speaking patrons. "Such a faith!"

Following the meal, John left money on the table with a piece of religious literature. When they left, Daniel asked John why he had left the money with the religious literature.

Mary answered for him. "We always leave a tip for the waitress. If she or he does a really good job serving us, we might leave a larger tip, but the normal minimum amount is 10% of the bill. Their wages are usually low, and they rely on tips to make a reasonable income. That is the way it is done in America. It's a normal expense of eating out and an excellent way to share the Gospel with people we may never meet again. Since we can't share the Gospel with them personally, we leave something for them to read that shows them how to be reconciled to God through faith in Christ."

"Oh, I guess that makes sense."

As they drove along on their way back into Chicago, Daniel was pondering in his heart the things he was learning from the Repenters regarding their faith.

After a while Mary said, "Daniel, you are so quiet. What are you thinking about?"

"Oh, I wasn't thinking of anything in particular. Actually, that is not true. I have been thinking about everything I have seen and heard. This will certainly be a most memorable day in my life!"

The next day, Daniel got up early with John and Mary to prepare for church. After breakfast, they headed out. There were far more people on Sunday morning than at the Wednesday evening service. He was soon to learn that not all the Repenters were of equal strength in their faith. Daniel also observed that John and Mary were among the most faithful members. He and his wife seldom missed an opportunity to be with the brethren.

They arrived for Sunday school and John sent Daniel to the College and Career Class. Most of the people seemed to be about his age, and he was the center of attention as many questions were asked about life in Romania. All of these young people had been born in America, so Romania was foreign to them. He enjoyed his position of centrality, especially when the questions came from the young ladies. There were certainly some cute ones in the class.

His fun was suddenly cut short when the teacher said, "Say, we had better get to our lesson. After all, that is why we have come together. You will have plenty of opportunity to get to know Daniel and hear of his stories of life in Romania and his escape."

The lesson was about the dual nature of Christ as man and God. His humanity was necessary so that he could identify with sinful man as he proclaimed His Gospel of the Kingdom. It was His message that took Him to the cross because the people refused to believe that the Messiah would come to them in the humble manner in which He had come. They would not accept the fact His understanding and interpretation of the Scriptures was because he was God incarnate in flesh. Daniel found himself fully captivated in the discussion. He had some questions, but was afraid to ask, less his ignorance of the Scriptures would become abundantly evident.

Following Sunday school, there was a time of fellowship with coffee and donuts. Daniel really liked this part of the program. Soon the playing of the organ upstairs in the sanctuary signaled the start of the morning service. Daniel gulped down the donut he was eating. He had been so busy talking with a certain young lady that he had not eaten it. This girl reminded him of "his" Veronica back in Romania. As he settled into the pew next to John, he wondered how Veronica was doing. Had she accepted that he was no longer available?

Indeed, she had not! A few hours earlier she was sitting in her church with Lidia and Mary. When Daniel was mentioned in prayer, she was wondering the same thing, "I wonder where Daniel is and how he is doing right now. Is he thinking of me? Does he still love me as I do him?"

Just as Daniel was battling with his decision about Christ, his father was in the beginning of his spiritual battle too. Lidia had come home the Sunday she accepted Christ and told him what she had done. He was shocked! How could she give up her faith? To be a Romanian was to be Orthodox. She was rejecting her heritage. All of their families had always been Orthodox. What would they say? What would their friends say? It would make him the butt of jokes at work. Repenters didn't drink, and he frequently liked to have a drink of his home brew, sometimes with the priest. How could she do this to him and the children? He was almost glad that Daniel wasn't there to share the embarrassment. How shocked George would have been if he had known the decision his son was about to make!

Pastor Virgil preached a simple message on the need of sinful men to be reconciled to God. He read several passages from the book of Romans. These were some of the passages he read during his escape. Following along, Daniel learned that these verses spoke of the fact all men were sinners and could not please God with their works. The pastor explained works to be things like giving money to the church, joining a church, attending services, getting baptized, and more. These were all good things, but until a person admitted his sin and his need for repentance and accepted Jesus as the substitute for him and his sins, these things were like filthy rags to God.

That simple but clear presentation of the Gospel put Daniel under great conviction. He had been confronted with the Gospel many times, starting in Romania with Veronica, and then with the Repenters in Serbia who were so instrumental in his escape. As he had shared with Mary a few days before, often during and after his escape he was plagued with the idea that he had experienced Divine protection. John's and Mary's testimonies were etched in his mind, as was Pastor Virgil's message!

He was grasping the pew as they stood for the final prayer. The pastor gave an invitation for anyone who wanted to be saved. His battle was not unnoticed by John, who boldly took John's arm and leaned over saying, "Isn't it time you stopped fighting God?"

That was all the encouragement he needed. "Yes!"

John led him out into the aisle and walked with him to the front to meet the pastor who had stepped down from the pulpit asking, "Daniel, have you come forward to accept Christ?" At that, Daniel began to weep. Finally, his burden would be lifted. The pastor asked John to end the service while he went to pray with Daniel. In a few minutes, Daniel was ushered into the family of God. He had finally surrendered his old, unsubstantiated atheistic beliefs.

His first thought was of Veronica. If only she knew what had just happened to him! Now he was qualified to marry her, but she was 5,000 miles away. He put those thoughts out of his mind as the pastor walked him to a waiting congregation.

It was their custom to wait when someone had gone forward for salvation. As Daniel and Pastor Virgil came into the sanctuary, all the people proclaimed "Amin" (amen) and "Alleluia" (hallelujah). John came down from the pulpit to be the first to welcome Daniel into the household of faith. He gave him a big hug and the familiar kisses on the cheeks. Those were not the only kisses he received. The attractive girl with whom he had talked before the service planted a couple, too!

Somehow, he suspected that there was more than an acknowledgment of his salvation symbolized by those kisses. He thought, "You don't understand. I belong to Veronica. That is, if she will wait for me."

After a time, the congratulations ended. John, Mary, and Daniel headed home for Sunday dinner. Half-way there, John suggested Mary could put the meal she had prepared in the refrigerator for the next day. They were going to a small restaurant near their home that served what they called "down-home meals." The prices were very reasonable, and the atmosphere was good for a Christian. This was to be a celebration meal!

Daniel wanted to communicate with Veronica and his family to let them know of his safe arrival in America and his new faith, but was afraid to attempt a letter. He was sure, even if the mail eventually got through, the Securitate would open the letters and not deliver them. Then they would undoubtedly hassle Veronica and her parents. Knowing he was successful in his escape, they would persecute his family or worse. His successful escape must not be confirmed by the authorities.

John agreed with him that it would not be wise to attempt such a communication. This was the reason so many of the church members also refused the temptation to communicate with their loved ones in Romania. They must wait until the day, Lord willing, when there would be a change in the government that would allow communication without persecution. That time could be a long way off, though there was indication that Russia was losing control over its empire because of an economic collapse. It was theorized that the desperation of the people might lead them to revolt.

Certainly, President Reagan's trade policies seemed to be achieving this goal. He and other public officials were predicting an ultimate collapse of the Soviet System. But when? It could be years before Daniel would be able to communicate with his family. Would Veronica still be waiting for him? How long could he expect her to wait?

The next morning, Daniel was up and anxious to be on his way with John to begin learning the trade of wood-flooring. Off they went towards the suburbs, fighting traffic all the way. When they reached the house they had visited on Saturday, Cristi, Eli, and Iacov were already there preparing equipment and materials for the day. They greeted him as Brother Daniel. That greeting certainly resounded with Daniel by giving him such a family feeling.

For the first part of the day, Daniel accompanied Cristy, watching him as he explained why they did what they did and what would happen if they didn't do things a certain way. Later that morning he was allowed to start inserting the tongue and groove oak boards, tapping them with a hammer, while Eli measured and cut the pieces. By the end of the day, he was beginning to feel useful. Finally, he was beginning to earn his way! He had received so much from John and Mary. He felt greatly satisfied with himself as they drove home amidst the ever-present traffic.

Days turned into weeks, weeks turned into months, and soon a year had passed. Daniel had learned the wood-laying business very well and was soaking up his new-found faith like a sponge. Living with John and Mary was such a help, because they had regular devotions, and Daniel was always invited to participate.

He was working through the requirements of applying for citizenship, which required five years of permanent residency. Regarding the requirement of mastering knowledge of the key United States documents, he accomplished that.

He was making good progress in learning English. Reading the Bible in English and Romanian was a great help to his language study and gave him an even greater understanding of His new Christian faith.

Not a day had passed without thoughts of Veronica and his family. Life was great, but without them, there was quite a void. John and Mary were doing all they could to fill that void, but it was not sufficient.

Though Daniel felt he was bequeathed to Veronica, as a normal young man, he had a few dates with some of the girls in the church. He was not interested in pursuing any of them. When he was with them, he could only think of Veronica. He tried to imagine he was with her. It didn't work. She was his until he learned otherwise, and no one else would do!

CHAPTER 29 NEW LIFE IN ROMANIA

Back in Romania, Daniel's successful escape was assumed by everyone. Not only had the Lord claimed Daniel as His own, but His Spirit had accomplished His work in Daniel's entire family. His mother's testimony before her husband and children had been used of the Spirit to bring conviction to them. After Lidia, Maria was the next to accept Christ. She turned out to be a real trophy of God's grace. She had taken the most persecution of any in the family. She was savagely attacked and shunned by almost all of her previous friends. If it had not been for Veronica, Maria did not know what she would have done. Veronica could identify with her, having suffered in the same ways. She became not only a friend but also a sister indeed! She soon found true friends in her new spiritual family.

The third to accept Christ was George. His battle against the Spirit had lasted for several months. John, the young man who had befriended Daniel, was instrumental in leading George to accept Christ. He did not have the courage to attend the Repenters' church, so the church came to George in the persons of John and his father. They came to help with the harvest. John's brothers had also come to assist them. Without Daniel, things had been difficult around the farm. Daniel's sisters could not keep up with the chores. The help and friendship of John and his father had opened the door of George's heart to the Gospel. He could resist no longer. He accepted Christ as his Savior.

He didn't have the courage to tell his co-workers at the factory, but they began to realize something had happened to him. He no longer took part in the unsavory talk that went on at every break. He no longer carried alcohol to work. The priest knew something was amiss because George didn't bring any home brew to share with him. George tried to stay out of the way of the priest so he wouldn't be confronted.

Before long the truth came out, and George became the butt of jokes. He was no longer included in the parties around the holidays, for which he was frankly glad. But the day-to-day shunning hurt. If it had not been for John and his father, he would have been most miserable. Their relationship was more family than friendship.

Then the inevitable happened. George was at the market selling vegetables from his harvest, and the priest walked up to him. "George, what is this I hear about you? You're the last person I would expect to be a traitor to the Church. How could you fall for their heresy? Didn't I teach you better?"

With boldness he didn't know he had, George said, "The problem is that you didn't teach us the Bible, only the man-made traditions of the Orthodox Church. Had you looked into the Bible, perhaps you would have found out you are the one teaching heresy."

The priest was taken aback and was speechless for a couple moments. Finally, he retorted, "Well, you are no longer a Romanian."

At that, George said, "The whole world is God's, including Romania. Perhaps I am the real Romanian here." The priest turned around without further word and angrily stomped off. George mused to himself, "Did I really say all of that?"

The two younger girls, Tabita and Luki, followed their father's decision. Now George and his entire family could pray for Daniel's safety and salvation. They were as much in the dark about him as he was about them.

CHAPTER 30 RENEWED HOPE

Daniel's second Christmas season in America was rapidly approaching, and he could not believe how the time had passed. This was to be the most memorable Christmas ever in the memory of all Romanians worldwide.

As predicted by many political analysts, but sooner than many expected, the collapse of the Soviet System and break away of the Eastern European countries had begun! The system had failed. There was unrest in all of the countries. The Poles rallied around Lech Walesa, threatening the Soviet- backed government. Then the world was rocked by the collapse of the Berlin Wall on November 9, 1989. Though this was of great interest to the Romanian community in Chicago, nothing could have gotten their attention more than to learn approximately a month later, there was rioting in the streets of the northwest city of Timisoara and in Bucharest, the Capital of Romania.

It began with a Hungarian preacher in Timisoara, who spoke against the government for not allowing more religious freedom. The crowning blow came when the army moved against a rally of thousands in the center of the city in front of the Orthodox Cathedral on Monday, December 18, 1989. No one knew what had sparked the shooting by the army, but some of the soldiers opened fire, and several young people on the steps of the cathedral were killed. As a result, the people moved beyond an orderly protest. As word of the tragedy spread, thousands more filled the streets, demanding that Ceausescu be taken down. The army, some of whom were from that area of the country, realized the tragedy they had perpetrated and refused to obey further orders against the people.

The news media refused to broadcast what was happening in Timisoara in other parts of the country, but the news quickly spread through Voice of America and Radio Free Europe broadcasts.

Once word got out, tens of thousands of people poured into the streets of Bucharest, many descending on the Ceausescu residence in the center of the city. As he stood on the balcony trying to subdue the people, the shouting and unrest only intensified. Suddenly, he was ushered back inside. Recognizing the seriousness of the situation, the Ceausescus' attempted an escape to Bulgaria.

They were caught and returned to Bucharest under house arrest a couple days before Christmas.

The Romanian Church in Chicago had its eyes on the news for days as these events occurred. A special week of prayer was called by Pastor Virgil. They would meet every evening. They prayed earnestly for the collapse of the Soviet system and the Ceausescu Regime. While the church was gathered together on Christmas morning for their traditional annual Christmas program, they got word that Ceausescu and his wife had just been placed in front of a courtyard wall and machine gunned. The leadership of the government was taken over by the National Salvation Front, which put forth Ion Iliescu as the new President.

Words were insufficient to explain the emotions of the people at the moment of that glorious news. Christmas would never be the same for Romanians worldwide. The question in everyone's mind was, what does all of this mean? Would Iliescu continue the past regime or was there going to be a rejection of Communism? Would Daniel be able to return home to see his family and his beloved Veronica? This had all happened so suddenly. Daniel had been resigned to not seeing his family or Veronica for many years. And now, it might be possible, and very soon!

After getting order in the church, Pastor Virgil suggested they should dispense with the planned service and go into prayer for Romania. They would come back in the evening for their normally scheduled program. They prayed for the next two hours for Romania's freedom and then sang Christmas carols before departing. That evening service was the most special in the history of the church. The news in Romania had brought every member and friend of the church out for the service, so there was standing room only. Daniel had a difficult time keeping his mind on the Christmas story. A story of his own was being formulated in his mind. He could not wait to see his family and his beloved Veronica. But was she still available?

If Romanians in America were excited about the turn of events, one can only imagine the ecstasy in Romania. Daniel's family and Veronica just wanted to know if Daniel, indeed, had escaped. If he had, they were confident he would return for a visit as soon as he could! All they could do was wait and hope. The burden of communicating was with him. They were at his mercy!

If Daniel came back without Christ as his Savior, he would still be out of reach for Veronica. She would be devastated if he had moved on with his life and found another to love, for then he could never be hers, even if he became a Christian. She had never doubted her love for him and his love for her, but not knowing where he was, her faith had faltered.

The next week was difficult for Daniel. He had trouble keeping his mind on his work. During the Wednesday service, Pastor Virgil reported on his attempts to get information from either the Romanian or American Embassies as to the meaning of what was taking place. The phones were flooded from all over the country, and it was impossible to get any information.

The Romanian Revolution, as it was called, was the main story in the news every evening. Clips of the killing of Ceausescu and his wife were now being shown.

President Reagan had been a prophet regarding the collapse of the Soviet Communist System, or better yet, perhaps he was speaking self-fulfilled prophecy. More than any other president, he had challenged the Soviets' right to subjugate the Eastern European countries. His "Mr. Gorbachev, tear down that wall," speech at the Berlin Wall would never be forgotten.

There were so many conflicting accounts on the various TV news stations, that during the Wednesday service, the church voted to send Pastor Virgil to Washington D.C. to make personal contact with the Romanian Embassy personnel.

He left on the first available flight for Washington D.C. and returned in time for the service the next Sunday morning. He reported that Romania had no intention of continuing with the Soviet system of government. It appeared that the doors to Romania would soon be open for uninterrupted travel from the West. The congregation cheered at his announcement. Daniel's heart leaped! He was going home to see his family and Veronica!

Daniel shared with Pastor Virgil his intention to make a trip to Romania as soon as possible. Pastor Virgil promised to stay on top of the situation and find out when it was possible to make a trip. They discussed the possibility of making a phone call into the country. Unfortunately, Daniel did not know of a single person who had a phone, and if he did, he knew of no phone numbers. So, making a call was essentially impossible.

Daniel then talked with John about his desire to take an extended leave as soon as travel was possible. "John, at this point, I want to spend time sharing the Gospel with my family."

"Is that the only reason you want to go back to Romania?"

Blushing, Daniel said, "You know the other reason. I love her and will be devastated if she has found another. I have done nothing but worry about it for days now that I may have the possibility to go back for a visit."

"I know, Daniel. Let's bring our concern before the Lord now. Oh Lord, I come to You on Daniel's behalf. You know Daniel's heart. He has followed Your leading in his life and taken You as his Lord. He has loved the woman You used to begin the process of reaching out to him. You know the state of Veronica at this time. If she has kept herself for Daniel even though the future was uncertain for her, will You prepare her to receive him? Lord, if she has chosen another, will You give Daniel the grace to accept this and find another woman of Your choosing? You do all things well and we trust You in this situation. Thank You for hearing our prayer and answering it even before I am finished. Amen."

"When the time is right for you to make a trip to Romania, we will miss you around here. You are a key part of the business now, but we understand. At this time, it is premature to set dates."

The other men he worked with also had family in Romania and wanted to go for a visit as soon as it was possible. John reminded them of his desire to make a trip, too! But for the sake of his flooring business, they couldn't all fly to Romania for a visit at the same time. They would have to work out a vacation schedule, and there would have to be some compromises.

Daniel had one potential problem that was not shared by the other men. Immigration rules normally did not allow for an applicant to leave the country for three years after applying for citizenship. The next week Pastor Virgil went with Daniel to the nearest immigration office to request an exception. Once again, God's intervention was evident. Because of the unusual circumstances of Daniel's case and Pastor Virgil's assurances, Daniel was given permission to leave for 6 weeks.

By February, Tarom Airlines, the Romanian airline, announced they would begin making trips to Romania from Chicago. It was now necessary for John to call a meeting with his Romanian employees to discuss how they would schedule vacation times. The result of the discussion was that Daniel should be the first to take leave. He had many reasons to visit as soon as possible - Veronica, Veronica, Veronica, and, of course, his family! The other men were married, some with children, and were well-established America citizens. Most of their relatives in Romania were distant and many they had never met. Therefore, they didn't really have urgency as did Daniel.

That night, John, Mary, and Daniel discussed his return to Romania. All he could talk about was Veronica! They had inquired with Tarom Airlines for fare rates and seats available. Not surprisingly, there were no seats available for a few weeks. Hundreds of others had already booked, and flights were full. Most of the seats in the previous flights were taken by non-Romanians. These included politicians, news media personnel, and corporate executives wanting to get a foothold on the huge new markets of the Eastern European countries, pastors, and mission board personnel. Daniel booked a seat on the first available flight and had a few weeks to prepare for his return.

On the way home from the church service the next Sunday, John said, "Daniel, I had a great idea this morning."

"My dear husband, weren't you paying attention to the sermon?"

"Yes, dear, I was paying attention. It was just a little idea but now I think it is really a big idea! Daniel, why don't you purchase an engagement ring to take with you? If everything is a go and the flame is still burning bright, you could make that first step immediately."

"John, you are a sentimental old man! I think that is a wonderful idea. How sweet of you to come up with that!" Daniel's response was a big smile.

Mary added, "Daniel, I think you are blushing. Let's do it next Saturday. I will go with you and help you pick out a ring. That is, if John will trust me out of sight with you."

"Oh, I am not invited, huh?"

"I didn't think you would be interested."

"And why not? After all, it was my idea. Besides, I am an expert in such things.

"Oh, you are, huh?" She leaned over and planted one on his lips.

The week went very slowly for Daniel. He was unusually quiet all week because his mind was continually on Veronica and his family. He kept playing over in his mind how he would meet them and what he would say. By the end of the week, he was well rehearsed.

Finally, Saturday arrived. After some lunch, the happy trio took off to find a jewelry store. After a couple hours of looking and debating, Daniel made a selection. It was decided they all had to agree on the choice. The ring was very modest in size and quality for two reasons. Cost was a significant consideration, but of equal consideration was the fact that what he was doing was a very Western thing.

Mary and John asked Daniel what he thought the response would be to the ring.

"Well, at most, Repenters would wear a simple, thin gold band, but only after marriage. An engagement ring would be out of the question, and one with a diamond! Oh my, this is going to be a scandalous event at best! But if Veronica is going to marry an American, she needs to get with the program! Well, I am not an American yet, but nothing will stop me from that goal!"

John and Mary gave a hearty amen! The purchase settled it. Daniel was going home with an engagement ring to snare a wife and create a scandal!

After Daniel's purchase, they stopped at the travel agency to pick up his round trip tickets to Romania. The tickets were from Chicago to Timisoara, where the revolution began. From there he would take a "milk run" train that stopped at every depot on the line. It would take him over 24 hours from the time he left Chicago to when he would get home. Though he had three weeks to wait, there was a positive side. This would give Daniel more time to make money. He wished to take as much with him as was possible. He could greatly benefit his parents. According to press reports, the purchasing power of the dollar was very strong against the Romanian Lei at this time. On the way home, Daniel groaned. "Three weeks - I will never make it!"

"I guess I will have to work you to death, so you don't have time to think about it." Thus began the slowest three weeks in Daniel's life. John and Mary promised to make it as miserable for him as they could. And, that they did! Every morning Mary would say, "How many days until you leave? Oh, that is still so long to wait!"

Daniel would say, "Yes, I know. But with God's help I will make it."

Back in Romania, Daniel's family and Veronica were becoming anxious, not having heard from him. Perhaps he never made it to freedom after all! That little Baptist Church was busier than ever uttering prayers for Daniel's safety and return.

CHAPTER 31 HOPE BECOMES REALITY

The time finally came for Daniel to leave. John took Tuesday morning off so he and Mary could take him to O'Hara Airport. They said their goodbyes with many hugs and kisses. John and Mary had unofficially adopted him. They almost saw him as the son they never had. Having seen the best there is in airline terminals and passenger planes; Daniel was in for some surprises on this flight. It was direct from Chicago to Timisoara, where he would de-plane. The plane would then continue on to Bucharest.

As he boarded, he quickly noted that the plane was very small in comparison to the plane he had taken to America from Heathrow Airport in England. He also noted that it was not very clean. There were some papers in the pocket in front of him from a previous passenger.

There was a fairly large group of people in the back, laughing and talking loudly in English. After takeoff, the man, who appeared to be the leader of the group, passed Daniel on the way to his seat in 1st class. Daniel asked him who he was. His name was Ralph, and he was taking a group of people who were interested in adopting children. He was videotaping the event, which was the reason for the excitement in the back of the plane.

There was another traveler sitting only a couple of seats behind Daniel who he had nodded to as they were putting their overhead luggage into the berth. Little did they know that they would meet again in unusual circumstances, which would lead to a relationship that only God could have orchestrated.

After a flight of about 10 hours, the plane landed at Timisoara. At touchdown, everyone, well almost everyone, was clapping. The waitresses began serving Champaign to the passengers, free of charge. Daniel asked a stewardess, "What is the occasion?"

"Oh, we were clapping because this was the maiden voyage of Tarom Airlines flying directly from Chicago to Romania without another European stop."

"Oh, I thought we were clapping because we made it safely." The stewardess didn't seem to think it was funny. She didn't respond and just walked away. He thought, "Well, I guess you can't win them all."

Daniel and a few other passengers left the plane and entered the terminal building. It looked like the Romania he had left. He found himself embarrassed at the conditions, however, having been in two of the best airport terminals in the world: Heathrow and O'Hara. Because he was a Romanian, he went through the passport and customs process fairly quickly, though he sensed a coldness which he interpreted to be jealousy. He had to admit a certain pride as he handed his permanent American visa to the agent.

He stepped out onto the front sidewalk, getting a cab going to the train terminal. He had quite a conversation with the cab driver about what was happening in the country. The man was very excited about the changes taking place. He believed it would be impossible for the government to re-close the borders as the hardliners wanted to do. Too many from the West were coming in, and the people now knew too much about the lies they lived with for so many years. The people would never again allow a Ceausescu-type regime. This time they were ready to die, if necessary, for freedom like the West had.

When Daniel reached the train station and paid the driver, he got out with his luggage and headed for the ticket office. He had given a tip to the driver with a sense of pride. The driver was speechless. Romanians didn't give tips!

As Daniel walked into the train station, he thought, "Little has changed. But then, why would I have expected anything different?" Everything was totally run down. It was a wonder anything worked. Finally, the train arrived, and he got on for the 5-hour trip to Orsova. Comfort was not to be his on this trip, but excitement was! He had not seen or communicated with his family and Veronica for over a year and a half.

Finally, Daniel's train pulled into the train station across from the ship-building factory he had worked in. He stepped off into the snow, taking in the sights. Everything looked as bad as when he left, but it was home! He was finally home! He stepped over to a cab and looked inside. It was an old acquaintance, Nicu. "I don't believe it. Daniel, you old devil! You are alive after all! Jump in. The ride to your village is on me. It's good to see you. How did you escape? Where have you been? What have you been doing?"

"Wait a minute. Give me a chance!" As they headed for his home, he explained very briefly how he had escaped and ended up in Chicago, Illinois, USA.

"You are a lucky man. You escape and then are able to come back to a woman who is still waiting for you. Half of the eligible men in town have tried to make it with Veronica and her only response has been, 'I am already taken.'" Daniel's heart leapt at the news. He couldn't wait to see her, but he must see his family first.

They soon arrived at his parents' home. Daniel insisted on paying Nicu, who, after very little persuasion, accepted payment plus a tip. Then he honked the car horn several times. Daniel got out with his luggage and started for the house.

Lidia opened the door. She just stood there for a moment in shock, and then as calmly as she could, she said "George! Girls! Daniel is home!" They then ran toward each other and embraced as tears flowed down their cheeks. A moment later, George was at the door, also in disbelief. He ran to his son with tears and open arms, giving Daniel a bear hug as well.

"Let me breathe, Dad," Daniel exclaimed. The girls came running out next with tears flowing. The hugging and kissing went on for some time. George grabbed Daniel's luggage and headed for the door.

They went into the house and sat down before questions started flowing. "How did you escape? Where are you living? Are you working? What is America like?"

"Slow down. First, I have to tell you something that you are probably not going to like, but I became a Repenter last year and am a member of a Romanian Baptist church in Chicago, Illinois.

After a short pause, the entire family said, almost in unison, "Praise God!"

"What is going on here?"

"Son, that is an answer to our prayers. We also became Repenters many months ago."

They began to hug all over again as they started telling how and when they had each put their faith in Christ.

In the midst of the rejoicing, they heard a car horn out front. George went to the door and said, "Daniel, I think someone is here to see you." Daniel leapt from his chair and went to the door. Stepping from Nicu's taxi into the snow was the woman he had thought of every day for the last year and a half. He stepped outside and George closed the door, telling the family that this was Daniel's private moment. Of course, everyone ran to the window to watch the reunion, so it wasn't really very private.

Daniel waved to Nicu as he sped off. Then, he turned his attention to Veronica, who was walking toward him with a torrent of tears flowing down her cheeks. He ran to her, and they embraced neck to neck. Daniel whispered in her ear, "My darling, I accepted Christ as my Savior last year." She looked into his eyes and he in hers!

"I knew God would answer my prayer and bring you back to me a saved man!" At that, they kissed. Oh, what a precious kiss it was! And there was another and another!

The door opened and his sisters taunted, "Daniel, we saw you kissing. Naughty, naughty!"

"Yes, naughty and nice."

They all went inside to talk for hours while Lidia prepared a feast. If they had a fatted calf, it would have been sacrificed for the occasion. Instead, it was a grouchy rooster that always got in the way.

Everyone was soon settled around the table. Daniel said, "I think we ought to give thanks and eat before the food gets cold." He insisted that he return thanks on this most memorable event. How special it was for them to all be praying together as Repenters! Daniel and Veronica sat together and held hands the entire time. It was a little difficult to eat that way, but what was more important - holding hands or eating? There was so much talking going on it was a wonder anyone finished eating.

Following the meal, Daniel passed out the gifts he had brought for everyone. To have a gift from America was a treat indeed. The gift in the little white box would wait for a special occasion.

By this time, they were well into the evening.

"Our Daniel is exhausted. He needs to go to bed."

The girls complained. "But Mom!"

"No but Mom! He is going to bed!"

"Yes, I agree. My man needs his sleep."

"What is this, my man needs his sleep?"

"It is as it sounds. I will see you tomorrow!"

Lidia asked Veronica if she was working the next day. "It is my day off. Isn't God good? He knew I would be worthless tomorrow, so He arranged for me to be off."

"Well, then, I have a great idea. You can spend the night here with us. I have an extra night gown you can wear. I need one of you girls to volunteer to give up your bed." They all volunteered at the same time. And so, it was settled.

Daniel, his family, and Veronica slept like they had not slept for many months. Daniel didn't stir until nearly noon the next day. His father had long ago left for work, and his sisters were in school.

He found his mother and Veronica quietly talking in the living room. When he appeared, Veronica said, "Behold, my answered prayer has arisen!"

"So, he has," Lidia said, jumping up and planting a kiss on his cheek before heading toward the kitchen to prepare him a breakfast fit for a king. After breakfast, Lidia cleaned the kitchen and washed the dishes while Daniel and Veronica sat arm in arm before the fireplace in spirited conversation.

Before long, the news had gotten around Orsova and the village of Daniel's arrival, thanks to the help of Nicu. Neighbors stopped by, and the same questions had to be answered over and over. Daniel thought, "I should have recorded my answers. I could have put them on a loudspeaker and saved a lot of time."

Late in the afternoon, Daniel and Veronica were finally alone. Daniel suggested they take a walk to get away from everyone. First, he went to his room to retrieve the small white box. He told his mother where they were going.

"In this cold? You had better dress warmly."

After fetching the necessary garments and taking her hand, Daniel led her toward a favorite quiet spot along the river, where he went when he needed to think. It was rather barren during the winter, but it was private and held a special place in Daniel's heart.

As they walked, he talked about life in America and all the girls who tried to get his attention. "Are you trying to make me jealous, or are you trying to tell me something?"

He brushed the snow off a tree stump, set her down, and knelt before her in the cold snow. "I am trying to tell you that those girls didn't have a chance. Will you marry me?"

She looked into his eyes with a sweet smile. "I thought you would never ask. Of course, I will marry you! That is all I have wanted since you left. I asked the Lord for you every day."

She leaned forward to her "husband-to-be," and kissed him long and sweet. "Remember your humble position before me after we are married."

At that, he jumped up! "Wait a minute, now!" Then he reached into his pocket for the little white box, opened it, and took out the ring.

"Oh, Daniel, what is that?"

"What does it look like?" As Veronica stared in amazement, Daniel slipped it onto her finger. She began to cry. "Don't you like it?"

"Oh, Daniel, it is the most beautiful ring I have ever seen. But we aren't married yet, and Repenters would never wear something like this."

"Let me explain how marriage is in America. This is not our marriage ring. This is an engagement ring. It says that you belong to someone. That someone is me. When we get married, you will get another ring without a diamond, and we will attach it to this one. Then people will know that you are married."

"I learned in our church that Repenters in Romania have misinterpreted Scripture. The Bible clearly does not say that the wearing of jewelry is wrong, but it should not be how we evaluate a person."

Veronica just looked at it admiringly for a long time. "Oh, Daniel, Romanian girls never receive anything like this for their engagement. It is so beautiful I cannot imagine what it must have cost."

"Yes, it was very expensive by Romanian standards, but in America, this is how men tell the world who they have chosen for their bride. I want people to know that you belong to me!"

"When can we be married?"

"I am not sure when I will be able to bring you to America, but my plan is for us to be married summer of next year if I am allowed to return again for a few weeks. After I return to America, I hope our marriage will give me the opportunity to get you a visa so you can begin the process of citizenship. I know my pastor and our church will do everything possible to help. If we have to wait until I get citizenship, I will only be able to visit you a couple weeks each of the remaining two years until I have citizenship. I think it is too early to know for sure. Can you wait on this process?

"I waited this long. With this ring on my finger to remind me of your love, I can do whatever is necessary. Let's go tell my parents first and then yours."

They walked slowly, arm in arm, back to the village and then taking a bus on to Orsova to see Vera's parents. Her mother hugged Daniel and said, "Welcome home my boy. All this girl has talked about after you left is you. Since she got her own apartment, I haven't seen much of her. If it had not been for Nicu, who stopped by to tell me the good news, I would not even have known you were back."

"I am sorry, Mother, but when Nicu came to get me, I had only one thing in mind, and it wasn't you."

Her mother hugged her. "I understand. I would have done the same thing in your place. Vera, what is that on your finger?"

Proudly holding her hand out, she said, "Mother, this is how men in America show the world that a woman is to be their bride."

"Oh, it is so beautiful. I have never seen such a ring. A Romanian could never think of purchasing something like this. Congratulations to both of you. Now, we will finally have a son. Wait until your father hears the good news. When will the wedding be? I will have to start planning."

Vera explained how it would not take place before summer of the next year.

"Then, I have time to save up for the celebration. You will be married in Romania, won't you?"

"Of course, Mother."

"I suppose you will live in America?"

Daniel responded, "That is our plan at this time. I can provide a much better life for Veronica and the children we hope to have."

"Mother, Daniel became a Repenter while he was in America, and he is a member of a Romanian Baptist Church in Chicago, Illinois."

"I suppose I should not be surprised."

After answering many questions over coffee and sweets and waiting for Vera's father, Veronica and Daniel headed for his home to tell his family of their marriage plans.

By the time they arrived, George was home from work. Walking into the house, Veronica put her hand up for Lidia to see the ring.

162

"Oh, my girl, that is beautiful! You didn't get married today, did you?"

Figuring it was time to stop calling her Lidia, Veronica said, "Oh, no, Mother. It is an engagement ring. In America, this is how a man lets people know that a woman will be his bride. It means I am taken and not available. In case you are thinking that Repenters should not wear such jewelry, Daniel explained that we have been misinterpreting the passages we use against wearing jewelry."

"Oh, that is better! For a moment you had me scared that you had gotten married without your family's participation. Congratulations! I am so pleased you will be my daughter-in-law." With that, she embraced her.

"George! Girls! Come and see what Daniel has given to Veronica."

After the family admired the ring and heard the explanation of its meaning, the questions started again. When will you be married? Will it be in Romania? Will you live in America? They would definitely be married in Romania, and yes, they would probably live in America. Daniel then explained again how he thought the process would work.

This was truly a happy day for the entire family. They all agreed that they would miss Daniel and Veronica after they married, but they would be happy to have Veronica in the family and to know that she would have a better life than they had.

Maria said, "Perhaps Daniel could find a man to marry me and take me to America."

The other girls chimed in, "Yes, and us too."

At that, they all had a good laugh.

Lidia said, "Oh, you all want to go to America and leave your mother and father here in Romania alone."

Luki said, "You can come with us." After some more laughter it was decided that they had better eat before leaving for the Wednesday evening service.

They quickly ate and headed for the bus stop. When they arrived at the church, there was no small stir as Daniel was recognized. Soon the whole village was talking, not just the Repenters. What a time of rejoicing they had that night! The Lord had answered their prayers that Daniel would be safe, that he would find Christ, and that he would come back to Veronica.

When Veronica showed off her engagement ring, several members said that she should not wear such a thing. Repenters did not wear jewelry, and she wasn't even married yet. Others nodded in agreement. Veronica explained how this was a custom in America when a girl was engaged.

They brought up the Scriptures that they were sure proved their point: I Timothy 2:9 & I Peter 3:3. Daniel interjected, "Brothers and Sisters, these passages were recently taught correctly at our church in America because some of the older members were causing dissention over the issue of jewelry. The problem is that you are simply taking these verses out of the Bible without considering the context, verses before and after. These verses are not speaking against the wearing of jewelry, but they teach that it is not the outward things that a woman is to emphasize, but the hidden beauty on the inside that was a reflection of the new birth they had experienced on the inside."

"But this is what Romanians believe."

Daniel replied that his church in America was also a Romanian church with a Romanian pastor. It is not what Romanians believe; it is what the Bible teaches. This is an example of why it is so important that we learn to properly interpret the Scriptures. Nevertheless, most of the members did not accept his explanations. It is difficult for generations of tradition to be abandoned, even when truth is revealed. Finally, Pastor Petrica suggested that he would look into the matter in the future and address it with the church. At this point they needed to get on with the service.

They had a joyous service that evening. Daniel looked at Veronica and his family, all sitting together, and realized how great God had been in their lives. Who could have guessed over a year and a half ago that they would be gathered together in the Repenters' church as born-again Christians, having put off the cloak of false Orthodoxy?

Daniel thought, "It's too bad that we don't have a church in our village to attend. Then we wouldn't have to take the bus twice on Sunday and again on Wednesday evening. If we had a church in our village, it might be possible more people could be reached with the Gospel. But even if we did, who would be our pastor?"

Like so many of the other Baptist pastors in the country, Pastor Petrica already had five small churches: the one attended by Daniel's family and John and Ioana, another in a bordering village, and three in remote mountain villages in the foothills of the Carpathian Mountains.

On the way home, Daniel shared his previous thoughts regarding the benefit of having a church in their own village. There was unanimous agreement that this would be an incredible blessing.

George agreed that it would be great, but their village was very small and certainly could not support a pastor. It would have to be someone who could preach with little or no salary. Pastor Petrica was already too busy to handle any additional responsibility. This was certainly a matter for future prayer. That discussion was to weigh heavy on Daniel's heart for a long time and have a significant impact on his future. The Lord was clearly working behind the scenes. Now it was up to Daniel to understand God's will for him. At this time, Daniel's plan was not God's plan.

Daniel's visit to Romania went quickly. How could six weeks go by so fast? He spent every possible moment with Veronica and his family, though he still found time, or rather, made time, to do some serious repairs around the house and help tend the animals.

He also found opportunities to meet with old school friends and tell them about Christ. In America, he had learned to be unashamed about his faith. The responses were usually the same - surprise! He always had the proud reputation with Radu of being a confirmed atheist. What had happened to him? He would gladly tell them! He didn't gain any converts, but he planted the seed. Perhaps in the future, someone else would harvest some souls.

CHAPTER 32 BACK TO AMERICA

The time for his departure arrived. After many hugs and kisses from his family, and some very special hugs and kisses from Veronica, he was on the train heading to Timisoara and the airport. He was traveling light on the return trip. He left his suitcases with Veronica because they would need them later.

All he had now was his carry-on with a few items of clothing and a prized picture of his family and wife to be. He had a perfect spot to display the picture when he returned. He would place it in a frame on top of his TV so that when watching it, he could look up during the commercials and see those waiting for him in Romania.

He could not wait to get through the terminal building and on the plane. It was so disgraceful. He hoped that when he returned, things would be improved. The plane trip was uneventful, but the difference was that they had a midway stop in Munich. Finally, he was in Germany, though not in the way he had originally planned.

It was good to be home in Chicago and see his friends and adopted family. He had taken many pictures of the people at the little Repenters' church to share with the church in Chicago. Of course, Veronica managed to get in many of the pictures. Everyone wanted to know everything about his trip. Pastor Virgil asked him to take some time in the first prayer meeting to share with everyone the events of his travel and the condition of Romania.

Daniel explained the state of limbo that the country seemed to be in. "There are those who want the old ways. They are the aged who are afraid that they will not receive the aid from the government they had received prior to the revolution. But the middle-aged and younger generations all want a new Romania. They want change and a good life like in the West. Everyone now knows what Communism has cost them as a society, and they are angry. It seems that there is no chance that the hardline Communists will ever seize control again."

"The majority of the young people want out of the country for a better life. They do not believe that the changes will come fast enough to benefit them. They will go to any country that will accept them. There are long lines every day at all the embassies of western countries. They usually start with the American

Embassy. If they fail there, they try another, and another. There is a frenzy to leave. It is hard for me to be critical, because I sought to leave myself. But now there is a hope that did not exist when I escaped. I think it will be detrimental for Romania to lose its youth, but the government cannot stop them if another country is willing to grant them a visa. Only time will tell the future for Romania."

Of course, being back with John and Mary was special. John was so glad for him to be home and back on the job. They had more flooring jobs promised than they could fulfill. God had blessed them for the quality of their work.

Daniel worked harder than ever on the language so he could pass the citizenship test on language with flying colors. He had already memorized all the political information he was to know about the functioning of the government and the constitution. He was careful now to save all the money that he could for his future marriage and round-trip tickets for he and his bride.

John and Mary had already promised him that he could continue to rent from them after he got married. He had planned to get a car, but now that was on the back burner. He needed to save his money. He would continue to ride with John, sharing the cost of gas.

Pastor Virgil decided to start a Bible Institute at the church to better train the members who were interested in expanding their knowledge of the Bible. Daniel and John agreed that they wanted to participate in the program. They started with a course in doctrines. Being a new Christian, Daniel soaked up the teaching like a sponge. He wanted to learn more about his new faith.

Some of the older members of the church in Chicago who had managed to get out of Romania either before or during the Communist Regime had really resisted challenges to their beliefs. It was as though they saw this as part of their loyalty to their homeland. Pastor Virgil frequently dealt with their error in his preaching and little by little some were beginning to "see the light".

Months passed and soon it was fall. It had been nine months since Daniel had been in Romania. Already some stores were beginning their holiday merchandising, which reminded him of the passing of another year.

He couldn't wait to return to Romania next summer to marry Veronica. He kept mulling over in his mind the fact that if he couldn't get a visa for Veronica after their marriage, they could be separated for approximately two more years until he obtained citizenship. The idea of being separated from her so long was very disconcerting and would influence his future decisions.

CHAPTER 33 REVISING FUTURE PLANS

There was one other problem with his future plans. Perhaps as a result of the Bible Institute teaching, Daniel had become burdened for his countrymen in their lost condition. He had gone through the courses on doctrines and personal evangelism. The last course had really changed his perspectives on life. He had begun to think perhaps he should return to Romania to try helping reach his own people with the Gospel. As he considered this idea, he knew that if he was to proceed in this direction, it would mean discarding his plans for American citizenship. After realizing his dream of freedom, could he give that up?

He had learned a trade, which was necessary in Romania with all of the construction that was taking place. If a person had skills in building, he could make a good living. Daniel wondered if he should consider starting his own business to support himself and help spread the Gospel. Perhaps he could even start a church in his own village. His father had enough unplanted land on which they could build a small church.

He shared his idea with John and Mary. At first, they were taken back by his proposal. They had looked forward with anticipation to his marriage to Veronica and continued life in America. John had even entertained the plan to have Daniel take over his business when he was ready to step aside and retire. That would not be too many years in the future. It was clear, at first, that they were not excited about the prospect of losing him. They said they all needed to pray earnestly about this.

A couple of days later, John and Mary asked Daniel to speak with them regarding their previous discussion. They noted that their first response was selfish. Though they would miss him and the opportunity to get to know Veronica, if this was of God, Daniel should follow His leading.

Daniel then shared his idea with Pastor Virgil. His response was, "Praise the Lord!" This had been a dream of his.

He told Daniel that he had recently talked with a director from a Baptist mission board in the south. Twenty-four Romanian students were being given a free education with a commitment to return after graduation to reach Romanians with the Gospel. Very quickly they were finding American girl friends. Their actions were creating doubt about their intentions of returning to Romania to preach the Gospel. If they married Americans, citizenship would be theirs, and they could abandon their previous plans.

"I know many Romanians in America, but I do not personally know of a single one who has a desire to return to Romania to take the message of salvation to our people. I have wondered if I should return to Romania myself, but there are so many Romanians here to minister to. Daniel, now you can see why I am so excited about your decision! I highly respect you and your maturity for such a young man. Only a man of God would consider giving up life in America to reach his own people."

"I believe our church would be willing to help support you until you get your feet on the ground financially. You would be our first missionary to the Romanian people."

Those words from the pastor, along with the encouragement he had received from John and Mary, really added fuel to his prayer life.

Pastor Virgil shared Daniel's plan with the church. The response of some, primarily the older folks, was the same as the pastor. They would be happy to help support him in his endeavor. There were others, primarily the young, who did not seem very supportive. The pastor wondered if Daniel's idea was bringing conviction to those who would not be willing to give up their life in America.

A little humor was introduced to the situation when some of the eligible women said, "Daniel may as well go back to Romania since he is not available to any of us." That amused him greatly, but he had to repent for indulging in thoughts regarding what a good catch he would be for one of those girls.

Daniel prayed even more earnestly about his decision. He shared his plans with his family and Veronica by letter. He explained to Veronica that if he made this decision, it would probably mean that they would never become American citizens. After three weeks without a response, he began to think that his letter had not been received. He also worried that Veronica would be disappointed not to return with him to America to enjoy a much better life.

Finally, he returned home one day to find Mary waiting for him, letter in hand. Now for the moment of truth! He opened the letter and began to read,

Dearest Daniel,

I read your letter with tears. They were tears of joy, not sadness. I have been so burdened for our people. I had secretly prayed that perhaps you would return home and help start a church. I was afraid to share my dream with you since I thought you were definitely planning to live in America. Of course, I would follow you anywhere. I know from all the things you have told us that America would be a wonderful place to live. To make my life with you is all that

I want. However, if you are looking for my approval to return to Romania, you have it with all my love.

Your parents and sisters were overjoyed at the prospect of us living here. Of course, my parents were excited as well, but do not share excitement for the same reason. Please pray for them! I know you do, but I am so burdened for them. They just don't seem to see anything wrong with their Orthodox faith, or perhaps just don't want to risk their status with their friends. They have seen the persecution that I have endured, and they have no desire to share in it.

They do not understand that I gladly bear the reproach. It is not hard for me because "I know whom I have believed in and am persuaded that He is able to keep that which I have committed unto him against that day." If only they could see that the persecution is nothing compared to my life in Christ, my wonderful Christian friends, and my sure hope of eternal life. Well, I must close for now. As you seek God's will, include me, for your desires are my desires.

With all my love, God's and yours only! Veronica

He stood speechless!

"Is something wrong?"

He handed the letter to Mary. As she and John began to read it, he sat down and thought to himself, "Indeed, she is the woman I want for my life's partner. She has a much greater spiritual depth than any of the young women in our church."

He praised God for His goodness in bringing Veronica into his life. Veronica's acceptance of his proposal convinced him to pursue his decision. He greatly considered her counsel. After all, she was the one who had pursued him for salvation, loved him, but chose not to violate her principles for his love. She was indeed a mature spiritual woman, and she was to be his!

As Mary and John finished the letter, Mary was the first to speak through her tears of joy. "Daniel, I must meet this woman some day! I have never seen anything so sweet. You must be the happiest man alive."

John grabbed his arm and pulled him out of the chair for a hearty handshake and hug.

"Well, there is the answer you have been waiting for. It was worth the wait, I would say. I think you ought to read the letter to the church, including the mushy parts. I think it would be an encouragement to many, and would bring conviction to some who love their life in America too much to ever consider such an endeavor. Perhaps you would inspire someone else in our church to go as well."

Indeed, the next Sunday Pastor Virgil had Daniel read the letter during the morning service. A pin could have been heard if it was dropped on the sanctuary carpet! Pastor Virgil had a season of prayer for Daniel and Veronica before continuing on with his morning message. He had decided for the occasion to bring a message on Matthew 28:19-20.

Daniel was now convinced that the Lord wanted him to return to Romania and be involved in reaching his people with the Gospel. The church was behind him and agreed to provide considerable support. Pastor Virgil knew the pastor of the Romanian Baptist Church in Atlanta, and arranged for Daniel to visit the church to present his planned ministry.

Little did Daniel know when he arrived in Atlanta that the man he had nodded to on the plane to Bucharest was only a few miles away. In fact, the Romanian pastor, a physician's assistant, told Daniel a prospective missionary to Romania, Wesley Benney, had visited the church some weeks previously. The name meant nothing at that point, but would later.

Daniel was not a speaker, so he just told the church of his plans. He was very well received, and the church was impressed. The people voted to provide $300 per month until such time he got his feet on the ground. He would then continue to receive support to build a church. When that was accomplished, the support would end.

Daniel returned home to Chicago and shared the results of the trip with John, Mary, and the pastor. They agreed that the $300 support from the church in Atlanta, along with the $500 per month support from the Chicago church would allow him to live with comfort until he got his feet on the ground with his own business.

CHAPTER 34 RETURNING HOME TO ROMANIA

Daniel was scheduled to fly to Romania the first week in June. He contacted his family with the date of his arrival. Their marriage would take place mid-July. He prepared to leave for his bride and life in Romania on a different economic level than he would have experienced in America. He had no idea what God had planned for him when His Spirit first began to intrude into Daniel's plans.

This trip was every bit as exciting, if not more so, than his last trip because of his anticipated marriage. He arrived in Romania without complication.

As expected, almost everyone Daniel met, thought he was crazy to give up American citizenship for his religious beliefs. It was really an indication of how unimportant religious faith was to the average Romanian.

Soon after his arrival, Daniel purchased a used 1979 Volkswagen van and began the process of building his new home attached to his parents' home. The challenges had nothing to do with money. In fact, the dollar had remained extremely strong against the Romanian Lei. The problem was availability of materials - finding what he needed was a real challenge. Daniel quickly found that in his quest for building materials, he should never assume a particular store would not have what he was looking for.

One day he was in a very small food store, if it could be called that, in a nearby village. All that was on the shelves were jars of pickles, tomatoes, beans, peas, and spotted peaches. Produce included dry onions, potatoes, peppers, carrots, and parsnips. Cooking oil was available in a large wooden barrel. The clerk would take the customer's bottle and fill it with oil from a ladle. Oil would overflow the sides of the bottle and fall back into the barrel. The clerk would then wipe the bottle with a rag or her apron and hand the bottle back. Daniel shuddered at the thought of how this process could pass bacteria from customer to clerk to the next customer. The revolution had not yet had any effect on cleanliness.

Beside this "great" selection of food items, however, was a large wooden box of nails the equivalent of an American 16 penny nail. Daniel had traveled to the city of Turnu-Severin, about 24 kilometers down the Danube River, looking just for this size nail in every store selling building supplies or hardware items without success. This was an example of what someone went through to accomplish construction. One positive aspect to building in most of Romania was that there were little to no building codes or approval processes to go through. Money plus materials equaled immediate progress.

Availability of benzina (gasoline) was another real issue. When the one pump station in Orsova had a supply, it was usually sold out by early afternoon. It was not unusual for Daniel to sit in line two hours or more, inching his way to the pump, using up precious benzina in the process. Often others would cut in line, sometimes bribing the car in front of them to get closer to the pump. Of course, the bribed individual traded one spot for the offered tip, and those behind received nothing for their loss.

Many threats were made by those in line, but few ever came to fruition. One of the reasons Romanians had accepted the despotic Ceausescu regime was the overall pacifist attitude of the people. The "might makes right" philosophy was practiced in every facet of life. Those with the biggest mouths, fists, wallets, positions, or connections with the government or Securitate usually got what they wanted, as their opponents would simply back down. All the fist shaking and name calling was like a theatrical performance enacted out in the daily lives of the people.

Daniel had purchased a 200-liter (52 gallon) drum. Any time additional benzina was available at the pump in Orsova or any other town he passed through, he would fill his car and a 22-liter (6 gallon) container which he would empty into the drum. He would often have to dip into it.

Having a car was a special treat for the family who had never owned one previously. It cut the time to travel to church by about 3/4. Daniel's family alone filled the van every Sunday and Wednesday. As time went on, that van would begin to take others to church as well.

July arrived quickly and there was a fever of activity in preparation for the wedding. In the Romanian culture, a wedding is an all-day/all night affair, according to what the family could afford. As in America, the bride's parents paid for most of it. However, if her parents were not able, the groom's family kicked in. In Daniel's case, his family had a farm, a garden, and livestock. Daniel had saved money for the wedding, as well as for the building of their home. It was to be a gala event, but without alcohol and dancing. The ceremony would take place at their little village church.

Food had already been taken to John and Lidia's home for final preparation and heating. The feasting went on well into the night for those who lived in the village. Those from Daniel's village had to catch a bus home, so missed out on the late evening festivities. Not yet having a home of their own or a decent hotel near their home, they drove to Turnu-Severin for a two-day honeymoon. Following the honeymoon, Daniel and Veronica shared his former little bedroom in his parents' home. It was cozy, to say the least, but that never seems to be a problem with newlyweds. This would have to do until he could complete their new home addition.

Daniel's two years of training in Sunday school, the preaching services in Chicago, plus the year he studied in the Bible institute, had prepared him to assist Pastor Petrica. He was quickly becoming acknowledged as a genuine spiritual leader.

The vast majority of pastors in Romania had received no formal Bible training. Almost no books from the West had been translated prior to the revolution. As a result, the doctrine of the Baptist Union pastors and members was not consistent with a historic interpretation of Scripture and the resulting Baptist theology. Daniel knew that the churches in Romania had considerable doctrinal error, and some even bordered on heresy. This had continued to be a challenge to Pastor Virgil as he led his flock in Chicago. Old beliefs and habits die hard, so he challenged Daniel to be patient with Pastor Petrica and others with whom he would work. Indeed, Daniel had to use great care not to offend his Pastor.

Since these doctrinal variances continued to surface, Daniel became curious as to why the Baptists in Romania had different doctrinal positions than the Baptists in America, when some of the first Baptists to evangelize in Romania were from America. When Daniel talked with old members who predated the Communist regime, they acknowledged that, following the imposition of the Communist political system under Russia following World War II, their doctrines changed.

Denominational "Unions" were established by the government to control all religious activity. The top union leaders were government agents responsible to keep all, within their denominational union, in perfect obedience to all government dictates.

The pastors were obliged to implement everything dictated by the union leaders and the government at large if they wanted to maintain their position or not risk harm to themselves and their families.

The Baptists originally believed in eternal security, but no longer did. This had kept them in obedience to the government, for they were told by the Baptist Union hierarchy that they could lose their salvation if they didn't obey the government.

Their doctrine included the teaching that a person was not truly saved until they had been baptized. Unfortunately, the pastors had authority over when a person was ready to be baptized.

Another Baptist doctrine violation was the priesthood of the believer. They were to obey their pastors in all things. Thus, the pastor took the position of the Holy Spirit in the lives of the people. This kept the members under the control of the Union and their pastor. The sin nature of the pastors encouraged them to readily assume and enjoy their control over the people. In fact, pastors were prone to exercise their presumed authority by meddling in personal family affairs.

It was certainly easy to see how the doctrine of separation of church and state would not fit into the Communist agenda.

It was easy to see how the belief in a millennial reign of Christ would not be allowed by a system that claimed it would rule the world for a thousand years.

The Bible presents only two spiritual offices, pastor and deacon. The imposition of union leadership violated this. There were lesser issues caused by the lack of understanding the Bible.

The government only allowed a couple new students per year in the Baptist Seminary in Bucharest. Needless to say, at this rate, it is easy to see why so few pastors had any significant training for pastoral ministry.

Daniel had several discussions with Pastor Petrica about these differences in belief, challenging him to search the scriptures to see if he could substantiate the Union's doctrines. It was difficult for him to accept Daniel's challenges to what he was teaching, even though Daniel was being very considerate with him. He was reminded that, with the change in government, there was no longer control over how they practiced their faith or what they taught and believed.

Deep down, Petrica was intimidated by Daniel, since he, himself, had no theological training. He greatly desired the opportunity of being able to have training, but did not see how this would happen any time soon. He could do nothing but teach the traditions he had learned and preach the Scriptures according to what he thought they meant.

The Baptist Union was receiving much aid from America and other Western European countries, but the money was being focused on Bucharest and other major cities, particularly in the region known as Transylvania. The southern region of Romania was receiving no more emphasis in spreading the Gospel than before the revolution. It didn't seem like there was much hope in the near future of receiving any help through the Union.

When Daniel made his decision to turn his back on American citizenship, return home to marry Veronica, and fulfill his commitment to the Lord, he was taking a big step of faith. He knew his country well and had no allusions that it would be easy to reach a very disinterested and ignored people with the Gospel. Because of the long history of Orthodox culture and the distain for anyone who challenged that culture, he knew that it would be an uphill battle. But he was prepared, and he was committed to trust the Lord one step at a time to fulfill his dreams with Veronica.

Those dreams included completing their home, establishing a successful flooring business, raising a large family, and establishing a church in his village.

Indeed, this would be a happy and God-honoring beginning for two lives committed to fulfilling God's plan for their lives. BUT their dreams turned to reality when an American missionary couple who committed themselves, in their middle age, to follow God's plan for their lives working with Romanian nationals, establishing a Bible institute, and a church planting ministry.

ESCAPE FROM THE MUNDANE

CHAPTER 1 MISSIONARY ON THE MOVE

Down in south-western Romania, things were going along in a rather "mundane" manner for Daniel and Veronica when, one day in August, Pastor Petrica approached Daniel and told him that a missionary from America was coming to their part of the country for a short visit. The Benneys, Wesley and his wife, Elizabeth, were making a survey trip to see the country. This was the first trip for Elizabeth. Wesley had made a trip to Bucharest a year earlier.

As Daniel and Wesley would soon realize, they had made eye contact on that first trip, when Daniel returned to Romania following his "Escape from Terror". Daniel's flight had terminated in Timisoara in Southwestern Romania, while Wesley's continued to Bucharest.

Wesley Benney, a former C.P.A. and Financial Controller, who had also received theological education, had walked away from a lucrative career to be ordained to preach and answer God's call to foreign missions. He was living in Atlanta, Georgia at the time. Not knowing where his family would go, Wesley and Elizabeth visited the headquarters of the mission board they had selected to help them. The mission board asked them to consider Romania, now that the borders were open to foreigners. They had learned that Baptist missionaries were being allowed into the country. This trip was Wesley's first exposure to the country and a necessary first step for him to confirm Romania as the Lord's choice. This was a big step for a man approaching 50 years of age.

Wesley did not know a word of the Romanian language, and had booked the flight without attempting to make any arrangements to be met at the airport. He was assured by mission board personnel that many people spoke English and that he would have no problem making contact with a Romanian Baptist pastor. All he would have to do was ask at the airport for assistance in making a contact. They could have not been more incorrect in their counsel!

Wesley was in for the trip of his life. He was surprised at the condition of the Romanian airplane. It appeared that the plane had not even been cleaned from the previous flight. It was a hint of the conditions he would find in the country.

Having landed in Timisoara first to de-plane the passengers not continuing on to Bucharest, including Daniel, the plane was refueled and began to taxi down the runway. Looking out his window, Wesley could now see the terminal building. It was very old and in disrepair. Then, he noticed a dozen Russian Migs. "I wonder why these Migs are parked here? I thought that the collapse of the Russian empire meant no collaboration with Russia." He felt a little uncomfortable. "Certainly, I was safe in coming at this time, wasn't I?"

The flight to Bucharest was short. Having flown approximately 400,000 miles during his business career, Wesley thought he had seen everything. Well, he hadn't! As the plane taxied toward the terminal building, he was shocked at the condition of the building. There were no ramps, so the passengers deplaned and walked across the tarmac to the terminal. There were military personnel with machine guns standing on either side of the path. The whole situation looked ominous.

As he walked inside Wesley noticed the filth of the floors, walls, and windows. Some of the florescent fixtures were partially hanging, and many of the bulbs were burned out. He never imagined that conditions could be so bad, even in a communist country. This certainly reflected how bankrupt the communist system was. He might have expected this in a third world African country, but not Eastern Europe. "How embarrassing this must be to the Romanians who have visited other countries."

Wesley walked up the stairs to the passport processing center. The passport personnel were in military uniforms with rifles over their shoulders. He thought, "Who are they trying to impress? If they got one look at Chicago's airport terminal and personnel, they wouldn't be so smug. They would probably want to crawl into a hole. I bet they don't know any better than I did, how backward Romania is." Wesley stepped up to the window and handed his passport to the officer, who scowled at him and asked why he came to Romania. When he responded that he came to visit Baptist pastors, he received a glare. He wasn't exactly expecting the traditional hug and kiss on the cheek, but he had expected a little more than he got.

After retrieving his passport with the appropriate stamps, he stepped into the next room to wait for his luggage. The turnstile that brought the luggage from below was in awful condition and very noisy. Finally, he got his two large pieces of luggage and stepped in line for Customs. When it was his turn, a short, stout woman with a cranky disposition said in English, "Open!" Wesley opened the first suitcase. The exposed half contained hardcover Romanian Bibles. The inspector said angrily, "What is this?"

"Bibles to give to Christians I expect to meet." Inwardly, he was thinking, "With the word Biblia clearly stamped on the outside, what do you think they are?"

She was quiet. "Close it," she said, and nodded to the other suitcase. She saw more Bibles and repeated, "Close it." After carefully inspecting the carry-on baggage, though missing the hidden pouch with $5,000 in American money, she waved him on.

Because of her surprise and perceived anger, she didn't ask to see behind the dividers in either suitcase. Had she done so, she would have seen nylons, shavers and blades, shaving cream, toothbrushes, toothpaste, and other items that were suggested as gifts for the pastors and wives he would meet. Obviously, God had protected him because he was told later that these items would have undoubtedly been confiscated.

He stepped out into a large waiting room with dozens of Romanians waiting for family members. At that point Wesley thought, "What in the world am I doing? I must be an idiot! I came to a non-English-speaking country like this without even planning for someone to meet me." Where were all the English-speaking people he was told he would meet? All he heard was Romanian. He was about to have a panic attack when he looked across the room and saw a short, stout man holding a sheet of paper with the name "Bannay" on it. Wesley's last name was Benney. This was awfully close. Could it be that someone was told he was coming? Certainly God knew! Was it possible that He arranged a great blessing?

Wesley walked toward the man who blurted out the name as written. Wesley responded by pronouncing his name correctly, and the man said, "Chat-tan-ooga, Tenn-es-see." Wesley thought, "That is where our mission board headquarters are located. Someone must have notified this man that I was coming, but who, and who is this man?" The man reached out and gave a hardy handshake. He then grabbed the large suitcases with a broad smile, charged out the door like he had precious cargo and headed for the parking lot with Wesley following with his carry-on, praising God all the way. He almost said out loud, "Lord, I don't know who this man is. He seems to know who I am, and I guess that is all that counts."

While Daniel was still on the train from Timisoara to his parent's home, Wesley was being whisked through the center of Bucharest with his mysterious "Angel of Mercy". As they drove past the Olympia Hotel, the driver took his hands from the wheel for a moment, gesturing as if he was shooting a machine gun, and pointed to the buildings all around them. Wesley observed bullet holes in all of the buildings on both sides of the street. A large building across from the Olympia hotel was burned out, and there were other signs of the recent revolution. He learned later that it had been a book publishing company. Wesley was thrilled at the realization of what had taken place just a few months ago, and he was experiencing the aftermath firsthand. From what he had seen thus far, there was obviously a long way to go.

After a half-hour drive, the man pulled into a parking lot in front of a multi-story apartment building. He and Wesley took a very small, cramped elevator to the correct floor. They stepped out of the elevator, and immediately the man opened his apartment. No one was there. Wesley was led into what appeared to be a combined dining-living room. The man put the luggage on the floor and pointed to the bathroom which Wesley desperately needed.

When finished, the man beckoned for Wesley to sit on the sofa. The man grabbed a pillow, puffed it up, took Wesley's shoes off, and laid him back on the sofa, making a gesture of sleeping. Thoroughly exhausted, Wesley willingly accepted the opportunity to sleep. The man put a blanket over him, turned out the light, and closed the door. Wesley was in the process of thanking the Lord again for His provision when he fell asleep.

He woke up a couple hours later, hearing sounds in the hallway. The door opened and twin teenage girls, as cute as bugs' ears, entered the room. They had learned some English, and between that and a lot of sign language, Wesley learned that their brother was a student at the Christian college in Chattanooga. When a mission board director mentioned in his church that a future missionary to Romania was making a trip to Romania, the brother, named Daniel, called his pastor in Bucharest and asked that his father pick Wesley up and let him stay in their home. He also had asked the pastor to introduce Wesley to the few Baptist pastors in the city, take him to their church services, and give him opportunities to preach.

Sometime later their mother entered the apartment, having just returned from her job as a nurse in a local hospital. Her second language was French which was of no help. As humorous as it was, the daughters translated for them. It was about as close to a "blind leading the blind" situation as was possible.

An hour later, Pastor Nicu arrived, and Wesley was pleased to find out that he spoke English fairly well. He reviewed the plans for the next seven days, which included having Wesley visiting the largest Baptist Union church in Bucharest and four other smaller churches in outlying areas. Wesley would preach in four of them and give a word of greeting in the other. He would learn that "a word of greeting" was the equivalent of a short message. Pastor Nicu would translate for him in these services. For someone who had stepped out in blind faith, Wesley was headed for an exciting week. He would even celebrate his 48th birthday during his visit.

While Wesley had been napping and making new friends, Daniel was approaching his destination: Veronica!

A couple days later, another missionary from Wesley's mission board arrived in Bucharest. He had been a missionary in an African French-speaking country and had to leave because his wife suffered from malaria. Since there was no chance of a return because of her susceptibility to a recurrence, he had been advised to seek another field of service. He was surveying the possibility of ministry in Romania, since the French and Romanian languages were both Latin-based (along with Spanish, Portuguese, and Italian, which happens to be closest to Romanian). Ben considered that he could learn the Romanian language quickly if this was where the Lord would have him go.

Now, what was the purpose of the $5,000 that Wesley had hidden in a secret pouch in his carry-on luggage? Trusting Wesley's corporate background as a CPA, the mission board asked him to attempt to purchase a piece of land in or near Bucharest, where a future Eastern European center could be established. There was a great level of naiveté in those days regarding the level of progress made by Romania to become compatible with Western Europe. It was assumed that property could be purchased like in Western European countries.

Therefore, Wesley's visit was more than just a survey trip. Ben's trip was more than a survey trip too! Because French was the second language of educated Romanians, Ben would be able to translate for Wesley if a hearing could be obtained with a proper government agency. Pastor Nicu advised that a meeting be sought with the Department of Commerce. With only a few days in the country, it was doubtful that such a meeting could be scheduled on such short notice. But with God, anything is possible!

Pastor Nicu took Wesley and Ben to the Department of Commerce. After explaining to the receptionist why they were there, they were asked to have a seat. To their shock, they were ushered a few minutes later into the office of the Director of the Department. Wesley felt a little intimidated to be in the presence of such a high government official. "Well, Lord. You got us here. Help us to accomplish our purpose!" They began their visit with a glass of Coke and a typical cup of espresso.

It seemed that the Director was as awed to be meeting with Americans as Wesley and Ben were to be in his presence. He was obviously pleased that he had Coke to serve to the Americans because he made special note of it.

Ben explained why they were there. After several minutes, they learned that the purchase of land was not possible for foreigners unless a proper organization could be formed with the government. Of course, such a process would take quite some time, and with the many changes being made after the revolution, the Director was not exactly sure at that time just what the procedures would be.

Learning that Wesley had held a significant corporate position in America, he had several questions regarding how business was conducted there. It was a very satisfying meeting, but the $5,000 would be returning home with Wesley.

Preaching in the church services was a thrill! Wesley had carefully planned a couple messages. He was careful, as warned, to make sure his sentences were short and that he did not use big words or technical terms that might not be understood or easy to translate. The people were so friendly. It seemed that everyone wanted to shake his hand. He certainly was made to feel welcome. It was clear that the people were awed to be in the presence of an American!

Wesley was struggling with two emotions. He was proud to be an American but at the same time ashamed of his feeling of superiority as an American. This was an emotion that he would struggle with in the future.

Wesley's trip quickly drew to a close. The condition of the city and the living conditions of the average city dweller appeared to be very bleak. There were open manholes in the streets and potholes almost big enough to swallow a small Romanian car. The main avenue leading to Ceausescu's unfinished 1,000-room palace was lined with dozens of massive multi-storied apartment buildings in various stages of completion, but only a handful appeared to be finished and inhabited.

These conditions weighed heavily on his heart. But his heart was even heavier when he considered the lost condition of millions who had never heard a clear presentation of the Gospel. This trip was very instrumental in sealing Wesley's decision to choose Romania for ministry, but Elizabeth needed to see the country herself before a final decision could be made. He would take a camera full of memories for his family, church, and friends.

Assuming that Wesley was experiencing the Spirit's call to Romania, the next big question would be where to locate. Of course, this would be a key reason for a second survey trip with Elizabeth. After Wesley's trip through the Bucharest airport, he determined that the next flight would be into Budapest, Hungary, where they would drive down in a rental car. He had been informed by mission board personnel that the airport in Budapest was almost as modern as many airports in America. Had they flown into Bucharest, they would have heartily agreed with Wesley's decision to fly into Budapest on future flights.

CHAPTER 2 DESTINATION ROMANIA

Wesley returned home in a state of euphoria. He couldn't wait to share his experiences with Elizabeth, his children, pastor, and church. Elizabeth met Wesley at the airport, and he talked non-stop all the way home. The pictures were worth a thousand words, especially the ones showing bullet holes where fighting took place in Bucharest.

The next Sunday Wesley was given the opportunity to share his trip with the congregation. The church was excited and already had the Benneys going to Romania before Wesley and Elizabeth had even met with the mission board personnel. Elizabeth shared Wesley's excitement, and based on her faith in God and trust in Wesley's judgment, also assumed Romania would be their destination. The planned future survey trip would not be for the purpose of determining whether or not Romania was their destination, but where to locate within the country.

A few days later, Wesley and Elizabeth drove to Chattanooga to meet with the mission board president, Dr. Roberts, and European Director, Dr. Hall, to report on the trip and return the $5,000. The men were intrigued with every aspect of the report and were excited about the Benneys' confirmation to go to Romania. Another middle-aged couple, the Humphries, were also on deputation for Romania and were raising support as fast as the Benneys. They too needed to determine where to locate because they had not yet made a survey trip.

Dr. Hall had recently returned from a trip to Timisoara in the western part of the country where the Romanian revolution had begun on the steps of the Orthodox Cathedral. Since the Baptist Union had full authority over who could do Baptist ministry in Romania, Dr. Hall had scheduled to meet with Pastor Gigi, who held a leadership position in the Baptist Union over the Baptist churches in the south-western region of the country. He was from the city of Lugoj 50 miles to the east.

Dr. Hall explained that the mission board had two couples well on their way to raising support to go to Romania and had to determine where to live. Pastor Gigi told him that when the missionary candidates were ready for a trip, arrangements would be made for them to preach in several villages in his region of the country.

As Dr. Hall shared his plan to acquire property in Bucharest for an evangelistic center, Pastor Gigi convinced him to consider his city. Lugoj was on the only route from western Romania to Bucharest and was one of only two major routes bringing goods into Romania from Western Europe. Timisoara was the most westernized major city in Romania, having been part of the Austrian-Hungarian Empire, and thus would be most comfortable for mission board personnel that might inhabit the planned evangelistic center. Timisoara was one of only a couple major cities that had an airport capable of handling international flights, though the best connections from America to western Romania were still to fly into Budapest and drive over the border.

It was decided that a trip would be planned for the Benneys and Humphreys to meet in Lugoj. At the same time, Dr. Roberts and Dr. Hall would meet further with Pastor Gigi and Pastor Tildi, the President of the Comunitate. This meeting would be to give serious consideration to establishing the new evangelistic center in Lugoj or Timisoara. And if a decision was made to establish the center in this part of the country, it would be logical for the Benneys and Humphries to consider this part of the country for ministry as well.

Pastor Tildi had scheduled the Humphreys to spend their entire time with Pastor Gigi preaching in Pastor Gigi's church and others in the area. The Benneys would drive to Moldova Noua and spend a few days with Pastor Dolphi to preach in some of his ten churches. Then they would travel back to Lugoj to meet someone who would lead them on the three-hour drive to Orsova to spend time with Pastor Petrica to preach in some or all of his five churches.

A couple weeks before the scheduled arrival of the Benneys and Humphreys, Pastors Dolphi and Petrica were informed that they would be hosting a missionary couple making a survey trip. Since neither of the pastors knew much English, it was of particular importance to enlist someone to translate for Wesley as he preached in the various churches.

Pastor Petrica immediately met with Daniel and told him the good news. Of course, he wanted the missionary to preach in his five churches.

"Oh, it sounds like you have already volunteered me to be the translator, and I suppose you want me to transport others to the meetings in my van?"

"Well, something like that. I knew you would jump at the chance."

"I sure will. I will be delighted. We must make a good impression! Wouldn't it be incredible if they would decide to come to our region of the country?"

It was decided that Daniel would take the train to Lugoj to get the missionaries after they concluded their visit with Pastor Dolphi.

There was a buzz of excitement in the little church and in Daniel's family. Daniel told Veronica and his family that they needed to pray that the Benneys would come to work with them. Thus far, no missionaries had been steered by the Baptist Union into their region of the country.

At this point, visiting pastors and missionaries had been directed to Transylvania, the northwestern part of the country. This was also the region of the country where the vast majority of the Baptist Union churches were located. Most of them were very small, many meeting in homes.

As great as the needs were in the north to maximize the effectiveness of the many churches, there was a need of a different kind in Daniel's region. His village was on the western border of Oltenie, representing about 20% of the country's land mass extending eastward almost to Bucharest and south to Bulgaria. About 35 kilometers to the east of Orsova, was Turnu – Severin, a major city of 115,000.

Since the Baptist Union had showed little interest in Oltenie under the Communist Regime, this was uncharted territory as far as the Gospel was concerned. Daniel had come to realize that he was quite limited in evangelizing his area. He did not have resources that missionaries would have, and he felt uncomfortable with his minimal Bible training. So, when it was announced missionaries were to visit their area, his excitement was understandable.

The reason that Transylvania had been much more evangelized was that it had been part of the Austrian- Hungarian Empire of the 19th Century. As a result, the people identified with western culture in economics, arts, and education, and had experienced a greater economy before the communist era. The people in this area had resisted the philosophies inherent in Communism to the extent that they dared.

They more quickly adapted to the freedoms that resulted from the revolution, and with their connections with the West, had access to western goods shortly thereafter. It was truly much easier for foreigners to live there because of the overall conditions. This would be borne out by the fact that the majority of missionaries of all denominations settled in this region of the country in the ensuing years.

When the time arrived for the trip to Romania, Wesley purchased tickets that took them through Amsterdam and on to Budapest. Indeed, the condition of the airport in Budapest was quite impressive - as good as many airports in America. A car was rented, and a map obtained. The Benneys were headed south for a three-hour drive to the border with Romania.

When approaching the border, they came to a halt behind a line of cars. They could not even see the barricade and processing center, so they suspected that they were in for a long wait. Both sides of the road were greatly covered with every type of trash imaginable. Apparently, as people would wait to cross the border, they would throw their trash out the car windows. After a couple hours, the Benneys reached the Hungarian check point. The process was fairly quick, so it was obvious that the holdup was on the Romanian side. The thousand feet or so between two border barricades was lined with cars, bumper to bumper. An hour after receiving the Hungarian passport stamps, they arrived at the Romanian crossing.

The agents were obviously intrigued with American passports and the rental car. They had incessant questions about where they were coming from and why they were coming into Romania. Their luggage was inspected. After receiving the proper stamps, they were cleared to continue on their way.

The Bennys immediately observed the same level of trash on the other side of the road where there was a similar long line of people leaving Romania. Road conditions also changed because the road was in terrible disrepair with frequent potholes of various sizes. What a difference! And it was that way the entire trip, with only slightly better conditions within the city limits of Arad and Timisoara. They were stopped several times along the way by the police in the cities and villages. Their late-model foreign car served as a magnet. Being Americans created interest for the police while they carefully studied the passports.

Finally, Wesley and Elizabeth arrived in Lugoj and found Gigi's home. After spending time with him and his wife over a meal, it was determined that the Benneys needed to turn in for the night. They were exhausted after traveling for 23 hours without sleep and needed to be well rested for their morning trip to Moldova Noua and meeting with Pastor Dolphi.

There were two routes that would take the Benneys to Moldova Noua. They decided to take one route on the way and the other route for the return trip so they would get more exposure to the countryside.

They arrived without incident to a great welcome. Dolphi and his wife were gracious hosts. Though Dolphi's English was not sufficient for translating, it was quite adequate for general conversation. Dolphi had ten churches and planned for Wesley to preach in five of them during their stay. His nephew had learned English well enough to translate.

Between services, Wesley was filming life in the villages with his video camera. For sure, he was capturing life totally unlike anything in America. There were the animals crossing the roads, horse-drawn wagons, and equipment used for farming that had not been part of farming in America for many decades.

Of particular interest was the fact all the villages the Benneys visited had dirt/gravel roads, no running water, and no sewer systems. Every home had an outhouse and a well or shared well. In addition, a large percentage had no telephone lines to their homes, though most could not have afforded a phone, even if available. Minimal electricity existed. Many homes had only one or two light bulbs hanging from cords, and the majority had no electrical appliances.

Most assuredly, the videos would be of specific interest to Timothy and Ellen, who would be accompanying Wesley and Elizabeth for a period of time.

Three days later, they were on their alternate route to Lugoj, through the foothills of the Carpathian Mountains. Were they in for a surprise!

Daniel left early that same morning on the train to Lugoj, and the train had to go through the foothills as well. When he got to Lugoj, he met with Pastor Gigi, Drs. Roberts and Hall, as well as the Humphries. They explained to Daniel that the Benneys were expected to arrive soon. Daniel paused for a moment and exclaimed, "Aren't they from Atlanta, Georgia?"

Drs. Roberts and Hall both responded in chorus, "Why yes, but how do you know that?"

"Well, that is a long story!"

"Since the Benneys aren't here yet, we would be interested in hearing it."

Daniel shared how he had escaped to America, given up his dream of American citizenship, and returned to Romania for his bride and an opportunity to help reach his people with the Gospel. Needless to say, everyone was shocked and impressed that Daniel had returned to Romania after having enjoyed the good life in American and the opportunity for citizenship. He mentioned the support he was receiving from the Romanian Baptist church in Chicago and the Romanian Baptist church in Atlanta, Georgia. While there, the pastor of the church had mentioned that a missionary by the name of Wesley Benney had shared his ministry plans in the church a few weeks before Daniel's visit.

Dr. Hall exclaimed, "Indeed, the Christian world is a small one!"

Ted said, "Maybe Daniel's area of the country is where we should go."

His wife Caroline responded, "It looks like Wesley and Elizabeth have first dibs since they have been scheduled there. Maybe the Lord wants us here to work with Pastor Gigi." Of course, he readily agreed with her assessment, and everyone had a chuckle over the direction of the conversation.

Gigi became concerned that the Benneys had not arrived yet. They should have been back a couple hours earlier. The trip wasn't that long, and the roads were actually quite good by Romanian standards. Pastor Gigi managed to get a call through to Pastor Dolphi. He confirmed that the Benneys had left in plenty of time to have arrived in Lugoj a couple hours earlier.

The anxiety abated when they heard the slam of car doors. They were here. As Pastor Gigi ushered them into the walled courtyard, Daniel looked at Wesley with a perplexing gaze and asked, "Have we met before?"

"How could we?"

After a long pause as each studied the other, they exclaimed almost in unison, "You were on the plane from Chicago to Romania a year ago!"

With a hardy handshake, Wesley said, "Wow, that is incredible!"

Dr. Hall responded, "Wow, indeed! What did I just say a few minutes ago about the Christian world being small?"

Daniel and Wesley were both thinking, "How could this not be a sign from the Lord?"

Once they got past that initial greeting process with Pastor Gigi, his wife, the Humphries, Daniel, and Drs. Roberts and Hall, the Benneys were asked why it had taken them so long to get to Lugoj. "You won't believe the story we have to tell!"

Not being a man of a few words, Wesley began to tell their story:

"We had been driving along, enjoying the sunny mountain scenery. As we crested a hill, nestled down in the valley, the city of Resita came into view. Thinking it to be a picturesque sight, I pulled the car over to take a quick video of the entire scene. At the moment I was doing that, we heard the screeching of tires and looked up. A man in plain clothes approached us with an air of authority. He said gruffly, "Pasaporti"! I handed him our passports and the man motioned for us to follow him."

"Needless to say, we were becoming a little concerned. What was wrong? We followed the man to a military base near the city. As we followed, I suggested that perhaps the man was concerned that I was taking a video. I told Elizabeth to put the tape in her purse and put a new tape in the recorder. We had nearly two hours of captured memories, and we didn't want to lose them."

"The man beckoned us to follow him. He spoke no English. Once inside the compound, there was a hustle and bustle of others coming in and perusing us as rapid discussion was taking place. We couldn't understand a word, except "espionage". What was going on? We were led to a basement room with no windows."

"Finally, a uniformed officer entered the room, trying to speak with what little English he knew. We didn't understand what he was saying, but he kept pointing to the camera. We decided that it was definitely the camera they were concerned about, so I handed it to him. He immediately looked in it and became agitated. It was obvious he understood the operation of the camera and knew there was a blank tape in it."

"We were not about to give up our two hours of memories without a fight. Elizabeth blurted out crying, 'They are just a bunch of Communists!' I responded, don't say that! It is a good thing they don't know English. The man left the room, frustrated."

"After some time, the man returned with another uniformed officer, who politely introduced himself in fairly good English. He explained there was an empty tape in the camera and there had to be another since we were seen videotaping the city. Elizabeth was still crying, and the man kept saying, 'Don't cry. Everything will be ok.'"

"I explained that everything was not ok! Yes, there was another tape containing two hours of memories, and we didn't want to lose it. I explained that we were planning to move to Romania in the future as missionaries, and we made this trip to get familiar with the country. We had been videotaping life in Romania to show our children and friends in America."

"Elizabeth gave up the tape and the man put it in the camera to review. Soon he was smiling and laughing at the things on the tape because they reflected some of the humorous things observed in Romania, like geese charging the car with their wings outspread and squawking, and sheep totally blocking the roadway as they slowly walked across."

"I noted that there was obviously nothing on the tape that should be of interest to Romanians. Why were we stopped, and why did we hear the word "espionage"?

"The man apologized and explained that Resita was the city where Romania had been trying to develop nuclear capabilities before the collapse of the regime. There is still sensitivity when foreigners pass through the city, especially taking pictures."

"Elizabeth, still angry, blurted out, 'have you ever heard of Desert Storm?' The man smiled and nodded his acknowledgment."

"What would Romania have militarily that America would want?"

"He laughed and said, 'You have a point! You are free to go, but we must keep the tape. Even though there is nothing on the tape of concern, the authorities above us will want to review it to their satisfaction. I am sorry.'"

"At that, we left, and continued our trip here more upset over the loss of the tape than the incident itself. We realize that we have an incredible story to share with our family and supporting churches when we get home, but without those two hours of videoed experiences."

Everyone listened to the story in amazement and Pastor Gigi asked, "Are you still planning to come to Romania?"

"Well, God protected us in Resita. I guess He can take care of us anywhere else in the future. We will trust Him. Yes, we are coming to Romania, though the exact location is yet to be determined!"

Following a short meal and some serious conversation with the Humphries, Wesley and Elizabeth got into their rental car with Daniel and started for his home. They stopped several times along the way for a view of the scenery in the mountains and, yes, more videos were taken. The entire trip they talked of Daniel's escape, trip to America, and decision to forego American citizenship to reach his people. Of particular interest was the fact that Wesley and Elizabeth both grew up in the suburbs of Chicago, and Wesley had graduated from high school in the suburbs where Daniel helped install floors.

Several times during the trip Wesley and Daniel revisited how incredible it was that they had met on the plane a year before and had been only a few miles apart when Daniel had been in Atlanta.

"Perhaps God is trying to tell you to come here when you come to Romania."

"We will see!"

By late afternoon, they arrived at Daniel's house to meet Veronica and his family. The first opportunity for privacy came when Wesley and Elizabeth went to the outdoor privy behind the house. They exchanged their thoughts regarding Daniel, and both agreed they should seriously consider this region of the country, especially since Daniel had told them there were only a couple of evangelical churches of any denomination in the entire region to the east of their village. They had determined that they wanted to work primarily where the Gospel had seldom or never been preached. This location certainly fit that description.

Meeting on the plane a year ago seemed to be more than a coincidence. They both acknowledged that Daniel's knowledge of English and the culture would make him a strong asset in ministry, and it would be a joy to work with someone of such strong Christian character. Daniel would make an obvious candidate for a potential pastor once a church was planted.

They were taken to meet Pastor Petrica. Daniel translated as the pastor explained his schedule of preaching. Wesley was to preach in his five churches during the next three days, the first that very evening in his largest church, Toplet, where Daniel and Veronica were members. Of course, Wesley and Elizabeth would stay with Daniel and Veronica.

After a quick meal, they headed for the packed church. Villagers had heard Americans were coming to preach, and that was enough to get all the members out, as well as many villagers who would otherwise never have considered being seen dead or alive in the church of the Repenters.

Wesley preached a solid evangelistic message with Daniel's excellent translation. Using a translator essentially doubles the length of a message, but time was not an issue with the people. This was one of the things Wesley would come to appreciate. The Romanians were not held hostage by time as Americans are. In addition, the Christians considered it a privilege to hear a message from an American, so again, time was not a prohibition.

John and Ioana invited Wesley and Elizabeth, along with Daniel's family, to their home for coffee and a pastry. They had a good time of fellowship. It was extra special for Daniel and Veronica since John and Ioana were their best friends. They felt like royalty having Americans in their home. Secretly, they were relishing the fact that everyone else in the village looked on with envy.

Because of the lack of a language barrier with Daniel, Wesley and Elizabeth were soaking up volumes of information regarding Romanian culture, both before and after the revolution. Daniel kept forgetting to translate his discussions with Wesley and Elizabeth for the others. Veronica was frustrated that she was missing out on so much of the discussion.

Wesley was busy capturing life in Romania again with his video camera to share with churches and family, since his original tape had been confiscated. The conditions he videotaped were so normal in Romania that the people thought it strange these things were of such interest to Wesley and Elizabeth. They didn't realize what was so normal in Romania was virtually non-existent in America.

After three days passed, Wesley and Elizabeth said their goodbyes and headed for the border crossing near Arad, where they had originally entered. The time necessary to cross the border was about the same as when they entered. The intensive questioning and inspection of luggage by the Romanian agents was the same. Once over the border, there was a sense of relief as they made the quick trip to the airport.

All things considered, from what was observed on this short trip, Hungary was much ahead of Romania. Hungarian roads were excellent in comparison. The size and condition of the houses and the cleanliness of the yards was most evident in Hungary. Farm animals were frequently seen in the front yards of most homes in Romania; however, this was not seen at all on the way to and from the airport in Hungary.

Wesley filled the car in modern gas stations carrying many food items and even a few American products. Many modern stores and shopping centers were seen along the way. Most exciting to see were a couple American fast-food chains already in the country.

Wesley and Elizabeth jokingly mused that perhaps Hungary was really where the Lord was calling them. But they would learn later that the language was horrific in comparison to the Romanian language. Some linguists claimed that Hungarian was the most difficult language to master, even more difficult than Chinese. With the difficulty they would have in learning Romanian, the Benneys were thankful that God had not called them to Hungary, even if life would have been much more comfortable.

After the Benney's left, Daniel and Veronica prayed earnestly for them to return and work in their region. Daniel said that, next to his decision to return to Romania, he never felt as sure of anything as he did about their return. There were too many coincidences and positive things causing them not to believe that God intended to bring them back.

Pastor Petrica and his churches were also seriously praying for the Benney's return to their region. He was hoping for Wesley's help in preaching and knew financial help usually accompanied the missionaries. Wherever missionaries located, there was usually a flow of visiting pastors and other representatives from supporting churches. It was hard for Americans and Western Europeans to be exposed to the poverty of the area and not leave money as they departed. The exchange rate of the Romanian currency against the dollar continued to be extremely beneficial to the recipients of dollars.

At the time of the Benney's visit, $50 represented a good monthly salary for a Romanian worker. So, what might seem to be a modest gift to the foreigners would represent a great benefit to the recipient. A $600 gift would not be considered a large sum by Americans, but it would represent approximately one year of wages for a Romanian. Even the godliest preacher struggled with his genuine motives for requesting help from missionaries.

Life was soon back to normal for Daniel as he worked to finish the construction of his new home. He needed to finish as much of the house as possible so he would be ready to put down wood flooring and begin his business when the shipment of flooring equipment arrived from America. Without the equipment, he could not really begin his business.

He was thankful for the support he was receiving from the two churches in America because his savings were being quickly exhausted in constructing the addition to his parent's house. Even with the very favorable exchange rate of the dollar against the lei, it was simply taking more money than he had expected. Of course, the difficulty finding building materials also took much longer to complete the work.

By October, Daniel had the walls and roof of his home addition built with the windows and doors in. His equipment had arrived in Constanta. After an eight-hour drive, he found that he would have to pay "extra" fees to get it released. But had he not paid these "extra" fees, it could have meant weeks of waiting. Such a period of time would also allow for the possibility of the equipment "accidentally" disappearing.

Unfortunately, the revolution had not improved the way business was conducted in Romania, nor the corruption and theft that was so prevalent. If one wanted things to happen when they were supposed to happen, money had to be paid. Many called it a bribe; Daniel called it good business if one could afford it. He defined a bribe as something paid to have something illegal done. Getting equipment that he paid for was legal, and thus he had to do what was necessary to get what was already his.

Daniel worked day and night to complete the interior of his addition before winter. He determined that he would get only the bedroom, kitchen, and eating area completed. Since he built his house against the outside wall of this parents' living room, he installed a door in place of the window from his home into the living room of his parents' house. He and Veronica would share this room with his parents until spring, when he could finish his own living room and the other bedroom for the children they hoped to have in the near future.

By the end of November, he had completed the interior of the three rooms, and it was just in time when the temperatures took a real drop. His parents could not get over how beautiful his wood floors were. He promised to put a new wood floor in their living room, too, but that project would become secondary to working on paying jobs.

With the Christmas holiday coming soon, Daniel was not able to get any floor contracts, so he went out and cut wood with the government forestry department. The pay was not very good, but he had opportunity to buy wood at a reduced price, and he was able to share the Gospel. He thanked God for the work. Veronica had her job, so they were quite comfortable with the day-to-day expenses, even with the ever-increasing prices.

CHAPTER 3 DESTINATION ORSOVA

Back in Atlanta, Georgia, Wesley and Elizabeth were busy with scheduled meetings to raise the remainder of their needed support and praying much about where to locate their ministry.

They had a couple options. The first was to move into a major city in Transylvania, rent an apartment, study the language for a year or more, and use that time to seek where the Lord would have them go. With better living conditions, it would be easier for them to assimilate into the culture.

The second option was to jump right into ministry with a translator while learning the language. They were both approaching 50 years of age and felt an urgency to begin ministry as soon as possible, even if on a part-time basis.

They chose the second option. Specifically, they decided on going to Orsova near Daniel's village. They weighed the circumstances of their trip to Romania for indications of the Lord's leading.

The following circumstances led them to their decision:

-They wanted to minister in a place not being reached. Orsova was right on the border of Oltenie, which had hardly received any evangelistic effort by the Baptist Union after one hundred years of Baptist presence in the country.

-Transylvania already had the luxury of several hundred little Baptist churches, and the present lion's share of visiting pastors, missionaries, and financial aid.

-Daniel, who was familiar with life in America and had a mastery of the English language, would make a great translator, co-worker, language instructor, friend, and potential national pastor.

-As a Romanian, Daniel would be able to help the Benneys with the culture and the language.

-Wesley and Elizabeth were greatly impressed with Veronica's spiritual maturity. She would be a real help to Elizabeth since she was rapidly learning English from her husband.

-Wesley and Elizabeth were impressed with the fact that Daniel was willing to give up American citizenship to return and help reach his own people with the Gospel. This was an incredible sign of spiritual maturity that would probably be hard to find elsewhere in Romania.

-Wesley couldn't get over the fact he had met Daniel with a nod and a smile on the plane to Bucharest. Somehow, that seemed like a sign from the Lord. What were the chances of this happening without the Lord's orchestration?

With approval from their sending church and mission board, the Benneys were going to Orsova! They were excited to tell their family, church, and friends of their decision.

They would be bringing their oldest son, Timothy, and their youngest daughter, Ellen, with them. Timothy had graduated from high school and was working for a cleaning company. Wesley and Elizabeth thought that coming to Romania for a year or so would be a great experience for him and would make it easier for him to accept his parents' departure to Romania.

Ellen had just finished her 8th grade in the Christian school operated by the Benneys' sending church. The plan was for her to complete the first three years of high school using a well-known home school video system and then return home to complete her final year and graduate with her friends.

Their youngest son, Stephen, would like to have gone as well, but he was enrolled in Bible College, and though the departures of his parents, brother, and sister were fraught with many tears, he was ready to get on with his education and preparation for life.

Kristin, the oldest, had graduated from Bible College, married and had a daughter. She and her husband accepted the departure of her parents with a level of pride that her parents had not put career and corporate gain in front of following the Lord's leading in their lives.

Wesley quickly wrote a letter to Daniel and Vera. He asked for a return letter so they would know if the letter with good news had arrived. Wesley let Daniel know the reasons for their decision as an encouragement to them.

Ted and Caroline Humphrey were also doing well in their deputation, having been successful in pastoral ministry for many years. They had determined to go to Lugoj to work with Gigi, and would be the mission board representatives at the property purchased by the mission board for the planned evangelistic center. They would be only about two and a half hours from the Benneys. Comfort from other Americans would be close by.

The Benneys had raised full support several months after their trip to Orsova. Preparation to leave required complete physical examinations. Truly, God showed His oversight by allowing the examination to uncover the necessity of surgery for Wesley's unknown physical need. This surgery could never have been safely accomplished in Romania.

Following a three-month delay, Wesley planned a trip to Romania about a month in advance of their planned departure to find a place to live. Having received and responded to Wesley's letter of decision, Daniel had already been researching options for him.

Wesley flew into Budapest again, rented a car, crossed the border, and headed for an exciting meeting with Daniel and Veronica. They talked well into the night because they had so much to share with each other on how the Lord was blessing in their lives and so excited with the anticipation of working together.

The next day they met with a woman Daniel knew. She had been an informant with the Securitate, having worked as the receptionist in the small hotel in Orsova. It was reputed that she no longer had any connection with them. According to Bucharest, the Securitate no longer existed, but, in fact, they were still in operation, as Wesley would learn soon after moving into the country. This woman, Tutrita, was of Serbian background and spoke Serbian, Romanian, Russian, Hungarian, German, French and English.

She knew a German family who had moved to Germany after the revolution, leaving their half of a duplex vacant. It was across the street from the Danube River on the main street into town and only a few hundred meters from the major route connecting the western part of the country to Bucharest. Tutrita felt this was the only option she found that an American would want. She knew the relatives of the owners and had obtained their phone number in Germany. Wesley contacted the owners through a missionary friend, who served as translator. A deal was struck, and all was set for the move.

The first floor included a living room, eat-in kitchen, toilet, and a large pantry. The upstairs had two bedrooms and a bathroom with a tub and hot water heater. There was enough room for the washer and dryer coming in the container. There was a door to a small balcony – sufficient for four lawn chairs.

The balcony overlooked the lake formed by the damming of the Danube River to create a hydroelectric power plant. Ceausescu and Yugoslavia's Tito had cooperated in accomplishing this major project. A second dam was built downstream near the border with Bulgaria. Between these two plants, most of the electrical needs of Romania were met.

The portion of the lake used by the Romanian Olympic Rowing Team was immediately across the street which would provide interesting viewing in the years ahead.

When the owners of the house fled to Germany after the borders opened, they left furniture behind that the Benneys chose to use. The key piece was a large king-sized bed with two straw mattresses greatly reflecting the sleeping positions of the previous owners. Anticipating having the mattresses rewoven with straw, Wesley and Elizabeth had not shipped a bed for themselves. The other important piece of furniture was a sofa in the living room that made into a three-quarter width bed. Two large armoires were also left behind. Closets were not built in most Romanian homes. There were two small furniture tables as well. The kitchen had a typical small refrigerator and wood-burning stove for cooking.

Tutrita told Wesley that his neighbor in the other half of the duplex had been the top Communist party boss in town prior to the collapse of Ceausescu's regime. Seeing what was done to Ceausescu and his wife, this man and his wife had hidden out at the local military base for 6 months. He had immediately received death threats when news of Ceausescu's fate was announced.

After President Iliescu came to power, this man was stripped of his position and forced into retirement. At that, he felt safe to return to his house.

Wesley said, "Well now, it will be an honor to live next to him. The Securitate will probably put listening devices in his walls or in the attic, common to both halves of the house. They will certainly get the Gospel if they do that."

Daniel was excited for Wesley and said, "I think this will be a great place to live. Your view of the mountain foothills, the lake, and the river will be stunning." By Romanian standards, it is a palatial place to live, though there were considerable repairs necessary. The idea of a palace stuck with Wesley.

The electricity would never handle the appliances Wesley would be shipping. All wiring was aluminum instead of copper so had much less resistance. There would be the threat of fires. Electricity through those wires during the Communist regime probably fueled no more than ceiling lights, lamps, the water heater, and refrigerator.

The living room floor was recessed, with the wood parquet having originally been placed directly over the gravel covered ground. Daniel said, "Replacing that floor is right up my alley. You leave me the keys, and I will have that floor finished by the time you return. I will take care of some of the other repairs too, like the one-inch crack in the upstairs hallway caused by a recent earthquake."

"I will have your neighbor's son, Mitruti, replace the aluminum wire with copper to handle the load of the appliances that are coming. Mitruti was the electrician I knew at the barge construction plant. He was helping with repairs on the gunboat when I crossed the Danube."

Wesley asked Daniel if he could also have the two mattresses refurbished with new straw and fabric. "Yes, of course. I know the people who do that work. They have been doing it for decades and really know what they are doing. I am sure that when they hear it is for Americans, they will do their very best."

All was set. At the end of the week, Wesley was on his way home with pictures of their new "palace". What would Elizabeth and their children think when they saw the pictures?

Daniel could never have imagined how the Lord would work in his life to bring about the answer to his prayer for helping to reach his people with the Gospel. Wesley and Elizabeth were old enough to be his parents, and he was impressed they would leave a life of financial comfort to live in Romania. It encouraged him regarding his own decision forsaking the comfort that would have been his by returning to Romania. Both of them had put the Gospel first.

Pastor Petrica and his churches were also praising God. Daniel reminded Wesley of the potential for wrong motives behind Pastor Petrica's interest in having him in their area. Often those wishing to justify their real motives maintained that the biblical book of Acts taught the sharing of wealth with those in foreign countries who were less fortunate. Because Western Christians were so well off, comparatively, it was only right that they should share what they have with the unfortunate in Romania. Some felt the Westerners actually owed this help to them.

Daniel and Wesley agreed they were not going to fall into the trap that comes with bringing aid. If people responded to the preaching of the Gospel, it would not be for material gain. After his arrival in Romania, Wesley would soon learn how right Daniel was with his warning. Indeed, his presence as an American was the real motive behind much of the excitement in attending his meetings. If aid wasn't the motive, being able to see, hear, and shake the hand of an American was powerful to people who had been totally barred from the West. Of course, those with false motives didn't come for very long.

Wesley would learn as time went by that many mission agencies and their missionaries would use aid as a "drawing card" for their ministry. Within a couple years, dozens of containers of every type of aid flowed into the country. Many new chapels or churches would be constructed with the money that followed the appearance of successful evangelism. Time would tell if the flurry of activity accompanying the initial influx of missionary activity would be permanent.

CHAPTER 4 DEPARTURE FOR ROMANIA

When Wesley arrived back to Georgia from his house hunting expedition, he showed the pictures he had taken of their "palace". Elizabeth couldn't understand why Wesley was so excited about their new home. It was in such disrepair.

"How can you call that a palace?" she asked, almost in tears.

"Don't you see the potential? When I am finished, with Daniel's help, it will be a palace by Romanian standards. It won't be by American standards, but this is Romania."

Up to this point, everything in the Benneys' life regarding ministry in Romania had been future and speculative: where, when, and how. This all changed. A date was set for departure, and the preparation became real. What was to be shipped, who would be the shipper, and when would the shipment be received? The answer to these questions would determine what would be taken on the plane to fulfill their needs until the arrival of the container.

Since the Humphries would soon be ready to leave as well, Wesley and Elizabeth began communicating with them regarding what they thought the needs would be for the first years of life in Romania, considering that little of value was available for purchase in the country.

Because electricity in Europe was 220 volts instead of 110 as in America, all appliances had to be purchased new. A major appliance manufacturer specializing in producing 220 electric appliances for shipment to Europe had everything they would need.

Wesley suggested that they share a 40 ft. container, since the cost was not significantly more than a 20 ft. container. They would save about 50 percent of what it would cost if each sent a 20 ft. container.

Since the Benneys would be leaving at least a month earlier than the Humphries, it was determined that the container shipment would be scheduled from Atlanta. The Humphries would send their goods from Tennessee to the staging area in Atlanta for the combined shipment. Pastor Gigi found a house for the Humphries to rent, and they accepted sight unseen, so all was set.

Until the Humphries arrived, their goods would be stored with the Benneys in the room designated as the future living room/bedroom. Ted's motorcycle would be stored with Wesley's in the little garage behind the house. Wesley purchased a large padlock for the iron gate protecting the back yard and garage. It was a brand manufactured and sold only in America, which hopefully, would make it very difficult to be compromised. Most of the cheaper popular brands sold in America were made in China, and the same brands were also sold in Romania; thus, there was the possibility of duplicate keys being available by people of ill repute.

The container was scheduled to arrive in Orsova from the port in Amsterdam, Netherlands (Holland) approximately a month after the Benneys' arrival.

The next important task was purchasing an automobile to ship. It was obvious that a four-wheel drive vehicle would be absolutely necessary to orchestrate travel in villages, especially during rainy times and winter. Essentially, no snow removal equipment existed in the country. Wesley found a four- year-old, four-wheel drive Isuzu Trooper II to ship to Bremerhaven, Germany on the North Sea. It was shipped with an expected arrival of a couple weeks after the Benneys' arrival in Romania.

After an incredibly busy month dampened with tears of sadness for some and tears of joy for Wesley, Elizabeth, Timothy, and Ellen, they left for Budapest. Upon arrival, Wesley rented a small car to use until the Isuzu arrived. Ron and Mary Price met them and helped take the extensive luggage to their home on the other side of Budapest. The Prices were missionaries with the Benneys' mission board and had arrived a year before to minister in Hungary.

After two flights totaling twelve hours of airtime and a three-hour layover in Amsterdam, the Benneys collapsed for a good night's sleep. The next morning, following a late breakfast, it was decided that grocery shopping and sight-seeing was in order. Having seen the food markets in Hungary during their survey trip, Wesley and Elizabeth were anxious to acquire canned foods, dry goods, and packaged meats. As Wesley and Elizabeth began filling the shopping cart, the Prices inquired why they were buying so much food. Wesley asked them if they had visited Romania yet. They had not! If they had, they would certainly have understood Elizabeth's spending spree.

Wesley explained it was obvious that the food available in Romania would not meet their needs. During the growing season, vegetables and fruits were in supply. Canned goods were not yet available in their area. Tomatoes, beans, peas, and pickles were the only things available in jars, and the jars had to be returned for reuse. The quality was very poor, and because the jars and lids were reused, Daniel had noted that too often the contents were spoiled because of poor sealing during processing.

The filth in meat markets was deplorable. Meat hung on hooks in the open air and flies had to be brushed aside to cut off the portion being purchased.

Chickens hung on a hook with feet and heads attached. Every part of a chicken was eaten. There was no assurance that pork, which was the main meat available, was free of trichinosis. It was rumored that a lot of the pork raised by the government was not regularly vaccinated in order to save money. That was not difficult to believe knowing the history of the Communist Government. The people who raised their own pigs were careful to have them vaccinated, even with the cost. Beef was seldom available and ground beef was unknown.

As a result, the Benneys would make bi-monthly trips to Hungary to buy provisions, especially meat, since it was packaged as in America. They would continue this practice until Romania's commerce system participated in imports from the West, and acceptable meats and other desired food stuffs were available. They would also purchase goods for Daniel and Veronica on these trips.

The Benneys anticipated being able to spend a couple days with the Prices during these trips because the fellowship would be valuable. Ron, Mary, and their three daughters assured the Benneys they were welcome at any time. One of the daughters was Ellen's age. Having American visitors would be a treat for them too. Ron said, "You will soon learn that it can be lonely in a foreign country without American companionship."

Wesley noted they would have the advantage of fellowship with Daniel and Veronica. Daniel had lived long enough in America, to understand the challenges the Benneys would have in a greatly depressed culture.

Later the discussion centered on life in Eastern Europe. Wesley asked why Hungary was "light years" ahead of Romania as evidenced by the airport, the road system, and the conditions of the homes. Many American eating establishments such as McDonalds, Dunkin Donuts, etc. were already in the city, and the stores were full of quality goods from Western Europe and America. There were even large stores on the order of small Walmart's.

Ron explained that the Communist regime in Hungary had been far more moderate than Romania. Approximately 40 percent of the Hungarian infrastructure was privately owned, so their society had a mixture of free enterprise and government ownership. In Romania, almost 100 percent of the infrastructure was owned or controlled by the government. The attempted revolution in Budapest in 1956 was squelched by the arrival of Russian military and tanks. The Russians finally backed out after threat of American intervention, leaving approximately 2,500 dead. Approximately 200,000 people, many highly educated and talented people, had fled the country, many not to return.

The devastating attempt to overthrow Communism resulted in a considerably moderated form of Communism, thus allowing much of the infrastructure to remain privately-owned. In addition, tourists were allowed to take structured tours of Budapest's many historic and cultural sites. The revenues from tourism gave a tremendous boost to an economy suffering from the inefficiencies caused by the stifled motivation that results from Communist philosophy.

In 1968, Czechoslovakia had experienced a similar uprising with a similar response from America, allowing them to share a comparable relationship with Western Europe for trade and tourism.

Ron also noted that Yugoslavia experienced a similar level of Communism, which was not the result of an attempted revolution, but rather resulted from Tito's refusal to institute Stalinist Communism. Because of his geographical location, which would make Russian intervention difficult, and because America was funneling money into the country as a "buffer state" with a commitment to provide military help if necessary, Russia practiced a "hands-off" policy.

After two days of memorable fellowship and touring ancient sites, it was time to leave for Romania. Obviously, it would take two trips to get the four Benneys and all of their luggage and purchases over the border. The Benneys were off to their first border crossing as a family.

Wesley and Elizabeth knew what to expect, but it was a new experience for Timothy and Ellen. The crossing was a replay of the previous trips.

The drive went as well as could be expected while dodging potholes. After a half-dozen usual stops from police in villages through which they traveled, the Benneys arrived at Daniel's home. After introducing Timothy and Ellen to Daniel and Veronica, they all headed to Orsova to see the "palace".

Upon their arrival, the Benneys were introduced to Mitruti and his parents, with whom they shared a common driveway. After the introductions, Veronica said, "Let's go into your "palace" to visit, and please call me Vera in the future. That is what my friends call me, and you are already my friends." Vera had brought some sweets she had made for this much-anticipated event.

As they entered, the first thing Daniel said was, "You must see my new floor. Well, your new floor! I promised I would have it ready for your arrival." Daniel had done a great job. Of course, only Wesley knew what the original floor looked like, so the others could not fully appreciate what Daniel had accomplished.

Timothy asked Daniel how he had put the new floor down. Daniel explained that he gathered some of the brothers from his church to mix concrete by shovel on the sidewalk in front of the house. The concrete was then hauled into the room by the bucket load. The job was very time consuming, but very Romanian. After leveling the concrete, the new oak flooring was pieced tightly together with Daniel's quality workmanship. But with the poor quality of the typical Romanian flooring - widths of boards were not standard – a filler was necessary. The only filler available at this time was fine sand. The coats of varnish put over the floor permanently sealed in the sand. Wesley and Elizabeth had to admit that the finished product looked good, even if it was quite unorthodox by American standards. After the arrival of the container, this room would be the living room during the day and Timothy's bedroom at night.

Since Daniel had previously delivered a load of firewood, the first thing he did after explaining his new floor project was show Wesley how to start a fire in the soba (ceramic furnace) in the room on the second floor that would be Wesley's and Elizabeth's bedroom. The sofa bed was moved up to this room, since it was best to save wood by heating only one room. It would serve as their living room and bedroom until the arrival of their container. Elizabeth and Ellen would sleep on the 2 straw mattresses that made up the "king size" bed, and Wesley and Timothy would sleep on the sofa bed.

Daniel then went to the kitchen to put a fire in the wood-burning stove, so water could be heated for coffee and tea to go with the sweets that Vera had brought. Daniel suggested that at the earliest possible time, the Benneys needed to buy a Romanian propane gas stove. Elizabeth heartily agreed with his suggestion. The meat products purchased in Hungary were put into the little refrigerator. It was so small, there was barely enough room. Noting the poor condition of the refrigerator, there was relief when it went on after being plugged into an outlet. Everyone said in unison, "Praise God, it works."

That evening would be one of the special memories of life in Romania, especially for Timothy and Ellen, since this was their first exposure to Daniel and Veronica. They would soon become family.

It was decided that the day after next, Daniel would follow Wesley with his van to the Budapest airport to return the rental car. They would go to the Prices' home to get the remainder of the trunks, and Daniel would purchase food supplies for himself and his parents. The Prices were anxious to meet Daniel. Wesley had shared the amazing story of his escape to America and decision to forgo life in America to help reach his countrymen with the Gospel. After spending the night, they made the quite predictable trip home.

CHAPTER 5 LIFE BEGINS IN ROMANIA

After having moved into their "palace" while awaiting arrival of the container, Elizabeth and Ellen spent most of the day in the bedroom because of the warmth. Elizabeth read books and Ellen did her schoolwork via the VHS tapes and books brought with them. Wesley and Timothy spent time during the day looking for materials and doing repairs to the house with Daniel's help.

At Pastor Patrica's request, Wesley immediately began preaching in his churches on Sundays and Wednesday evenings. This provided exposure to Romanian poverty and lack of cleanliness standards for Timothy and Ellen. They inquired about the strange odors they noticed within the churches and were informed that it was body odor. Village homes did not have indoor plumbing and facilities for taking baths, so most of the people did not clean themselves completely for many weeks during winter months. Many of them lived in their inner garments, seldom shedding them. The outer garments would be cleaned as necessary, and the definition of "necessary" was quite different than in more progressive countries. Lack of indoor plumbing was also the major issue limiting the cleaning of clothes or bedding during the winter months.

Each church contained a bucket of water with a metal cup for public drinking. The members would reach in and fill the cup for a drink. The remaining water and cup were put back into the bucket for the next thirsty member. As Wesley would say many times in the future, "We don't know where those hands were before reaching into the bucket for the cup."

Wesley was informed that no phone lines were available. The current phone system was installed in the 1940s and had long ago maxed out. It was manned by a bank of women who had the opportunity to listen in on any calls they "wanted to." Rumor had it they "wanted to" a lot! It was easy to see how beneficial it was for the Communist government to keep track of everyone, even after the revolution, because of the neurosis that still existed.

Those with phones agreed that the change in government had certainly not stopped the operators' interest in listening in on phone conversations. The people knew when their conversations were being infiltrated. Again, even though the government insisted that the Securitate was no longer operating, everyone knew who was behind the invasion of privacy.

With multiple family members living together, even the death of someone would not make a line available. Having a phone was such a privilege that no one was going to give up a line for any reason. As a result, Wesley was told not to hold his breath waiting for a line. Mitruti's parents had a phone, so the Benneys still had access to service, such as it was. That number had been given to family in America, the container company in Amsterdam, and the auto shipping company in Germany. It took more than having the availability of a telephone to get calls; it also took the Lord's help. The Benneys waited by faith for phone calls regarding the arrival of the Isuzu and the container.

A couple weeks after the Benneys' arrival, Mitruti came running to the door exclaiming, "Mr. Benney, a telephone from Germany!" Wesley's heart was beating overtime as he ran to Mitruti's house. The Isuzu had arrived! Wesley would leave immediately, and Timothy would remain home to assist his mother and sister. Of course, Daniel and Vera were there to provide oversight.

The Romanian train trip was another adventure. The cars were World War II vintage – dirty, run down, and very noisy. Looking into the toilet revealed the gravel below the train, so it was obvious where refuse ended up.

Just like the border crossing by car, there was a considerable process of reviewing passports to get over the border into Hungary. It also included the inspection of luggage at the whim of the conductor. The train terminated at Budapest. After a several hour wait, another train was taken from Budapest through Austria and into Germany, where yet a third train was taken through to Bremerhaven, located on the North Sea. The difference between the Hungarian train and the Romanian train was like night and day, but not much different than the train in Germany. This was additional proof that Hungary's Communism was not the Stalinist Communism of Romania.

Having retrieved the Isuzu with ease, the trip home was accomplished quickly because Wesley determined to drive home non-stop. The autobahns in Germany and Austria rivaled the best interstate highways in America. With no speed limits outside the cities, the trip was unnerving. Wesley drove about 75 miles per hour in the right-hand lane while everyone passed on the left, leaving him in the dust.

The major thru fare in Hungary from the Austrian border to the highway leading to the Romanian border was similar, but with limited speed limits. The border crossing into Romania was rather typical, except for extraordinary interest in the Isuzu because of American license plates. It appeared that the border personnel had probably never seen an Isuzu, and probably had seldom, if ever, seen American license plates. Everyone was called out to see it!

After the crossing, Wesley was stopped many times in the cities and villages by police who were also mesmerized with the car and American plates. Of course, they all asked questions that they really had no business asking. Wesley had determined that he would take control of these "visits" with the police. He reminded them that the country was no longer a repressive Communist Regime, and that their questions were seeking information that was not their right to know. The police usually backed down quickly. After 32 hours without sleep, Wesley arrived home to an anxiously awaiting family.

The interest in the Isuzu with American plates on the trip home was eclipsed by the interest in Orsova. The car was parked in the driveway in full view of anyone passing. It became the center of everyone's attention. When driving anywhere in town or anywhere else, for that matter, people would stop "dead in their tracks" and gaze at the car until it was out of sight.

The arrival of the Isuzu precipitated the greatest challenge to Elizabeth's faith she would experience in 10 years of living in Romania. Wesley was advised that, as quickly as possible, the catalytic converter needed to be removed because lead-free gasoline was not available in Romania. If the converter was not removed, the engine would soon be permanently damaged.

Daniel knew a Christian mechanic three hours away in Pojejena where his cousin lived. He had the capability of removing the catalytic converter and constructing a pipe to put in its place. The decision was made that Wesley, Timothy, and Daniel would leave the next morning to have the work done. It was assumed this could be accomplished the same day and they would be home that night.

After dismantling the exhaust system, the man realized he wouldn't be able to finish the work that day. There was nothing that could be done but to spend the evening with Daniel's cousin. Unfortunately, it took until evening of the next day before the work was finished. Since it was dark when the repair was finished, the men were advised to stay over that evening, as well. Road conditions along the Danube were dangerous at night and occasional robberies took place by thieves coming out of the remote foothills. Since Daniel's cousin didn't have a phone, it wasn't possible to call Mitruti and contact Elizabeth. The entire incident caused an unavoidable dilemma.

When Wesley and Timothy arrived home, they found Elizabeth and Ellen sitting at the kitchen table crying. Assuming one evening might have been necessary, a second evening seemed very ominous. Knowing that the road along the Danube was dangerous, they thought perhaps Wesley, Timothy, and Daniel were at the bottom of the Danube. They had been in the country only about a month and the worse had been feared.

Since delays were not unusual in Romania, Vera was not concerned when Daniel didn't arrive as expected. Since Daniel's parents didn't have a phone and Vera didn't drive, she had no way to know that Elizabeth and Ellen hadn't been contacted. Had she known, she would have taken a bus to see them and calm their concerns.

Needless to say, there was great rejoicing, but a very serious lesson was learned. Wesley assumed, quite incorrectly, that the change out of the catalytic converter would be a relatively simple thing. Accordingly, he had given Elizabeth and Ellen a specific return time of late evening of the same day of departure. He would be most careful in the future!

Soon, it would become evident that most things in Romania took longer, if not much longer to be accomplished than would be expected. This was Romania, not America.

CHAPTER 6 DIVINE INTERVENTION

Two weeks after receiving the Isuzu, Mitruti came running over again saying, "Mr. Benney, a telephone from the Netherlands." The voice at the other end of the phone explained that the container had left Amsterdam a day and a half earlier and would be at the border of Romania in a few hours. Someone needed to meet the truck to help the driver cross the border and lead him to Orsova. Wesley and Timothy made the trip to the border to meet the truck, while Elizabeth and Ellen stayed behind.

They arrived in the early morning after driving all night. Wesley explained to the border control personnel that they did not want to cross the border with the car but were there to meet a truck on the Hungarian side with a container from the Netherlands. He was instructed where to park the car. After some discussion between the agents and stamping of the passports, Wesley and Timothy were permitted to walk across the border to the Hungarian Port of Entry.

As they neared the Hungarian side, a tall agent approached them to learn the reason they entered the country on foot. After explaining, the agent, who spoke English very well, suggested that they walk out toward the end of the line to look for the truck. He instructed Wesley to tell the driver to cut line and bring the truck up to the border crossing, and he would expedite them. He said that without this, it would take the truck at least two days to cross.

Wesley and Timothy could not believe their ears. Why would this man, whom they never met, do this, especially knowing how the Hungarians disliked the Romanians? Wesley thought that being a missionary to Romania would have caused the same response as being a Romanian. He and Timothy agreed that the Lord was clearly manifesting Himself, keeping His promise to meet the needs of those He has called to service.

Wesley thanked the agent. "Well, Timothy, let's go for a walk and hope the truck has arrived." They estimated the line to be about one mile long. Walking the entire length of the line, they discovered the truck was not there, so they walked back. Seeing the agent, they explained the truck was not there yet. He suggested they return after a while. Wesley and Timothy walked back over the border to the Romanian side, explaining to those agents that the truck hadn't arrived yet and that they would try again later. They sat in the car, ate their lunch, and slept for a couple hours.

"Well, Timothy, my son, let's start the process all over." Again, they had to explain why they were there and were allowed to walk to the Hungarian side. By God's grace, the same agent greeted them and acknowledged that they were going to walk the line again. The one-mile walk was made, and behold, the truck had just arrived a short time before.

Wesley told the driver that an agent had instructed them to have him break line and bring the truck up to the front of the line.

The driver laughed and said, "No, I won't do that!" He explained that some years earlier he had done a similar thing and had the windshield and lights on his truck destroyed by the other drivers in the line. It was in the dead of winter. "If you can get someone to come back with you to lead me in, then I will do it."

"Timothy, I think we are in trouble because no one is going to walk a mile out here with us."

Breathing a prayer as they arrived at the Customs Center, Wesley asked an approaching agent, "Where is the tall agent we talked with?"

He had finished his shift and had left for the day. With a feeling of total panic, Wesley explained that the agent said he would allow the truck to come to the beginning of the line, but the driver refused the risk of an altercation with other drivers. This agent went into the office and came back with another man who was not in uniform. It turned out this man was actually in charge of the new shift. He had a three-inch diameter medallion around his neck with the seal of Hungary on it.

After explaining, again, the promise made by the agent on the previous shift, this man said, "Well, since he has left for the day, I will allow that for you." When Wesley told the agent that the driver would not break line without an official to bring him in, the agent said, "Well, then, let's go get the truck."

Wesley and Timothy could not believe their ears! This was a one-mile walk, and this man was going to walk all the way out there when he was in no way obligated to do so, and when he was the man in charge? He certainly could have sent someone else to do the honors.

This was clearly the hand of God in action! After they walk out, the three men climbed into the truck cab, sardine style. The agent said to the driver, "Proceed! We won't have any trouble."

The driver started up the engine and began to pull out around the truck in front of him. Immediately, the driver of that truck and other drivers jumped out of their cabs with wood clubs blocking passage. The agent leaned over the dashboard, lifting the medallion so they could see it and motioned for them to step aside. This process was repeated all the way to the front of the line. Upon arrival at the Customs Office, the official gave instruction to process the truck next.

As instructed, the truck was taken next, and after only a few minutes, with the interaction of the official, the truck passed through the Hungarian border and onto the Romanian side. Wesley and Timothy thanked him and walked back to the Romanian border, praising God the whole way. They had just witnessed an incredible event, but this was only the first of a couple more incredible events before the container was unloaded at the Benneys' house.

The process of passing through the Romanian customs went well. Wesley told the driver to expect a 6-hour drive, and they would probably be stopped several times in the process by police in the cities and villages. He certainly did not exaggerate the delays.

They arrived in Orsova that evening too late for the customs office, in town, to begin their process, so the driver would sleep in his truck.

The next morning, Friday, a very excited Wesley and Daniel led the truck driver to the Customs Office near the ship building factory. They were fortunate to have one in their town. The Danube River was the only reason. Goods were being shipped down the river on barges, so a customs office was necessary as the first point of contact when coming into Romania.

After hours of waiting and discussions with different agents, it was determined that Wesley needed to go to the Customs Office at the hydroelectric dam and border crossing into Serbia, midway between Orsova and the city of Turnu-Severin. The office in Orsova had absolutely no idea how to receive such a container. Processing goods shipped into the country was one thing, but processing the belongings of people coming into the country was another thing! They had never experienced a foreigner moving into their jurisdiction.

Wesley informed the truck driver, and they were on their way arriving at 12:30. Daniel feared that no one of authority would be there after 12:00. On Fridays, officials of position vacated the government offices at noon. As they entered the lobby, the officer in charge was coming down the stairs to leave for the weekend. When Daniel confronted him concerning the entourage, he immediately became interested and shook hands with Wesley. He admitted he had never had such a request either and had no idea how to handle the customs process.

He said he would call the Customs Office in Bucharest and to try to reach the Director of Customs for Romania. He was sure, at this time on a Friday, the Director would have left for the weekend. However, when he called, the Director was still there. After only a few minutes of discussion, the agent hung up the phone, shook his head in amazement, and said, "The Director told me to tell the Customs Office in Orsova to accept the container and call the Customs Office in Bucharest on Monday for instructions on handling the official paperwork." He said he would immediately call the office in Orsova instructing them to stay open and process the container as instructed by the Director in Bucharest. At that, Wesley, Daniel, and the driver departed again for the Customs Office in Orsova.

Daniel exclaimed, "I cannot believe what just happened! Maybe this would happen in American, but not in Romania. We just saw the hand of the Lord again! Finding the Customs Director at the border crossing and the Director of Customs for Romania still in their offices on a Friday afternoon was a miracle. It is a stamp of God's approval that you came here to work with us! But then, God was just answering my prayers, so you should thank me for all that is happening."

"Wait a minute. What about my prayers? Maybe God is answering me," Wesley retorted.

"Ok, I guess God is answering both of us."

They had a good laugh together as they rejoiced in the process thus far.

When they arrived at the customs office, the officials were ready and suggested that they immediately take the truck to Wesley's home. Upon arrival and positioning of the truck for unloading, the neighbors showed up to take part in the spectacle. Imagine Americans moving to Orsova!

The customs official holding the packing slip was checking off the items or boxes as unloaded. They began opening every box, but soon decided to randomly open the remaining boxes when they realized there were a couple hundred. The appliances caused incredible awe! The officials and bystanders had never seen such large and beautiful appliances. These items were not yet available for purchase anywhere but Bucharest, and then only for the privileged. The two motorcycles created no small stir, either. Most assuredly, the Benneys would become the talk of the town for a long time.

About half-way through the process, one of the Humphrys' boxes was opened upside down, and there were two shotgun shells sitting on the bottom of the enclosed files. Now that caused a real stir! The three customs agents conferred and decided guns must have been shipped into the country. This was a serious problem! As Daniel translated what was being discussed, Wesley felt a mixture of fear and anger at Ted for packing shotgun shells. It was a box of files that had undoubtedly come from a file cabinet.

If the box had been opened right side up like the others, they would have never found them in the first place. All Wesley could do through Daniel's adept handling of the situation was to assure them Americans understood well that guns were not allowed in Romania, and that, indeed, no guns would be found among their goods. They were not foolish enough to break the law in this manner when coming to do religious ministry. Wesley noted that Ted was an avid hunter in America, like many Americans, and he had probably accidentally dropped the shells in the box when emptying his files.

After some time, the agents agreed to continue the process, but they were going to open every single remaining box. This activity slowed the process down considerably, but after some time, they decided to pass the boxes along rather quickly again as their normal quitting time was approaching. They noted that when Ted came for his possessions, he should answer to the Customs Office regarding the shotgun shells, which they took with them. Papers were signed, the truck driver took off, and gifts of coffee purchased by Daniel were given to the agents in appreciation for the service they provided.

CHAPTER 7 LIFE SETTLES IN

The exciting process of emptying boxes began like Christmas for the next couple days. It was difficult to orchestrate the process with the living room filled wall to wall to the ceiling with the Humphreys' belongings. The first-floor hallway from the stairs to the kitchen was also stacked with boxes, leaving a narrow two-foot-wide passageway.

Within a couple days, the duplex was beginning to look and feel a little like home, except for the living room and first floor hallway. Ted's arrival could not possibly come soon enough!

Familiar pictures on some of the walls were a comforting improvement. Elizabeth and Ellen moved to Ellen's bed in her room, leaving Wesley and Timothy to sleep in the master bedroom. Fires were now started in two sobas.

A couple days after the partial arrangement of belongings, Wesley went to the open-air market with Daniel to see what cold storage vegetables were available. He observed a poor elderly woman with some paintings for sale. Daniel learned that her husband had painted them many years before, and now he had passed. She needed money, and Wesley was delighted to purchase something original, even if not professional quality. Wesley was saddened to see her letting go of something she cherished because of her poverty. What she was asking might have been reasonable in the economy of the time, but the price was a mere pittance against the dollar. As a result, he gave her far more than she was asking, along with a Gospel tract in the Romanian language. The joy that his generosity gave her was matched by the joy it gave him to put forth a testimony that would be shared with her friends. These purchases would be cherished as reminders of life in Romania.

A couple weeks after receipt of the container, Mitruti came running over saying, "Mr. Benney, telephone." It was Ted calling to say he and Caroline had arrived in the country earlier than planned, and with Gigi's help, had acquired a rental truck. He wanted to know if tomorrow was ok to get his belongings. Wesley responded, "Is tomorrow ok? Is a bullfrog waterproof?" Tomorrow it was!

At noon the next day, Ted arrived with a man from Gigi's church to serve as a translator. Of course, Daniel was there to help and share in the fellowship.

After lunch and a couple hours loading the truck, Ted was on his way. When reminded that he was to go to the Customs Office to answer for the shotgun shells, he said, "If they want to talk with me, they can come to Lugoj to see me." Well, the shotgun shell situation never came up again. The Customs people had apparently dropped the issue.

There was joy in the Benney home! Now they had a living room and Timothy had a bedroom! Not only that, but now there were 4 more walls and a hallway for hanging pictures, including those recently purchased. It really was feeling like home! For an American, however, what is a home without a pet?

Wesley had recently noticed a cat frequenting the shed behind the house, and he had a suspicion there were kittens there. He investigated, and sure enough, there were 3 kittens, two large grey males and a much smaller calico female. The calico was very undernourished.

The family decided the small kitten needed a new home with sufficient food to survive. Milk was not available to purchase, but Elizabeth had shipped many boxes of powdered milk. She removed a needle from a syringe brought in their medical packet, and life-saving milk was made and fed through the syringe. The Benneys had a pet!

Elizabeth had brought skirts with large pockets for casual wear. "Princesa" (Princess) found a warm birth in those pockets until she gained enough strength and size to venture out on her own. Allowing a cat to live in the home of any Romanian was scandalous, but this was the home of Americans. The scandal did not end there.

Wesley asked Daniel to find a veterinarian to provide injections against cat diseases. The one he found in Orsova laughed and said that cats and dogs in Romania are not given injections. If they died from diseases, as many did, there were always others to take their place. Cats and dogs were necessary to kill mice and rats and to warn of anyone encroaching in their yard or garden. Bonding did not take place with most of them, and they certainly did not live indoors. The veterinarian's job was servicing farm animals such as pigs, cows, and horses. He was not interested in acquiring the necessary injections for a cat. He walked away laughing and shaking his head.

Wesley and Elizabeth were anxious to see the Humphreys' home. On their first trip, Wesley shared his plight regarding finding injections for Princesa. Ted noted that he had found a young veterinarian who had access to injections for dogs and cats. Ted had found him after purchasing a German Shepherd puppy. Wesley met with him about bringing Princesa to Lugoj on a future trip. He said he would be glad to acquire the necessary inoculations. However, when Wesley asked about having Princesa's front claws taken out and neutering her, he was aghast! How would she protect herself? Of course, Wesley noted that she would be a house cat and would not have to protect herself.

The veterinarian noted that neutering cats or dogs was almost unheard of in Romania. He said that he had training in those two procedures, but had never actually performed them in his short time as a veterinarian. He was not aware of anyone else in his area either. He was willing to proceed if Wesley would acknowledge the risks due to his inexperience. An agreement was made, and a date was set for a future trip to Lugoj. Indeed, a couple weeks hence the surgeries were performed successfully. Thus, the Benneys had the privilege of being allowed to present the young veterinarian with his first opportunity to perform these "specialized" surgeries.

After some weeks, the interest in the Isuzu seemed to have abated, that is until Daniel bought a copy of a newspaper produced in Bucharest containing a picture of the Benneys' home and the Isuzu in the driveway. The article claimed the car and home were that of a political candidate in the upcoming election. The car was supposedly given to this candidate as a bribe. Of course, the Tennessee license plates were not visible. This was a real eye opener into the corruption taking place in Romanian politics. Wesley sent a letter of chastisement to the office of the newspaper for printing such a false story. No retractions were seen in forthcoming papers, nor did the office ever respond to Wesley's letter. Because newspapers were the only source of news available to the masses, they carried the aura of absolute proof, so it was easy to see how mistruth could be spread.

Soon after establishing their home, Wesley and Elizabeth began to study the language with the self-study books they brought from America. Dr. Roberts, the mission board president, told them that, statistically after age 40, mastering a foreign language was not possible unless the person was already bilingual. The Benneys were near 50 years of age and knew only English, so they were facing the challenge of a lifetime. It was noted that Wesley's two years of Spanish in high school would not present any particular advantage in learning Romanian, even though they were both Latin based.

Noting their challenge, Tutritsa introduced them to a Romanian high school English teacher named Radu. Wesley suggested meeting weekly for language study, which was readily accepted by Radu when Wesley offered to pay him $25 U.S. dollars per month. Since this sum of money was much beneath their budgeted amount for language study, and since it was equivalent to half a month salary for a full-time worker, both were winners. Of course, Daniel and Veronica were also providing much help with the language, since they spent so much time together with the Benneys.

Soon after beginning lessons, Radu, informed Wesley and Elizabeth that the Securitate, which supposedly did not exist, was alive and well. Wesley said that Daniel had already apprised him of that fact. Radu said that after the arrival of the Benneys, the agents had been positioned five days a week in a car with a listening device one street behind them. Wesley noted that at such a distance and doubting they had sufficient technology in the first place, it sounded like there would be little return for their investment in "equipment" and salaries of the agents. Radu showed his agreement with a broad smile.

Since the occupant in the other half of the duplex was the previous top communist official and the equivalent of a mayor before the revolution, it seemed the most obvious method of spying would be to put bugs in the wall between the units or in the open shared attic. Wesley and Elizabeth had already assumed this was being done so they weren't intimidated by Radu's disclosure.

They would regularly say things they wanted any listeners to hear. If, indeed, Wesley and Elizabeth were being bugged, the listeners were getting many doses of the Gospel and confirmation that the Benneys were "really" there without any connections with any U.S. governmental agencies. They were really Christian missionaries, not spies.

Wesley had decided that, before starting permanent ministry, he would study the language and do as much preaching as possible with Daniel translating for him. Pastor Petrica's opportunities for Wesley to preach were already being fulfilled, but there was Dolphi with his ten churches. His need for help was certainly more critical than Petrica's. He, too, was imploring Wesley to preach in his churches as often as possible. Wesley determined he would try to help both pastors, but his caveat was flexibility.

If he was to meet this opportunity for preaching, he would have to have a translator available at all times. Wesley suggested to Daniel that he could meet some of his income needs from his ministry support fund if Daniel would provide more translation time for him.

With support from the two churches in America and what Wesley would pay, Daniel could put aside his plans for a flooring business. He had not progressed very far in starting his proposed business anyway. He needed and received a commitment from the two churches to continue the support for the unforeseeable future. The churches were delighted to support Daniel in such a ministry. Daniel's total compensation actually exceeded what he could make in his flooring business, which had obvious benefits for his and Veronica's lifestyle.

For Daniel, it was far more than the financial benefits. The opportunity to have a key role in reaching his people with solid biblical teaching was his main motivation. After all, he had given up the opportunity to have American citizenship to do this. Every message he translated was a verification of God's call for him to return. What else might the Lord have in mind for Daniel?

Everything was organized for Wesley to conduct ministry on Sundays and other days of the week fitting in his language study and general responsibilities as father and husband. As with Daniel, he had the challenge of acquiring the necessary petrol (gasoline) for the trips to Dolphi's churches, which averaged two to three hours away. Wesley followed Daniel's advice by purchasing a 50-gallon drum, which he kept filled with extra gasoline in the little garage. Like Daniel, he took a large gas container everywhere he went with the goal of getting additional gasoline.

Wesley spread his preaching between Petrica and Dolphi, but after several weeks, he determined that he wanted to slow his pace. Elizabeth and Ellen were becoming weary with his schedule. Though Timothy usually went with Wesley and Daniel, Elizabeth's home schooling kept her at home with Elizabeth. Wesley and Timothy would often arrive home quite late. Not knowing the language very well, Elizabeth was uncomfortable, and without a phone she felt very vulnerable, especially considering that everyone in the town and surrounding villages knew about the Americans, including the vagrant Gypsies camped in the outskirts of Orsova and in the nearby foothills of the Carpathian Mountains. Many roamed throughout the country living in their wagons. The government allowed them great latitude in their movements. Though some of them engaged in transient labor as they moved about, many did not.

Of course, food was a necessity, so they practiced a form of socialism called theft. People in the villages near their camping sites were assured of providing provisions against their will. Even barking dogs were not sufficient to protect their gardens and hen houses.

Gypsies often knocked on the Benney's door seeking handouts. Elizabeth insisted that she would feel much better if a large dog became part of the family. Of course, Timothy and Ellen readily agreed that their family needed to grow, and Wesley was easily convinced. After some discussion, they agreed on a Rottweiler because of their fierce look and reputation of being loyal guardians. On their next trip to Budapest for provisions, they asked the Prices to scour the newspapers for availability of a Rottweiler puppy with a pedigree.

Wesley and his family had hardly arrived home when Mitruti announced a call. It was Ron saying he found a litter of Rottweiler pups soon to be available. They had a strong pedigree, so the price was $250 American dollars. Wesley would be allowed first choice if he returned quickly. Because of the sum in the Hungarian economy, it was assumed the pedigree certainly must be significant.

Undoubtedly, the fact that Wesley was an American influenced the price and offer of first choice from the litter. Wesley and Timothy made a quick return trip to Budapest to adopt their new family member. The pedigree did seem impressive, and the parents were strong, beautiful specimens. The father weighed 64 kilo (140 lbs.).

The Benney men chose the largest female. Upon arriving back home, they decided to name her Lady. As time would tell, she was no "lady," but became very endeared to the family, Daniel, and Veronica. Without question, her fame challenged that of the Isuzu. When Lady was taken for a walk, people would cross to the other side of the street. Needless to say, as Lady reached adulthood, Elizabeth and Ellen would be quite comfortable when Wesley and Timothy were away. Lady's presence had become known "far and wide."

CHAPTER 8 BIBLE INSTITUTE MINISTRY ESTABLISHED

Wesley, after a considerable discussion with Daniel, planned to preach regularly in the two of Petrica's churches closest to Orsova. Toplet, Daniel's church, and Filet were separated by a land barrier and a river emptying into the Danube near Orsova. Wesley would preach the morning service in one and the evening service in the other, and switch the order every other week. He would preach in the Wednesday evening service in each church every other week as well. He still preached in Dolphi's churches from time to time, but focused more on learning the language and getting to know the church members in the two villages, serving in a quasi-pastoral position assisting Petrica.

Having the opportunity to learn the culture along with the language and to teach correct Bible doctrine through his preaching was truly a blessing. The people very quickly accepted his ministry to them. Daniel's great translating abilities gave Wesley freedom in his preaching. His relaxed style could be called more preacher-teacher, and the members of the churches liked his style over the authoritarian and rigid style the Romanian preachers mimicked from the Baptist Union officials.

One of the practices that Wesley rejected was the manner in which a Baptist Union pastor would enter the church and approach the pulpit. The people would stand and bow their heads in an attitude of prayer. The pastor would kneel in front of the pulpit in silent prayer. Then he would stand and ask the people to be seated. Wesley interpreted this as elevating the position of pastor in a manner emulating the status of Catholic and Orthodox priests and hierarchy. His practice was to simply walk to the pulpit, greet the people along the way, and open the service in audible prayer. Both Petrica and Dolphi soon began to imitate Wesley's practice.

Things were going along quite well with Wesley's preaching arrangement. In addition to the regular preaching services, he was having many opportunities to provide spiritual counsel to the members. Many opportunities were based on doctrinal differences that were surfacing during the preaching. Most of the younger members and youth were quite open to accepting the changes, but wanted to see proof in the Scriptures. Wesley and Daniel were delighted when it became necessary to mimic the Bereans. The older brothers and sisters often were not going to give up their beliefs, regardless of scriptural documentation. Culture was stronger than truth for many.

This was also very true of the people under the state Orthodox Church. For sure, their 1000-year cultural background provided many obstacles to accepting a truly biblical approach to salvation and daily living. These obstacles included many holidays, obeisance to a myriad of saints and Mary, burning of candles, confessing of sins to the priests, and last rites which were necessary to help keep one out of hell at death. The many icons in their churches and homes served as obstacles to accepting a truly biblical approach to salvation and daily living.

One day when Wesley and Daniel were passing out gospel tracts in the streets of a nearby village, a policeman objected. This had been illegal during the previous Communist regime, but those prohibitions were long gone and were well known by the populace at large. Apparently, this policeman thought he could throw his weight around, so to speak, perhaps in defense of his Orthodox faith. He demanded that they stop passing out the tracts.

Wesley, not to be thwarted, asked Daniel to translate his objection and intent to continue what they were doing. When the policeman lifted his rifle and pointed it at Wesley's head, Daniel suggested that the discussion needed to end. Seldom had Daniel suggested anything more appropriate than this recommendation. As they walked away, Wesley insisted that Daniel tell the policeman they were going to report him to the authorities. Of course, they did not really intend to do so, but were sure the warning would be enough, because an American was involved. This village was visited many times in the future without incident.

Approximately four months after arriving in the country, Wesley and Ted discussed the idea of starting Bible institutes. Each of them had contemplated this ministry, and now seemed the time to put plans into motion in their respective regions of the country. Both men had brought college-level materials with them, some from their own education.

Wesley also received permission from two Bible colleges to use some of their syllabi for the Bible institute and purchased courses from a Bible publication company. His plan was to take the best materials from each source and redesign his own courses if he felt an improvement could be made.

He planned to begin the institute in the fall when schools normally start. This gave enough time for the necessary preparations to begin teaching the first two courses.

A four-year Pastorology program for men was planned, which would be the equivalent of the 36-hour Bible program taught at the Bible College Wesley attended for his Bible degree. There would be a four-year Christian service program for women as well. In place of the Pastorology courses, there would be courses designed specifically for women in ministry, and Elizabeth would teach the women's courses. The equivalent of four to five hours of course material would be taught each of two semesters per year with summers off.

Furthermore, the institute would be taught in two locations. The first location would be in the church in Pojejena, where the replacement of the catalytic converter took place. Pastor Dolphi would be a student. As with Petrica, he never had any Bible training before becoming a pastor. He took the position of pastor out of desire, and certainly not because of any credentials.

The institute in Pojejena would meet on Friday afternoon for approximately five hours. The trip would take about five hours round trip, so with the teaching time and fellowship time, it would be a long day. As previously noted, reaching this village required traveling along the Danube River. With almost no railing and very narrow gravel roads, extreme care was necessary, especially during winter months. By this time, the threat of robbery along the way had become a thing of the past. Police had been active ferreting out troublemakers in the villages of the foothills.

The second location would be in Toplet, where Wesley preached every week. The classes would be taught on Saturdays. Of course, Petrica would be a student.

Petrica and Dolphi were ecstatic over the opportunity to study college level courses, take exams, and meet standards for graduation. Tests were a sham in Romanian schools at every level. Students were allowed to cheat, and bribes bought whatever grades being sought. Passing grades and graduation meant little in such an atmosphere. Students never really knew their level of competence nor how they compared with fellow students.

Needless to say, Daniel was elated at the idea of a Bible institute. He would translate for the teaching and participate as a student. His Bible institute training in Chicago prepared him for jumping in again, especially since the institute would begin with basic doctrine courses he had there.

As Wesley continued working with Daniel, it was becoming quite evident that he would be a perfect candidate as a pastor to take over the church he hoped to plant in the near future. He invited Daniel for coffee at a small cafe along the Danube to discuss his future.

"Daniel, I think you should seriously consider a life of ministry as a pastor following the completion of the institute program. I hope to start a church in two or three years, and it would be an excellent place for you to get experience going along with the institute training. In time, I will have you preaching, and as the church grows, I will need an assistant. When the time is right for you to take over as pastor, that will be our signal to start another church or return home, depending on the timing and our age."

"You have no idea how exciting this sounds! When I contemplated returning to Romania to help reach my people, I guess I never dreamed of doing so as a pastor. I just assumed I would start a flooring business and assist as a layman."

Daniel quickly went to tell Veronica of his conversation with Wesley.

"So, what do you think?"

"I have secretly prayed that something like this would happen. I couldn't be happier! Being a student in the Bible institute will prepare me to share in ministry with you."

The issue yet to be solved was how Vera would attend classes after the birth of their first child which would take place soon after the institute program began.

Planning the Bible institute program was the easy part. All of the syllabi class notes that would be given to students to fill out would have to be translated into Romanian. The syllabi would range from 200 to 300 pages, depending on the course being taught.

Daniel did not feel as qualified for the task since his grammar wasn't as good as he thought it should be. Besides, his traveling to translate with Wesley was basically a full-time job. As usual, the Lord provided. A good Christian friend in the village of Toplet spoke very good English and had a sound grasp of grammar.

Wesley proposed to pay her to translate the written materials and notes for the students. Though she had a full-time position as a bookkeeper, she was delighted for the extra income, and also for the opportunity to be involved in such a worthwhile ministry. It was too good to be true! Eleana and her husband Adrian would also be students in the Institute.

After Eleana's translation, Elizabeth's work would begin. She would type the translated material using a European font purchased for use with the Romanian language. Not knowing Romanian very well and having to read the writing of the written materials, this would be a slow process. Of course, the translations would take place a semester at a time.

After typing the material into proper format as she thought they were written, Eleana would come over to review the material, and Elizabeth would make the needed corrections.

Initially, in both institute locations, many men and women began the studies. Within the first few weeks, when they learned that they would have to pass stringent exams and realized the commitment for attendance that would be required for four years, many dropped out. The serious students included ten men from Dolphi's churches, and six men and two women in Petrica's village.

Most of the men were deacons and responsible for preaching when their pastor or Wesley was elsewhere. It thrilled Wesley, Daniel, Dolphi, and Petrica to know that there would be direct and immediate benefit to those churches as the deacons' preaching would reflect what they were learning on a weekly basis.

The strong bond that had developed between the four men soon included the students.

As time progressed with the Bible institute ministry, Elizabeth's part in typing the syllabi gave her a clear edge on Wesley in learning the language in written form. She could understand the written language, especially theological terms, far better than he could. But he was clearly ahead of her in communication skills because of his continual association with Romanians in all venues of life.

As anticipated, shortly after the beginning of the institute program, Vera gave birth to their first child, a daughter they named Daniela Rebeka. Elizabeth was quick to step into the role of a grandmother. Daniela served somewhat as a surrogate for the granddaughter living 5,000 miles away.

Unfortunately, real tension developed between Elizabeth and the biological grandmothers. Elizabeth and Vera had become very close. Vera asked many questions regarding her pregnancy and trusted Elizabeth more than her parents because she was increasingly convinced that some of the cultural ways were not correct and that there had been a level of deception under the previous Communist government. She was disgusted with the lack of training that Romanians had received in basic cleanliness and health related issues. Some of these issues came to the surface as soon as Daniela was born.

The first issue to create consternation between Elizabeth and the grandmothers was the issue of how children should be clothed in the first months of their lives. Babies would be wrapped in blankets and kept in a heated room, even during the warm months. Of course, Elizabeth challenged this cultural norm and Vera was willing to follow her advice. Vera really established her motherhood by challenging her mother and mother-in-law.

Wesley had wondered if this tradition had an effect on the metabolic development of children because many villagers were observed working their gardens in the warmer months in woolen garments. The women especially could be seen in long length skirts and heavy upper garments, including sweaters.

Another custom was to bind the legs of babies for the first several months to keep them off their legs to assure they wouldn't become bow-legged. It was no wonder children crawled and walked very late compared to American children. Elizabeth and Wesley assured Daniel and Vera that their children would not be bow-legged and encouraged them not to bind their baby's legs at all.

Again, the grandmothers were extremely upset with Vera for listening to the Americans! But when Daniela was walking soon after her first birthday, everyone marveled at her progress, and she was not bow-legged! Vera and her "American mother" were vindicated. It is interesting that only a few months later, there was a special TV program that criticized the binding of children's legs because it hindered their progress in walking and development of motor skills - further vindication!

Following the first year of the institute, Wesley and Elizabeth took a three-month summer furlough. The primary purpose was to take Timothy home to get a job and get on with his life. Another computer was purchased for use by Eleana, which would greatly enhance the process of translating Bible institute materials. Now Eleana could type her translations directly into the computer, thereby bypassing much of the work that Elizabeth had previously done.

The first three years of the institute ministry seemed to pass so quickly. They were great years of spiritual growth for the students and for Wesley and Elizabeth in cultural and language issues.

Making the weekly trips to Pojejena presented several challenges. Three times rockslides blocked the road. However, this was not known until reaching the blockage. Wesley and Daniel had to retreat and take an alternate route through the mountain foothills, greatly increasing the travel time. Each time this happened, the students were found patiently waiting because there was no way to contact them. Everything was set back so it would be the wee hours of the morning when Wesley and Daniel finally got home.

A frequent and expensive challenge was punctured tires, caused by sharp stones in the gravel road. Often the punctures were so large that repairs could not be made. Inner tubes were put in tires that could not be repaired, but these would puncture as well in time.

The tires used on the Isuzu were not available in Romania for the first few years and had to be purchased at a Goodyear store in Budapest at a cost of $250 per tire. Wesley always made the trip to Pojejena with two mounted spare tires, just in case it was necessary. The possibility of being stranded was not an option, though two flats in one trip never happened. During the first two years, as much money was spent on tires as on food.

In the third year of the institute, the road was paved with asphalt. This greatly improved safety, wear on tires, and the time necessary to make the trip. Approximately two hours in travel time was saved each trip as a result of the pavement. Every trip began with "Praise the Lord for the paved road!"

During these years, Wesley's preaching requests were not diminished. Daniel began to preach with assistance from Wesley. He quickly grasped the concept of sermon preparation and was becoming expressive in his presentation and hermeneutically correct in his exposition of the Word.

CHAPTER 9 A GOAL ACHIEVED – THE PLANTING OF A CHURCH

At the end of the third year of the institute, two major events took place.

First, Ellen was taken home to finish her last year of high school in their sending church's Christian school. She was to live with close family friends and graduate with her former classmates.

Second, Wesley and Daniel decided it was time to start a church. Daniel's desire to start a church in his village had long since been put to rest. As George had said a couple years before, the village was simply too small to warrant a church. Veronica had acquired a driver's license so could take Daniel's family to church when Daniel was with Wesley. Other people would have to rely on the bus service, as inconvenient as it was.

The decision was made that a church should be planted where there was the greatest potential for reaching the lost. With only a small Baptist Union church and two very small Pentecostal churches in Turnu-Severin, this was the obvious place to go. Even though there were dozens of towns and villages with only four small Baptist churches in the 300 kilometers to the east of Turnu-Severin until Bucharest, there were more people in this one city of 115,000 than in all of those towns and villages combined. Once a church was started, Wesley and Daniel envisioned reaching out into some of those villages.

The first thing Wesley did was to purchase an apartment in Turnu-Severin. By Romanian standards, the apartment was considered to be in one of the better parts of the city. It required interior repairs, but when finished would be quite comfortable, except in summer months when the interior temperature could be in the high 90s, depending on the weather.

After getting settled, Wesley put an ad in the city newspaper for two weeks announcing the start of a new independent Baptist church. A room was rented in the large hotel in the center of the city. The day of the first service, three Orthodox people came out of curiosity, and an elderly couple, members of the Baptist Union church in town, decided to attend. The older couple responded to the preaching with great interest and proved the genuineness of their interest by asking many theological questions following the service. They attended the next Sunday with their son John from Timisoara.

Following this second service, John and his parents further questioned Wesley regarding his theological position and plans regarding a church. One key question was whether or not Wesley would be working with the Union. Wesley's response to this particular question was the key to the future for them. When he stated his absolute independence and desire not to be identified with the Union's theological errors and authoritarian methods, there was a clear meeting of the minds.

This couple was old enough to remember the doctrines before the Communist intrusion into the Baptist community when the Union structure was created, and doctrinal changes were imposed on them. Now that the government no longer controlled their faith, they wanted a church that would practice those original biblical doctrines.

After the discussions with Wesley, this couple was prepared to come on board. They noted that there were some other Baptists in the city who had the same concerns and desires.

John then noted that some years back he had purchased an 80-year-old house in disrepair with an attached empty lot on one of the major boulevards. He had purchased the property with the hope of starting another church for his parents and other Baptists who were also dissatisfied with doctrinal and control issues of the Baptist Union.

Assuming this would probably never happen and needing money for his business in Timisoara, he had decided to sell the property. When his parents called him about the new church start, he determined that perhaps his original goal could be realized after all, but his need for money required a fairly quick sale. He was prepared to make an offer to Wesley.

"You need to see this property. It is perfect for a church. You can use the house until the church outgrows it, and then you could build a new building on the empty lot. I would like to show you the property now and discuss terms I need before I return to Timisoara."

Was this real? Wesley pinched himself and said, "Well yes. There is no way we could purchase property now, especially since we have only had two services. But, yes, I would like to see the property anyway."

On the way, Wesley said, "Daniel, I don't know what to think! This is unbelievable!"

"Yes, it is so incredible that it must be of God. If God is in this, there must be a way to do it. We will see what John is willing to do to enable you to buy the property."

"Well, if John is willing to do some fancy financing, perhaps it would be possible. This is all so fast and beyond my wildest dreams! In fact, when he mentioned the property, I pinched myself to make sure I wasn't dreaming. I guess I wasn't."

They pulled up in front of the house on the corner of the boulevard, and Wesley expressed his thoughts.

"When John said it was in disrepair, he sure wasn't kidding. Seeing the outside, I hope the inside is in better condition."

The building was truly in disrepair. There was a wire fence around the perimeter, completely overgrown by weeds, vines, and tree saplings. The attached lot was so overgrown that it verified the property had not been occupied for decades.

A tour of the old house disclosed that the inside was dry, and the house seemed to be structurally sound. The closed solid wood shutters had fully protected the windows from weathering or breakage. Having some experience in building a garage and an addition to a house, Wesley was sure he could do the repairs with Daniel and others at minimal cost.

It would be an excellent meeting place. Two large rooms were upstairs, and two smaller rooms with a small alcove for storage and a bathroom were downstairs. Immediately, Wesley could see removing the shed in back and building on an additional room that could be used for socials and youth activities. The front room upstairs would be used for the sanctuary, and the back room would serve as an overflow room as the church grew. When the church outgrew these rooms, there was the adjacent empty lot to build a new church building.

The property was located on one of the three major bus routes, which would certainly give good exposure.

Though the asking price was more than he could possibly come up with in the timeframe being asked, Wesley knew he would never get an opportunity like this again. This had to be of the Lord!

"John, I don't really know how supporters could raise the money in the timeframe you are proposing. I think your asking price is reasonable, but"

John cut in, "But, you haven't prayed about it yet or talked it over with Daniel and your wife or your supporting churches. I guess I could revise my original timing for a sale to allow you time to figure out how to make this happen. I just feel that this is of God. The way this has worked out, it just can't be a coincidence. This seems to be an answer to our prayers. In fact, I am so sure that this is right, I want you to start using the house for your services while you work out the finances. Besides, I bet you are paying a fortune to rent that room at the hotel."

Wesley looked at Elizabeth, Daniel, and Vera, seeing the anticipation in their eyes. Even John's parents were looking at him awaiting his response.

"Well, yes, let me see how we can make this work. Since I have already paid for the hotel room for next Sunday, we will have two weeks to get things ready in the house. I am confident that this will be enough time. I will put another ad in the paper after next Sunday announcing the change in meeting place. Then there is the matter of how to raise the money within the required time frame."

John's parents said they would help with repairs and cleaning, and they had friends who would do so as well. The deal was made. John said he would leave the keys with his parents. Daniel got their address. They had a phone, so communication was possible.

After John and his parents left, Wesley said, "We have seen the Lord do some incredible things to get us this far, but this really takes the cake."

"What is this about a cake?"

"This is an expression we use to say that something is unbelievable or incredible. I am surprised you never heard that expression when living in America."

Elizabeth said, "Wes, I keep telling you that you use too many euphemisms, especially when you preach!"

"Yes, dear, but Daniel knows most of them and knows how to accommodate when he translates for me. He may as well know all of them. Besides, when I put my messages together in Romanian, I don't include them, because I can't figure out how to translate them."

With a chuckle, Wesley suggested they head for home.

It was clear there was simply no way Wesley could contact his supporting churches with a plea for funds in time. However, there was an answer also provided by God's blessings. Having retirement investments as a result of his successful career before surrendering to the mission field, Wesley determined that he could borrow the necessary funds to purchase the property from his investments, with the intent of returning them to the retirement account over a period of time as money could be raised from supporting churches.

He also sent out a plea to his supporting churches and individuals. The results were amazing. Several of his larger supporters stepped up with significant contributions.

Wesley contacted his daughter, Kristin, who had access to his investments. Within four weeks the property was purchased. In anticipation, major improvements had already been made in the yard. The wire fencing with vines, weeds, and saplings etc. were removed with no small amount of work. What a change!

Wesley was startled when one of the helpers found the skeletal remains of a very small baby. The remains were obviously very old since they were found in the soil under the vines and overgrowth. Wesley determined the best thing to do was to bury the bones and not mention this to anyone. It could only create bad press and senseless investigations. As it was, their presence was creating quite a stir in this part of the city. Being a major route, Cicero was traveled frequently by busses, exposing the travelers to what was happening at the old house that sat empty and rundown.

The results of the improvements were so impressive that it was hard to believe what was there when they began. Many neighbors came by to offer their congratulations because it had certainly improved the whole neighborhood. Wesley had expected these close neighbors to visit the services, but most of them never did.

In the days that transpired after driving throughout the city with Daniel, Wesley noted that there was not another structure with an empty lot anywhere in the city. Truly God had brought this property to them!

Almost immediately, a new sign was affixed to the front of the house saying Biserica Crestina Baptista Independenta Libertatea - Turnu-Severin. Within a few weeks, a new 1.25 meter (4 ft.) high block wall surrounded the property with a new iron gate sufficient to allow admission of a car. Necessary repairs to the house were completed as well. Then work began to tear down the shed which would be replaced with a concrete block addition of approximately 4.5 x 9 meters (15 x 30 feet).

Now that the building was ready, the emphasis was on evangelizing the area by passing out brochures printed with the address and an invitation with the schedule of services. Very quickly Wesley had a full range of services: Sunday school, morning service, evening service, Wednesday evening prayer service, and a ladies' meeting every other Friday evening.

Because Daniel was also gifted in piano, he began a small choir. Mandolins were purchased for him to begin a small mandolin orchestra with children and adults. Learning to play mandolins for Christians in Romania was almost as normal as breathing. The main reason mandolins were so popular was they were very inexpensive to acquire, compared to other instruments.

Wesley had no idea of the interesting history regarding the house. One day, when he and Daniel were working around the property, a car drove up and a woman in her 90s was escorted out of the car. Wesley and Daniel walked over to greet them. The woman, who now lived in Timisoara, had owned the house. It was built by her family early in the century. They were Jewish and had been very wealthy before World War II.

They had owned all the land surrounding this house where all of the large apartment buildings were built during the previous Communist regime. Her family had a granary selling the corn they and others raised. When the Communists took over the country after the war, her husband and two sons were put in prison, where they died. Their land was all confiscated and she was left with the house and the lot that Wesley had purchased for the church. She said that even though she was Jewish, and the house was being used as a Baptist church, she was glad it was being used for a good purpose. Wesley saw this meeting as a further sign that the purchase of the property was truly of the Lord.

Following that encounter, Wesley was encouraged to do some investigating of the Jewish presence in Turnu-Severin. There was a Jewish cemetery nearby. It was immersed in weeds, vines, and tree saplings. The number of headstones gave evidence that there was once a fairly significant Jewish presence in the city. Undoubtedly, the ancestors of the elderly visitor were buried there.

Wesley learned in his inquiries that, indeed, there had been many Jews in the city prior to World War II. During the War, most of them had been rounded up by the Third Reich and sent off to the camps in Poland and Czechoslovakia for extermination. Following the war, a few who had survived the holocaust had returned.

As the nation of Israel was establishing a strong economy, it began to offer money to the Soviet Union countries for release of Jews wanting to immigrate to Israel. The Ceausescu regime allowed for the release of every Jew wanting to leave. Most took the opportunity, and now only a handful of Jews remained in the country. It was not known if any yet remained in Turnu-Severin. Thus, the condition of the Jewish cemetery was to be expected. The Jewish synagogue in the center of town had been locked up for decades also giving evidence of disuse.

Shortly after the renovations of the church were completed, having been finished during the last year of the Bible institute program, the graduation ceremony was held on the church property. Wesley rented a bus to bring the students from the Pojejena location to Turnu-Severin with their families. Those from the Toplet location were brought by Daniel. The graduates included Pastors Petrica and Dolphi, Daniel and Vera, and Adrian and Eleana.

It was a very exciting time for everyone. When reflecting on the five-to-six-hour round trips every Friday for four years to Pojejena, Wesley and Daniel agreed that it had been more than worth the investment in time. The events and memories could fill a book. Through everything that happened, the hand of the Lord was clearly evidenced.

Though apartment living didn't have the serenity and beauty of the environs of Orsova, it had its benefits for the Benneys. For the first time in five years, they had a telephone. The apartment was located only a couple minutes by car from the church, and there was easy access to church members, and ever-better supplied stores. The fresh vegetable and fruit markets usually had an abundance of products, even in the winter. Fruits were being imported from South America and Israel, and other products of all kinds from the West were now available in major cities.

The main drawback of apartment living was the temperature during the hot summer months. Whereas the duplex in Orsova was far better insulated and had air flow through the attic, the temperatures in the apartment would reach the mid-nineties. Wesley was chastised by other missionaries for not purchasing window air conditioner units which were now available.

None of his members had such luxury, including Daniel. Wesley simply could not indulge is such comfort when his people couldn't. How would it look when they came to visit? He and Elizabeth learned to live with a couple fans directed on them during day and night with screened windows open at night.

They learned that many of the comforts Americans are accustomed to, are not as necessary as perceived. Perhaps the pride of "keeping up with the Joneses" rather than need was behind much of the quest for the good life. It was strange how easy it became to live in the Romanian culture with some of the deprivations. They learned by experience rather than by proverb that true joy comes in personal relationships, following God's leading, accepting the consequences, and in acknowledging God's greatest goodness – eternal salvation through faith in Jesus Christ.

The church grew slowly but steadily during the next four years. Baptisms were always an exciting and challenging time. Because it was not possible to put a baptismal tank in the house, Wesley had a tank welded out of metal and put it in the adjacent lot. He surrounded it with a concrete wall for esthetics. Each baptism became a viewing spectacle for neighbors and those passing by on the busy sidewalk. This was a good testimony time as tracts were passed out to the bystanders. Unfortunately, baptisms were limited by the weather.

During these years of church planting, Daniel and Vera were blessed with another child, a son who was given Wesley's name, thus, revealing the relationship that Daniel and Vera had with Wesley and Elizabeth. They thought of these children as their Romanian grandchildren. That was only natural as they came to think of Daniel and Vera as their Romanian son and daughter.

CHAPTER 10 SOME JOYS AND SORROWS IN MINISTRY

Many interesting, and sometimes sad, incidents took place during those years of ministry. For example, one day a man staggered on to the church property while Wesley, Daniel, and a couple church members were making some repairs on the outside of the building. The man's speech was slurred, and Wesley could not make out what he was saying. He called Daniel over, who even had a difficult time making out what he was saying between his profanities. One of the members walked over and said, "I know who he is! He's one of the young priests at the Orthodox Church a few blocks away."

Wesley would probably have been surprised if it had not been for the fact that about a year before, when he and Daniel had a service in a rented city building in a small town to the east, a similar incident occurred. A woman and her daughter were among the visitors. About midway through the service, a man came staggering in, walked to the front of the room, and demanded that the woman and her daughter leave immediately. She got up, apologized, and hurried out with her daughter. As the man staggered after them, one of the visitors noted that he was one of their priests.

Though this had been a unique experience for Wesley, Daniel was not surprised. Having grown up in the culture, actions such as these with priests were nothing new to him. He would often say that it was no wonder the people lived as they did when considering the lifestyles of many of their religious leaders.

During this same time period of growing the city church, Wesley and Daniel began to reach out into surrounding villages to preach and locate possible sites for satellite churches. These experiences were sometimes discouraging and sometimes joyous.

The most discouraging experience happened at a village to the north. This village had a high percentage of Gypsies, so Wesley was particularly intrigued with the possibility of reaching a people who had even rejected Orthodox Christianity over the past 1,000 years since emigrating from the country of India. They met a Gypsy man who had a small auto repair shop specializing in the small Romanian Dacia. He had built a small building with the hopes of having a grocery store for the village. Since this had not come to fruition, it was empty. He willingly allowed Wesley to use the building for weekly services on Sunday evenings prior to the evening service in Turnu-Severin.

In the beginning, the building was always packed with 30+ children and adults. First, they would hold the service for children with singing and flannel graph or flash cards stories. The adults were as enamored with the stories as the children. Next would be a service for the adults. Several women prayed to accept Christ but absolutely refused to be baptized, which was disconcerting to Wesley and Daniel. It caused them to suspect that perhaps the decisions were not genuine conversions. Things were consistently going so well a search was made for a house that could be purchased to establish a church.

Then the other foot "dropped." After exactly one year of continuous services, Wesley and Daniel arrived for the normal service, and no one was there but the owner of the building. Not a single child was there. Knowing how much the children looked forward to these meetings, it was clear they were being held back from coming. When asked where the people were, the man said he had no idea. Both Wesley and Daniel knew he was lying.

The next week, Wesley and Daniel went to visit the village people who had been coming. All kinds of excuses were made, but there was no ring of truth to any of them. Most of the people said they would be in the service the next Sunday. The next Sunday came and was a replay of the previous week. Again, the owner had no idea why no one came. Again, it was obvious he was lying.

A second visit was made to the same people in the village. Again, they received the same excuses and promises to attend the next Sunday. That third Sunday was an exact replay of the previous two.

Wesley and Daniel made a third attempt. They approached two homes of Gypsies who had previously been faithful to the services. The wives were two who had prayed for salvation but refused baptism. They noted the men were mixing cement and putting in a sidewalk to the street. They were making mocking comments as Wesley and Daniel arrived at the gate.

When asked, the men expressed the truth behind the empty services. They boldly accused Wesley of being a stingy American. They said, "We came faithfully to your services for a year, and you never brought a container with aid to our village like other missionaries have done in other parts of the country. We gave you what you wanted, and we expected you to give us what we wanted in response."

Wesley reminded them what he had brought was what they really needed, a relationship with Jesus Christ as Savior. They said they were not interested and would not return, nor would they allow their children to come.

Wesley and Daniel visited the other attendees in the village who essentially repeated what the two men had said, though they weren't as direct. No one indicated any interest in Wesley and Daniel returning in the future.

Now, that was a very painful experience! It also explained why the women who had prayed for salvation had refused to consider baptism. Baptism was a sign of true acceptance of the Gospel and identification with the Repenters.

Wesley and Daniel determined to "shake the dust off their sandals." Some weeks later, they felt that perhaps they should make another attempt. When they went to talk with the owner of the building, they were informed that the building would not be available. This seemed to verify that the man had only allowed use of his building with the hope of gaining from aid as had the others who had so faithfully attended for a whole year. Perhaps he even imagined if aid came, it would be distributed from his property since he was the one who offered the meeting place and had a facility for distribution.

While absorbing this disappointment, a similar outreach in a village about 20 miles to the east of Turnu-Severin had a completely different outcome. Several Christians in this village greatly desired a place of worship. The people noted that a small two-room house and shed with about two acres of land was available following the death of the widow lady who had lived alone. The cost was $4,000. Though the house was in bad condition, it could be repaired for use.

Many of the little two room houses in the village were constructed of clay. Large saplings were cut and placed in the ground with other smaller saplings interwoven through them. Then, special clay, the type used in making bricks, was packed around the saplings to a thickness of approximately one foot. The sides were smoothed with water inside and out and covered with a white lime compound.

Accommodations were made for a couple small windows and a door. A roof with tiles covered the house and hay was packed in the ceiling for insulation. The dirt floor was packed down and hand- woven rugs were put directly on the packed dirt. A single light would hang from the ceiling(s), and a small earthen fireplace was built for cooking and heating in the wintertime. In the summer, cooking was done outside in a clay oven under a lean-to.

Contrary to what Wesley assumed, Daniel told him the clay provided very good insulation. He noted such construction was common in many of the poorer villages. From the outside, one would not suspect the construction.

Having prayed about the possibility of building a camp facility, it was determined a small church could be established in the house and a camp building constructed later. The decision was made to purchase the property.

As commitments to support the camp ministry came in during the ensuing weeks, construction of the facility was initiated.

Part of the preparation was drilling a well because the original family never had one, having obtained water from neighbors. The process of drilling a well was an intriguing process. Men from another village were recommended for the work, but to Wesley's surprise, they did not come with any heavy-duty drilling equipment.

They arrived with a horse-drawn wagon and their "equipment." They set up a tripod contraption with a drill turned by two men walking in a circular motion pushing the handlebars. As the drill was raised, the dirt was removed, and the drill dropped back in. Some of the dirt around the hole would cave in, so after a few hours the hole not only got deeper but also got wider.

When they reached a depth slightly below the water table, a man was let down to break away loose dirt in the shaft and to fill a bucket with the loose dirt as it fell to the bottom. The bucket was hoisted up and dropped down again and again until the process was complete. This took two full days. The final depth was approximately four meters (13 ft.), and the width was approximately one and one fourth meters (4 ft.).

The next step was to construct a brick wall around the opening to a height of about one meter. Then a wooden roof was constructed about two meters above the hole. A wire mesh covering was put over the opening to keep leaves and other trash from falling into the opening.

In the future, someone could be lowered into the shaft to remove any additional dirt that had collapsed over time. The whole process was a reminder of the failure of Communism.

During these church planting years, Daniel was promoted with many preaching and teaching opportunities in Turnu-Severin and in the village church. He handled the camp ministry with the help of Vera and was proving himself to have a gift for preaching and teaching.

Another of the Institute graduates, Iacov (Jacob), was also a member of the church and was being given opportunities to conduct the Wednesday services. He was also given the opportunity to preach in the village church using one of the two church vehicles.

Though not as talented as Daniel, Iacov was very willing to serve in any capacity desired. His job allowed him to be available all evenings, Saturdays, and Sundays. He was a valuable asset.

Wesley began to seriously consider stepping aside and allowing Daniel to be the pastor of the church. Iacov could work into an Assistant Pastor position as the church grew. These thoughts came to the forefront when Wesley received an invitation from the President of the Bible College, from which he had received his Bible degree, to take a teaching position within a year. Elizabeth's aging mother, who lived in the same town as the college, would soon be in need of assistance because Elizabeth was the only sibling who could provide the needed care.

In preparation for turning the reigns over to Daniel, Wesley realized he needed to begin construction of the new church they had been discussing. The old house meeting rooms were filling, and there was little room for growth.

Wesley had a good idea what he wanted with the structure, so he sketched out the plans to scale, and an architect put the plans into architectural configuration. Thus began the hoops necessary for approval from the city, all of which included "generous" payments of fees.

Wesley had been saving ministry funds toward the construction and put a plea out to his supporting churches for additional funds to complete the work. He had a good estimate of cost. In Romania, the cost of construction was approximately 75 percent labor. All the work would be done by Wesley, Daniel, and the church members at an incredible savings. It would be absolutely necessary to have the new building finished before leaving the country. Without Wesley serving as construction contractor, the church could not be finished.

The first step in construction, and the only phase requiring outside help, was the digging of the foundation with a backhoe. Then, mixed concrete was ordered and poured. Following this initial step, the work proceeded reasonably well. About three months later, the large single room structure was essentially finished, and services transferred to the new sanctuary. Maximum seating would be 120. The most significant feature of the church was the baptistry built into the front of the church. No longer would weather dictate when a baptism could be conducted. The downside was that neighbors and passers-by would no longer be able to observe the services.

CHAPTER 11 PASSING THE TORCH

Following completion of the construction, a grand opening was planned and advertised in the local paper. Signs of invitation to the grand opening service were posted, and brochures were printed and distributed.

Baptist missionaries from other parts of the country came to the memorable service. Wesley decided it would be appropriate for Daniel to bring the key message since the work would soon be turned over to his leadership.

An ordination service was planned for two months later. Wesley explained the significance of the ordination service and planned the ordination council to be made up of himself and two missionary friends. The ordination council was held on a Sunday morning so that all the church membership could attend.

The members, some of whom had been in the Baptist Union for decades, had never seen an ordination council such as the one that day. Though not unlike an America ordination, it was definitely a rare event in Romania. The Baptist Union was in charge of who was ordained and when. The local church did not play any significant role in the process. One of the reasons the Union so disliked the independent Baptists was their independence from a higher authority. The Baptist Union and pastors had come to enjoy the power they had under the Communist Regime and continued after the revolution. Not unlike the Pharisees in Jesus' day, they loved their control over the requirements for salvation, baptism, membership in the local church, and meddling in members' personal matters.

The actual ordination service was conducted during the evening service, with laying of hands on Daniel and a prayer of consecration. Daniel delivered a message. Following the service, people enjoyed a time of food and fellowship.

The stage was now set for the church to be turned over to Daniel's leadership. He was increasingly pushed by Wesley into the forefront. A couple months after Daniel's ordination, when Wesley announced his intent to move on and his recommendation that Daniel was ready to take the helm, the decision was unanimously accepted. Though the people were loyal and very grateful to Wesley and Elizabeth for having sacrificed for their benefit, having one of their own as pastor, was immensely satisfying to them. Daniel was easily voted to be the pastor, and Wesley was given the honorable position of Pastor Emeritus. Once again, the concept of the indigenous church was in process.

Soon thereafter, Wesley and Elizabeth concluded a grand epic in their lives, one they could never have imagined when they had walked to the altar of matrimony 37 years before. In the process, they had acquired an adopted son and daughter in the faith and two adopted grandchildren. The Benneys returned to America where Wesley taught in the Bible College and Elizabeth served as a secretary.

The relationship with Romania was not ended because Wesley and Elizabeth would return to visit for a month during summer break. At those times, Daniel would step aside from the pulpit and Wesley would, once again, enjoy ministry to those he had come to love in the Lord.

As Daniel and Vera would often recount, they could never have imagined how God would have worked in their lives. It was like a fairy tale come true. Politically, Daniel had escaped from bondage to freedom in America, but in the process, he had spiritually escaped from bondage to Satan to freedom in Christ! Daniel's plans had not been God's plans, for which he would be eternally grateful!

THE END

Made in the USA
Middletown, DE
21 May 2022

66026179R00139